The Happy Numbers

of Julius Miles

ALMA BOOKS LTD
London House
243–253 Lower Mortlake Road
Richmond
Surrey TW9 2LL
United Kingdom
www.almabooks.com

First published by Alma Books in 2012
Copyright © Jim Keeble, 2012

Jim Keeble asserts his moral right to be identified as the author of this
work in accordance with the Copyright, Designs and Patents Act 1988

Printed in England by CPI Antony Rowe

Typeset by Tetragon

ISBN: 978-1-84688-181-7

THE HAPPY NUMBERS
OF JULIUS MILES

JIM KEEBLE

ALMA BOOKS

The Happy Numbers

of Julius Miles

To JGK, for the happiness you bring

1

Some things change and some things don't. In my experience it's never the things we expect. These streets have changed, the dark tarmac is less scarred, the once dull rain of London's East End now silver against chrome and glass. And I've changed – I do this now. I find people love.

They need it, as jobs vanish, accounts empty and passion is crunched in the rush to survive. It's a calling, don't think it isn't. I know this because when they touch for the first time I feel the hit. Like a seventy-proof shot or the first pill of the day. The electric. The beautiful fuzz.

The polaroid wouldn't tell you anything. A woman in her early forties, dark-brown hair cut in a bob more fashionable than not, flat masculine face like a lifelong nun, but hey she's got a smile that saves the day. Jeans and trainers, blouse and anorak. Social worker, religious pesterer, private detective. You don't look at me twice in this city. But I'm the real deal. A Cupid. A god of love.

I walk the streets of Bethnal Green, the soiled, boiled gutter of London, where all gets swept eventually. I grew up here, kissed here, lost my heart here. My father killed here. And now I sit on my bench and wait for the job to start.

He's on his way, the latest on my list. I notice him from afar, two heads above the Bangladeshis, a head above the Somalis, bowed like a monk doing his liturgical rounds, in meditation, not prayer. Julius Miles breathes in numbers and spins out silken mathematics that swirl and settle around him like armour. His business, statistical summaries. If they were spells, this guy would be the High Wizard. And who am I to say such magic does not exist? I'm no Einstein. Numbers make me laugh.

It's a spring day, which means low clouds over the tower blocks and yellow smears of daffodils ripped by kids or dogs from their half-dug council beds.

But Julius doesn't see such artistry – he's the Emperor of measurement, a professional statistician working for the Barts Health NHS Trust based at the Royal London Hospital, Whitechapel, East London. His face is simple, square. English. Spade of a nose. No beauty intrinsic in his features, but those dark, sad eyebrows draw us ladies to him. Broad shoulders, bowing calves like a butcher's hams, trunk slouching forward to conceal his height. Six foot four. 1.93 metres. Size 13 shoes.

Julius has the big man's desire for small women. But this giant is clumsy, except in his head. The pixies he's attracted to he pushes away. Nervous jokes, clumsy quips intended to be witty, but they simply grate.

"I like your cardigan, was it your grandmother's?"

"I find vegetarianism fascinating, is that why you're short?"

"You do know smoking doesn't actually make you thinner?"

A dinner party, a newly converted Queen Anne house five minutes from the hospital, eighteenth-century red-brick, Corian kitchen, French painted walls, Italian table, and a redhead, five two, finally turns to Julius.

"So what do you do, Julian?"

Usually he'd correct, chide even, but not her: he wants to squeeze her. "I'm the hospital's statistical expert reporting to the Director of Corporate Services."

"Oh, I love experts. What, league tables, improved targets, that sort of thing?"

"Exactly. I churn out numbers so the powers-that-be can argue about what they mean."

"Do *you* know what they mean?"

"Sorry, no. I can't afford to think about that, it's not my job. I can't give the figures meaning. I just collate the data. Nothing more."

At the end of the evening, Julius conspired to be next to her as she put on her coat. The connection can be instant, that mix of pheromones, perfume and visual mapping. Something told him that this configuration of circumstances – the presence of a petite, unsuccessful travel writer and a giant NHS statistician at a gathering of newly promoted doctors, his fragile state of intoxication that left him with just the right amount of testosterone in his bloodstream, the minute or so of general confusion as people hugged and bid goodbye, giving Julius a moment to speak without anyone else hearing him – would never occur again. He had to act. It was, from a statistical point of view, a once-in-a-lifetime opportunity.

"Do you have a phone number? I mean, of course you do, but could you give it to me?"

She smiled at him – and he forgot every equation he ever knew.

"Oh, that's sweet, but the thing is, I've got a boyfriend."

Julius knew this was a lie. Nine out of ten women who come alone to dinner parties wearing black bras and drink more than six glasses of wine are single. But he kept quiet as the door closed slowly behind her.

I open my journal. Thrill of empty white paper, let's kick off the adventure. Each time is the same: I think it's impossible to understand them, to categorize another soul. But I always get there in the end.

Julius Miles is straightforward. Just three words and he's not even passed my bench yet. Who he is, what he is, what he will no longer be when I'm done with him.

Big Lonely Rock.

A seventh wave must crash into him.

He's upon me now, looking to the pavement, avoid the gum, the dog do, the cracks. His eye on his watch, on his monthly record.

Fastest Time Taken to Walk 2.1 Miles to Work in May: 28
minutes.
Average Time Taken to Shower: 6 minutes.
Brush Teeth: 50 seconds.
Apply Roll-on Deodorant: 7 seconds.
Polish Shoes: 2 minutes with 30 seconds airing between polish,
application and buff.
Eat Crumpet with Honey Once Butter Has Melted: 45 seconds.

In government circles it's called "analysing performance indicators". If the whole world is a machine, how can we speed it up?
Here are a few of Julius Miles's other statistics:

Total Lifetime Relationships Longer than a Week – 7.
Total Sexual Relationships – 4.
Time since Last Sexual Relationship – 2.5 years.

I leave the walking to the man called Miles. I'm Felicity, so I catch
the happy bus. The 66D takes me west along the "Roman Road",
so called because the Romans built it, legions of skirted men
imposing cubits and digits on an Icenian world of devil-worship
and roasted foxes.

Julius likes the Romans, and not just because his father and
grandfather were named after Emperors. He likes their arpents
and yokes and sesters and scruples. He sees history as the struggle
between calculating men of mathematics and reckless dream-sayers.
Worships the scientist.

Even Julius would have to admit that in Bethnal Green arithmetic and geometry lost. The Romans' beautifully straight road
still intersects with the River Lea on its way to their garrison of
Camulodunum, now site of the UK's "finest roller-skating rink",
Colchester Rollerworld. But today it is flanked by examples of
human beings waging war on sense and structure, a continuous
mess of half-baked businesses and tax dodges, most surviving less

than six months. "To Let" is the brand of the area. Smorgasbords of shopfronts and signs, buddleia and ragwort poking from rooftops amongst naked television aerials and half-attached satellite dishes – nothing consistent, nothing planned.

The bus coughs past the market stalls in the concrete square and on past the Golden Shoe Thai Restaurant, Hakan's Supermarket, Tolga Supermarket, Tolga II Supermarket, Hassan Ali Hairdressers, Gentle Life Yoga Centre, Crockett's Washing Machine Shop and Electrical Warehouse, and the London Buddhist Centre, housed as if the punchline to a music-hall joke in the red-bricked Victorian splendour of the former Bow Police Station.

The bus disgorges most of its passengers at the traffic lights, and I hold my nose to avoid the stale belch of Bethnal Green Underground station, the breath from the depths, the gasp of the beast. I inhale again only as we pass Liby Gardens, where Large Girl in Headscarf Practises Free Throws on the lumpy basketball court. Beneath the bridge three fat Bangladeshi men sitting together on an orange sofa stare at my passing reflection, daring me to tell them nobody loves them.

I get off on Whitechapel Road, where the street market is just beginning. Julius loves this place, but do not think it's because of the chaotic splendour of the bright stalls brimming with gnarled foreign fruits and bulbous foreign vegetables, the pavement thronged with tiny Bangladeshi burqa mums and lofty Somali dames in chadors dragging reluctant offspring to purchase okra and peas and strange, bloody fish heads from the Indian subcontinent serenaded by battery beat boxes blaring Bangla and pirated expat Somali rap. No. Julius likes Whitechapel Market because it's a pie chart of the world. Only one in six people on this stretch of road is white. Five sixths are brown or black. Welcome to your planet, Julius Miles will tell you. To your future.

But there's no time to linger like a tourist in my own city. I have work to do. I cross the road to the hospital, waiting until three stubble-chinned drunks scuttle clear of the revolving door, spinning round like ancient liars to eye me with disdain.

Perhaps they think the manly girl in her new jeans and new Asics is a cop. More likely they sense somewhere deep in their shaking minds that I am not like them, not like any of these citizens of the world, except for maybe the other freaks and fallen angels hiding away in the forgotten rooms above the money-transfer offices and the sari shops, who glance out once a day at the building where they grew wings, in reverence and despair.

I'm post-op, you see. Born male, but have become female, although even after three years of HRT I still have to shave. Electrolysis is not my friend.

Don't be surprised that I'm transsexual. Us minor gods are carefully selected. The Storks often resemble fat babies, the Money Spiders tend to have golden tans even in winter, and the Grim Reapers possess deathly teeth, full of cavities. There's no need to overcomplicate things, I'm sure you'll agree. Life these days is difficult enough. Us Cupids are nearly always transsexual. The job description requires intimate knowledge of both sexes. Hermaphrodites are also chosen, but have a reputation for being a little highly strung.

This East End hospital didn't make me. I went west, with my father's money, to where oil paintings guard you every metre of the corridors, and Kenny G's Haydn serenades you on the way to the operating theatre.

The Royal London would like to be as modern as the West End hospital where Felicity found herself. But despite its New Labour extensions and future-proof blue-glass towers, it's still the place where the Elephant Man was carved into little trunky bits, where the Ripper sent Catherine Eddowes's kidney along with a letter addressed "From Hell". There are still corridors where electrical entrails hang from gaping vents and damp walls peel like a leper's back – a place where you start to feel that horror is not just something in the films.

Room 717B lurks halfway down one such corridor. On the door is a sign that reads "Department of Diagnostic Statistical Research", black Arial lettering on white. Julius likes the sign, but despises his office. Room 717B is small, cramped and airless. Too hot in summer, too hot in winter. Just a single medium-sized window that opens onto a puke-yellow wall; you can touch the brick without leaning out.

Inside the window, the office furnishings are shabby, fraying and forlorn. Every surface wants to be somewhere else – the white polystyrene ceiling panels loose and flapping in the air-conditioning breeze like sullen surrender flags, unfurling ferns of plastic veneer on the desktops curling away at the edges. The floor buckles in places as if mini-earthquakes occur each night. Lino bubbles towards the door, attempting to escape. And the walls are blistering, paint puckering damply beneath the small fog cloud puffed anxiously ceilingwards by Julius's nine-gallon recirculating humidifier.

The dampening and the blistering and the peeling scares Julius a little. As if Nature, with its viruses, bacteria and amoebas, is lurking just beneath the surface of every man-made object, microscopically multiplying and exhuming until it takes hold and rots everything within the smell of its spores.

Julius keeps his computer sealed in plastic. His printer and scanner and backup drives beneath Tupperware tubs purchased from the country's largest DIY online retailers.

The only personal items Julius permits in Room 717B are a bumper sticker on the noticeboard that he purchased in Arizona which reads "Drink coffee and do stupid things faster with more energy" and a plant that his mother gave him when his last girlfriend left him three years ago. Hoping to drown it, to overwater it to death, he soaks it every day using a catheter linked to the tap that one of the Urology guys rigged up for him. Yet the yucca is thriving. Some plants are like that. Some people too in my experience. Try to hurt them and they feel alive. Nurses and doctors and orderlies hurry past the door to 717B and its sign because they can't quite believe that anyone could be working eight hours a day five days a week dissecting statistics. As if those who carry out such abstract work in a hospital might in fact be part-machine themselves.

You and I would rather stack shelves, but Julius Miles does not find his job boring. As far as I can tell, he loves his work. He collates data from the different hospital departments weekly, and in some cases daily. He processes the figures, comparing them to historical data from each department, and to data from other London, UK and European hospitals, not to mention the government's ever-changing national target figures.

Numbers. Order. Sense. An island of reason in an ocean of mess.

Julius has much to clean up. Billions of numbers sting through his Dell PowerEdge servers. The NHS is the biggest single employer in Europe, fifth biggest in the world after the US Defence Department, the Chinese Military, Walmart and McDonalds. 1.2 million people on its payroll even after government cutbacks. If it were a country, the UK's National Health Service would be the thirty-third biggest economy in the world. And the grumpiest.

Julius lays out multilevel Poisson regression models explaining lengths of stay over time and across surgical firms and trusts within the Strategic Health Authority whilst adjusting for patient variables such as co-morbidities. He includes control charts for each trust illustrating the variation over time, even though his boss, Richard Lovall, Director of Corporate Services, usually moves Julius's detailed and statistically rigorous work to an appendix, asking instead for over simplified multicoloured pie charts. Richard Lovall likes pie charts, simple mystical wheels that he can wave at people, the chief executives, the politicians and disgruntled patients' representatives with their ill-fitting twinsets and weight-watcher eyes. Richard calls Julius "invaluable" and "a sterling asset to the Trust's management team", although Julius suspects that he's just being nice because Lovall is clumsy like Julius, and is usually nice to everyone, as his name suggests.

He was less nice when he explained that the Department of Diagnostic Statistical Research was being considered for closure under the Trust "Restructuring Plan".

"Wouldn't be redundancy, Julius. No, nothing like it."

"But you'd be firing me…"

"And you'd be picked up by any number of companies, whom the Trust would then approach to hire you out to do exactly the same job you're doing now, for more money but without the pension noose around our neck. Think of it as a transfer. Moving house. Changing lanes."

Julius doesn't want to leave the hospital. Despite its yellowing worktops and peeling walls, he doesn't want to leave Room 717B. He knows it's a hiding place, but nobody blamed Anne Frank for wanting to stay put. He is afraid that the Trust will kill his job in the next round of firings.

Seriously Depressed Man Considers Making Up Figures to Render Himself Invaluable.

I heard him first two weeks ago. No sound that you could detect, no sob, no shiver: the long-term lonely are hardened against expressing their pain, they know the hard way that after a tipping point tears make sadness worse, not better.

We're sniffer dogs. Coal-mine canaries. Cupids feel the pulse of a heart that yearns, vibrations on wind and water. Sometimes it's just a taste on the tip of the tongue, burnt metal.

The nights hurt him most. Upright on his queen-sized bed, two in the morning, three, four, five o'clock. Shadows tilting around walls, big lump of man as rigid as a dial around which the empty room turns. Blames himself, the list concise, damning. His vital statistics. Cowardly. Graceless. Arrogant. Even despises himself sometimes, hurts the palms of his hands with his fingernails. Prays to something to be lighter, warmer, gentler. Julius stands at the window bathing in the low groan of the city that's alive despite the devil's hour, placing his arms around his thick chest, fingertips tapping his back. He hugs himself. Closes his eyes. Imagines his fingers drumming his back are a woman's touch.

A quick fix, why wouldn't he be?

I might be still a little woozy from the cocktail of oestradiol, progesterone and Spironolactone, my perception most likely fuzzed by hormones and hope and the odd benzo, let's not kid ourselves, to massage the post-op pain. But I give myself a couple of weeks, tops.

I'll hang around the lifts on Staircase C, notebook in hand. Lunch from the Marrakesh Café, back of the managerial block, two customers behind him. Maybe use the clipboard, stroll the linoleum outside Room 717B noting paintwork, loose electrical sockets, window locks ill-installed. Nobody will question me, nobody will look twice. I've done this too long to be noticed.

And at 5.30 p.m., not a minute before, I'll follow him home and start to plan his future.

Don't worry, Julius Miles. The path of love is never straight, but mostly it is true.

2

I cannot choose the ones you fall in love with any more than I can change the direction of the wind or the length of your feet or nose. Bows and arrows are for Hallmark Cards, as no doubt you suspected.

What solidifies attraction into love, sometimes instantly like lava hitting water, sometimes over months and years, tectonic plates shifting, is a sap none of us can tame. I am merely the gardener, pruning, dead-heading, planting to ensure the garden flourishes and renews. The mechanics of plant botany and biochemistry are mysteries I have no interest in unpicking.

In my experience, which is vast, the clumsier the initial meeting the better the chance of success. If it works, it does so in six words or less.

He was left-wing, felt right.
In the morning, she cooked porridge.
Surfed Facebook hit her wave.
Fell in love picked ourselves up.
Drank to lose myself found her.
Forgot myself he didn't.

I knew from an early age why I was here. The tubby ten-year-old boy with an interest in soft furnishings and a talent for whispers by schoolyard walls prodded many an ardent Andrew into the arms of a bashful Belinda. The football boys beat me up, of course, but they all came round eventually, by the canal, stammering clumsy apologies and grunting their desires. I learnt early that you can never tell who someone's going to go for. The star centre forward had no interest in the big-bosomed captain of the netball team, saving confused hopes for the mousy clarinettist with lisp and specs. Which meant, symmetrically, that the chess team substitute had eyes only for Whitney the wanton Wing Attack.

It surprised me. How easy it was to be a high priest of love. If the wall is going to tumble, the smallest of nudges will set up the fall. Job satisfaction is high. Most of us love our work.

Early evening in the well-heeled East End enclave of Bow, half a mile from the diesel guts of Bethnal Green. Warm breeze from the south, pink clouds, geese labouring homewards to the marshes beyond the Olympic Park. I like this patch. Neat streets, rows of three-storey Victorian townhouses built as speculative subdivisions in the East London real-estate boom of the 1860s by lawyer Joseph Rogers and builder William Bruty, men of exactitude and dispassion, except when it came to making money. Slap-them-up-quick Billy, cash-in-quicker Joey. So the world turns.

First keys handed to butchers and tea dealers, Victoria's fresh-faced merchant class, sweeping up the five steps to new front doors with puffed-out cheeks and toothless old folks, pregnant daughters hanging to their coat-tails. Whole families marching to the entrepreneurial drum. By the 1930s the same houses carved up, partition walls, beds stacked like shelving, brimming with mewlers, pukers, scullery maids, schoolteachers, dockers frying stolen halibut in the hallways.

Today, just one soul sits in silence at number 42 Woodstock Road. Radio 4 on every floor, spraying house plants. Deaf to the chaotic ghosts of former inhabitants that scream and shout and screw and fling cake and shit and sing and smash and drink and die around him. My Julius.

But this fine evening I'm not interested in him. Action speaks louder than words, to do is to be. On the corner of sleepy Woodstock Road and the architectural potpourri of Roman Road is a small shop. First a scalemaker's, next a jeweller, then a pawnbroker's, it has since 1972 carried the same sign on the façade, painted black with perfect gold lettering, the pride of Uncle Gus, his delight, his life's work. Domus Decorus. The only Roman remnant on the Roman Road, a Latin incantation that locals born in the last forty years nod at knowingly as they pass.

"Means 'Bewtiful 'Ouse' in Latin…"

At first glance, you cannot tell what the shop sells. At second glance, you cannot tell that it *is* a shop. Wooden chairs of different ages, sizes and makeshiftness hang above the door, two missing seats. Leather coats, fur wraps, men's jackets from cheap high-street stores, dresses of polyester and sequins dangle on either side of the entrance like costumes from some forgotten Eighties play. The two large windows, at right angles to one another, door in between, exist as frames to precarious stacks of gnarled footstools, rows of grimacing Toby mugs, broken 1960s chrome lamps, teak sideboards, metal trestles, a stuffed eagle (missing one leg), a small chaise longue (missing one leg), vases that might be Ming or Marks & Spencer, chipped plates from at least five different Royal Weddings (one of them Swedish), hunting horns, old copies of the Guinness Book of Records and at least six different sizes of grandfather clock, the hour and minute hands at six different angles as if delineating the time zones of a demented mind.

It could be an art installation by a Turner Prize nominee. Or the home of a hoarding monkey. But it is a shop, owned by Julius Miles, inherited through the will of his Uncle Gus. Julius rents out the shop space and has crossed its threshold only three times since he became its owner, five years ago next month.

The business is listed under "Antiques" in the Yellow Pages, on various internet search engines. But scroll down the Google page and you're a click away from discussion threads that are not inclined to extol the virtues of Domus Decorus.

This is NOT an antiques shop! Junk Junk Junk!!! Imitation Royal Dalton and plastic Presley memorabilia. Junk Junk Junk!!!

Do not believe Feiner's London 2010. It is definitely not "worth the trip to the East End to this lovely eclectic emporium, run by an ancient but effervescent antiquarian who seems to know more about English history than any Oxford Professor". No antiquarian, just a lippy cow with dubious piercings. Update your guidebook, Feiner's!

Bought an "authentic Eames-style office chair" from Domus Decorus. At home realized there was an Ikea label that someone had tried to peel off. B**ch running the place refused to take it back. AVOID. TYPICAL ROMAN ROAD RIP-OFF MERCHANTS!

The mishmash of objects and furniture makes Julius feel physically sick. He sees it as a symptom of mental illness and walks the other direction from his house, taking a detour just to avoid the shop, past the screaming six-year-olds at the primary school round the corner onto Merryweather Road, to get to Roman Road. Same dogleg, an extra 425 metres give or take, on his return each evening. He thinks about selling up, but sees his uncle sitting in his armchair outside the shop on hot summer's days, reading Proust or Goethe, and cannot bring himself to part with the place.

I like the façade of Domus Decorus. Looks like every object in someone's life has been thrown from a car speeding towards Essex and landed against the walls and windows. A shop overstuffed, under-loved and overpriced. A tangle of creativity representing that wholly human greed for amassing what-shall-we-call-it... stuff. It thrills me. Says how far from the jungle we have come.

I'm across the street, no need to hide, can of super-strength White Ace in hand, just another cider-touting dropout in a London full of such folk. Tomorrow it might be the fluorescent vest. Dark fleece with Housing Association logo. A simple laminated name badge, plastic clip, 55 p. There's no end of labels in the modern world designed to make us anonymous.

I down the cider, don't get me wrong. She's no saint this nun-face, 500 ml of White Ace will kick-start any evening. A drink built for comfort, not joy. The small rage in my belly as the last gulp hits, I toss the can on top of the dirty Chinese takeaway boxes outside the dirty Chinese takeaway and cross the road to the shop door, fifteen minutes before closing.

Pause at the tsunami-detritus window, a pair of beaten Clarks shoes for £60, a CD player £40. My eyes linger on two small pottery clogs, a KLM freebie from a business-class flight Gus took to Buenos Aires in 1982. Single blue windmill on each toe, birds flapping across empty skies above Arnhem fields. Flights of fancy.

"How much are the clogs?" I ask.

"What clogs?"

The voice of a smoker, a drinker, sexier for it. From behind a phalanx of porcelain dolls, their heads inches from a line of hanging baskets, spider plants raining downwards onto the dolls' unruly hair, Planet of the Plants. "What clogs are you talking about?"

"The pottery ones, in the window."

Silence. Then a clatter of books and magazines cascading to the floor.

"Shit."

And she emerges. The first on my list of Julius Miles's possible maidens.

Daisy Perkins, thirty-nine years old, 5"5', fifty-five kilos, butter curls, jammy lips, breasts like beacons. Black camisole beneath unbuttoned blouse, you can't help staring because they're there to stare at. Daisy ran the shop for Gus during his latter years, Gus said they were close; how close Julius tries not to contemplate.

Daisy has leased Domus Decorus from Julius since he inherited the freehold. Lives at number 40, next door to him, claims it's happenstance not a provocation, the rental came up at the right time. Thinks herself bohemian, loves art but has no artistry, craves taste but has none of her own. Beautiful limpet. Daisy between roses.

"Oh, those clogs. Ten quid."

"I'll liberate them from you for five."

Her look, hand on haunch, haughty and naughty. Hot black eyes. Lips painted for action. Three years ago she would have parted those lips, shoulders back, chest out. When I was a man. Got a feeling Daisy likes men. Loves them infrequently. Needs and uses them. Seductive to all, but few trust her. Has no strength, lets anything go. Except her son, Arnold. Daisy loves Arnold like the best idea she ever had. I'm surprised there's no picture of him in the shop except in her wallet, but people are strange when it comes to kids. Flaunt them like BMW convertibles. Or conceal them from the marketplace like a secret belief in the Church of Scientology.

"Sorry. Ten's the price."

She doesn't like me. Disdains women, I sense, despite the row of feminist classics on the shelf above her desk. Defines herself by beating them to it. Makes Daisy feel big when she belittles another sow.

"Is there someone else I can talk to?"

"Does this look like Comet Electrical Warehouse? It's *my* shop."

"Do you own it?"

"Yes."

"I thought it was rented."

Cocks her head to one side, curls bounce. "Who are you, Companies House?"

"Maybe I should talk to your landlord. Julius might give me a deal…"

Black eyes cool. Arms cross over cleavage, that shop's shut for now.

"You're a friend of his? Of Julius Miles?"

"No. Met him once. Told me about the shop. Was in the area, thought I'd check it out."

She doesn't believe me. She's trouble, Daisy; Gus liked trouble. Maybe Julius needs trouble. I find it happens often that we need what we don't want.

"Eight quid. Since you and Jules are such good friends."

"I don't like your manners," I remark politely.

"I'll not sleep tonight for the worry."

"Is Julius single?"

"You want a tilt at him? Good luck with that…" Her laugh an exhalation of Benson & Hedges.

"He's solid. Something to hold on to."

"Big men don't all have big ones. Trust me, darling."

"I don't trust you. Yet I think I'd trust Julius, despite his pedantry. Do you see the difference?"

"Yeah well, it's been a delight, Mother Superior." She turns, heading back to the desk, steps over the slide of books scattered across the rug without picking them up. Can still see me in the mirror behind her chair, of course. Black eyes darting. My job begun. The picture of Julius in her head is different now, however slight the shift. It works like this – the desire of others breeds desire in those uncertain of their own aesthetic.

"Thanks. Like your shop, despite what they all say."

She doesn't rise to it. Disappears beneath the line of protective dolls, her Foreign Legion. I exit, just a jerk of hand, who could tell, slipping the clogs into my pocket. If she saw me steal them, she doesn't say.

You see that I know what I'm doing, don't you? The Private Dick with no dick never starts a job without a full bag of ideas. A couple of days on the scent usually does it. The preliminaries, sketch out the list. I knew all I needed to about Daisy Perkins before I set foot in there. Follow and sweep, ask and you shall be told, keep it simple, amicable, non-intrusive. Whether it's this age of reality TV or just low-down human cattiness, never underestimate how much someone will say about you to a complete stranger if she knows how to ask. And I know how to ask. Don't think I don't.

The other possibles:

Awa Yasin, twenty-three years old, 5"2', forty-seven kilos. Pretty little doll, nursery assistant and Arnold's nanny when the boy isn't in school. Hopeless with numbers, confuses corner-shop change, no plan, no boyfriend, no fear. Gets people like some Paddies get horses, understands their tick, their tock, their terrors and hopes. Laughs like tropical rain. Born in Somalia, arrived at Heathrow before her first teeth. A dark button.

Rukshana Begum, thirty-five years old, 5"3', 5"5' in her heels that she takes off only when sleeping, showering or having sex (always when sleeping, usually whilst showering or having sex). Costing and Income Accountant at the Barts Health NHS Trust. Dreams of acceptance. Pretty-ish, Bangladeshi-ish, Easy-ish. Prides herself on her temper, which she has to fake most of the time.

Nadia Florescu, twenty-seven years old, 5"2', sixty-five kilos. Cleaning Supervisor for Managerial Offices, Royal London Hospital. Broad as tall, muscle not fat. High-school weightlifter in Romania, petty criminal in Bucharest but merely to fund the train ticket west. Part-time degree at East London University in Multimedia Design Technology. Hold on to her coat tails, Nadia's heading places. A workhorse with a heart the size of a horse.

Gwendolyn Lank BA, MA, PhD, Cantab, thirty-two years old, 5"8', fifty-five kilos, Julius's first girlfriend, now lecturer in French Literature at University College London. Shaved head, stick insect in tweed, hips like a rentboy, breasts no bigger than profiteroles. Uncle Gus's favourite, which is why his nephew clung to her long after she shook him off. Her passion is French Surrealist poetry of the 1920s. Julius the mathematician hung off her every sigh. "Leave everything!

26

Leave Dada! Leave your wife! Leave your mistress! Leave your hopes and fears! Leave your children in the woods! Leave the substance for the shadow! Leave your easy life! Leave what you are given for the future! Set off on the road!" Barren, infertile, fruitless, lank like her name. Mother given diethylstilbestrol during pregnancy, Gwendolyn given reproductive-tract abnormalities whilst in the womb. Vaginal adenosis, she will tell you, more than once. Who better for Julius than a passionate geek whose favourite word is vagina?

Richard Lovall, thirty-eight years old, 5"10', eighty-seven kilos, Director of Corporate Services, Barts Health NHS Trust. Sings in a choir at weekends, Handel and Bach, not show tunes. A hugger not a kisser. First wife died of breast cancer at thirty-two; Lovall moved into the health service from KPMG six months later. Second wife the second-best friend of the first. Large hands that knead needlessly, ancestors probably bakers on one side or the other. Receding tight-curled hair, a badly shorn sheep, but this Richard sees himself as a Lionheart.

Don't get me wrong, I don't think Julius is gay, but I've screwed up before, lack of preparation. No sense in making that mistake twice. Blame it, if you want, on the HRT, back when I was a little distracted. Now I cover all the bases.

Not much point in hanging around tonight. A Tuesday evening. He won't be going out. Here is the routine of Julius Miles:

7 p.m. dinner in front of Channel Four news, Tesco's Finest Beef Stroganoff, sparkling spring water and an apple, Cox's orange pippin. Wash the plate, the glass. Dry both, place back on the table for breakfast, add teacup, cutlery. Mix the tea leaves, three parts Earl Grey, a part Darjeeling, a part Lapsang. Fill the kettle for the morning, halfway between the three- and four-cup level. Iron two shirts. Open gas bill, compare the same quarter's usage with previous three years, pay gas bill online. Check broadband

download and upload speed on the Speedtest website, record the results on the Speedtest forum.

The lonely plan their time.

Elsewhere on Woodstock Road I hear laughter, howling children, shouting lovers, edgy guitar music, classical symphonies, chatter of dinner parties. The professional couples, straight and otherwise, graphic designers, writers, property lawyers, minor bankers and major secretaries from Canary Wharf proud to be living in a Conservation Area because it conserves the level of their investment. Houses pushing £700K with the Olympic bounce. Gentrify, gentrify, the estate agents' love call.

Julius's Uncle Gus despised the Conservation bunch, painted the front of number 42 pink one year, railings purple, front door day-glo orange. Sat on his steps in a wizard's hat pointing a hazel branch at the bespectacled council frump in denim jacket and skirt, at the suited council blimp, threatened to turn them into toadstools, who wants the first hit? Hung his brother's medical-school skeleton from the streetlamp, had schoolkids throw conkers through the pelvic cavities. Played Tchaikovsky from a record player on his roof. Spent July and some of August entirely naked, even to water his window boxes.

Augustus Miles purchased number 42 Woodstock Road in 1948 from Florence Swaby, who was born in the house three years after her parents bought it from William Bruty in 1865. Uncle Gus paid the eighty-year-old £5,000 cash, profit received from the sale of a small Mondrian sketch at Sotheby's. Gus vague as to the drawing's provenance – "the War, old boy", outskirts of Paris somewhere near Vincennes, grateful flophouse madam or German Infantry Captain, depending on the day and audience.

Uncle Gus, the sparkler, the genie in the dull old bottle of the family, Julius's father's older brother, invited warmly to birthdays, reunions and Christmas on the understanding that he would never show up.

Julius was five when he made his first visit thirty miles from St Albans to Gus's East End, father fussing over seat belts, and suddenly there's a face in the glass, blocking out the sun, a nose – or is it an aubergine squashed almost flat against the window of the Ford Escort Estate. White moustache and teeth rich with pipe smoke.

"*Bienvenue, chère famille!*"

Loved children, Gus the bachelor king. Loved Julius most of all. Quiet, myopic Julius, a starer, a blinker, a big clumsy owl amongst day birds. Gus practically hugged him out of his car seat – "This must be joyous Julius!" – bore him up the steps, legs dangling, Julius's face deep in an armpit that smelt of tobacco and sweat and rose-petal water. Aubergine swinging down into view again as Julius landed on the carpet, multicoloured light from the stained glass in the top of the door bathing the hallway as in a medieval chapel, eyes following nose, so blue, so sharp, Julius had to blink.

"*Bonjour petit ange.* I'm your Uncle Gus, and I'm here to make a fuss…"

Julius's father was unable to resist a frown, seeing in Augustus's flamboyant embrace of his son the sunny older brother's familiar admonishment of the wintry middle brother: "Nouse not rules Claude, you're suffocating the swain".

Gus died five years ago. Buying rambutan, durian and dragon fruit from the Star Night Supermarket and Video on Mare Street in Hackney, whistling *The Dream of Gerontius* as he stepped out between two white vans unpacking rice, straight into a number 38 Routemaster on the day before the hop-on-off bus was withdrawn from service.

"Rouse thee, my fainting soul, and play the man;
And through such waning span
Of life and thought as still has to be trod,
Prepare to meet thy God."

Julius snipped out the short paragraph in the *Times*, still stuck to his fridge half a decade on. "Pensioner Killed on Routemaster's Last Journey". Hopes Gus is happy with the epitaph.

Julius didn't attend the funeral. Preferred instead to install the new server at work, a second Samsung monitor, numbers flickering across the two screens in a perfect digital ballet. Shortly afterwards, a phone call from his father, choking back tears. "I leave number 42 to my nephew. The shop also."

Everyone told him to sell the old house, cash in, cash in. An albatross, his mother called it, around your windpipe. Father was less categorical, sensed the hole in his son's thirty-five-year-old heart, the same shape a secret in his own. Went with him to Gus's solicitors in Mayfair, permitted no noses to look down in Julius's direction.

They came to Woodstock Road together. Father and son ascending the steps to number 42, Julius nervous, clumsy, dropping the keys at the door, two grown men bumping heads as they crouched simultaneously to retrieve them from the worn "Welcome" mat. Smiling at one another. Both remember that moment as the beginning of the beginning, the warming between them that continues to this day. One of the many magics of Uncle Gus.

Julius unlocked the duck-egg door, stepped into the shadows. Pausing to smell the stale air of the hallway, his Uncle Gus distilled. Father behind him but nostrils just as wide. Ever noticed how scent can be as loud as a sound...

They ascended, descended stairs, both startling at a creak of a board outside Gus's bedroom. Remained in doorways, never crossing the threshold. His father's fingers lacing through a beam of late afternoon sun, touching the dust.

"Like a museum already," he said to Julius. "Are you sure you want to do this?"

Julius nodded. Didn't know how to say no. Went downstairs at his father's bidding to make tea, as Nephew had done for Uncle most Sunday afternoons since that first one in 1978. The kettle boiled, but Julius could not move, staring at the open tin of Dar-jeeling. Two floors above him Claudius stripped the bed of the sheets his dead brother had slept in, plucking a single white hair from the pillow. Placing brand-new cotton across sagging mattress, pausing only to wipe his eyes.

"He'd understand if you don't want to", his father's last words on the doorstep as night crept along the street. "I'd understand…"

Julius shook his head. "I'm at home here, Dad." Hadn't meant it as a rebuke. His father smiled to tell him he had not taken it so.

So Julius lives in the museum of Gus. 1888 Steinway upright. Ewer and basin from J.H. Weatherby & Sons, Tunstall, 1891. Antique Rabat carpet from Morocco, 1750. Stanley Spencer sketch of Augustus Miles, 1946. A battered tuba, a Chippendale bureau, a huge brass cooking pot hand-hammered in Mombasa, six empty birdcages, one of them gilded. Bang & Olufsen BeoGram 4000 record player, BeoMaster 4400 Amplifier, and BeoVox 5700 Passive loudspeakers all purchased in 1972. 789 records, classical, jazz and the Rolling Stones. Everything Mick and Keith recorded between 1963 and 1982.

Books on shelves, shelves on books, stacked up walls and in corners, spines like saplings and redwoods felled by storms. First editions amongst airport thrillers and racier detective pulp, the oldest a *Wuthering Heights* from 1847, the same as one that sold at Bonhams for £11,400 three weeks after Julius moved into the house.

A gold mine. And he'd not even looked in the attic. Sat and scru-tinized every object over and over, not touching, never touching. Their beauty was strange and opaque, but he looked and found in each a number, a date of manufacture, a product code, a series classification. The numbers helped, the only sense he could take from the jumble of beautiful things, it helped him breathe more easily. Took his digital Minolta through every room, the dark house lit by artilleries of flashes, all night long. Cataloguing every item, every fork, every glass, every ladle.

Sent Claudius the photographs and a short letter. *Anything you want, Daddy.* Father's reply by return: *Will come and see.* The two men staring once more at the Aladdin's cave, each willing the other to rob it. But neither moving a muscle.

"He'd understand," said Julius. Father nodded, hand to chin, like father like son. Took just one bowl, crude pottery that Claudius had fashioned at school in 1939, ten weeks before their father was killed crossing the road from his doctor's surgery. A statistic of the War. In the last three months of 1938, 2,494 people were killed on Britain's roads. A year later, three months after war was declared, this rose to 4,133, thanks to the blackout. One victim, Julius's grandfather, Dr Felix Miles, aged thirty-nine, the age Julius is now. Another statistic, if you want to see it that way.

Daisy Perkins lusted after the contents of Gus's house after he died. Enquired on a weekly basis, if only to infuriate Julius. "Anything you want to let fly? Twenty per cent commission, I'll get you top coin!"

Julius tries to purge the treasure trove each spring. One or two artefacts make their way to the front door, where they remain hopefully for several days before retracing their steps to the creases in the carpet, the light circles on the dark wood shelves, the bright clean squares on the grey walls where they live. Return to where you belong.

The only things Julius binned at the outset were the domestic electrical appliances – fridge, toaster, kettle, television, radio. Gus never bought for the technology but for the look, whereas Julius values performance, environmental ratings, hard facts, data. Has subscriptions to three separate consumer-report websites. Cross-references, compiling his own database that collates the number of stars a device or appliance is granted by his Holy Trinity of advice sites. Thinks wistfully from time to time of setting up his own meta-website to report on the consumer reporters.

This boy needs a girl. A woman's eye. Gus knew beauty but not when to stop. I'm a poet but I have learnt restraint. I'd give Julius five minutes to list every item in the house he recalls by memory, stopwatch the fool. Then sell all that slips his mind.

I might take something from the collection for myself, the gilded birdcage perhaps, a little something to remember Julius by. Budgies, or a parakeet called Nelson, I'm thinking. Yes, I've been through the house one morning while he was at work, why wouldn't I? Ask any cop, a credit card unlocks most residential front doors. For everything else there's Mastercard.

Relax. I'm no creeper. Mine is vital work.

* * *

The morning is wet. May drizzle, none finer. I'm late, past eight thirty, steaming at myself, must have forgotten to set the alarm. Nursery opens at ten to nine, time to check out the little Somali, what was her name? Anorak pockets empty, no journal. More steam. It's Friday 13th – I could have, should have stayed in bed.

I'm looking for the girl from the tower block, the one who child-minds Daisy Perkins's son. The boy's name foggy too, my brain like the air today – soft.

Julius exits his house, locks the front door behind him, walks down the five steps of his house and up the five steps to next door. Number 40. The house Daisy rents from ageing Mrs Eaves. In his hand, an opened envelope, Thames Water logo prominent. He seems agitated. I suspect Daisy Perkins has failed to pay her water bill. I suspect Julius is angry. I suspect he is going to give her a piece of his mind.

I watch, intrigued to map for my charts the anger boiling within him – I imagine that his fury at a missed payment, an ignored deadline, could be volcanic. The big man hesitates, hand over chin, reciting Pi to fifty decimal places, I can almost hear his whisper.

"3.14159 26535 89793 23846 26433 83279 50288 41971 69399 37510…"

Take out my journal, jot a quick note.

Could Daisy Perkins be the diameter to his circumference?

He goes to knock, hard, manfully, the landlord of a commercial property confronting his wayward tenant. The door swings open. Unlocked.

"Hello?"

Julius stands, puzzled, on the threshold. Scent of coffee and flowers from within. He steps onto the brown and sky-blue Victorian tiles, a geometric pattern of triangles and swirls.

"Daisy?"

He almost collapses over her, grabs the banister to stop his fall. Daisy Perkins is lying, asleep on the floor. She is stark naked.

Julius stares despite himself. He stares at her body, eyes delineating the curves of her hips and breasts. He looks at her belly and below and is surprised to see that her pubic hair is dark, unlike her hair.

Tattoos. Humming bird. A scimitar. Chinese characters, something about rebirth…

To his left, a noise. Through the half-open doorway into the lounge Julius sees a small boy climbing out of a cupboard under the well-stocked bookshelves. The boy blinks as if a creature emerging from below ground – Daisy's son, Arnold. Three, almost four.

Arnold stares at Julius. Julius looks back at the boy and thinks that he does not look like an Arnold. Arnolds are old and Jewish or Austrian or both.

Julius shivers. Something about the small boy unsettles him deeply. Arnold has turned and is standing over the prone form of his mother on the tiled floor.

"Wake up, Mummy," he admonishes. "Silly sausage. Time for school."

As Julius watches to see if the boy's prodding succeeds in waking his sleeping mother, he notices something that will change his life for ever. Daisy Perkins is lying in a pool of blood. Time accelerates, the room closes in at the speed of light. Julius reaches out, touches her neck, but it is cold stone. No jolt, no quiver. Dead cold.

He cannot breathe. As if sharing her state. Staring as much at the boy who is now crouched, tickling the blood on the floor, marvelling at the redness between his fingers.

Julius does not hear the footsteps behind him. No one can blame Arnold's child-minder for jumping to conclusions. She sees only her employer lying naked in a pool of blood and a large thirty-nine-year-old man stooped over her with his great fist clenching, unclenching by her throat.

Had Julius seen Awa Yasin before she saw him, he would have cried out: "Stop! Only three per cent of all deaths in the UK each year are due to accidental or violent causes, approximately 16,000 out of a total of 533,500, and only 700 or so are murders! Think about it, there is merely a 0.1312% or one in 762 chance that you've stumbled across a killing!"

But he does not see her, so he has no chance to explain the probabilities involved. Instead, Awa Yasin reaches in her bag, whips out a can of Mace and sprays it into Julius Miles's face. She jabs him fiercely in the stomach and kicks him hard between the legs.

As Julius falls backwards from the house, his head striking the last step obliquely, causing him to pass out like the giant from a beanstalk in front of several children and parents on their way to the primary school at the end of the road, the last thought that flickers through his brain before it clouds up for a while is that this is exactly the sort of misunderstanding that occurs when people are not in possession of the correct statistics.

3

This has never happened before. I put my first couple together at the age of ten. In my thirty-one years of melting and stitching souls one into the other no one has ever died on me.

If I'm honest, I'm a little angry with Daisy Perkins. She was high on my list of possibles. She wasn't what Julius wanted, but could have been what he needed. The kink in his line.

A week on from her death and I'm sleeping less than four hours a night. My new breasts ache. Head like chopped beef frying, spits of ideas but everything's angry. And I can't find my journal. Again. Turned the flat upside down, came across three scribbled scraps of paper in a fleece pocket.

Julius likes Bach. Violins.

Awa Yasin: suffers from hay fever. Prettier when she sneezes.

Daisy can be convinced. Jealousy is a motivator with her.

Or it used to be. Before my top pick hit her head on the tiles of her hallway floor and vanished from this world. And my list.

There have been failures before, naturally. Even Elvis screwed up his movie career. Remember the tree surgeon who cut off two fingers just before his clinching date with the dental technician (it was going well – wait for it, they both loved pulling

36

roots). And the Spanish flight attendant who ditched the skinny blond male immigration officer at Stansted Airport for the skinny blonde female immigration officer at Bydgoszcz Airport in Poland. Not to mention the Latvian gasman who lit the boiler but not the heart of the shivering nail-salon girl from Dulwich – she went for a Bermondsey baker; his hands were perpetually warm.

After each of these near-misses I suffered, a couple of weeks at least – diarrhoea, hives, intermittent dizziness. But I was able to find consolation in the knowledge that the Dumper had ended up happy, and now I could cast out my net in favour of the Dumpee. Second chances sometimes taste sweeter.

And so I coaxed the dental technician into a stumbling relationship with an ambitious optician, and Charles the skinny immigration officer ended up with Idriss, a 250-pound asylum seeker from Chad, who, it turned out, shared his passion for early-Eighties German electronica. The Latvian gasman found a Lithuanian online, they're now the happiest couple in Swindon. Which is saying something, as Swindon is a surprisingly happy city.

I open my new journal, smoothing down the skin of the page, fingertips taut with anticipation. Rewrite the list, Felicity, shuffle the pack. I'm an optimist. I see opportunity not affliction in all things. The pale page the hue of a naked bottom just waiting to be smacked. But still the beef fries. Try to remember the names, girl, what's wrong with you? Women's faces flicker behind my eyes, but not monikers. Gwen. Gwendolyn. A wet string bean with dimples. Who is she to Julius and Julius to her?

One name I cannot forget. Daisy Perkins. I saw her dead.

In the immediate aftermath of violence there is often adrenaline and trembling and sometimes great strength. Awa Yasin maced the man from next door, then swept up Arnold Perkins with one hand like a rugby forward, at the same time dialling her phone with the other. Bounded downstairs, tiny and ferocious.

Out on the street a pair of East End mothers knelt by Julius Miles, wide one rolling him carefully into the recovery position whilst lean one carefully took a picture on her smartphone, in case the unconscious giant tried to sue them later for having caused or added to his injuries.

In the general kerfuffle, I climbed the steps to the front door of number 40 behind them and slipped inside, easing the door shut behind me. A simple click.

The house was still and quiet. Small scuffling sounds and murmurings from the Somali girl and the boy on the floor below me. In front of me, a woman lying naked on the floor, but she might as well have been piles of clay. No human presence other than flesh spread out in parts with names like leg, arm, hand, breast. Mouth half open as if on the cusp of a pithy rejoinder.

"Dead's not bad, what would you know about it? Wallflower!"

A dead person is a sculpture, nothing more, nothing less. The object has the power to frighten and agitate but is in itself opaque. Some of you know what I mean, those who've seen the dead. You just need to know where to look; hospital wards, retirement and funeral homes, the air the same in both, dry and mephitic. I saw my first corpse at the age of nine, road-traffic accident, the old man and I on the bus back from the Ritzy, Charlie shouting at the driver to stop, his voice a policeman's bark even out of uniform. Told me to wait by the grubby launderette as he took charge, first response, commandeering the teetering cabbie's radio to call it in.

I looked. I think he knew I would. Maybe even wanted me to.

A woman, same age as Daisy Perkins give or take, mid-thirties. The front of the black cab had mounted on her crushed bike as if having sex with it. She lay to one side, cast away by the gutter. Blood pooled like resin beneath her bike helmet. Skirt up round her tummy, knickers for the world to see, and don't think they didn't. I looked. Didn't even ask Dad to smooth down her hem out of respect for her. I stared in terror formed of a simple fear.

That this woman had died without finding love.

I leant in closer, seeking a sign, anything in her eyes or mouth or the general mist still clinging to her body that would tell me that she had died in Grace, not flung asunder into the cosmos without wings. She wore no wedding ring to give a hint. No one understood the depth of my tears, assuming childish shock, a thick wool coat around my shoulders and a bosom hug from the large Jamaican woman running Speedy Clean.

But I was desperate to know. Had the cyclist been loved? Was it possible to tell? I suspected it could be, because anything is discernible if you have the energy and time to uncover it. A lifer with a window can give you the minute of the day just by the shade of his walls.

From Dad's notebook I found a name, Samantha Doherty. Didn't take long to look up the relatives, her parents. Attended the funeral, saw a man her age, and a child, each weeping buckets. Slunk away, the only one overjoyed. There was no doubt she would be missed.

After my old man was made detective, my research intensified. Found post-mortem photographs almost every week in the folders locked inside his briefcase, a simple combination, shame on you, Detective Sergeant, your birthday backwards. Stared at the glossy colour prints. Photocopied them and stared some more at the portraits of pulverized meat, governmental snuff shots. The bashed with blunt instruments, the stabbed with six-inchers, the gunned, the strangled, the bottled and the hung. Police snaps slipping between my fingers like the secret pages of a conjurer's book.

Became lost in dead eyes. Were they at peace? Had they been loved at least once? Most had, I decided in my teens – most had.

In her hallway, spread out on the Victorian tiles, I could see that Daisy had been loved. I had no doubt. A softness around her oculus and mouth. A relaxation.

Her son Arnold loved Daisy Perkins, obviously. My guess is that Uncle Gus had loved her too, in his own way. My relief was complete – her soul had departed this world on wings young and old.

* * *

Julius Miles is summoned to the inquest into Daisy Perkins's death as a witness. He attends Poplar Coroner's Court in one of Uncle Gus's suits, a black two-piece circa 1987 from Martino's on Bethnal Green Road (now the Masjid Mosque and Cultural Centre). Sits in the front row, feels as if he's looking at himself, a stiff reflection, moulding his chin with one hand, then the other.

"I was passing my next-door neighbour's house on my way to the corner shop to get some milk when I saw that her front door was ajar. Having called out to her at least five times, I entered the house to discover Ms Perkins dead and naked in the hallway."

The Coroner records a verdict of "Accidental death". As if all other dying is planned.

* * *

Daisy Perkins's funeral takes place on a muggy Monday afternoon at the beginning of June. Julius receives official permission from the Health Trust to attend. "After all, you did find the body," concedes his boss, Richard Lovall.

"And we were friends. Of sorts…" adds Julius, matter-of-factly. "She was close to my uncle Gus…"

"Right…" nods Richard in a tone that invites Julius to elaborate. But Julius remains silent, rubbing eyes still sore from the synthetic analogue of capsaicin sprayed into his face by the Somali nanny Awa Yasin.

"Do you know the dead woman's family?" Richard continues – why wouldn't he, all managers are addicted to information from almost any source, they don't actually do anything, but survive through knowing who everyone else is sleeping with.

Julius shakes his head, bowed uncomfortably in the small chair. "Daisy was an only child. Parents had her late, they're no longer with us."

"Oh. Sad. Many friends?"

"Don't know. Don't think so. After all, the Vicar asked *me* to say something at the funeral. And I'm just her neighbour really."

"And you're her landlord, no? For the shop? What does it sell, antiques and things?"

"Oh. Yes. The shop." Julius nods into his chest. "Yes. I am."

"Do you know what you're going to say? For the eulogy?"

Julius shakes his head. "My uncle had a diary. Might glance at it, see if he mentions her at all. Steal his lines. He was funny. Much funnier than me."

"Really?"

"Yes. Can you believe it?"

Richard smiles. His words come gently but not without pain. "I spoke at my wife's funeral. At first I told them I wasn't going to... that I couldn't. But in the moment, I couldn't help myself. I think it made things a little easier in the long run, you know. Lifted something..."

"I really didn't know Daisy, Richard," Julius sounds suddenly testy. "The Vicar asked me to say something, that's all, I suppose I could have said no, maybe should have done. But... but... she was Gus's friend." Richard nods. "And she has a son. He's three, almost four. Maybe I can say something to help..."

"Three years old? Shit. That's awful. Just awful..." A moment as Richard reaches for his bottle of Evian, unscrews the lid hurriedly, sipping. Julius straightens, looking his boss full in the face. Wonders if those are tears welling in Richard's eyes. Then remembers...

"Oh. I see. How's it going, Richard, the IVF? Mandy coping all right? Any bite yet?"

Richard looks back at Julius. "Thanks for asking, Julius." And smiles once more. "We're doing fine."

* * *

Augustus Miles's diaries are written in simple ten-stave music pads. On average, one pad a year since 1973. Daisy Perkins came onto the scene in 2001, two days after the Twin Towers fell. Gus notes on 13th September that he'd just met the sort of woman buildings tumble for. It was, Julius recalls, a time when anything and everything seemed touched by the dust from New York.

Julius yanks five volumes from the cardboard shoebox, 2001 until the last one in 2005 (only half-filled). Lays them out on the kitchen table. His uncle's brilliant brain spilt onto pages and pages of tight neat lines, an irresistible swirl to the Ys and Qs. Julius opens "2001". Gazes at tiny handwriting. But sees no words. Letters refusing to connect in his head, this English might as well be Mandarin. His hesitancy overwhelming his optical nerve.

He closes the diary. Piles the music pads back one on top of another into the shoe box. Places the shoe box back on the top shelf of his wardrobe, behind the dusty board games and Gus's weather-beaten binocular cases.

He cannot read the diaries. He does not want to alter the work of art that is his Uncle Gus in his mind.

Julius sits up most of the night with an open Word document on his laptop. "DAISY PERKINS" blinking at him from the top of the screen. Types a few words, deletes them. Retypes. Deletes. Finally he searches on Google and finds a website: "Eulogy Examples 101". Fifteen minutes later his speech is written.

* * *

Julius heads out to buy new deodorant for the funeral. Usually he avoids the Roman Road Market with its crazy-paving scattering of drunks, marching drug addicts, barking fruit-sellers and fighting dogs, preferring the faux-marbleized vacuum and straight lines of the Westfield Centre in Stratford. But Daisy cherished the local market for its chaos, and Julius thinks it might be a tribute to her to buy something there.

At Superdrug next to the Quicksilver Mini Casino he sniffs seven brands of underarm deodorant before settling on a Gillette

Triple Protection System Clear Gel Cool Wave (No Marks Even on Black). As he strides back through the market assiduously avoiding the dark bloody spots on the grimy tarmac that are not blood at all but gelatinous phlegm laced with the dark-red paan chewed by older Bangladeshi women on their way to go online at the Bow library, Julius passes a neat little stall selling plastic toys. Lines of grimacing dolls on steroids, ranks of multicoloured plastic tricycles with long handles for fervent parents to push, files of red fire trucks waiting for a miniature disaster somewhere. In pride of place alongside the knockoff Barbies and spade-and-bucket sets is a large toy machine gun. "Sale Item, was £15.99 now £5.99!" Julius pauses by the box, walks on, turns around, looks again and buys the machine gun for Daisy Perkins's son.

He catches the number 25 bus from the Royal London Hospital to the funeral. It takes thirty-seven minutes to get from Whitechapel Road to the City of London Crematorium at Manor Park. I am already sitting at the back of the bus when Julius gets on, not even a glance in my direction. The bus busy with schoolchildren in crimson uniforms jostling and chewing gum, tossing vague obscenities at passers-by like boasts. I watch Julius, bowed in his usual stoop by the stairs, clutching the box containing the gift, attempting to appear invisible, which is not difficult in London, even when you're six foot four and carrying a replica machine gun.

We jolt through the streets of East London, and I think about Julius and his life of lines and numbers and I take out my notebook and scribble.

Takes buses even though he could afford taxis without a thought. Maybe to confront disorder? Or is he attracted to disorder? Like convent girls to men with motorbikes?

The noise on the bus increases as the schoolchildren near their stops, last-minute flare-ups, threats, offers and agreements made with each wheeze of brakes and suck of opening doors. As we pull away from Stratford Broadway, a group of lanky purple-uniformed boys of various ethnicities start teasing another boy in dark-blue school clothes who might be from somewhere like Romania or Albania or anywhere where boys are large and dumpy and have dark fuzz on their top lips even though they're only eleven.

They knock off the boy's glasses. They take his school bag and empty its contents onto the floor of the bus. None of the adults intervenes for fear of being knifed. Faces turn anywhere but. I glance at Julius. Head bowed by the stairs, hair almost rapping the ceiling.

He's the biggest thing on this bus. The bullies know it, a couple of them glance his way as they smudge the boy's exercise books into the chewing gum on the floor with their trainers. And the boy knows it too, looking up at Julius, silent but imploring. I see one of the textbooks mashed into the plastic, pages ripped and bent. *Framework Maths*. The boy has personalized the back cover with stickers of African animals.

Julius does not react. Bowed like a statue. He thinks about the excess waiting-time statistics for route 25 as a percentage of the minimum standard set by London Transport of 1.7 minutes. He stares out of the doors, which are fogging up with the breaths of around eighty pubescent kids, lips moving as he calculates that each person on the bus is breathing an average of fifteen times a minute, meaning that in any one second at least twenty people are misting up the glass. He counts the electricity poles and the increased prevalence of semi-detached houses with faux-Elizabethan frontages as the bus gets nearer to the green expanses of Wanstead Flats. Amassing numbers, square footage, house prices compared to national trends, number of cars per resident for each street we pass.

I stay focused. Don't even think of looking at me, Fuzzlip. On a job I cannot break cover.

As the ringleaders get off three stops later, the boy gathers up his books, attempting to smooth down the pages, stuffing them hurriedly into his bag, and I glimpse neat block capitals on one of the covers. Adem Yilmaz. I scribble the name on a page of my notebook, tearing the paper from the spiral, folding it neatly and placing it in the back pocket of my jeans. When Julius is seen to, I'll spend a couple of days, no need for more, find someone for Yilmaz. A first ever kiss before summer's through, to help ease the pain.

* * *

I wait until the sombre opening hymn seeps through the double doors before creeping into the back row of the crematorium. I go unnoticed.

Tall vaulted brick ceiling, skylights half open, beaten and bruised sky semi-conscious and low on this heavy June afternoon. Twenty or so mourners. A small turnout for an old person, let alone a woman under forty. A few faces I recognize, the headmistress from Arnold's school, dolphin earrings leaping and diving as she belts out 'Lord of All Hopefulness' louder than all; Janice, the corpulent head of Early Years Foundation Stage, blinking over her Ray-Bans; the shaven-headed droopy-lidded Bangladeshi hairdresser who runs Noor Barber's next to Domus Decorus; a couple of local mums Daisy got drunk with on occasion, clad in tight dresses of grey and black better suited to Christmas Parties, heels to match, make-up of shade and intensity that suggests they've taken inspiration from recently watched episodes of *Gossip Girl*.

The Vicar, early thirties, balding, has intelligent eyes and shoes. Probably a do-gooder slumming it in the East End to make himself feel better about his Oxbridge education.

Julius is alone, as usual. Front row left. Front row right, the small Somali girl, black dress which might as well have Primark written on the sleeves, black tights, black flats. Black headscarf. Heavy serious eyes ringed with heavy serious make-up. It's clearly her first Christian funeral, hand as uncertain and wayward as a gasping fish out of water, flapping at the boy's back, his arm, then his hair, back to his arm again.

The boy, Arnold Perkins, is dressed in a small grey suit, pale face, fixed frown. Dwarf bank manager rejects a loan. Eyes cast down at his shiny shoes, he's keeping dead-still for his dead mother in the coffin six feet from his seat. The wood dark, could be oak. Top of the range. Wonder who paid for it?

Coffins are like underwear adverts, dead cats and the mentally ill, things we cannot help staring at. Picture what's under the lid, try not to. Waxwork dummy, or decaying meat?

Life stops quickly. It takes three to seven minutes for brain cells to die once the heart stops pumping the red stuff around the body. Decomposition commences immediately, intestinal fauna digesting gut and stomach, clostridia and coliforms invading the rest of the body. The pancreas eats itself. Decomposing tissues release verdurous substances and gas, the skin turns greenish-blue and blistered, starting with the abdomen. The front of the body swells in a grotesque parody of pregnancy, the tongue protrudes and fluid from the lungs oozes out of the mouth and nostrils.

This is when the embalmer begins. Wash the corpse with disinfectant and germicidal solutions. Bend the legs and arms and massage them to relieve rigor mortis (it is unlikely Daisy Perkins was buried wearing her trademark Converse – feet are usually too swollen and refuse to sit perpendicular to the legs after death, making shoes difficult to put on). Pose shut the eyes using an eye cap. Stick shut the lips with medical adhesive. Once the features are set, begin the embalming.

First the chemicals, formaldehyde, phenol, methanol and glycerin, injected through the neck and right common carotid artery. Displace blood from the right jugular vein. Pump embalming solution through the body, whilst again massaging the limbs to ensure proper distribution.

Make a single small incision just above the navel, push the trocar into the chest and stomach cavities to puncture the hollow organs and suck out their contents. Fill the cavities with a concentrated formaldehyde solution. Finally, insert a trocar button to fill the hole in the chest. Keep it simple, effective. You're servicing a car.

As the Vicar intones Psalm 23 – "Yeah, though I walk through the Shadow of Death, I will fear no evil" – I re-focus on my mark. Julius Miles stares blankly towards his hymn book thinking that 23 is the atomic number of Vanadium, the sum of the first six (2x3) digits of Pi, the angle of tilt of the earth's axis and the average number of seconds it takes for blood to pass through the human body. A Holy number.

Silence now in the crematorium chapel. Thick air, sweat between shoulder blades, women waving white service sheets in front of their noses as if frantically surrendering. Everyone has to be thinking it's the furnaces, but more likely it's just the unseasonably muggy weather. The promise of thunder appropriate, I believe, for a woman as stormy as Daisy Katherine Perkins, late of Bow.

Julius eyes the Vicar, who nods once then turns his back and takes a practised puff from the asthma inhaler concealed in his cassock. Julius folds himself out of the pew like a piece of elongated machinery. Head inclined, he approaches the small lectern. This is why I'm here. To see how my mark copes under pressure. A reality-TV moment – can Julius extol the life of someone his much-loved Uncle loved but he himself disliked intensely?

My suspicion is that Julius is a choker. If so, I'm looking for a conqueror to kiss steel into his blood. But if he pulls it off, perhaps I need a flake, a bailer, a woman less good under fire who will covet the big statistician's strength in battle and grow herself through his example. Do not think me callous. Daisy's dead, nothing's bringing her back. There are other ladies out there.

"And now Julius Miles, a friend of Daisy's, will say a few words…"

Hand to his mouth, his refuge and defence. Eyes stuck to the printed sheet of A4. Vicar's hand soft on his shoulder, and Julius remembers, finally, to look up. Blank gazes from the small congregation. He peers far over the boy's head – who wouldn't. One deep cough and he begins.

"Daisy lived an amazing life, even though it was rather short. Daisy was a great friend; the kind of friend that stands by you when you need somebody to be there. She always had a smile. And a friendly wave."

The Droopy-lidded Bangladeshi barber nods. Others await a punchline.

"I remember once Daisy said she had travelled the world. Lucky world, I say. She loved Africa. Particularly the animals. But also the people. She lived in Paris for several years and liked eating French food…"

Julius looks up as if expecting a laugh. When none is forthcoming, he returns to his page, ploughs straight his furrow. I'm impressed, he's a man whose internal timetable can defeat his fears.

"What is it that we remember when we think of Daisy? I'm sure everyone who knows her well would agree with me on this. It was her sense of humour. She was the kind of person that would make everyone laugh so hard that they'd end up crying. Who could forget her mother-in-law jokes? How about all her environmental jokes? Goodness! Just thinking about those environmental jokes still makes me laugh…"

Mourners glance at each other to see if they're alone in failing to recognize this side to Daisy Perkins. Which is unsurprising, given that Julius copied every line in his speech from the online template, his only piece of creativity being to insert the name "Daisy".

"This is what I will truly miss about Daisy. That she could make me laugh when I was really sad. She always cheered me up when she knew I'd just had a bad day. That's the trademark of Daisy. She always wanted to make people happy…"

In the front row, Arnold listens intently to these words. Staring up at Julius with big grey pupils.

"Daisy's death was sudden. I simply could not believe it. Daisy was too young, but I have realized that Daisy did indeed live her life wonderfully. Daisy was well loved and she had done so many things on earth and I'm sure she'll do much more in heaven. I will be for ever grateful to have known Daisy. I will be for ever grateful for having spent time with a friend like her. All the memories I have shared with her will be for ever cherished and remembered. Daisy will live for ever in my heart... In our hearts."

Next to Arnold, the Somali nanny is crying. Big round tears down her small round cheeks. Her shoulders actually judder. Julius continues, at pace now, his voice louder, owning the moment...

"Daisy is in heaven now, and here we are at her funeral. This is not the time for us to grieve her death but it is our time to celebrate her life. Don't ever forget Daisy. She never wanted to see people cry. She wanted to make everyone happy. So at this juncture when we are about to lay her body to rest, let's all think back and remember how Daisy touched our lives. How she made us laugh and how good Daisy was as a person. This is not the moment for us to shed our tears, but we should all be thankful that we were given the chance to have known a woman named Daisy."

A noise to my left makes me jump. Thought I was alone at the back of the show in seats reserved for mischief-makers and cold-hearted observers. Which one is he, I wonder? Silver-haired, early fifties, pale-blue shirt, dark-blue suit, rock-star sharp. £3,000 titanium Chopard Mille Miglia watch dropped straight out of a GQ page. He retrieves his fallen hymn book from the floor, apologetic but unabashed, as if that's how he lives. Cary Grant. The man my old man always wanted to be.

"Daisy will be for ever missed, but I know in the right time I will meet Daisy again. We will all meet Daisy again and she will make us laugh in tears again."

Julius sits down abruptly. Somali nanny tries to compose herself, dabbing her eyes with a black handkerchief. Arnold Perkins looks back down at his shoes. And the Vicar steps in for the kill.

"I want to thank Daisy's good friend Julius for that very moving eulogy. I myself will be brief. I did not know Daisy before her death, but I've had the great fortune to learn much about her in the past few weeks. I have learnt of her love of beautiful objects.

Her enthusiasm for new projects however challenging or outlandish. Her love of the music of Icelandic electro-folk legend Björk. Her fierce temper, her infectious laugh and her highly photogenic hands."

Cary Grant is nodding, his air of amused detachment wearing thin on me – and we've only just met.

"But there was one light that eclipsed all others in the palace of Daisy. The love of her life. The centre of her own joyful storm. Her son Arnold."

Murmurs from mourners. Arnold blinking, could be uncomprehending, could be fighting his own young tears. Can a three-almost-four-year-old understand the death of his mother? Can he own the emptiness she's left behind?

"Daisy said she loved Arnold like she loved sunshine. She soared when he smiled. She fought without fear when he was in need. And she told her friend Larry one time that Arnold helped her see God in the world, even though God and her had not spoken in a long time. I think that is a very beautiful way of putting it."

I look around the six men present. Unless Bangla Barber has given himself a Ready-brek English name, there are only three candidates for "Larry" in the chapel: seventy-something trembler in three-piece next to twinset Maggie Thatcher blow-dry – East End neighbours of the deceased I'm sure; stern late-forties slob in inexpensive dark suit who scratches the back of his neck whilst hymn-singing; and Cary Grant. Any one of them could be Larry. Or all of them. What's the probability, Julius? Three Larrys at a funeral numbering just twenty mourners?

"When someone dies like this, accidentally, suddenly, in good health, we talk of tragedy. A flower plucked, a child orphaned. The God who let this happen is cruel, we think. I think it too, of course I do. Yet this God who sits back and watches us die is also the God who created us. Not for nothing do we call him Father. For like a parent, he gives us life and then lets us go. To be ourselves. To make our own mistakes and our own successes. We all die. It's who we are before the end that counts. What we do with the life God gives us. How we change. How we laugh. How we love."

I raise my head. The Reverend seems to be looking only at me. Soft and earnest, a good man. A perspicacious man. Is he on to me? Does he sense I'm the competition?

"I leave you with the message, for me, of Daisy's death. Shakespeare summed it up in his Sonnet number 73: 'This thou perceiv'st, which makes thy love more strong: To love that well which thou must leave ere long.' Let us love more, deeper, better in the knowledge that the only thing that is sure is that there will be a time when we will no longer see those we love. And that the only thing that survives of us is love."

* * *

Thunder rumbles as we trudge from the chapel, bruised sky finally starting to cry, teardrops smudging the concrete flagstones.

Julius waits under a tall tree counting the drips from the leaves, the even intervals between drops reassuring to him – ten seconds, ten seconds, ten seconds. When the Somali nanny exits the church, holding the child's wrist in one hand and a large rainbow umbrella in the other, Julius steps from his arbour into the rain, robot-strides towards them.

Awa Yasin is chatting with Twinset and Three-Piece. Julius seems to know them too, old folks who live on the same street, probably friends of Uncle Gus's from way back, because who wasn't a friend of Gus's? Julius waits, shifting from foot to foot in a puddle. Twinset and Three-Piece nod and smile, Twinset's hand on Awa's shoulder, thirty or more funerals to her name, practised in the much underrated art of consolation.

"Takes time, love, always does. Time's the healer. No doubt. No doubt."

Finally, Awa senses Julius's presence. Looks up, face paler, round cheeks drawn. Seeing Julius does nothing to improve her complexion.

"Oh!" she exhales. Julius finds himself staring down at her lips that form a near-perfect zero, the last number to be adopted into the modern numerical system because human beings find it easier to accept the concept of presence rather than absence, even though personally I have found that absence is often the predominant force in our lives.

"Hello," begins Julius, bowing low because the Somali nanny is five foot two. "Could I have a word?" Neither he nor Awa Yasin register my presence ten paces behind them, the ghost in the photograph.

"Er, thanks Daphne, George," Awa says to the neighbours, calmly. "I'll bring Arnold round end of the week like normal, yeah? Sorry, I've got to talk to Mr Miles a sec…"

Awa Yasin takes hold of Julius's arm. Julius steps back, shaken by the physical contact, but her grip is firm. Fingertips warm, dark against his blotched, worried skin. She eases him round 180 degrees so their backs are turned to the old folks.

"Look, sorry, I meant to call, no hard feelings about spraying your face, yeah?"

Julius shakes his head. "It's fine. I should have seen you coming. I'm sorry about your employer. Sorry about Daisy."

"Thanks," murmurs Awa. Her eyeliner has run, two insolent streaks down lovely skin. Tears welling again and it's clear that Julius would like her to stop crying, but he does nothing, which is the right thing to do, because tears born from emotion contain larger amounts of manganese and the hormone prolactin than those wrung from pain, and if the body releases manganese and prolactin it can enhance the weeper's mood and in some cases increase her sexual libido.

Not that I've decided the Somali is for him. But there's no harm in seeing which way the wind blows.

On average, women cry sixty-four times a year. Men just seventeen. This means statistically speaking women are four times more likely to weep than their male counterparts, which seems about right. Ever since I started Hormone Replacement Therapy I've been crying more. Possibly four times more. And I have to say, hand on heart, I feel better for it.

"God, look at me, you'd think I'd just won an Oscar or something," Awa laughs weakly, swiping her eyes, eyeliner devastation. "Truth be known I'm a bit of a weepy Wendy at the best of time, bawl at almost anything, limping kittens, Britney Spears songs… er, clouds…"

"Clouds?"

"Yes. Clouds can be sad, can't they?"

Julius looks at her for a brief moment. Then nods. "I suppose they can."

She gazes at him, curiously, as if for the first time. "I liked your speech. I didn't know you and Daisy were… you know, so intimate. I thought…"

"Yes. Well… The Vicar asked me to say a few words, it was my uncle really that she was close to… Before he died, obviously."

Only now does the boy Arnold look up at Julius from the loose collar of his suit. It takes Julius a couple of seconds to realize the small creature is staring at him. Gratefully he turns.

"Got something for you here, young man!" he declares loudly in a parody of insouciant enthusiasm. "Here!" Julius conjures the boxed machine gun from beneath his coat, thrusts the large plastic weapon towards the small boy. Arnold looks up at Julius, confusion flickering up and down his wan features. Looks to Awa. Awa nods back at him.

"I'm sorry," Arnold states slowly, measuring out his words like ingredients of a familiar recipe. "I'm not allowed to play with guns. They're violent."

Julius is surprised by the boy's eloquence. And annoyed.

"Why not? The world's a violent place."

"But it doesn't have to be," interjects Awa. "We prefer that Arnold grows up in a gun-free environment, so that he can go out into society knowing that you do not have to resort to physical violence in order to get what you want."

"But sometimes you do have to resort to physical violence to get what you want. Sometimes physical violence is the only language the dumb-wits understand."

Awa chuckles, fingers to mouth, not to protect herself like Julius, but rather to curb her first true instinct: laughter.

"Thank you, Mr Miles. The toy was a kind thought. But we cannot accept the gift."

"Who's this 'we' you keep talking about? You and your dead employer?" Julius's voice almost a full octave higher. Faces turning to look. Words are like buzzing bluebottles to Julius, he swats them but never hits hard enough, only stunning them momentarily before they fly away from him again. "Look, please, just take the gun... Arnold wants it. Don't you, Arnold? You want the gun Arnold, don't you? Don't you, Arnold?"

The boy appears torn, hand twitching millimetres from his side. Then he shakes his head, empathically. "No. No thank you."

"Oh, for goodness sakes," Julius groans as he rips open the box, tearing the plastic machine gun from its packaging ties. "It even sounds like the real thing! Rat-A-Tat-Tat!" Red flashes from the barrel as he pulls the trigger. "Rata-Tat-Tat!"

Everyone is looking now, old folks, hefty headmistress, stern schoolteachers, Bangla Barber and assorted hangers-on. Frozen in intrigue as the tall man in the black suit direct from 1987 totes the plastic machine gun in the air. Rambo the Geek.

"Excuse me," murmurs a cheerful male voice behind Julius, and I sense a hint of Estuary in an otherwise clipped accent. Julius turns to point the gun at Cary Grant, who raises his hands in defence.

"Woha! Don't shoot! I come in peace."

Julius lowers the gun. Cary Grant holds out his hand, and the next thing that makes me suspicious of him is the length of his thumb. Longer even than the index finger, a curving instrument like something a dentist might use to check under your tongue. A menacing digit. Capable of malice.

"Larry Silk. Friend of Daisy's. And you are?"

"Julius." They shake. "Julius Miles."

"Julia Smiles? Or Julius Miles?"

Julius shudders. Three decades of teasing, a rot within him that has never dried out.

"Sorry, Julius, heard that one before, I suspect. You're the long-suffering landlord. Must have been sparky dealing with Miss Perkins…" Larry Silk smiles like he means it, although I'm not sure he does. Julius looks down on him.

"My uncle trusted Daisy, admired her 'pluck' – I think he called it. I tried to do the same."

"Well put, well put indeed. Pleasure to meet, despite the circumstances. So… Miss Yasin, the Reverend would like a word, wants to know if he can drop in on young Arnold later this week?"

Larry Silk's hand on the Somali nanny's arm, people touch at funerals, see for yourself, they need a pulse. As the man and woman turn, Arnold walks away, a deliberate separation. Stops by the pavement, gazing up at the tall chimney as if seeking out the smoky ashes of his mother snaking into the dark sky. I know what he's thinking. If Mummy was by my side I could turn my head into her skirt and the world would be dark and warm and safe.

Maybe Julius realizes this too, because he hides the weapon in his coat and walks up to the boy. Man blinks, boy blinks.

"Sorry. About the gun."

"It's okay. You didn't know."

"I should have realized it was the wrong present to get you. Maybe sometime in the future I can get you the right thing. Okay?"

"Okay."

In the boy's black pupils and dark-brown irises Julius sees himself, twice. At the sides of Arnold's forehead, thin pulsating purple veins retreat under a thick mat of light-brown hair. Julius reaches out, gently touches the boy's shoulder. Arnold flinches slightly. Julius touches his shoulder again. This time Arnold does not flinch.

"We all die sooner or later, Arnold. You will see your mum again one day, I promise. I'm sorry she died. She was a fine antiques dealer."

Arnold scuffs the toe of his once shiny black shoe against the kerbstone, back and forth, back and forth. Wanting to hurt something, if only his leather Clarks. Julius senses he needs to say more.

"I'm a statistician, Arnold. Do you know what a statistician is?"

Arnold shakes his head. Awa Yasin reappears, poised to intervene, tiptoe ready.

"I count things and then I put those things in order and it helps people decide whether the things are in the right place or not. Okay?"

"Okay."

"And I know because I've counted them that most people do not die like your mother, in an accident. Statistically speaking an accident like hers is very rare. You have a one in 3,750 chance of dying accidentally in this country. So you need to realize it is very unlikely such an accident will ever happen to you. Okay? It's most likely, given the year you were born in, that you will live until you're at least eighty-seven years old."

This time Arnold doesn't respond. Julius frowns as if he knows the truth is there but just beyond his grasp. Then his face relaxes, the idea good and solid and real. He takes a small paper pad from his jacket pocket and writes something, ripping off the piece of paper, handing it to Arnold. The boy staring at the black lines on white.

$$(1 + 1) - 1 = \infty$$

"One plus one minus one equals infinity," explains Julius. "I think that's a good way to describe how you're feeling, at least mathematically speaking. Keep it. When you're older maybe it'll make more sense."

"Come on, Arnold," says Awa firmly, enlacing the small boy's hand, and they walk with Larry Silk back towards the small groups of black-suited mourners who huddle under the ever-darkening sky. I watch the older man, the straightness of his back, the clack of his heels, the cut of his jib.

Julius turns up his coat collar and plods through the puddles out of the crematorium to the bus stop. When the number 25 bus pulls up, he asks the bus driver if he has any children and the driver asks why and Julius says, "Because I bought a toy gun for someone, but they're not allowed to be violent, so if your children are allowed to be violent they are welcome to it," and the bus driver grins and says, "They like to play a bit of cops and robbers now and again," and he takes the plastic gun and hides it under his bag so the other passengers will not get scared.

I do not follow Julius onto the bus. I leave him to rest his head against the misted window and count the lamp-posts all the way back to Bow. I stay to watch Awa Yasin and complete my notes.

Orphan's only carer. Capable, no doubt. A cupful of joy, could be annoying, half full for a lifetime? Probably religious. What's her family situation? Traditional Muslim? Could be a hiccup if she's the one for JM.

Awa kneels down by Arnold, tissue-wipes his nose. Tugs down his tiny suit. Hugs him. Ushers him into the minicab car seat, tightening buckles with strength and speed. Climbs in herself, bodyguard and angel.

The crematorium car park is empty now but for one vehicle. BMW 760Li, black, tinted windows, chrome hubcaps. Very expensive wheels for East London, footballers' wheels, barristers' wheels. Or the wheels of someone making money that Her Majesty's taxman isn't necessarily aware of.

Larry Silk exits the crematorium and points his key fob at the BMW. Pauses at the driver's door, looking about him. Doesn't see me, no one would behind the gargantuan horse chestnut tree by the gates. But I watch him. And this is the surprise. Silk is crying. Sodden, shuddering tears.

I'm beginning to suspect that Larry knew Ms Perkins very well. I have no doubt that summer flower Daisy liked a winter romance.

The older man wipes his nose on a handkerchief, inhales deeply, blessing the air in his lungs. Then gets into the car and drives off at speed.

My hand on the bark of the tree, dizzy suddenly. Unrest, rush of wind above, swirls of pale blossom rolling like froth on green ocean waves. I shiver, but it's not the breeze. Steady on, girl, steady...

I walk out across damp desert tarmac to the middle of the car park; you can smell the electricity in the air. Alone in front of the brick crematorium. A factory with a cross on top. Chimney still and empty now. All quiet except the flanks of threshing trees.

Black and vacant are the doors to the crematorium. I stare and stare, willing her to walk out alive.

And I am back in that house, staring at her body white and dead on the green-and-white tiles.

The police arrived ten minutes after Julius found Daisy's body. Two uniformed officers took one look at the scene and uttered the words "Accidental Death". Found the shower had just been used, wet towel dangling from its hook in the bathroom. In the hallway where she died, barely three feet from her outstretched fingers, a plastic beaker surrounded by a small pool of water. Tap still dripping in the kitchen below. Report written in their heads before their laptops.

"After her shower the subject was thirsty. She walked down two flights of stairs to the kitchen, filled a plastic beaker with water, came upstairs to the raised-ground-floor hallway, the water was spilt, the subject slipped on the wet tiles, tumbling backwards, and struck her head on the floor. Died instantly."

A simple story, told by those first tin lids, accepted and repeated down the line and up the chain, because like all good stories it sounded entirely true.

But I hear my old man's voice. His morning mantra. "Find the absence of the normal, Kevin. The presence of the abnormal."

Two images have been itching at the back of my head since Daisy's death. Her head wound. And the soles of her feet.

The gash that bled onto the tiles was located at the back of Daisy's skull, where the occipital curves away from her neck. There were classic signs of basilar bone fracture, periorbital bruising around the eyes, dabs of dried blood at her nostrils and her ears. Yet this kind of skull fracture is rare, occurring in less than five per cent of serious head traumas.

And her feet were dry. If Daisy slipped on spilt water there would have been water about her toes.

Another thing. Forensics found blood and a tiny bone fragment in loose grouting between the floor tiles. Yet other than in cartoons, people do not slip and fall backwards with enough force to crack the base of their skulls against the floor. Daisy's legs and feet would have had to windmill a good three feet off the ground to create enough momentum. Unless of course she was pushed, her head dashed against the floor by some external force.

The boy was hiding in the cupboard when Julius entered the house. What if he was hiding from someone? Someone who pushed his mother to her death?

I understand. Even murder cops get bored. They're as keen as the rest of us to go home and watch television. It's not the gunslingers who solve crime but the pedants and the bores, my old man explained. "The evidence is always there, son. Most cases are solved by a pig-headed copper going back one last time."

There is one more thing he told me, my cop father. Because it acts as an alibi, and because they get a kick out of seeing the pain and grief they've caused, killers often attend the funerals of their victims.

4

Awa Yasin lies in a nightdress in the sagging brass double bed that Daisy Perkins purchased six years ago at a car-boot sale in the car park of Carpetright in Braintree, Essex. The window of her dead employer's guest room looks out to the lights of three soaring 1970s council tower blocks behind the low Victorian streets. Three simple rectangles against the orange London night, monuments to linear structure, ordering the skyline.

Awa knows these towers. She tries not to imagine the old man with his lists of odds and horses' names on the twenty-first floor of Albion House. Fifteen nights she has spent away from him since Daisy's death. The only nights in her life. Never intended to. The first evening she held Arnold's hand tight in the lift, nothing new there, sometimes she brought him to the tower, they rode the lift up to the flat, gave him supper with her dad. Daisy would come and collect him after shutting up the shop. Said she liked her son seeing London from up high. Liked him getting that perspective.

On the first dreadful new night she cooked the boy his favourite: chicken, rice and beans. Her father slower than normal to chew each spoonful, Arnold staring at the puppets on television, the two diners framed by the setting sun over the capital city. Awa fighting back tears as she scrubbed the pans at the thought that when the same sun had risen that morning Daisy had still been alive.

When the boy looked up, squinting, she heard herself tell him that his mummy was with the sun now, watching him always. "You know how it is, even when you can't see the sun, it's always there?" So it was with his mother. And like the sun she would always make him warm.

Ignoring her father's scowls, she showed Arnold to the bed, her bed. Tried to get on his pyjamas. Which was when the boy started to scream. Her father shouting at them both in Somali, arms waving furiously, until she lay alongside one, then the other, waiting for both to doze into sleep. Sat on the floor of the hallway between the two rooms, hugging tight her heart.

The next night no different. Her father angry at her, not the boy. In the morning, both rubbing eyes, she and Arnold went to the nursery, where she told the Early Years leader that she had to take an hour, her father was unwell. Hurried back to Albion House. Sat down with him, cross-legged before him on the floor.

"He needs me, Adabe."

"I need you."

"Adabe, right now he has no one else."

"I have no one else." Ensconced in his armchair, face of a retired cherub, pencil moustache, bald patch. A gleaming mahogany egg. In a brown suit. A man called Mohammad Ali, but this one no fighter.

"You're sixty-seven years old, Dad. He's three."

"If your mother were here, it would be different." Nodded to himself, to reinforce the truth of his words. Long fingers that once played violin at high school in Mogadishu cradling his round belly, pregnant with beer and bariis. "But as we know, she is not coming back..."

"Come on, Dad. Mama's in Dubai, not heaven. Even the social worker said Arnold needs continuity. Anne Sheldon's from the Council. Unlike us, this sort of situation is not new to her..." Hoping the mention of her father's former employers might soften him. Tower Hamlets Council. Mohammad's respect, even love, for the Holy Order of THC that took him from a Heathrow plane, asylum seeker number 403 with grumbling wife and two wide-eyed young girls, gave him housing, money and before long a job delivering internal mail in a white Ford Escort van with air conditioning. Tower Hamlets Council. Working at the right hand of God in Mohammad's eyes.

"What the hell you think people see, Awa? A girl like you. Playing mother like a clown jokes in a circus? A girl like you…"

"Like what, Dad? Brown? Young? Ditzy?"

"Like… Like you know what I mean…"

Awa stormed from the flat, took the boy in his superhero night clothes back to the house where his mother had died. Phoned her father only after the boy was asleep in his own bed in his own home. Standing in the empty kitchen, drinking a dead woman's coffee.

"I'm staying at Daisy's house, Adabe. For Arnold. For now." Winced as her father slammed down the phone.

* * *

She feels the lights in the tower block as eyes watching her. Drifts into sleep finally, dreams of dancing with John Travolta in *Grease*, but not in Los Angeles, they're at Woodstock Primary, the students just nursery age but each three-year-old hand-jives like an expert.

Wakes to the boy's whimpering. Goes to his door, fingertips it open. Shadows of swallows fluttering anxiously above his head, a child's mobile of small wooden birds Daisy found at a car-boot sale in Canterbury.

"Mama. Mama…" His whimper.

She lies down beside him once again. Strokes his warm hair even though he's not awake, damp wisps between her fingers. She isn't Mama. Never will be. Wishes she could speak to her own mama, but Faduma went to see her daughter Faduma in UAE to help out with the baby grandson. Who is no longer a baby, but a boy older than Arnold, five full years old. Now Faduma The Elder speaks only through

Faduma The Younger, Mrs Man-with-the-Restaurant. Sister Faduma, Faduma the Fortunate, Faduma the Fat, Faduma the give-you-an-opinion-especially-when-you-don't-ask-for-one.

"Mother's happy here, Awa. No rain. You know how she hates English rain. I'll bring her back when she's ready, don't worry. And tell Dad to get on a plane, Rafiq wants to see his granddad."

Informed her father, who barely nodded.

Back in the spare room, Awa finally dreams once more, Travolta kisses amidst warm surf of a somewhere beach. Wakes and goes into the boy's room with a smile. All she can do for him.

* * *

I watch them leave the house, 8.45 a.m., as they do each school day. Not the world's longest commute, past five front doors to the Early Years entrance. Into the main building, Awa reappearing at the side gate that she unlocks, always a little late, 8.52 a.m. Smiling at the nursery pupils as they charge into the playground like babbling puppies. Dark-brown headscarf framing her almond eyes, cK, cK, cK like some ancient spell around her head, fake Calvin Klein, a one-time peace offering from Dubai.

At 9 a.m. or thereabouts Awa locks the gate once more. One glance back at the street, perhaps sensing she's being watched but no idea how closely. She's on my new list. My new question: who killed Daisy Perkins?

Larry Silk: a quick internet search at the Bow Ideas Store library tells me that Silk is an accountant, has his own company, First Financial Services, based in Canary Wharf. Nothing untoward that I can find. Larry's married, of course, some heifer named Jacqui. Perhaps Daisy was going to tell Mrs Silk she was bedding her husband, so Larry dusted her. Or perhaps **Jacqui Silk** discovered this herself and struck down the Jezebel with a sharp shove to her shoulder.

Trevor Nugent: Daisy's helpmate at the antiques shop, charity case. Nineteen years old, still spotty. Daisy employed him to deter local troublemakers, because Trevor is himself a local troublemaker. Suet eyes, string body, tracksuit whatever the weather. Looks hungry, always. Perhaps hungered after Daisy. Sexual advances rebuffed leave naked women with cracked skulls all the time. Read your newspaper.

Grace Chewitt: Daisy's cousin from Liverpool, overweight and underpaid, benefits clerk who might just benefit from Daisy's will. Failed to attend the funeral because she had an optician's appointment – tinted contacts took precedence. Tell me that doesn't sound unsound.

Frank the Lank: ageing alcoholic who walks past Domus Decorus at least six times a day in a worn leather jacket and stonewash jeans circa 1989. Ogles women, snarls sometimes, even at estate dogs. But he's as thin as Jesus without the beard and barely capable of lifting a can of Special Brew these days. Daisy could have crushed him with her little finger.

Awa Yasin. Just fifty kilos, 110 pounds, but something tells me Mohammad Ali's daughter packs a punch. But why kill the hand that pays you? Perhaps Daisy decided she needed to cut back in these recessionary times, fire the nanny – the kid's old enough to hang out at the shop after school, he could feather-dust a few figurines? But without Arnold, what is Awa Yasin? A nursery assistant who hurries home to her depressed father, locked in her lofty prison, the forgotten princess in the tower? With Daisy dead, might she be able to cling to the Prince-and-Heir for ever?

Notice that Julius Miles is absent from my list of suspects. This is not favouritism. It is a fact that he could not have killed Daisy Perkins. She died half an hour before Julius entered her premises at 8.25 a.m., according to pathology – body temperature as measured by first responders at the scene had declined just one degree below normal, clear livor mortis on the underside of her corpse suggested recent demise. Witness statements concur – Arnold told the family liaison officer that the last time he saw his mummy alive she was going to take a shower and he was watching *Thomas the Tank Engine*, not a DVD but the telly, which according to Channel Five's schedules for the day put Daisy's shower at sometime after 7.50 a.m. Julius was having breakfast at 7.50 a.m. Wearing a dark-blue V-neck sweater over a grey T-shirt. I remember it clearly.

I remember it clearly.

How does such a thing come to mind when I cannot recall where I left my purse this morning?

* * *

Julius makes dinner like he prepares statistics. Cut away the fat. Slice into exact segments. Grind, measure and weigh. Line up the ingredients. Stick them in the pan, fry at high heat and serve. *Jersey Royal potatoes boiled for 13 minutes. French green beans, 4-minute steam. Diced organic chicken thighs, Cajun style, Jamie's recipe from the latest TV show. Each day's meals inscribed on the calendar above the toaster, no repetition within 14 days, strict 21-day rotation, seasonal variations every 3 months.*

He takes care of himself, Julius. Healthy yet varied dishes from around the world. Now and again he allows himself the treat of setting out two plates instead of one. Conjures up a guest in his mind. She smiles back at him through settling steam. Nods with satisfaction at her first bite, and they talk of spices and poaching pans and Michelin stars in Vietnam and Argentina. She looks French, maybe southern German with just a hint of an accent, and tells him casually that she's just been made Associate Professor of Applied Mathematics at Harvard. Would Julius ever consider coming with her to start a new life in Cambridge, Massachusetts? Maybe even go back to college, get his PhD?

After eating, Julius clears the table, pulls on yellow rubber gloves, ties the half-apron about his waist and washes his glass, plate, cutlery, then the pans. Always the same order. Sets the table for breakfast. Straightens the tablecloth.

It's Thursday evening, one of the nights in the week when Julius works after dinner. Bach's Cello Suite number 1 to spur him through the last spreadsheet edit. *The Effect of Inherited Bleeding Disorders on Pregnancy and Childbirth*, ordered by Dr A. Rachida of the Department of Obstetrics and Gynaecology, a woman Julius has never met but trusts, because she signs her emails "Yours Truly". She's on the hospital management board. A good pie chart cannot harm his prospects of keeping his job.

The knock on the front door startles him. Quick, furtive. Julius grimaces; only temporary postmen and itinerant youths brandishing baskets of overpriced dusters, sponges and batteries knock rather than ring the doorbell, always in a hurry. He remains at his desk, using formula-auditing tools to convert text string to numeric value in SQL. Watching the numbers align, the final step towards purity.

Another knock, short, taut. Julius strides to the front door, unbowed, knowing how to intimidate as long as he's on the right side of his own doorstep. Head almost touching the frame, chest full. He swings open the door, King of His Castle.

The doorstep is empty. Julius blinks in tangerine streetlight.

"Please. Mr Miles."

Julius looks down. The boy barely reaches his thigh bone. Strigine eyes gazing up at him with an expression Julius finds puzzling. Anger? Resentment? Concern? A stressed child, for whatever reason.

"Oh. Hi Arnold. Is everything all right?"

"Come. Now. Mr Miles. You must come…"

Pulls at Julius's trouser leg, David dragging Goliath. "Come…"

"Why? What is it? What do you want?"

But Arnold Perkins is gone, holding on to the railings with one hand, sliding his feet to the edge of each step before slipping down the next, red flashes with each tap of his dinosaur soles on the concrete. Julius admiring the evenly spaced blinks from the kid's shoes as Arnold struggles up the steep steps next door, pausing at the top. Face screwed in tension and disbelief: "I said come on! Now!"

Julius gazes up and down the street, seeking other adult assistance. I remain in the shadows, where I belong. A sigh, and Julius lumbers slowly down the six steps, up the six steps. Hesitates, then enters Daisy Perkins's house.

The hallway dark. The small white face of the boy by the stairs to the lower ground floor. Pale hand beckoning in this house of ghosts.

"Come on, Julius. She's down here…"

Julius peers down the stairs after the boy, the open-plan living room lit by a single standard lamp in one corner. Long shadows across swirling carpet. The room is empty. Julius hesitates; he's descended these stairs just once before, angry as a hornet at Daisy's lateness in paying the rent.

"Come on!"

The boy urging him, and suddenly Julius can hear moaning, a guttural choking. He grips the banister, terrified that this is Daisy Perkins, surged from beyond. Then he sees the body in the shadow of the dining table.

Julius hurries down the stairs but stops halfway across the room. Staring at Awa Yasin, her thin arms jerking from her body, one leg snapped beneath the other, chin jutting vertically, then the moaning again. Head jacking left and right as the seizure rattles her body. A spew of froth seeps from her lips.

Julius stares, desperate to decipher a pattern to her movements, a regularity, something that could be strung along a graph, charted, boxed or diagrammed. He is overcome by the chaotic spasms of her limbs, the shake of her head, the saliva stringing from her mouth. This insane puppetry.

"What time is it?" Julius turns to the boy as if in a dream. Arnold Perkins repeats himself like a frustrated schoolmaster. "What time is it? She needs to know. You have to write it in her book."

Julius looks at his watch. "9.23 p.m. What book?"

"In her bag."

"Is she okay?"

"She has epil-seepee…"

"Epilepsy." Julius's head filling finally with the relief of numbers, rattling them off as the woman's left hand rattles the metal table leg. The World Health Organization reports fifty million epileptics in the world, a percentage of 8.5 per 1,000. 402,000 individuals in the UK registered with GP practices as having epilepsy, 6.2 per 1,000 people, or one in 161 inhabitants. Epilepsy's rate of occurrence increases with age: around three per 1,000 in under-sixteens, but twelve per 1,000 in the over-sixty-fives. Blackpool Primary Care Trust has the highest rate in the UK at 8.6 per 1,000 people. In London it's much less, 4.4 per 1,000, perhaps on account of the capital's younger population. In 2008, there were 973 deaths from epilepsy in England, 565 men and 408 women. Half of these deaths occurred among those aged between fifteen and fifty-four.

"Did she tell you what to do?" Julius asks. "If she's having a fit?"

"A seizure. It's called a seizure."

"Yes. You're right. Sorry… seizure. What did she tell you to do?"

"Get Mr Miles."

"Okay. I'm here. Now what?"

Arnold bites his lip, narrow eyes in concentration. "A pillow. Under her head."

Julius clutches a pillow from the sofa, crouches down. Tries not to look at the eyes of the Somali woman that gaze at him blankly, as dead as dead, but she's not, her body straining, demons dancing, neurones flaring.

With great focus and determination, Julius reaches beneath her headscarf, cups her skull in one hand, head and palm a perfect fit, how light and fragile compared to his own thick cranium. Slides in the pillow. More foam oozing from her mouth, he reaches for her...

"No. Don't touch her mouth. She said. Don't touch her mouth."

"What about her tongue, what if she swallows it?" Julius scrutinizes the small boy, now fearful that Arnold knows nothing, even though he sounds as certain as a monk.

"Don't move her tongue, she said! Don't touch her mouth!" Julius nods. Steps back.

They wait. Hulk and Pixie by the fitting woman. A silent vigil. After a while the puppet jerks slow.

"Push her that way," says the boy, mimicking lying on his side.

"What, like this?"

Julius reaches out, suddenly aware of his big meaty fingers on her dark skin. Gently he turns her slight body, just a nudge, her mouth slackens, drool spooling onto the floor. Her breathing more regular now, at rest, at rest. Eyes shut. She could be sleeping.

Arnold sits cross-legged, arms crossed too. No wonder nor apprehension. A tiny sentinel.

A few minutes later she stirs. Julius fills a water glass. Kneels down. Dark brown eyes focusing upwards, searching his face. She mumbles something. Julius leans closer.

"Thank you," she whispers again. "Thank you."

* * *

"I'm fine. It hasn't happened in a long time. I'm fine."

Julius nods, states without emotion: "Last year eighty per cent of epilepsy sufferers registered at GP practices were recorded as being seizure-free for at least twelve months. Although this figure tends to be less in more deprived areas. In the Knowsley Primary Care Trust near Liverpool, for instance, the figure was merely sixty-three per cent. Nobody's quite sure why."

Awa smiles. "You work at the hospital don't you? Statistics or something?"

Julius shrugs. Wonders what he's still doing here sitting at the table while she sips water and tugs at her headscarf. Arnold asleep on the sofa, SpongeBob playing quietly on the small TV.

"Statistics. Wow. Cool."

"Sometimes it is."

"Well you're talking to someone who's a complete waste of space at maths. Didn't even get a GCSE. English, music, art – that was me – crap at maths and science, not one of my skill set I'm afraid, got the short stick there. My sister Faduma, on the other hand, she's sharp as a tack with numbers, did maths A level, could have been an accountant now, but she does the books for the restaurant her husband owns, they live in Dubai, United Arab Emirates…"

"Hmmm. Well I should…"

"Me, I can't even add up some days, don't get me started on long division. Thank God for calculators, hey?"

"Thank God." Julius stands, tries to move quietly, but his knee knocks the chair, scrape of metal on tile. Arnold does not stir.

"Don't worry. He's out. Amazing how they can sleep through anything, isn't it. Beautiful, really. I'll carry him up to his bed in a tick."

"Do you really think you're okay to stay with him?"

"Told you. I'm fine. Afterwards, I'm always fine. I get a bit chatty, as you might have noticed, funny some people are knackered, they just need to sleep, but me it's like a shot of something, I feel energized somehow, little Miss Chatterbox, me…" She stands firm, arms across her small chest as if to prove her solidity. Not much bigger than a child herself, thinks Julius. She gestures to the sleeping boy. "How about my little hero, yeah? Did me proud. I told him when I first started working for his mum, told him about my condition, said if it happens when we're alone, just you and I…"

"You and me."

"Sorry?"

"You and me. Not you and I."

The Somali woman looks at Julius, he hurries to cover his embarrassment. "You said when you first started looking after him, you told him…"

"Yeah, right, told him 'just find someone'. A grown-up. Tell them the checklist, I got him to repeat it, he likes repeating things, you know, nursery rhymes, even adverts off the telly, 'Go Compare, Go Compare, to be sure when you first insure Go Compare… do you know it?"

"No. I don't watch much television."

"Don't blame you. It's rubbish mostly. Anyway, I told him to tell the grown-up the checklist. 'Time'. 'Pillow'. 'Recovery Position…' Actually I don't think I said 'recovery', because I wasn't sure he knew the word, but of course he only had to hear it once, he's scary with words, you just have to say something, just one time and there it is, straight back at you, I think he's gifted, well with language anyhow, probably other things as well… So I just said make sure the grown-up pushes me on my side, and I showed him. Did he show you?"

Julius nods. Awa smiles. "Good boy." Pulls a blanket over Arnold's legs, covers his toes.

"Well, you know where I am if you need something." Julius heads for the staircase, reaches the top stair, a metre from where Daisy Perkins died.

"Julius."

Julius stops, turns. She wants something from him, but he cannot think what it can be.

"See, the thing is, Julius, no one knows about my condition, and I'd appreciate it if you'd keep it to yourself. I mean, I know you're not exactly Mr Tell-Everyone-on-the-Street, but if you are speaking to anyone, George and Daphne, Freya, the French couple… It's not something I'd like to broadcast. Okay? Thanks. Appreciate that."

"Did Daisy know?"

"No."

"You think that was very responsible? Considering you were looking after her son? I mean what would have happened if you were out somewhere, or on the Underground, or by the canal, you could have fallen in, what would he have done?"

Awa steps towards him, two steps at a time. A glare on her far bigger than her size.

"Or simply crossing the road, a busy road like the Mile End Road, holding his hand and then you get a seizure and you let go of him and there's a truck coming…"

Julius recoils as the small woman glares up at him.

"I don't get it with you. You make that lovely speech at the funeral, all strong and heartfelt about Daisy…"

"It's a 'eulogy', not a speech. And I told you I didn't know her…"

"…and now you're burning me for being reckless with Arnold, when everyone knows I wouldn't even breathe if I thought it'd hurt a hair on that boy's head. You're lucky I'm prepared to let it go, just this once, because I know deep down you're just worried about him…"

"Am I?"

"What are you so afraid of?"

"I don't know what you're talking about."

"You don't have to hide it with me. I know everything. She told me, Daisy told me…"

"What did she tell you?"

"Four years ago you came to her house, early September. You got drunk with her. One thing led to another and you had sex. Nine months later, Arnold is born…"

Awa talks breathlessly, not seeing the big man's face freeze. "That's right isn't it, Mr Miles? You're the dad? You're Arnold's father? That's what Daisy told me…"

Julius hears the words but sees numbers, the woman's face suddenly a binary code, 0 and 1 played out in flickering waves. Her eyes blinking, zero and one, zero and one. Across the road I hold the cherry tree like a stick insect in a wind tunnel.

"…She told me you didn't want to be a father, it freaked you out, you shut the door on her. That's what she said. Said you were crap with adults, even crapper with kids. When you tried to give Arnold that machine gun at his own mother's funeral, I could see what she meant…"

Still Julius's eyes stare blankly at the small dark woman who's chuckling carelessly in front of him. Outside, I flick open another can of warm White Ace, the only thing for it.

"What's the matter?" says Awa, noticing Julius's frozen features for the first time. "Think I told the whole street? Think I cared enough to spread the word that Arnold's father lives next door, in the very next house, but doesn't have the balls to own up to it? Can't accept the responsibility?"

"No," says Julius, finally breathing again. "I didn't think that."

Awa looks at him, puffs out round cheeks. "What then? Angry someone else knows your dirty little secret? Ashamed? Or maybe you're just really disappointed in yourself that you bailed out before he was even born. And now Daisy's gone you're wondering, was there another, better, brighter life for you? Another way…"

"You're wrong. I never knew."

"Sorry?"

"I didn't know that Arnold was… I didn't know that I was… I never knew."

Awa stares up at Julius, confused. "You never knew?"

"What you're saying, that I'm… Daisy never told me."

The young Somali woman tilts her head to one side. Then the other.

"Oh crap," she states, simply.

* * *

On the desk Julius's laptop screen gleams in the shadows. *The Effect of Inherited Bleeding Disorders on Pregnancy and Childbirth* spreadsheet perfect in front of him. He sits in his desk chair, scanning the figures one last time, the columns, the rows. Attaches the file, writes a short message to Dr Rachida. "All Best Wishes, Julius Miles BA/Hons." Send.

Beyond, the eyes of the tower blocks look down on the sleeping houses without emotion, without remorse. As Julius stares up at them, one of the eyes closes, a light turned off. He climbs the stairs, brushes his teeth, gargles mouthwash, fifty-eight, fifty-nine... sixty seconds. Spits out, puts on clean ironed pyjamas and climbs into bed.

Twenty minutes later he hears a child's cry through the wall, footsteps ascending the stairs. A door closing. The crying subsides. He turns into his pillow and tries to produce an infinite family of quartic elliptic curves containing a length-10 arithmetic progression: *Let us consider a curve* $E : y^2 = f(x)$, *where* $f \in Q[x]$ *and f is not a square of a polynomial. We say that points* $P_i = (x_i, y_i)$, $i = 1,..., k$ *on the curve E form an arithmetic progression of length k if the sequence* $x_1; x_2,..., x_k$ *form an arithmetic progression...*

Half an hour later he falls into a fitful sleep.

5

Men think about sex every fifty-two seconds. Women think about it just three times a day, or once every eight hours. I suppose Julius would be unimpressed with this statistic given that I've just gleaned it from a women's magazine plucked from a bin outside Bethnal Green Underground Station. The article lacks any scientific references and footnotes, but it does have quotes from women named Tamsin and Scarlett, most likely staffers who work alongside the writer in the magazine's offices and spend their time making up stats and interviews for each other's articles.

Yet the statistic rings true. When I had a penis I thought about sex a great deal. But since my cock has been sliced and folded back into a vagina, branch into blossom, I find myself much less concerned with the idea of getting my rocks off. The dull ache from my breasts doesn't help my libido.

It took four years to get the operation. Twelve months of ebb and flow with Dr Fitzgerald my GP as we both tried to understand who and what I was, then the "Real Life Test": three years of psychiatric evaluation in conjunction with courses of HRT that caused my breasts to enlarge and my moods to swing like an executioner's axe. I wore wigs, dressed in women's clothes, went to a speech therapist who coaxed a more feminine lilt from my larynx. Then a year ago I had the silicone breast augmentation, and finally, six months ago, the vaginoplasty.

I'd never had an operation before. Even the dentist scared me as a child. I took the Underground to Chelsea & Westminster hospital, staring at my reflection in every tunnel. Walked out amongst the everyday shoppers on the Fulham Road, who barely glanced at the slender middle-aged man, stepping, certain, uncertain, towards the hospital.

Sweet eyes from the receptionist, sharing the hope, the faith that change can be true. They checked for blood clots, liver problems, they checked my heart. I told them no need, it's the one part that doesn't require realigning. My heart is bigger than anyone's. My old man always said so.

Read the statement in Dr Kamaljit Pillai's waiting room. "A patient must have a solid sense of their own gender identity. They should not be at the early stages of questioning, exploring or thinking things through. They should have enough mental stability to make an informed decision about their medical care. It is important to have the coping skills and supports to withstand the typical stresses of Sex Reassignment Surgery."

They assessed me, I passed. I'd prepared well. I stood upright at the toilet bowl for the last time in the shiny bathroom of Dr Pillai's office, let drop my penis and felt no sadness for the limp dangle of flesh – cut the fat from the steak. Lying on the trolley in the anaesthesia suite, I felt nothing between my legs, gone was the swell-surge that is a constant of the male condition. A flutter of excitement as the Propofol sang into my veins. No stress, no regrets, ninety-nine, ninety-eight, ninety-seven, fuzzy magic, slipping numbers, a spell of reinvention, frog into princess, beast into beauty...

* * *

Daisy Perkins had sex with Julius Miles. JM is Arnold's father?

A note by my bed. Takes a minute or so to figure it. Julius I know, big man, bowed head, my mark. But "Daisy Perkins"? A name like a business, stuff for sale. I do not recognize her. Seek out my journal, eventually find it in the rubbish bin under the sink. Peel off the carrot shavings, flicking through the pages I am surprised to find most of them blank. The cover seems new. In the bin again, a paper bag, receipt from W. Houseman Stationers – my supplier of fine-bound writing books, from the shop where Bethnal Green police detectives used to buy their notepads back before mobile phones, when it was the style and size of your blotter that said what kind of cop and man you were.

On my dresser mirror I find another note, tacked with tape. *Daisy is dead. Someone killed her.* Pull it off, seeing myself in the glass. A smile on the stern woman's face. Something is happening, Felicity. Something is happening.

* * *

So Julius had sex with Daisy Perkins. I remember it now. Who she is, was. The dead siren spread on the rocks next door.

From the kitchen I watch Julius pulling up weeds in his tidy-rowed garden. I've been in Daisy Perkins's house most of the morning. The Somali nanny left with the boy at 8.45 a.m., the daily rhythm, bright as a button as usual. My credit card got the front door unlocked in seconds.

I sit on Daisy's sofa unable to resist a smile. Daisy Perkins had sex with Julius Miles. Proves I've still got it, no need to doubt. Daisy was top of my list. See it right here.

"Daisy Perkins, thirty-nine years old, 5"5', fifty-five kilos, butter curls, jammy lips, breasts like beacons."

I told you. It's a calling. Most like me are born into it. They sent Feinstein the piano teacher to reveal my true vocation. Sitting at Stanley's old upright playing the Polonaise, trying not to gag at the scent of mothballs and pipe tobacco. Stan ceased humming, tapped the piano wood for me to stop and informed me that I had little talent for Chopin, but a calling for bringing men and women together. His conclusion: that whilst I was a hopeless musician, I was attuned to the lyrical song of love. "Kevin, you're a musician of the heart." And with that line from a Seventies rock ballad, my world shifted into focus for the first time.

The past is impregnable. But there is much to unravel here and now.

Julius is Arnold's father. Impregnated Daisy on the carpet where I now rest my Nikes. Calculate the probability, Julius. It's no story, no fairy tale. The impossible happened like this…

A warm October night. A file of bank statements. The big man struck low with bile. Marching. Knocking. Bowed fury. Ready to rumble with his flippant deceiver of a shop tenant.

"Miss Perkins! Open the door! Daisy! I need to talk to you! For God's sake!"

Has spent two hours formulating a three-point plan. Firm but fair, give her a week, full seven days, to pay the two months' arrears. £1,500 cash or electronic transfer, no cheque, no nonsense. Sign the direct-debit mandate he's printed and filled out for her for all future rent instalments. Or she's gone. No ifs, no buts, no kiss-my-disgruntled-big-behind. He'll find another tenant, a solid unremarkable business, another convenience store, newsagent, even one of those lettings agents specializing in Ukrainian and Polish clients.

It's late, after ten, but even if she were a nun who recited bedtime prayers before eight, Julius is angry enough to keep knocking. He knows Daisy's no woman of the cloth. Sure enough she opens the door in denim hot pants and low-cut T-shirt, glass of Sancerre dangling like a bracelet from her hand. She knows what she's doing, this one. The goods out and on the shelf. Leans back against the door post, not a bra in sight but plenty to catch the eye.

"Hey JM. What's cooking?"

"I'll tell you, shall I? Exactly what's cooking? You're two months behind with the rent. Again. Do you remember what I told you last time?…"

"Sorry Jules man, bit of a breeze out here tonight, finally turned chilly hasn't it, what a summer we had, felt like the bloody Balearics, not England. I've got a shiver, brrr, do you think we could carry this on downstairs?"

"...I told you it wasn't acceptable, in fact it was completely unacceptable, I told you it couldn't happen again. I said that. *This can't happen again.* And do you remember what you told me, what your reply was?"

"Mmmm..."

"You said of course, Julius, will do Julius, won't happen again Julius... actually you probably called me Jules. How many times do I have to reiterate it's not Jules, it's Julius!"

But she's gone, humming gently to herself in a saunter down the stairs to the lower ground floor. Julius follows, big and hot and angry, only pausing at the bottom step because he can go no farther. Daisy is bent over in front of him, picking at something on the carpet, full bottom raised.

"Bloody fluff, where does it come from, what do you do with fluff?" Persistent fluff no doubt, because she remains bent over a little longer, backside still floating until she uprights herself finally, pirouettes round to face him.

"I hear you Jules, old boy. Time for a finance chat. Absolutely." Steps back to allow him off the step, hand through hair, finger hooking to her front tooth. "I'm sorry Julius. I am, really. Sorry."

"You said that last year. I don't want to hear your sorries..."

"Stuff your sorries in a sack..." Daisy smiles. Julius casts his eyes down to his feet. There are times when he doesn't recognize them as his own, great clunking paddles. Suddenly his limbs feel leaden, his heart heavy.

"That was one of Gus's favourites, wasn't it Julius? 'You can stuff your sorries in a sack, mister...' Think he heard it on an episode of – what was that American series he loved..."

"Seinfeld."

"Seinfeld. That's the one. 'Stuff your sorries in a sack...' – ha, ha, ha..."

Julius nods, blankly. Sits down at the table. Staring at the numbers he's underlined on the bank statements. The printed direct-debit form. Smooths out the paper, a gesture both calming and empowering. Feels something tighten nicely in his shoulders.

"There's no use squirming out of it, Daisy. It's here, black and white. £1,500 you owe me. And I have decided that from this month onwards the rent for the shop will have to be paid by direct debit into my accounting account…"

"Your accounting account. Wow, Jules." Daisy's shrill laugh. "Okay. Accounting account it is then, why not?" Julius looks up at the glass of wine that's materialized by his side. Daisy raises hers. "But we'll get through it, won't we?"

"Get through what?"

"Our differences. For Gus. For Gus's sake." She toasts. "To Augustus Archibald Miles."

Julius drinks. The power of the much loved dead to spur us into actions that we'd otherwise shy away from. The wine is very cold. A loving punch to the back of his throat. He sips again as his uncle would have.

"Glad you're here, because I got you something…" Daisy in the kitchen now, busy, flouncing. "Just a little something…"

"Daisy, I'm not going to mess about here, I've work to do tonight, important work… It's an ultimatum I'm afraid. Clear and simple. Sign the direct debit. Or you're out!"

The smile of Daisy Perkins. She cleavage-leans across the table, places a small black cylinder carefully next to his sheets of annotated paper. Stands back, hands on haunches. "Know what that is?"

Julius reaching out, despite himself. The black cylinder in his great paw. Turning handle at the top, slats and numbers encircling the cylinder. "It looks like a maths grenade," Daisy declares. "The earliest calculator, it was…"

"…designed by Curt Herzstark, Austrian Catholic-Jew, imprisoned in Buchenwald in 1943…" Julius turns the cylinder slowly, religiously in his meat mitts. "But the head of the concentration-camp works department heard about Curt's ambition to create a hand-held calculating machine, told him if Curt could do it they'd give it to Hitler as a present when the Nazis won the war, and Herzstark would be made an honorary Aryan. He survived the concentration camp because he was working on a calculator."

Ogling the shining black object: "He called it the Curta. Daughter of Curt. First one was manufactured in 1948 in Lichtenstein, it can do addition, subtraction, multiplication, division, even square roots, it works off a complement-addition algorithm based on the addition of the nines-complement of the subtrahend. Beautiful. Just beautiful…"

With the eyes of a child he pulls the first three sliders down to the number two. "See, two hundred and twenty-two… Turn the pepper-grinder once… Look here, up on top, 222." She nods, leans in closer, and he can smell her, cannot help but smell her, some perfume he doesn't know because he doesn't know perfume, but it smells so sweet and so feminine to him: so everything that he is not. "Now we're going to multiply this by three, two more spins of the pepper-grinder, because we've already turned it once, see…" Turns the handle again, ratcheting clicks, like a heart opening. "There it is, 666."

"Right on, Jules, you're so demonic."

He smiles. "OK, so let's not be so sinister, we can get rid of that number by subtracting 222, we lift the pepper-grinder… See, the red line appears, so now one turn of the handle is a subtraction, that's the way the mechanics work, and, there you go… four hundred and forty four."

"Found it at a fair in Amsterdam, thought of Julius Miles…"

Julius lifts his head, sensing sincerity. "Gus used to have one."

Her mouth an O of surprise. "Really? No. Friggin' coincidence, huh? But then there's not much Gus didn't have." Julius not hearing the innuendo. Enraptured by the machine in his palm.

"I used to play with Gus's as a kid," he muses. "Every time I came here to the house. His was a Type I like this, 1952. The Type II had an eleven-digit data entry, eight-digit revolution counter, fifteen-digit result counter, but it was heavier, less streamlined. My uncle preferred the Type I. The original. Me too..." Cradles the black object, Daisy marvelling at the thickness of his fingers, wondering. "Got me hooked on maths, really. Used to play with it for hours..."

All at once her fingers are around his, small, strong, pushing the big ham knuckles closed over the smooth black case.

"It's yours, Julius. A present. Been meaning to give it to you, but I hardly see you these days."

Her fingers hot around the club of his fist. He must not, he cannot look up. Eyes misty with something swirling and unsure and ancient and new. Breath caught in his chest like feather down. His calves tightening already in preparation for flight, but then his chin is lifting, a tectonic movement, granite surfacing from his stupor as her hand raises his face to within an inch of her nose.

"Julius." Her warm breath on his face. "Julius," and this time his mouth stumbles upwards, parting against her lips. Even Daisy is surprised. He kisses her and she pulls at him and they stagger and she is in his arms and he feels like a lifeboat, a great big vessel designed to save lives, many lives, a massive hull launching onto a vast choppy sea.

"Jules, that's, that's..." she moans, unzipping him, unable to resist a glance before she lowers herself down. "Good God!"

At 10.32 p.m. on Tuesday 16th October, Julius Miles and Daisy Perkins start to have sex on the carpet. Four minutes later they stop having sex, because Julius has come, the mechanical calculator that saved the life of the inmate of Buchenwald still gripped tightly in his hand.

* * *

He left the Curta on the kitchen table. Beside the direct-debit form. Took the sheath of printed bank statements and departed without a word. Daisy never signed the mandate. Paid the rent for Domus

Decorus the following month, but no mention of the £1,500 she still owed him. Julius crammed an angry note through her letterbox early one morning, but made sure he avoided her from that day forth. Never passed the shop. Stepped the long way round.

Daisy knew what she was doing all right.

One crisp Sunday morning in early December, the doorbell rang. Julius bounded up the stairs two at a time, expecting the Jehovah's Witnesses with whom he'd been happily debating the statistical implications of 144,000 souls being selected to be born again and rise to heaven from the billions who have lived and died and are still to be born, from here until the day of Har-Magedon. Disappointment when it was her. Followed by rising distress.

"Hello, Julius." She seemed different. He could not be sure, a new haircut or make-up or new earrings? Something women do. Her features rounder, healthier even.

"You look… fatter than the last time I saw you," he said, before anything could be done about it.

"Thanks, Julius." Coat buttoned, no lipstick. "I'm pregnant."

He pressed return and the computer in his brain sourced words, and he asked her whether she was happy to be pregnant and she said yes. He asked her who the father was and she said that she had done the calculations and she was a hundred per cent sure that it wasn't him.

"What calculations?"

"Come on, Julius. Don't be a lump. It's not yours."

He wasn't sure why she sounded angry. Muttered a form of congratulations and excused himself, closing the door behind him. Sick with relief.

*　*　*

Julius stands outside the shop. His shop, he keeps telling himself, without much conviction. 6.30 a.m., sun easing into the early-morning June sky, slow yawn. Glass towers of the City on the

83

horizon glinting with promise of sunglasses and money to be made. A motorized street-sweeper trundles by, chugging whirls of dust and crisp wrappers. Beyond, students in skinny jeans and sparkling tops stagger in a line towards a cash machine, drunken post-club laughter.

Julius starts with the wire mesh padlocked to the door frame, stands it to one side, jiggles the large key in the ancient lock. Opens the door. Gets hit on the head by a Toby jug falling from the hook above the entrance. Picks up the broken pieces wondering if this is where Daisy's spirit dwells. Daisy didn't want to die, he's sure of that. Would certainly linger if she could.

"Oh my," he exhales in the doorway. Particles pirouetting in the newborn sun, they say dust is the skin of the dead. Unprepared for the disarray that faces him. Might be better to let burglars in, he thinks, surely the place would be cleaner after they left.

He looks down, the concave wooden step into the shop entrance, worn by a hundred thousand feet or more since the door first opened in 1874. Unable to add to that number. Blocked by the piles of furniture and pots and vases and bookcases and ungodly plastic things and clothes undoubtedly riddled with moth worms and fleas and diseases of every itinerant and hopeless hermit who sold their possessions to Daisy Perkins for a few coins and a smile from a lady such as her.

Julius Miles scrutinizes the shelves, the walls, the floor, desperate to locate a straight line. But everything is skew-whiff. Not unlike Daisy herself, he thinks.

Shivers at the violence of the disorder.

Finally he takes the plunge, moves forward, his head strikes a basket, then a birdcage, he's unstoppable now, legs knocking umbrella stands, an old brass fireplace, a wooden figurine of a Native American chief smoking a half-broken pipe. Julius makes it to a clearing, a square foot of bare floor. Unable to imagine the homes that such dispiriting ugliness came from. Nor those who would want to pay money to carry it back to their own hearths.

He glances at the small white tags, handwritten prices dangling innocently. £110 for the birdcage. £30 the basket. £780 the fireplace. And a Half-Pipe Sitting Bull to you for £95.

Picks up the Indian Chief. Not heavy in his hand, made of some light wood composite, maybe even balsa. Poor paint job. The base cracked too. Perhaps the price tag is a mistake, he wonders. Everything in the shop is expensive, as if Daisy the guardian of human discard could not bear to part with her objects, chasing prospective buyers away with a shop-wide, sky-high pricing structure. Eventually he locates her desk, beneath the curtain of spider plants, still guarded by porcelain dolls.

"She's not coming back. Sorry," he hears himself murmur. The dolls' faces stare back at him insolently.

No computer in the shop. Daisy prided herself on continuing Gus's regime – no electronics, except for a battered CD player playing Brahms or Chopin. The desk drawer is not locked. Paper clips litter the inside like desiccated insects. And real desiccated insects next to the paper clips. A wizened apple core. Some kind of fungus growing on what might be a stain of yogurt in the shape of Africa. An open packet of tampons spill forth with reckless abandon.

The right-hand section of the drawer is stuffed full of papers: bills, invoices, flyers, some bank notes, £10, £20, an incongruous $50 bill poking through like a lost refugee in search of a better life. Julius's queasiness is not subsiding. He cannot find energy enough to tidy up this rat's nest. Wriggles his fingers through the mire of papers, gropes and finds what he's looking for. A large spiral note-pad, the word ACCOUNTS neatly stencilled across the front cover. Tries to pull it from the drawer, but something is stuck at the back, he tugs, once, twice, and the bottom of the drawer falls out. The floor now a shower of papers and paper clips and every tiny memento Daisy saw fit to bury in the most organized place in the shop.

"Fantastic."

Julius sits down on the swivel chair. Stares at the mess he's created, adding to the wreckage that is Domus Decorus. Amidst the papers, a black object. Julius picks it up. The Curta calculator. The top dial reads 444. The number he created the night he had sex with Daisy.

He turns the Curta in his hand against the morning sun that dapples the walls, the shadows of the birdcages like the bars of some ancient seraglio on the walls beyond. The machine is pristine, no dents from the fall. Unharmed.

Julius sits in the threadbare swivel chair for a long time. Clicking down the sliders, turning the pepper-grinder handle, multiplying, dividing... the only sound in the empty museum of a shop. And almost inaudible amongst the silent still objects that watch Julius work, the low noise from the Roman Road, traffic building towards rush-hour growl.

"Life goes on, don't it?"

Julius looks up. A gangling silhouette against the morning sun. White Adidas tracksuit – sky-blue insignia and piping-white New York Yankees baseball cap too big for the shaven pinhead it crowns, long nose like a drainpipe down a pimply wall, tallow eyes, gold tooth lower left first bicuspid. The sort of youth who scares Julius and most of the middle-class frontiersmen and women in the Woodstock Road Conservation Area, because they sense that young men like this mock the very codes most normal people live by. Offended by his expensive sporting gear, failing to understand the comfort and tribalism of wearing the same look every day of your life.

Trevor Nugent peers at Julius from under the brim of his cap. Halo of dust above his head. "Gonna get rid of this stuff? 'Rent Me' sign going up?"

"Sorry, it's... Actually I don't remember your name. You work... worked here, didn't you? At the shop? Friend of Miss Perkins?" Julius looks at his watch. 8.30 a.m. Feels foolish. Two hours lost to the click-clack of the Curta.

Trevor Nugent ambles towards the desk, jangling. For a moment Julius thinks perhaps it's the percussions of the youth's pokey bones striking one another as his thin limbs click. Then he notices the chunky gold chains around Trevor's wrist, the necklace hanging from his scrawny neck.

"Helped out. When it suited me. So you gonna close the gaff down or what?"

"Possibly. I don't know yet. You've worked here awhile, haven't you?" Trevor shrugs. "You didn't come to the funeral."

"Nah. Creeps me out that stuff. Dead uns. Specially the burn house, hate the burn house, they incintegrated me nan there."

Julius is suddenly afraid. That the Adidas lizard is going to rob the shop. Nugent knows the stock, knows better than Julius what's really valuable, Julius is certain. Something in the way the young man's eyes flick back and forth is reptilian, a cold-blooded need.

"Shit, man, somebody broke in?" Trevor has seen the broken drawer, the piles of discarded paper. "Man, that's evil, everyone knows she's kicked it, that's not right, snatching from the deceased."

"No. It's nothing like that. It was my fault, I broke the drawer, I was trying to open it just now."

"Oh. Yeah, it's a piece of shit. Here, I'll…" And in a blink, Trevor is down on the floor, hands and knees, scooping up invoices and bills and order dockets as well as paper clips and all manner of strewn objects.

"No, it's all right, I'll do that…"

"Sit tight. I owe her a day – Miss P. paid me in advance."

While Trevor arranges the papers on the desk, Julius takes Daisy's ACCOUNTS to the least cluttered corner of the shop. Unfolds awkwardly into a small armchair, upholstery ripped, bleeding pale wadding. Flicks through the spiral notebook. Surprised by the neat notation, the exactitude of columns and rows, dates, prices, every transaction for the last two years noted in small but perfect lettering. More surprised by the figures. In several months the columns show an income exceeding £15,000. Other months £7,000, £9,000, £11,000. A yearly turnover of almost £200,000.

"All done, guv. Could sweep the floor for you if you want, needs a good brush…"

Julius closes the notebook. Trevor squinting through sunlight. Julius gets to his feet, clutching the account book. "Thanks… you never did tell me your name."

"Trevor. Daisy called me Trev."

"OK, Trevor, I'm locking up now. Give me your number, I'll let you know what I decide to do with all this stuff. Probably going to need a hand clearing it out down the line. I'll pay you, of course, same rate she did."

"Fair dos. My number's on the desk. Leave a message. I call you back." Trevor lopes to the door. Julius picks up the keys, but Trevor still remains in the doorway. Shifty now? Julius's heart picks up, sudden tautness in the youth's face, thin gaze. How quickly these people of the street can harden. A charge from Julius could bowl him, but what if a knife flashes free of that Adidas suit, slashing, spiking into his abdomen?

"I'm sorry… Julius, innit? I don't mean to do this to you but…"

Hand in pocket and out before Julius even sees it. He winces, anticipating the shiv to his belly. When no pain sears, he looks up to see a brandished envelope. "Could you take a look at this for me? Please?"

Julius takes the envelope from a red-faced Trevor, hands damp with receding nerves. "It's me dad's results."

On the envelope Julius sees a familiar logo, "Barts Health NHS Trust". While Trevor scratches behind his left ear, Julius scans the letter from the hospital's urology department.

"I'm sorry, Trevor, I'm not a doctor, I just work in the Department of Statistical…"

"Nah. That's fine. I just wanted to know what you thought…"

"It's just an appointment letter, nothing more. Your dad's prostate test."

Relief softening the pimpled face. "Okay. Great. Thanks… When?"

Julius looks at Trevor. The youth's eyes dart away, to the road. A realization from Julius. "Do you want me to read this to you?"

Trevor sighs, says nothing. Julius reads out loud. "This letter is to confirm an appointment has been made for Mr Roy Nugent on Tuesday 14th…" Footsteps towards him. Julius stops reading. Trevor is right in front of him now, chin high. Breath caught in Julius's throat.

"She helped me. That's all." Trevor takes the letter from Julius's unsteady hand. Folds it neatly, back into his pocket. "Thanks." And is gone.

* * *

Julius waits at the side gate of the school with the Bugaboo mums and the smoking childminders and the small Bangladeshi women Bengali-chattering beneath black burqas. Steps back as Awa Yasin unlocks the gate and the parents shuffle forward to collect their clamouring children from the nursery playground. She sees him now, curious.

"Just one question," he says. "When's Arnold's birthday?"

"Aw, that's sweet." Smooths down her headscarf. "August 21st."

"Thanks." Hurries away from her and the surge of oncoming children down the street to the silence of his house. Taps impatiently on his laptop. www.conceptioncalculator.co.uk. Enters Arnold's birth date, almost four years before. Clicks "Calculate".

Pulls down a box file from the shelf, flicking through neatly clipped bank statements, five years old. Finds what he's looking for, a page on which two payments are circled in red pen, ballpoint indentations deep and angry – the months Daisy Perkins failed to pay her rent for the shop. Looks at the header on the printed page: date and time of printing – October 11. 21.30. Back to the screen:

"*Probable date of ovulation: October 12. Possible dates of conception: October 8 to October 16.*"

Numbers do not lie. Not to Julius. He sucks his cheeks, leans back in his chair so far that he topples over and crashes to the floor. Lies on the carpet, unable to turn for the shooting pain in his neck.

* * *

Julius waits until evening, but the pain does not subside. Forlornly skirmishing through cupboards, two woollen scarves wrapped around his neck, some kind of comfort. Cursing himself for not re-stocking on aspirin, paracetamol, ibuprofen. He needs a better system, more detailed lists, checks and balances.

Julius plunges into Gus's most comfortable armchair, looks through his phone contact list. Eleven numbers, six of them local businesses necessary to his existence – minicab, doctor, dentist, Golden Bangkok Thai takeaway, Tower Hamlets Council, London Transport. Considers calling the minicab number, asking the Turks to go to the chemist's for him, fee payable. He hesitates, feels it would be too complex to explain. Another contact: Mum & Dad, but his parents are in Australia on their "Ski Trip".

"Spending the Kids' Inheritance, S-K-I, get it, Julius?" his mother could not stop chuckling.

Another contact: "Daisy Perkins Mobile". His finger hovering over the button. He calls the number, but it does not ring. Just a woman's voice: "This number is no longer available."

I see him through the window, bowed in the chair, pain sometimes the closest we come to true prayer in our lives. I cannot intervene. To talk to a mark is to alter the balance, pull back the curtain, reveal the wizard. I watch as he curls up on the floor, big slug, knees into his chest. Staring at a floor vase next to the fireplace adorned with flying cranes flapping west. I pass the window, barely a shadow, then back again. That Julius has no one to call is his fault, of course, yet the fault is small and ancient, the simple cumulative expansion of isolation and loneliness that grows across the years.

I walk to the Costcutter on the corner, buy a packet of paracetamol and ibuprofen, returning a little breathless, preparing to push
them through the letterbox to number 42 and run. But when I get
back to the house he is outside, dragging himself up the steps to
next door. He knocks. A long while before the young Somali woman
appears. He tries to be friendly.

"Don't know why, but I thought maybe you'd have an idea what
to do. I cricked my neck."

The white smile. "Cos I'm from Africa? Ointments, sheep's
intestines, strange herbs from the brown boys in Whitechapel
Market, that sort of thing?"

"No. Because you're next door and I don't have anything in the
house and I don't think I can walk to the shops. Sorry."

"Really? My dad swears by acupuncture. Had needles for a mi-
graine one time, said he walked out of there on air."

"I'm phobic. Of needles."

"Cup of tea? And some pills, then?"

He hesitates; the pain stabs him again.

"Okay. Yes. Thanks."

* * *

Julius sits on the sofa in front of the carpet where he had sex with
Daisy Perkins and where Awa Yasin had her seizure. Staring at the
swirls, looking for the pattern, the alchemy that makes women
shudder on this spot one way or another. The boy playing in his
bedroom two floors above them. Awa has made tea. She sits opposite Julius, stirring the leaves round the pot, round and round.
Too many circles, thinks Julius. There is no chaos like the chaos
of circles.

"Confusing time, huh?" She keeps stirring. Julius does not respond. Awa pours the tea. He takes the cup from her, pops into his
gaping mouth three ibuprofen capsules. Sits tight, keeps quiet. For
a long time. Awa Yasin maintains her silence. A kind of stand-off

between them that Julius does not fully understand. She stares at him and he stares at his shoes.

Then eventually she says, "When I'm afraid, I try and figure out what it is I'm afraid of doing, the action that corresponds to that fear. Then I try and do exactly that."

"Mm."

"Only way to defeat the bully. I didn't want to take the job with Daisy, didn't want the responsibility of looking after the boy. Because of my condition. Was terrified I'd have a seizure out with him somewhere, like you said. So I took the position, took him everywhere I could think of. Ta-dah! No seizure."

"Until the other night."

"One in three years." She shrugs.

He sips his tea. "Cardamom?"

She nods. "*Shah Hawaash*. Somali tea."

"I like it. Never had it before." She smiles warmly. Julius frowns: "Did you know Domus Decorus was making over two hundred thousand pounds a year? Even in Gus's boom years he didn't take in more than eighty."

Awa Yasin looks at him. "Two hundred thousand pounds? Wow. I didn't know…"

"That's what her accounts say."

Awa laughs. "Must be a mistake, she was always cutting out coupons for Tesco's. Accounts must be wrong. Daisy was as bad as me at the numbers…"

Her mobile phone rings. She picks it up from the table, heads to the end of the kitchen looking out over the garden, the slender trees baked golden in the setting sun. Julius listens as she speaks quietly.

"No, Adabe, it's five to, I call you at seven, remember? Yeah I know, but it's not seven yet. Your watch is fast. Yeah, five minutes fast…" She turns away, cupping the phone. Somali words fast and insistent. When she sits down again she peers into her cup before looking up at Julius. The smile that says "nothing fazes me".

"Spirals," Julius says quietly, almost to himself. "That's what it feels like right now. It feels like spirals."

"You mean the swirly things?"

"Yeah. The swirly things. Like this carpet."

"Bending round and round for ever."

Julius nods. "There's something called a logarithmic spiral, it never changes its shape however big or small it gets. It's quite re-markable – a straight line from the centre of the spiral, the pole, will dissect the spiral curve at the same angle at any given point. But the thing is, you'd never get to the pole, because the shape of the curve replicates exactly, it would just keep going to an infinite smallness…"

"You don't talk. Then you talk about mathematics."

Julius scratches his chin. Awa stands, goes to the fridge, taking out a milk bottle.

"Arnold's going to bed soon; he has his milk first. Would you like to give it to him? I mean, he drinks it himself, but you can take it up to him if you like."

He stares at her. Lost. "I don't think so, no. Thanks."

"Understood. Well, let yourself out. Hope the crinch gets better."

"The crinch?"

"Is that not a word?" She laughs, disappearing up the stairs.

* * *

Julius waits. Awash with unease. At sea. Many years since he was the lifeboat, feels more like a drowning ox. Needs rescuing himself now. He climbs the stairs as quietly as he can, approaches the front door. Then hears her voice, singing to the boy.

"As I was going to St Ives, I met a man with seven wives, every wife had seven sacks, every sack had seven cats, every cat had seven kits…"

Pauses to hear her finish the verse. Then she begins again, same words, same lilting tone. Drawn to the voice, Julius climbs the next flight of stairs to the small back bedroom that is Arnold's room, stops in the doorway. Sees Arnold lying on the floor staring up at the bird mobile, Awa cross-legged on the bed. Headscarf lying beside her, naked hair curly, like black endive, Julius thinks.

"Kits, cats, sacks, wives, how many were going to St Ives?"

"2,802."

She starts, hand to her scarf, dragging it quickly around her head. Arnold gazes up lazily at the large man in the doorway.

"No. You're wrong," he says to Julius.

"No I'm not. 2,802 were going to St Ives."

Arnold Perkins shakes his head, yawns. "It's one. The answer is one. Kits, cats, sacks, wives, man, they're coming *from* St Ives." Arnold laughs, looking at Awa, who smiles back at him. "Not *going* there. There's only one going there, and that's you. Everyone knows that."

"Perhaps Mr Miles hasn't heard it before, Arnold…"

"Of course I've heard it, I'm thirty-nine years old, who hasn't heard it? But as a matter of fact, the rhyme doesn't say the man and his wives *aren't* going to St Ives." Arnold wrinkles his nose in mock disgust. Julius continues: "In which case, the man, his seven wives, their seven sacks, seven cats, seven kits… seven to the power of zero, plus seven to the power of one, plus seven to the power of two, plus seven to the power of three, plus seven to the power of four, which is 2,801. And if you include the narrator, that makes 2,802."

Arnold puts his tongue between his lips, blows a loud raspberry.

"Arnold. That's not nice." Awa pulls the headscarf straight and the doorbell rings below them. "Pyjamas on, young man." Awa exits, turning her body to squeeze past Julius down the stairs to the hall. Arnold yawns again. Julius remains in the doorway. Notices the framed photograph of Daisy next to the boy's low bed. Something scrunched up next to his pillow. A woman's bra. His dead mother's underwear to protect him during the deepest hours of the night.

Suddenly, Julius feels empty, because he has nothing to give to the boy, not even a word. Empty and leaden, both at the same time. At the front door he hears Awa unhitch the latch and a man's familiar voice, bright, confident.

"Sorry to disturb you, bad time, good time?"

I recognize the voice as well. Kneeling beside a Renault Espace, I watch the man at the door to number 40, eyes narrowed. The accountant with very long thumbs.

"Evening, Mr Silk, what can we do for you?" Is that a small degree of resentment I detect in the young Somali woman's voice?

"Well, my dear..." replies Silk, stepping into the space Awa has left for him in the hallway. "I was rather wondering if I might see my son..."

6

Larry Silk watches Arnold shoot bubbles from the snout of a bright-green bubble gun. The boy's small fingers slipping on the trigger, scowls of frustration. Silk sees the mother in the boy, feels pain in his gut, grief spiking through him. Yet his tone is patient, as it was with her.

"Pull the trigger lots of times, Arnold…"

The bowed hulk of Julius Miles sits opposite Larry Silk, watching as the white-haired man in the charcoal suit crouches down on his haunches by the boy. "That's it, Arnie…" Silk coaxes gently. The boy pulls the gun trigger once more, chuckles. Now Julius disappears in a cloud of bubbles.

The big man watches his own wide face reflected back at him in a dozen oily shining circles that drift upwards towards the ceiling. Larry Silk laughs too, eyes never leaving Arnold, who turns, continuing to pull the trigger of the plastic toy, bubbles trailing off now into the shafts of summer evening light streaming through the front window.

Beyond, Awa Yasin perches on a high stool by the breakfast bar like a tennis umpire, gazing back and forth, Larry to Julius, Julius to Larry. Wondering why these weak men keep giving the boy firearms. Silk's is the only voice in the room. A pleasant sound all the same, honey-coated confidence. I peek in at him through the front window, careful that my shadow does not fall across the glass. No doubt to me that he loved Daisy Perkins. Which doesn't mean that he didn't kill her.

"It's broken!" barks Arnold. "You broke it." The trigger jammed, he eyes both the toy and the older man angrily. Shakes the plastic gun, now spraying himself with detergent.

"Give it here, son, I'll fix it," Larry reaches out to tousle Arnold's hair. Julius notices Arnold pull back, Silk's hand suspended mid-ruffle.

"Time for bed I think, Arnold." Awa slips down from her stool. "Say a big thank you to Mr Silk for your Bubble-Nator..."

"Thank you, Mr Silk."

"Now up those stairs before I nip your bottom like a Somali crab, you know crabs from Somalia are the biggest and the meanest and the craziest in the world, here he comes, nip, nip, nip..." The young woman's fingers out like pincers, chasing the squealing, slipping, wriggling child up the stairs and away from the heavy male silence of the living room.

The two men listen to the footsteps, lighter and lighter until they are sounds no more up the next flight of stairs to the bedrooms. Their eyes anywhere but on each other. Larry Silk wipes his mouth with a handkerchief. Takes out a comb, re-carves his side parting.

"Thank Christ for that girl, hey?"

Julius shrugs. Silk takes out his habitual handkerchief, dabs craggy eyes. "I miss her. Daisy. No point in being bashful. Your next-door neighbour was a crazy little jewel."

Julius does not remember Daisy Perkins this way, but he nods slowly, distracted. In his head he is hearing Larry Silk calling Arnold "son", over and over. The white-haired man shifts forwards in the armchair, tugging the stuck hem of his suit jacket from under him, pulling it taut on each side. Comfortable again. Correct.

"I'm going to adopt him." A quiet comment, simple statement, without pride or antagonism. "Whatever it takes." He stands, a conductor leaving the stage. "Whatever it takes." Heads towards the stairs.

"Daisy told Awa that *I'm* Arnold's father."

Larry turns. Julius stands, and it might be the length of his shadow, but he seems bigger now as he faces Larry Silk. Bear to lean wolf. Silk's smile painted crooked. "Say again?"

"Arnold's mother told the nanny that I was the father."

Silk flexes his fingers, as if preparing to grip something hard. "Daisy said Arnold was *your* son?" Julius nods. Then bows his head, bear shrinking back into man. Hand to chin, then mouth. Larry Silk takes out his comb, redresses the side parting, pockets the comb. Voice faltering, plaintive now: "She told me I was the father; I didn't doubt her. I mean, I thought I was the only one…"

"It wasn't anything," mutters Julius. "Just a mistake. She owed me rent money and she had sex with me instead of paying up…" Larry Silk straightens, rigid; Julius continues, stumbling like a teenager, "I mean, she didn't pay me with sex, I didn't mean that, it wasn't like that, it's just she was late with her rent and I was angry and she confused me with wine and a Curta, it's a kind of mechanical calculator, a collector's item really…"

"A mistake?" growls Larry Silk. "Nothing I did with Daisy was a mistake. Everything we did together was right. Perfect."

Julius speaks from behind his hand. "The date fits. When I had intercourse with her. I checked on the internet."

"I checked too. After she died. I checked."

A fiery shape between them now, burning, flaring, intoxicating. A shape with large breasts and a hippy shake. A shape called Daisy Perkins.

"A DNA test, Julius." Larry Silk's grey eyes now watery. "There's nothing else for it."

"Sorry?"

"A paternity test."

"Hmmm."

"Come on, boy. What's the problem? Everyone does paternity tests these days, it's practically the national sport…"

"No, it's not that, I'm not against a test in principle. I'm just concerned…"

"Why? Because deep down you know you're not Arnold's dad?"

"No. It's just, I'd like to know will the company who perform the test even use Bayes' Theorem? I mean will they be assuming a prior probability before testing that you or I are the father to be 0.5, i.e. one in two? Because strictly speaking that doesn't follow the principle of indifference."

A blank look from Larry Silk, but Julius is a man used to blank looks, and it simply causes him to accelerate and gear-shift upwards: "I mean, take the likelihood that I am the father. Either I am the father, or I'm not, right? This suggests two equal probabilities. But actually they are not equal in any way. Because I could be the father. But then so could every single man in the world, so long as they're not shooting blanks..."

"Hang on, mister, let's not speak ill of the dead, Daisy was no slapper..." Silk loosening his tie, perhaps ready to fight for the honour of his dead lover. Yet Julius remains undaunted, clearly happier now on home turf, the unassailable logic of numbers to convey...

"I'm sure Daisy wasn't a slapper, Larry, but I'm afraid statistically speaking she had the potential to be. Therefore, as several high-profile court cases have attempted to prove, Bayesian approaches are often either left out or improperly used in many paternity tests. With a prior probability of 0.5 it's not difficult to end up with a 99% probability of paternity, whereas simply adjusting the prior to a more modest figure of 0.1 can leave you with a probability of 91% – way outside the bounds of certainty."

Larry Silk looks at Julius. "I didn't know that."

"I'll make some enquiries, I work at the hospital..."

"The Royal London. I know."

"I can get a testing kit posted to your address."

"Actually, I think I'd rather use a company that neither of us picks."

"Why?"

"I sense it would be better..."

"Why?"

"Oh come on, Julius, think about it, if you choose a company and the result from their labs comes back saying you're the father, I won't trust it. And the same goes, I suspect, vice versa..."

"I hadn't thought about that."

"Let's ask Miss Yasin to find us a testing lab. We'll pay her for the service."

"Will we?"

"Why not? She's a smart young lady, she'll track down a reputable company. I'll see if she's amenable." Larry Silk bends, long thumb scooping his coat from the back of the sofa. Turns back to Julius, stretching out his hand, Julius hypnotized momentarily by the arching pollex. "I suppose you know about Arnold's sports day?"

"Yes," Julius lies. "Daisy told me all about it."

"Well, I'd appreciate it if I could have sole access. It's been in my diary for weeks."

"Right..." says Julius. "Okay."

"Well, Julius Miles, happy swabbing," concludes Larry Silk warmly, finally shaking the big man's limp damp hand. "May the closest genes win!"

* * *

The accountant gets into his expensive BMW and starts the engine. But doesn't drive away. Just sits there. For a moment I think he's on the phone talking into a hands-free. But then, eyeing him from behind the skip outside number seventeen, I realize he's talking to himself. I can just about make out his words even through toughened German glass.

"He's mine, he has to be mine. Why wouldn't you tell me? Jesus, Daisy! You bloody bitch!" His tone hard and violent. My hand slips from the side of the skip and I stumble forward. When I look up from the gutter, Larry Silk is staring down at me. I meet his eyes in the hope that he will see me as just another beginner transsexual drinking super-strength cider by a skip in East London. But he doesn't look away. His glare sharp and menacing. Not a breath of fear about him.

A sudden revving-up of engine, I step back and Larry Silk swings the BMW out from its parking space, almost knocking me down. As the black car tears away, I see him looking back in the driving mirror, watching me until the very end of the street. I feel the bite of his eyes even after he's turned the corner and vanished.

7

Still at number 40, Julius sits alone on the sofa in Daisy's living room. Staring at the television even though it's switched off. I'm beginning to know this look on his face – a wide blankness, but check out the vacillation of the pupils. He's retreated into percentages, Julius's drug of choice.

The UK has seen a 2.3% rise in the number of obese children between the ages of two and nineteen in the past five years. 5.1% of five-to-ten-year-old British boys are clinically obese. 10% of boys are likely to have a mental disorder compared to 6% of girls, rising to 13% among ten- to fifteen-year-old boys. 15% of eleven- to fifteen-year-old boys have admitted using drugs. One in four sixteen- to nineteen-year-old boys regularly uses cannabis. 25% of eleven- to fifteen-year-old boys drink alcohol at least once a week. Between 1991 and 2001, the number of new episodes of sexually transmitted infections seen in Genito-urinary Medicine (GUM) clinics in England, Wales and Northern Ireland doubled from 669,291 to 1,332,910. In London it costs over £300,000 to raise a child to the age of eighteen, without counting paying for private education.

"Penny for them…" murmurs Awa, quietly. Neither Julius nor I had noticed her return; she is stealthy and light of foot, the step of someone used to moving quickly and unobtrusively – a second daughter of selfish parents.

The shadows have lengthened. It is getting late, the sun now casting a reddish shadow across the dark russet bricks of the back wall of the garden.

"Sorry. I'm off." Julius stands to go.

"I'll organize the test," says Awa, simply. "Larry asked me, he says it's a swabby thing, you rub it inside your mouth, pop it in the tube, send it off."

Awa waits, but Julius says nothing more. She goes to the fridge, takes out a can of lager and tugs at the ring pull. Tries to angle her small index fingertip under the metal ring, but it's not strong enough to prise up the tab. Julius takes the can from her, yanks the ring in one jerk. They listen to the fizz of widget and beer. Awa picks up the can like a specimen bottle, sniffs the opening and takes a sip. "I don't drink beer," she says.

"Me neither."

"Daisy drank beer. She drank it quite a lot."

"It does not surprise me to hear that."

They sit down opposite one another, two small glasses of Carlsberg in front of them like sacrament. Long silence. Neither drinks.

"He should be Arnold's father," Julius mutters, finally. "Not me."

"Really? Why?"

"He's got everything."

"He's weird. Too nice and too happy to be nice and happy."

"He's rich. He likes children. He drives a BMW."

"He's pompous."

"So am I," says Julius. "In my own way."

Awa smiles. "Yes. You are." She drinks. He drinks. "Do you like Arnold? Do you actually like the boy?" she asks, her tone serious now. "Do you want the best for him?"

Julius knows that he should not tell her the truth. But he's too tired to lie. "I do want the best for the boy," he says. "But I'm not sure I like him very much."

* * *

The morning is hot. Heat haze already buzzing off the metal pyramid atop the soaring Canary Wharf tower, steel against blue. The thrusting bank edifices shine like cash in the sunshine. Cropped bankers in short sleeves, Ray-Bans, suit bags, Range Rovers. A cacophony of masculinity. Even the fountains are ejaculating.

I dab my make-up with a pink handkerchief that I'm pretending was my mother's, smooth down my summer frock like Marilyn. I'm thrilled and terrified to be wearing a dress, purchased online from Zara (I do not go into women's clothes shops yet, I'm still too rude to the staff, a crude form of self-defence I know, but come on, many of us attack when we're vulnerable). Cute little pink flats from River Island, clutch purse from Next.

My heart pinches with each glance, but no one looks twice. I pass, it seems. I get a smile even, from an elderly security guard – okay, he wears glasses, thick glasses, but it makes my heart skip and I float along to the coffee stand. I'm a little high today, if truth be known, in the castle of high finance.

Across two bridges, cradling my takeaway coffee like a pet. Gleaming metal everywhere magnifies the heat, some kind of transplanted North American dream of steel and sunshine. Which subsides as I descend farther south onto the Isle of Dogs, and the steel disappears into red brick and sandy London brick and rusted corrugated-iron and wire fences, 1950s faux Elizabethan timbered semis and the pugnacious buttress of white working-class pride that is Millwall couched against the advancing super-armies of international capitalism. Flags everywhere here, in two designs – the cross of St George and the blue-and-white of Millwall Football Club. Its motto the same as the inhabitants of this hernia in the East End of London: "No one likes us, but we don't care."

Larry Silk's office is less impressive than you'd imagine from his website. A row of 1980s commercial units behind an oriental-food-distribution warehouse. Faint spray of soya sauce in the air. Three of the units "To Let". An industrial-flooring distributor – "Five-Star Flooring". And next to this – "First Financial Services". The embossed plastic sign by the peeling door just a few centimetres off horizontal.

Larry Silk wasn't always in the side streets. For twenty years he shook the world, working his way through three of the biggest international accounting firms on the planet. Hong Kong. Dallas. Toronto. Geneva. But never made partner. Perhaps because he was born in Billericay, Essex, schooled in Chelmsford, went to university at Queen Mary College, East London. I heard the wash of Estuary in his larynx the moment he opened his mouth. My father's own patois.

Larry left his last job five years ago, set up his own outfit, First Financial. There's not much you cannot find from an hour or so on the internet, if you know where to look and are willing to tap in a credit card number or two. I came across the court record for Larry's divorce from Jacqui Silk, dated a few months after he sold his four-bedroom in Fulham; he put the cash into his new company.

A quick cross-reference of Jacqui's maiden name and, wouldn't you know it, there's the announcement of her next wedding, page 27 of the Surrey Advertiser.

Mr and Mrs Ronald Masterson of Godalming, Surrey, are pleased to announce the marriage of their only daughter Jacqui to Mr Jean Pelforth, son of M. and Madame Yves Pelforth of Geneva, Switzerland...

Yves Pelforth has 22,892 more entries on Google than Larry Silk, as befits a senior partner in the multinational accounting firm Larry departed just before he and Jacqui got divorced. You think love is complicated. But I'm here to tell you that people act consistently with who they are. A woman who insisted on Jacqui, not Jackie, from the age of ten was always going to move swiftly up the food chain.

Jacqui Silk, now Pelforth, is off my list of suspects. She didn't kill Daisy Perkins – Jacqui would have been only too happy to learn that some ditzy second-hand-furniture saleswoman from the wrong side of town had got herself knocked up by lanky Larry. It would have confirmed the righteousness of Jacqui's decision to dump him. Larry was always leaning back East. Whilst Jacqui Masterson has been strutting West since the day she was born.

But Larry... Larry is right up there on the murder ballot. His anger was violent. His stare from the BMW scared me. And I'm a tough skin.

Yet it's no slam-dunk, there is a crimp in the seam, as my old man used to call it. Arnold Perkins is not scared of Larry Silk. The boy laughed and played with him. The boy let Silk ruffle his hair. If it was Larry who pushed Daisy to the tiles, over some sharp gnarl or affliction in their relationship, why isn't Arnold shaken to the core by the sight of him? Julius found Arnold climbing out of the cupboard in the living room when he came across dead Daisy in the hall. The boy had been frightened enough of someone to conceal himself. At the risk of speaking like a statistician: something doesn't add up.

I keep watch on Unit 3B from across the road. Today I have the hi-vis fluorescent waistcoat and clipboard. Plod the length of the street, noting cracked tarmac, misaligned kerbs. Scribble on my clipboard, dictate into the small hand-held voice recorder. Occasionally I crouch – knees together, Felicity, you're a lady now – spray a small yellow circle around a particularly lethal-looking paving slab. No one questions me. Ne'er a stare from the office windows. Today I appear a cog in the industrial wheel, and there are few things more invisible than that.

No one goes into Unit 3B. No one comes out. If Larry has a secretary, she's virtual, fielding his calls from some call centre in Hemel Hempstead. The sun relentless now, bouncing off my fluorescent disguise. Clouds building, London trying to be tropical. My make-up is running, I glimpse my reflection in the window of Foo-Hun International Importers. A crying clown in a pink smock stares back at me.

My hand is jittery – your mistake, lady, no one finishes Venti triple-shot Americanos, not even American fighter pilots. My boobs sore in the cheap bra. Nothing for it but to reach deep into the dark fold of the handbag, pop out a mazzy, swallow hard.

Painkillers strangle you slowly and deliciously. The buzz of numbing. Lean back against the warm brick, hear the blackbirds sing.

At 2 p.m., Larry Silk exits Unit 3B. Walks past his car and away down Marsh Wall. I follow, thirty paces behind, slipping off the hi-vis, dumping it along with the clipboard in a bin. He turns down Mastmaker Road, across to Millharbour and over the Pepper Street Bridge to Crossharbour. Something tells me this is no lunch appointment. He glances back at intervals, clearly checking if anyone is following him, and not because he feels someone is following him – I'm too good for that. My old man had me trained from an early age. "Line of parked cars, Kev, cross the street from the subject, walk ahead of them. Only slow when the cars run out, let them overtake on their side, they won't suspect a thing, then you cross back behind 'em…"

I fall back as Silk passes the DLR, wait at the station entrance glancing at the map of local amenities, then turn off into the ASDA car park as he continues south. I exit by the barriers and pick him up again – now I'm twenty yards behind but fear nothing, for I have him ahead of me, widescreen. He looks back one more time, and I keep walking, using his hesitation to make up lost ground whilst appearing for all the world like I'm listening to music on my iPod, whereas in fact the headphones are connected to a bag of crisps in my pocket. "Ears peeled, eyes wide, Kev, easy does it…"

As anticipated, Larry starts walking ahead again before I reach him, so we're back in step, Larry ahead, Felicity behind, just ten yards and a sex change between us.

Then everything turns. Suddenly Larry veers left, up steps that lead through a line of dense hedges and small trees that border the main road, heading somewhere unseen. My heart speeds up. It's a smart move from the suspect: if I follow along the narrow concrete path, he could jump me at any point, right out of the bushes, unnoticed by the wider world. But if I don't follow, he's gone to do whatever he's so nervous about doing.

Adrenaline bounces off the benzos in my blood – fight or flight. And for the first time since the operation, I sense the masculine surge up within me once more. Fingers become fists, stomach clenches in anticipation, nostrils flare, sweat appears under my arms. This is not me, but it is me. As if my body is returning to itself, to the male from where it began.

Back in the day, I could handle myself. Soft-bellied, pansy hands, but of course my old man showed me parry moves and a duck punch, two fingers sharp to the neck, throat jab that could choke a bull. But then I was Kevin, and now I'm Felicity. What will happen to the girl in the pink dress if she strays into the woods in search of the wolf?

I start up the path. The trees and bushes breathing warm air, scent of jasmine and stale urine from somewhere. Keep going, girl, straight down the line, show no fear, no compassion.

As I get to the top of the incline, the bushes part and something comes for me, fast.

"Rape! Rape!" I scream. A large dog gazes at me heading to one side, as if wondering if this screech is a command. A German Shepherd, coat thick and shiny – macho-pet, not a kill-guard. The Alsatian sniffs derisively in my direction before bounding away into the foliage, distant laments of his owner now audible somewhere beyond the greenery.

Breathing out, shoulders heaving, I locate Larry Silk once more, now almost four hundred yards farther on, strolling across an open field, green after the recent thunderstorms. I'm about to follow him when I realize I don't have to. The space is so open, so unlike anything I've seen in London, that I have a fix on Larry for half a mile or more.

I'm looking down over a wide green meadow, three gently rolling hills dotted with sheep. Beyond, wooden fences and more animals.

It could be rural Sussex, except for the nest of soaring Canary Wharf skyscrapers behind us.

It's time to take my time, stroll down the long grass past the fifteen or more grey-white sheep in the lie of the hills. Beyond the grazing flock, in the shade of a row of hawthorn trees, stand four Friesian cows, tails idly flicking the flies that craze around the fresh dung piles. Smell of warm grass and suncream.

I remember now, I think. I've been here before. Perhaps as a child, perhaps later, in the years of confusion and distress. Mud-chute Children's Farm. An English field in the heart of polyglot Docklands, rolling pastures out of Hardy in Dickens's backyard. Ahead are paddocks and pens of animals, the enclosures of the kiddie farm, a scattering of families with prams and children under various levels of control scattered along paths between wooden fences. I stop still. Kneel down in the long grass, take out my small binoculars – call me Safari Queen. Wolf hunter.

Larry Silk leans against a dull metal gate, gazing into a small corral of white and brown llamas. He watches the chewing animals, their jaws left, right, left. The llamas watch Larry chewing gum, jaw right, right.

After five minutes I start to wonder if Silk is simply here because he likes llamas. After ten minutes I start to wonder if Larry likes llamas a little too much. He picks some grass, tosses it towards the animals, who barely glance down at his offering. Then he leans back against the gate once more.

The man appears from nowhere. Stands five feet away from Silk, hands firm on the other end of the gate. Younger than Larry, maybe mid-thirties, neatly pressed sky-blue polo shirt, equally well-seamed grey trousers, crisp brown deck shoes. Hair short, black. A very good-looking man, East London smooth. I've known his type since childhood, lusted after them almost as long. A smile that could crack an egg. Each one a joker with no fear of locks, riches or codes of honour and practice. Such men will break the bank, your heart and their word in an afternoon.

Larry Silk doesn't look over. Keeps ogling his llamas. If you glanced at the two men on your way to the pig wallows, you would say they were simply professionals of some description on respective lunch breaks, taking the air, no link between them, just a coincidence of time and location. No body language to suggest connection, both looking ahead at the chewing animals, both relaxed, shoulders low, feet straight.

But I can see their lips move. They're talking to each other. Fast. I focus the binoculars in on the younger man. He seems to hold the power in the relationship, for when he listens he does not nod, but when he talks Larry Silk nods a great deal.

It could be innocent. A chance meeting of old colleagues. A friend wanting financial advice ahead of a divorce. A handover of kit for a five-a-side football team the older man manages, the younger man captains. It could be. But it isn't.

Because I see the large bull head in the dark-leather coat standing by the wooden gate beyond the llama enclosure, eyes always on the man in the sky-blue polo shirt whilst simultaneously scanning every dad, mum, kid and grandparent who passes within ten feet of his boss. A minder. Mindless muscle.

Two minutes later the man in the sky-blue polo shirt turns and walks away from the llamas. Quickly I click-clack a dozen long-lens snaps of him as he reaches Bull Head, and the two of them disappear towards the tea room and the guinea-pig petting area.

Still Larry Silk rubbernecks the llamas. Rips up one last clump of grass and tosses it towards them without hope of thanks or recompense. Low rumble of thunder now, air thick and damp. Larry turns and walks back through the meadow towards Crossharbour station. He doesn't see the woman in the pink dress buying a Mr Softee ice cream with raspberry sauce and two chocolate flakes at the van by the park exit. He walks right past her, clearly deep in thought.

* * *

Two nights later, Julius stays up late working on a report examining the number of hysterectomies and endometrial-ablation procedures performed at the Royal London Hospital from 2004 to 2005, to identify trends in cases of heavy menstrual bleeding. It is after 3 a.m. when he closes the file and sends it to Richard Lovall's mailbox.

Julius likes this time. The hole in the night when his head empties, even of numbers. Outside the window, east towards Hackney Wick and the Olympic Park, a hint of light in the dark-wash sky, first breath of a new day. A bird singing in one of the garden trees, eager for dawn.

I like this time too. After three, the streets belong to me. Most of the teenyboppers are still dancing or shagging and the older pub crowd retired long ago. Even the blade-carrying head cases pumped up on brandy, Red Bull and meths give the shuffling she-man a wide birth. I think they can sense that I am a god, with all the backup that comes with the title. It doesn't hurt that I have my wooden staff with me, courtesy of my old man, the antique walking cane with the brass handle that he maintained was one of the original night sticks given to the Bow Street Runners back in 1749.

"The nuts that's cracked, son! Imagine! A bagful, I shouldn't wonder!"

In the weeks since I took on Julius's case, I have come to savour Woodstock Road. I never feel cold here, even on chillier nights – the old London brick seems to capture the heat of the day and releases it kindly during the hours of darkness. No one has complained about my presence, the New Labour freeholders in the attractive Victorian houses are mindful that they've chosen to live in one of the most deprived boroughs in the country and are thankful that the only sign of danger they have to endure is a thin strange woman in an expensive North Face raincoat drinking cider by their Audis and brand-new Minis. One of them, a stooping media lawyer with an expensive fold-up bicycle, even gives me a pound coin from time to time. Little do you know, Gilbert, that I invested much of the money from my old man's life insurance in Tesco shares, and am currently sitting on a high six-figure nest egg, even with the credit crunch.

My spot for my night-time vigils is sacred. Back against the wall of the only council block on the street. Some copper asked me to move on a few weeks ago, but I demanded his name and rank and he decided to back away. If you sound like you know the ropes, most Plod will leave you alone. They're not priests, they don't have to believe in their work.

I believe in my work. Love makes the world go round. Everything that happens is down to love. Wars, revolutions, massacres, election campaigns. A man goes on strike because he needs money to feed those he loves. Or needs their respect, which is a vital ingredient of love. A politician reaches out for acclaim because his father failed to love him enough. A country invades another because it feels unadored by those neighbours it looks up to.

But love is not something you can force, it's not on demand, not clickable. If you're still waiting, don't count down, don't chase your tail. Chances are you won't even realize it's happening. For some of you it will be like walking from a darkened room into sunlight, a slap between your eyes. For others you'll remain in the dark but gently find yourselves able to discern shapes in the vortex, the darkness no longer opaque but warm and snug and comfortable. Even Julius will tell you, statistically speaking we all fall in love more than once in our lives. In more than one fashion.

I hear his sighs, his loneliness. It's all right being alone when you're in love with someone. When you're in love, being alone is thrilling, because your isolation is filled with fantasies of when you will be with the one you love. You see yourself as the romantic hero or heroine on the verge of conquering your beloved's heart. But when there is nothing but empty space and insolence beyond those walls, solitude feeds pain like damp breeds bacteria.

Julius is depressed, that much is clear. But it is not so much a sickness as a lack, a simple deficit that can be remedied as easily as giving a diabetic insulin. He needs to be touched.

I dream of someone touching me. Not sexually, it wouldn't have to go that far, although I wouldn't complain – who would? A hand on my arm. Finger on cheek. Arms around my rib cage. Just imagining it makes me smile. I haven't been touched in a long time. I feel sometimes as if I'm not real, as if I'm the one who is dead, Daisy dear, watching the living. I don't self-harm or anything to remind myself that I'm alive, but I have been known to run the back of my hand over rough surfaces, just to feel the scrape.

I walk up to Julius's front door. I want to ring the bell, again and again, and when he opens the door, blinking in the 5 a.m. street light, I want to hug him tight.

But I stand there, my hand outstretched against old wood.

8

My bag has been stolen. Should have seen it coming. Rush hour, crowded bus, jostling shopping bags, pushchair handles, jib-jab, could have been anyone from the lippy Bangla teenagers to Silent Drunk swaying between the burqa mamas. Or the Russian painter-decorators nursing beer cans below hard blue stares.

Rajiv lets me in via the buzzer. Santos hands me my spare key from the tin in his room, I unlock my door, return the key to his big red palm. Fasten my door behind me, double click, chain across. Flustered and flushed. This shouldn't happen to a lady.

Call the card companies, change the internet bank passwords. A soothing flick through the TV channels, but the feeling won't go away. Not dread, but the same sensation in the opposite direction – a sense that something bad has happened in the recent past but I cannot make out what. It's smeared as if through gauze.

I open drawers, shake books, run my fingers along the highest shelves. Discover three pieces of paper torn from different notebooks.

Daisy Perkins was killed by Larry Silk or someone Silk knows. Why?

Eggs, milk, Cup-a-Soup, tonic water, jumbo Smarties, artichoke hearts.

Rukshana Begum. Nadia Florescu. Gwendolyn Lank. Jenny Giannopoulos. Awa Yasin.

A second, then two, three, then I remember. My possibles. The women of Julius Miles. Minus the one who died, of course. At least now I know the source of the bad taste in my mouth – darling Daisy, cut down in her meadow.

It's time to get back on the job. I'm lagging behind, out of focus. I have no superior, no controller, just my own conscience, but luckily for you lot she's a hard-arsed harpy with a whip for a tongue.

"Forget the dead un," she says to me in the mirror. "Julius needs a girl."

Two names are singing to me.

Rukshana Begum. Costing and Income Accountant at the Barts Health NHS Trust. Dreams of acceptance. Pretty-ish, Bangladeshi-ish, easy-ish. Prides herself on her temper, which she has to fake most of the time.

Gwendolyn Lank. Who better for Julius than a passionate geek whose favourite word is vagina?

Calm has returned. I'm back in the saddle.

* * *

Julius is finishing up the Oral and Maxillo-facial Surgery figures at his desk in Room 717B. "O and M" – mouth, jaws, face, neck. When he first started working for the Hospital Trust, he was dazzled by the intricacies of modern medical specializations – experts above the shoulders in eyes, in ears, in noses, in throats. Experts in brains, tongues, teeth. Below the neck, even more virtuosos: cardiologists, pulmonologists, gynaecologists, urologists, proctologists, gastroenterologists, rheumatologists, a seemingly endless list of professionals for every corner, every crevice of the body.

Today they can replace a heart, lungs, even a face. Create artificial eyes, man-made brains. They can turn a man into a woman, a woman into a man. Soon, it seems, humans will be like those toys that you can change from anything into anything. Nothing will be fixed for evermore. We will all be in a permanent state of transition. We will all be free.

Except of course we won't be. The longer Julius has spent at the hospital, crunching the numbers – the renal-failure rates, MRSA increases, the rising incidence of common cancers – the more he has come to see the legions of doctors and scientists as merely uniformed guards tasked with creating the illusion of security rather than actually protecting anyone. Fix a hole in the fence, the prisoners escape elsewhere. Put up bigger fences, the intruders still get in. Human beings still shatter. Still wither and die. Our flesh still disintegrates into dust.

The only thing that remains behind is love. I know I'm hardly an objective commentator, but my calling gives me certain insights, I think. This is what I believe. That there are connections within us, call them DNA strands, call them the electrical pulses of all those couples before us who loved and had sex and created offspring – an eternal line of small ebbing lights tracing back into prehistory. This is the eternal. A string of love, coiled deep within us.

I'm here to tell you it is the invisible, not the mappable, that makes us who we are.

Julius is taking his time, you can't rush precision, completing a table of figures for zygomatic fractures that show as they did last year that men are four times more likely to suffer fractures to the cheek than women, mainly because men drive cars at higher speeds, play more contact sports and get into fights more than women. As he underlines and emboldens the headline figures, there's a loud knock on the door.

There are only two people who knock on Julius's door: his boss Richard Lovall and the cleaning supervisor, Nadia Florescu. Richard knows only too well not to interrupt Julius during mid-quarter processing. Nadia doesn't give a fig about Julius's need for tranquillity and solitude during the mid-quarter computations, but she's away on holiday in Constanta on the Romanian Black Sea coast with her father and five brothers. I checked.

Nadia's off my list – a woman with so many men in her life could never be for my Julius. He needs gentleness, not a surrogate brother with a penchant for arm-wrestling.

After three further knocks, each louder than the previous one, Julius rubs his wide chin vigorously. "Go away!" The knocking stops. Then another loud knock, clearly designed to infuriate.

"Oh, for bloody hell's sakes!" Julius bellows, throwing open the door, hands on hips, sweat on brow. A warrior's fury when the numbers are disturbed, but only then. Staring up at him, two burnt hazelnuts housed in a fireball – Rukshana Begum in two-inch killer heels, Prada skirt and jacket combo off eBay Fashion Outlet. Nails the colour of nuclear residue, jet-brown.

"No need to shout, Julius." Her voice pure London, bobbing and knock-you-down.

"Oh, it's you." Julius knows the small Bangladeshi woman to nod to, has had meetings with Begum and Richard Lovall, even shared a joke with her at the management party last November to celebrate the hospital's new Advanced Trust status. "Here's a statistic for you – one in three East Enders weighs as much as the other two!" Rukshana laughed, sincerely, into her cranberry juice.

But now she frowns up at Julius, mimics his gruff voice: "Hello, Ms Begum, nice to see you, Ms Begum, I assume, since you bothered crossing smokers' alley to a completely different building and climbed two flights of stairs in your Choos because maintenance were cleaning blood from the lifts, that you must have a good reason for knocking on my door, especially since you've recently been made Senior Executive in charge of costing and income for each of the three hospitals!"

"Have you? Congratulations. I didn't get that memo."

"Ha. You're the biggest clown I know."

"I find that hard to believe, Rukshana."

Begum gazes upwards. The stooping giant barely fitting the door frame of Room 717B. She bares perfect white teeth, polished to a deadly gleam.

"Julius, I need a favour."

"Hmmm."

"Can I come in?"

"No."

"Sorry?"

"This is my workplace. I don't receive call-bys."

"Jesus, Julius, you run the statistical-analysis department of a public hospital, not some top-secret weapons facility. I need to talk to you!"

Julius leans against the door post, blocking all light from the room behind him. And waits.

"Jesus, Julius. Jesus…" But Rukshana is smiling, and I'm beginning to feel so much better, I'm not losing it, I've still got the shakes, it's an instinct, like good taste. Begum is digging Julius, his fastidiousness, his impassivity, his bulk. Julius's natural state is turning her on. An "angel fit", as we call it in the trade.

"Okay. We'll do the doorway shuffle. Whatever you like…" Rukshana continues, feigning annoyance.

"I have sensitive data in my office, ask Richard Lovall…"

"I said we'd doorstep disco, relax. So why am I here?" The words cast up to Julius's bored indifference. "I'm here because I got an email from some journalist on the *East London Journal*, it's a FOI request…"

"What's that? FOI?"

"Freedom of Information Act, pain in the petunia as you might guess, but we're a state institution, so we have to oblige. Journo wants to know quarterly figures for each department as a percentage of yearly total Trust budget, plus ward breakdowns and, get this, catering costs…"

Julius shrugs. "I have all that. You could have just emailed me."

"Oh." Rukshana raises a perfectly trimmed eyebrow. "In her message she apologized for asking for so much information, said she knew it would be a nightmare for whoever had to collate the data."

"Your journalist clearly doesn't understand statistical processing."

"Clearly."

"Do *you*?"

Rukshana Begum looks at Julius Miles. Hand smooths skirt, delicately. "It is the mark of a truly intelligent person to be moved by statistics," she says.

Julius Miles looks down at her. Hand across his mouth and back again. "George Bernard Shaw."

"'There are three kinds of lies: lies, damned lies and statistics."

"Mark Twain."

A wrinkle of her nose. She sighs. "Statistics are human beings with the tears wiped off."

Julius is silent. Then he nods. "I like that one. Who said that one?"

"Paul Brodeur. An American writer."

"It's good. Very good. How do you know all these? Did you Google 'statistics quotes' before you headed over here?"

She shakes her head, sadly. "Don't flatter yourself, big head. I like quotes, that's all. I've always wanted to be a writer myself…"

"But you're an accountant."

"And you're a statistician."

"But that's all I want to be."

"Really?"

"It's who I am."

Rukshana Begum thinks about this. Then points the toes of her shoes away from Julius, straightens her small back. "You'll send me the data?"

"Yes. Of course."

"Thanks."

"You're welcome."

Julius tries to smile, but his jaw seems to lock with his lips only half-upturned in a grimace like a stricken children's entertainer. Two hands soar to his defence, covering his mouth and chin, paddle fences. He likes Rukshana, I know that much, admires her spikiness, the pretty Bangladeshi cactus. Believes in her honesty, at least with him.

She passes me as I bend to tie my shoelace at the staircase, nods a "morning" and is gone, heels tapping down the stairs like a secret code.

It keeps me warm that I keep people warm.

* * *

I haven't been to my old man's nick since his funeral. The police station is located on London's famous street of upmarket tailors, Savile Row, but you wouldn't know it. A long time ago the schmutter merchants lobbied for the street name to be kept off the cop shop for fear it might tarnish their upmarket brand. So the police station is known as "West Central Station". Not a tweed nor coattail in sight.

My father worked at West Central for fifteen years, travelling the four miles from Bethnal Green on the Underground or the number 8 night bus, depending on the shift – as any London copper will tell you, you don't shit where you sleep and you don't sleep where you walk the beat. Especially not in the East End in the mid-Sixties, when the Krays and their pitbulls spat and prowled.

My father liked "The Row", as they called it back then: it swung in those days with crazy new fashions and the hip young London crowd. The Beatles opened their Apple Corp office at number 3 – Dad was one of the Plod who shut down the band's live performance on the roof of the building in front of the film cameras.

One of the few bits of live footage I have of my old man is a snippet from the *Let It Be* documentary. See him yourself if you want to rent it, he's one of the three cops who walk up to the door of Apple Corp, but you don't really see his face apart from a quick glimpse towards the end of 'Get Back', just before the police leave the rooftop and the impromptu concert ends. He looks so young, even younger than the Beatles themselves.

In the Seventies my aunt Mabel took me to see *Let It Be* at the cinema, I couldn't have been more than six. Miserable Mabel was always proud of her older brother, the upstanding policeman. I shrieked when I recognized him on the big screen. He walked up onto that rooftop in front of the sneering Beatles groupies and their smug management team, back strong, helmet pulled down right, just above his eyes. He wasn't just good at his job, my old man, he looked the part too, proper police, tall and pious. I was so proud of him. I told him as I ran through the door and he picked me up in his arms, looked me in the eye and said: "Nothing to it, Kev old son. Those Beatles were doing what they do, I was doing my thing. No secret. No harm done."

I'm wearing jeans, my Asics and a three-button suit jacket over a black shirt. Not so feminine, I'll grant you, but this is a threshold I have to cross at my own pace.

Stepping into the police station, I'm transported back thirty years; the smell is the same – disinfectant, stale coffee and the faint odour of armpit. I inhale as deeply as I can.

Detective Chief Inspector Edward Knowles sits behind a large metal desk. He drinks from a dark-blue plastic cup, red flask of coffee standing to attention on the shelf as it has done for three decades or more. He smiles as I enter.

"Hello, Felicity."

"You can call me Kevin, Eddie," I reply, firmly. DCI Knowles shakes his head.

"That's not your name now. You know me, I like to get my facts right."

I cannot help smiling. I suspected Eddie would be like this. For a guy with a face as long as a rat, head shaven like a skinhead or gay barman, he is one of the most thoughtful souls I've ever met. My old man's Deputy Sergeant. Now Detective Chief Inspector.

I knew my father used to talk to his junior about me, about his boy who'd lock himself in his bedroom, weep at breakfast, sing Kate Bush in the shower and every few months leave a note on his desk with the name and phone number of a woman who'd be perfect for my old man.

He told me just before he died, said on his cancer bed, "I talked to Eddie about it, and he said you can't help how you're born." Had to lean close to make out his next whisper. "I think he's right, and that's why you've got to go for it."

So now you know, it was the tough old copper who pushed me to have the operation, twelve years before I started hormone treatment, fifteen years before finally I went through with the surgery itself. He was the one who did the research about babies born with mixed-up chromosomes. The one who sat me down one Sunday morning when I was fifteen and told me everything he'd uncovered about gender dysphoria.

"You're born a woman in a man's body, Kev. It's your DNA."

He'd gone over the evidence like the detective he was, put it to me straight and simple. His tone the same he used when explaining case developments to murder victims' parents.

"We are born with twenty-three pairs of chromosomes in each cell of our body, one of which determines sex. Typically every foetus gets one 'sex' chromosome from the mother, which is always 'X'. The second 'sex' chromosome comes from the father, and it can be either 'X' or 'Y'. Normally a foetus having one X and one Y becomes a boy, because the Y chromosome triggers this whole flood of androgens, they're the hormones that make you male, like testosterone. These hormones give the kid both his gender and his sex. On the other hand, two X chromosomes lead to a whole lot of female hormones, causing a little girl to be born."

I nodded, insides dancing.

"So the way the foetus develops depends on its own particular sensitivity to specific hormones, and whether those hormones are available to it. For most people this works just fine. Masculine hormones make a boy, female hormones a girl. What you see is what you get. But sometimes the pregnant woman has additional hormones in her body, say from particular medication she might be taking or from the environment. Or the foetus can sort of be immune to the hormones triggered by the chromosomes. Sometimes babies have more or less than forty-six chromosomes, and having one more or one fewer sex chromosome screws the whole thing up. They could be XXY or XYY – or just a single X one."

I could see it, as he explained, the tiny chromosomal spirals inside me, all vertiginous and confused.

"Kevin," he said, taking my hand. "I think the hormones got all mixed up when you were in your mum's womb. Maybe the androgens were blocked or you didn't react to them in the way most people do. They worked enough to give you the physical sex of a boy, but they didn't manage to touch those parts of your brain that make you think and feel like a man. Instead you've got the mind and the feelings of a woman."

"So I'm a girl with XY chromosomes?" I asked, suddenly getting it. My father looked at me and beamed.

"You're very clever. Always have been. My little brainbox…"

"Thanks, Dad," I said, feeling a swell of love for my old man.

He looked at me, and it may be an invention of memory – so many years have passed since then – but I think I remember tears welling in his grey sick eyes.

"When I stepped up on that roof," he said, not changing his inflection, so that it took me a moment or two to understand that he was referring to his visit to Apple Corp in 1969, "I was ready to dislike that bunch of spoilt long-haired hippies. But they had something, John and Paul. A confidence. Some kind of sheen. It was like they knew things none of us did, and they weren't afraid to say them."

I looked at him, concerned that my level-headed copper had suddenly gone soft on me.

"All you need is love," he murmured gently, resting his cheek against the top of my head. "They were right about that one. That's the one thing you need."

Over the top of his red plastic cup, DCI Edward Knowles isn't afraid to look me in the eye, unlike some who knew me before.

"So what's cooking, gorgeous?"

I show him the photographs. He looks at them for a long time, then looks up at me. "You don't know him? Pretty boy?"

I shake my head. My snaps of Larry Silk and the man in the sky-blue polo shirt, Mudchute Children's Farm llama enclosure, 14.24 on 7th July. Eddie Knowles smiles.

"I was trying to remember, how long since your op, Felicity?"

"Eight months."

He nods. "Still pain?"

"Some. Nothing like I feared. They know what they're doing at the Chelsea; my surgeon's one of the best."

He nods. Picks up one of the photos, re-examines it.

"So this fella next to him, older man in the grey suit…"

"Larry Silk, he's an accountant, has an office half a mile from the farm. He's in Canary Wharf – well, the fringes anyway…"

"How do you know him?"

"It's a long story."

"I like stories."

My turn to smile. "Your lot have already had a spin around that track, Eddie. Called it natural causes."

He waits, a man of wiles and experience. I continue: "Woman called Daisy Perkins, lived in Bow, E3 postcode. Hit her head on the floor, didn't get up."

Eddie sips his coffee, realizes the cup is empty. He unscrews the lid of the red flask, pours half a cup, rescrews the lid.

"And how do you know this Daisy Perkins?"

"Don't. I'm a friend of a friend."

"Hmm. There's a few of them in my business."

He sips the coffee, smacks thin lips. Something has changed in the room, but I'm not sure what. "This Daisy Perkins. Saint or sinner?" he asks, suddenly cheery once more.

"Wild enough, I'm sure. Only met her the once, but she sang loudly. Had plenty to keep the audience happy, if you know what I mean."

Eddie looks at me, trying to read something. A smile on his lips, but not in his eyes. Quickly, I point at the photograph. "You know pretty boy, don't you?"

"Not personally."

"A friend of a friend? I thought he might be a P.O.I. Walked light, like he's used to a scrap and a scarper."

Knowles nods. "Spot on, Felicity. He's a Person of Interest. Jay Munnelly." Peers over his coffee cup.

I return the peer. "You sound like I should know him."

"Do you?"

"Told you, I know the other fella. Never heard of Munnelly."

"Nephew of Declan Munnelly?"

"Son of, brother of, nephew of. Still doesn't mean anything to me – sorry Eddie."

The old Detective Chief Inspector frowns, puts down the plastic cup, kneads the back of his neck. "Really? You never heard of the Munnellys?"

I shrug, shake my head. Knowles watching me every step of the way.

"The Munnellys are messy. West Essex drugs. Used to be happy stuff, Es, dexies, peachies. Recently moved into harder candy. Nasty shit. Shame really, they were amicable at one time or another."

"So this guy in the polo shirt's a drug dealer?"

"Not necessarily. Can't tell you the ins and outs, mainly because I'm not aware of them from behind here…" Gestures at the desk.

"But suffice to say, gentlemen who share his DNA are doing unpleasant things."

"You think the accountant Larry Silk's part of their firm?"

Eddie shakes his head. "Doubt it. From what I recall, the Munnellys prefer Paddy power. You have to be a Mun or Mac to get close to them. Their bank bender's McGraw or McGaffery or something like that."

I look at the photograph of Jay Munnelly, slick hair, smart face, nice strides. Have to admit to a flash of attraction in the nether regions, the cop's son – now daughter – has always had a thing for bad boys.

"What game are you fixing here, Felicity? Anything I need to lose sleep over?"

"Don't fret, thanks Eddie. I'm not one to go off piste. You know that. Dad knew that."

"Did he?"

His head tilts left. Work face now, long jaw tight. Something creeping me out a little, like he's reading a page I haven't written.

"How are your boys, Eddie?"

"You know, I don't get to see them as much as I'd like, given where I'm at… Brian's in Canada, loving it there, he's staying for the duration I think. Jed's down in Southampton. Wife's pregnant. I'm going to be a granddad, you know…"

"That's great, Eddie. Congratulations."

DCI Knowles smiles. "Thanks, Felicity. I know it's nothing really to do with me, but I can't help feeling a little bit proud."

* * *

The antiques expert, Grégoire Chazelle, is already waiting outside Domus Decorus when Julius approaches. Julius consults his watch, sick that he might be late. Yet the dials tell him he's a minute early for their appointment. Chazelle pushes his bifocals back up a large veiny nose, then runs a hand through hair long thinned to threads.

"I'd forgotten how quick the Central Line can be, Mr Miles. Fair shot all the way from Lancaster Gate." Gazes up at the cluttered shop window. "Nearly walked past the place, didn't recognize it."

"Daisy went a bit overboard after Gus passed away. She was… enthusiastic with her stock."

Chazelle nods, bifocals slipping back down his nose, but with a practised scoop he prods them up once more as Julius unlocks the shop door. Stands in the doorway, breathes in. "Can I still smell him?" Sniffs the air, the Master of Wine that he is. "Possibly. The pipe smoke I would say…"

"It's been five years, Greg."

"Has it? Seems less. Or possibly longer. Well then, let's commence the numbers game, get this lot appraised."

Julius sits at the battered desk while the antiques expert turns vases, gently lifts chairs from the rusty nails, tuts over Persian carpets and grimaces at the lines of porcelain dolls. Flicks a finger along the cases of paperbacks and then hardbacks. Takes out a small digital camera that he cradles in one hand as he stalks the shop, stopping once or twice to eye an armchair, the leather Chesterfield, a small writing desk buried under grubby copies of *Elle Decoration* from the mid-'90s.

Picks up an old meat grinder, turns the handle. Crank of steel. Laughs, to himself, replaces it on the pine table covered in metal boxes brimming with buttons.

"Ah-ha!" he mutters, five minutes later. Julius looks up from the mouldy Sudoku puzzler he found on the floor under the desk. Chazelle is sniffing a small rusted box. Before Julius can ask him what he's found, the Frenchman holds aloft a smoker's pipe.

"It was Gus's, yes? I'm sure of it."

"Maybe. He had several."

"Mmmm. I think this was his."

"Quite possibly. Er… would you like a cup of tea? I knew this would take a while…"

Chazelle does not answer. Walks up to the desk, fingers playing through the dangling fronds of the spider plants above Julius's head as if tapping a head-height piano. "No need."

"It's no trouble, I was going to make a brew for myself…"

"No need, because my work here is done."

Julius's hand to chin. "And?"

"And nothing. It's junk. Complete and utter junk. As perhaps you suspected."

"Oh."

"This girl, Daisy…" he pronounces "Daisee" with extra French dismissiveness, "she was as you say 'enthusiastic'. But not a pinch of taste. It makes me angry just to think of what she has done to Augustus's magnificent emporium. Really very angry."

"But is any of it worth something? Is any of it valuable?"

"This lot," declares Chazelle, swinging the camera round by the cord attached to his bony wrist, "is nothing but a pile of sh*ee*t!"

* * *

A small thud on the brown doormat. Julius climbs the stairs from his lower ground floor and opens the package. Inside, a plastic envelope, two small plastic swabs.

Julius considers DNA analysis to be the miracle of our age. He is delighted that modern science is turning to mathematics to explain the deepest truths of humankind. It thrills him to think that even the most sacred secrets of our bodies and minds are slowly being uncovered by hobbit geeks like Julius himself in stuffy little rooms all over the world. Alone in his office, he feels part of something, a tribe of new explorers digging into the core of numerical existence.

He swabs his mouth carefully. The swab tastes of plastic. He is careful to rub it on both cheeks, his tongue. The roof of his mouth. Puts the swab back into the small clear plastic bag, seals it and places it back into the envelope.

Julius is happy to give his DNA sample, because he does not believe that he is Arnold Perkins's father. He does not believe that his seed could have penetrated Daisy Perkins's egg. He does not believe that his spermatozoa are more vigorous than that of the sprightly Larry Silk. He imagines his own sperm to be weak, sickly worms, barely able to wriggle. Whereas Silk's are zip-zapping fireworks, despite his more advanced years.

Outside, I lean back against the warm wall and open a can of White Ace, invaded suddenly by despair. I am feeling sad, because I know many things but I don't know if Julius Miles is wrong.

9

When he was a student at Cambridge University, Julius Miles attended a guest lecture given by Dr Uri Schindler, a white-haired skeleton with the chuckle of a Viennese rat-catcher. Dr Schindler's lecture was entitled 'Possibility or probability – is your friend dead?'

A ship, let's call it *The Bonny Babe*, has been lost at sea. Forty of the fifty passengers have drowned. You know that your friend, Mr X, a successful businessman, had booked a berth on the ship to attend a conference of ball-bearing manufacturers. What is the probability that he was one of the drowned?

Easy. 40 in 50, or 4 in 5. Not good odds, particularly if your friend Mr X owed you money. And what is the chance that he was saved? 10 in 50, or 1 in 5.

Yet slowly more information concerning the tragedy drips in (there are no twenty-four-hour news reports in probability case studies). The next update states that 20 of the 40 dead were members of the crew. Good news: the chance that Mr X has drowned has now decreased to 20 in 30, or 2 in 3.

Then another bulletin arrives, stating that 5 of the drowned passengers were women. The probabilities relating to your friend have changed again. The chance that he is alive has improved even further, it is now 10 in 25, or 2 in 5. And the likelihood that he is at the bottom of the sea is 15 in 25 or 3 in 5.

At this point, a bulletin is received from the ship's owners in Bangladesh, stating that the initial roster was only provisory and that there were in fact 20 passengers and 30 crew on board when the ship left harbour. Since we know 40 people drowned, 20 of whom were crew, all twenty of the passengers must have drowned, including the unfortunate Mr X. You start composing your sympathy card, dust off your black suit and call your accountant to instruct him to write off the money you were owed.

Finally, Mr X's wife telephones. She's been calling up all his friends and colleagues to let them know the happy news that Mr X changed his mind about the trip at the last minute and flew to the conference instead. He is safe and well and enjoying his golf on the Algarve, and at no time was there any possibility of his having been lost on the good ship *Bonny Babe*.

What changed as each news bulletin came in was the "probability" of an outcome, even though there was only one "possibility" that Mr X was alive and well.

Julius feels that the probability is that Larry Silk is Arnold's father. But there is only one possibility.

* * *

There was never any doubt that I was my father's son. My hands are his, birds' wings. Feet likewise, like knotted rope. I had his Adam's Apple, before it was shaved smooth. I suspect our penises were similar, although I never saw his. Stanley "Charlie" Hopkins was a private man.

But now all that is gone. He's dead and buried, and Kevin is Felicity – the name I've called myself in secret since I was three. The 2004 Gender Recognition Act gives trans men and women the right to a gender-recognition certificate and a new birth certificate. My country is one of the most progressive in the world, at least in terms of gender rights. We can now marry in our newly recognized gender. I've applied for a new driving licence and a new passport as a woman. Not that I drive much or that I ever travel anywhere.

I just want to see my new name and face in print. Julius would be proud of me. I want to be a statistic.

* * *

The phone call from Gwendolyn Lank shakes the big phlegmatic tree that is Julius Miles. Her number still programmed into his phone. He knows the yellow ribbon should have been cut long ago – she was never coming back, but she was Gus's favourite, and part of a story Julius still tells himself when drunk. Gwen and her emperor Julius, poetry and mathematics in perfect harmony. A reunification, west and east, science and art, thick and thin.

"Heard you'd inherited Gus's old place in the will, figured you hadn't changed the number of the beast, so thought I'd give it a shot..."

Her voice remains a dancing burlesque show. She laughs for no reason. The breath catches in Julius's throat. "Sorry, it's been simply ages, hasn't it – oh mighty Caesar..."

Surprised, shocked even by the stirring in his loins after all these years. Images of their first-time debauchery sneaking around the explicit-content settings in his head. Her naked panting smile.

"Gwendolyn. A surprise. A... a... nice surprise."

"Blasts from the past, *le temps perdu retrouvé*... Guess what? Weirdness came calling on me, Big J. I got a letter. A singular one."

"Really? What kind of letter?"

"Simple white envelope, London postmark. Addressed to me, which isn't the strange part. It was the 'and'. Guess who was the 'and'?" She doesn't wait for an answer. "You! 'Gwendolyn Lank and Julius Miles'. How warped is that?"

"Who sent it?"

"Dunno. No name, no return address. A blank white envelope. Secretive, *non*?"

"What was in it?"

"And so to the crux. A cheque, my jolly lean giant. Made out to *moi* and *toi*, G and J, the good ole Lank & Miles show back on stage."

"What's the name on the bank account?"

"Nexus Holdings Ltd. Googled them, nothing. Called the bank, they said they couldn't give out any info."

"How much is it for?"

"A thousand pounds. A grand. Or a 'bag' as I'm reliably informed it's called these days. 'Bag of sand', a 'grand'…"

"But we don't have a joint account. We never did."

"Not that I know of. You didn't set up some secret little stash hole somewhere, did you, Julius? Some accounting fiddle? Or romantic lingering? I have to admit it did cross my devious little mind that you might have sent it to me yourself, knowing that I'd call you…"

"What? I didn't! I can assure you!"

"Clearly, judging from your outrage at the mere possibility."

Julius is confused and angry and sad and glad to hear her voice again. Feels like he's in his own dream, slipping down a well that might be empty or gloriously full. Seeking fingerholds wherever he can.

"So what are you going to do with the cheque, Gwen? You should destroy it."

"So quick to find the absolute, Julius, as ever. Is that what you want me to do?"

"Yes. Someone's playing some sort of trick…"

"You sound uncomfortable. Is anyone listening in perchance? A sigoth?"

"A what?"

"Significant other. Mistress, boyfriend, wife?"

"Oh God no. I'm not married…"

"Why not?" Her tone as light as a summer swallow. Now Julius wants to hang up. He's about to say goodbye when Gwendolyn speaks quickly.

"I'm engaged, JM. He's Professor of Ancient History at Oxford, I'm moving down there, hopefully getting a position at St Hilda's. His name is Odwyn, which is odd…"

"It's Welsh. Like your name."

"Spot on, big fella. Well done! So… anyway… six weeks to the day, we're doing the deed in Dyfed. Ms Lank shall be Mrs Jones, thank Christ. Strange I should get the cheque now…"

Julius looks around the room at the bookshelves and the antique vases and the mahogany hat stand and the wrought-iron French poker. And comes to the realization that one of the reasons he has not sorted through his uncle's possessions and sold them is that somewhere at the back of his mind he was holding on to the dream that one day it would be Gwendolyn Lank who would tell him what to keep and what to give up. Has fervently imagined Gwen sitting beside him at the fireplace, French poems on her lips, French poker in her hand, French kisses on his lips.

"I wish you all the best, Gwen. And to Odwyn too."

"Thanks. You always were a gent, Julius. Your uncle taught you well."

"Tear up the cheque."

"Will do, Scooby-Doo."

Julius hangs up the phone just as she is saying goodbye. He turns, eyes lingering on one of Gus's favourite paintings, a small John Minton sketch of a naked woman, her eyes doleful yet serene. "My empress," Gus used to call her.

Julius continues to stare at the painting as minutes slip by, five, ten, fifteen… Then, without warning, his shoulders rise again, he opens his laptop and types fast into the Google bar. Scrutinizes page after page until he finds what he's looking for. Prints out the article and hurries down to his kitchen, three steps in a bound, rips a box of twelve eggs from the old Electrolux refrigerator, pulls out Uncle Gus's most trusted Le Creuset, puts it on the hob and starts to boil a very large pan of water.

* * *

Awa Yasin does not smile when she answers the door at 8.25 a.m. She wears a white frilly blouse and long beige skirt, beige headscarf hastily thrown around her face. "Hello, Mr Miles. Everything okay?"

"Yes. Good morning, Awa." Between the young woman's legs Arnold appears, squirming shyly into her thighs, small round head pushing up the long skirt. Julius looks away quickly.

"Arnold! Please! Careful!" Awa exclaims, pushing her skirt back down.

"Hello, Arnold," Julius mumbles. "I was wondering…" He turns, eyes on the Somali woman now. "Perhaps I might walk Arnold to school?"

Awa frowns. "It's five doors away. Less than a hundred metres. If you were that Jamaican runner… can't remember his name… you'd do it in less than ten seconds…"

Julius shrugs. The bear with no tongue. Awa sucks in her lower lip, a tug on Arnold's ear. Weighing the past and the future.

"Okay. Arnold, get your sweatshirt, don't forget your packed lunch, it's on the side…" Pats his shoulder as carefree as if she were really his mother. The boy turns, scampers back into the house. Awa remains on the doorstep. Julius feeling the sun on the back of his neck already. Flushed and damp.

"You look… nice," Julius remarks, awkwardly. Awa does not smile. "Special occasion?"

"No. Just another day in paradise." Her tone flat and stern, Julius feels admonished. Anger flushes his cheeks, the boy's not *her* child, she's just a port in a storm. Whereas he, Julius, could be the dock on the bay.

Arnold reappears, squirms back to the safety of the young woman's legs, clutching a small backpack with some superhero or other flying across the front pocket. Gently, like wool from briars, she prises him loose.

"Have a nice day, Arnold. I love you."

* * *

Awa steps back into the cool shadows of the lower ground floor. Her father still sitting at the kitchen table staring out through the large window at the garden, plants and lawn unruly since Daisy's death, ragged and riotous and unfurling in every corner as if suffering some kind of burgeoning grief. She waits for Mohammad Ali to continue but, as she guessed he would, he remains silent.

"I'm fine. I've been fine," she says eventually, conceding to his need for her to give in first, Somali daughter to her father. And now he turns, sadness drooping from heavy-lidded eyes.

"You had another fit."

"Seizure, Aba. Not fit. I didn't."

"The way you move your tongue in your mouth, I see it, Awa. Your tongue, it still hurts from the biting." His round face softer now – and she feels the nauseous guilt for having cast him as blind to her, seeing only what he wanted to see. "I know you, Awa."

She blushes, rolls her tongue round her mouth despite herself.

"I was… It was fine. The boy went to fetch the neighbour…" Her hand to her mouth as she says it, seeing his face harden. "It's Mr Miles, the big man next door, he said he wouldn't tell anyone, he doesn't have any friends round here anyway, he won't talk, he's a little stuffy but he's okay…"

Silence again from Mohammad Ali. The dark space between them familiar to Awa from these past five years, a void shaped with the curves and bustle of her mother Faduma, Faduma the tormentor of them both. Knows how much her father misses her. And how little he will admit to missing her. Knows too that it has been her role as next-in-line to fill the space, feign-play the part her mother made her own before exiting the stage so abruptly.

"I can't let what I have drag me down, Dad…"

"You cannot pretend you do not have the illness! It is in you, Awa, it marks you…"

"What? It doesn't mark me, it's not who I am, Aba. I am me, not the epilepsy. Why can't you see that?"

"Why can't *you* see what is real?! Not stick the head in the sand? It is this modern culture that deludes you, that is it! They make you think everything can be changed, everything can be fixed, every-thing can be made better. Bigger, shinier, 'sexier'! Such nonsense. The world does not change. People do not change. What we are born with we take to the grave."

"How can you say this, Aba? You bet on horses every day. You worship chance, you pray that you will win, win big, as if somehow that will change your life, transform who you are…"

He stands, furious now, Ali the fighter only when the truth slaps him hard in the face. "Who can listen to such nonsense? Who told you I 'bet', as you call it? Who said such things, I want to know – names, dates, places where such things are talked about…"

"Come on, Aba, everyone's seen you… I've seen you… some days you never even make it to the mosque…"

"You are wrong. You are ignorant, you ignorant, corrupt young woman! We should never have brought you here for a better life, never made the sacrifices! I could be back there now, a big man, a great man, a farmer of much land, but your mother and I, we fear for the future of our girls, so we make the sacrifices Allah requires of us…"

"That's it, isn't it? It's all about Mum. You miss her, Dad, of course you do, why not just get on the plane – I've got money, I've got money saved up, I mean what do I spend it on? And Fada will help with the ticket, they want to see you, your grandson wants to see you…"

"You insolent girl, you foolish girl, you monstrous girl… yes, that is it, the monster within you makes you blind even to its existence and to its power. Open your eyes, Awa, there are demons, such things exist, of this there is no doubt. Demons who seek out pride and greed, the two great sins of this western society, the pillars of American-led capitalism, and use them to devour you through such weakness…"

Awa cannot help her laughter. "Stop talking like Sheikh Fazul at the mosque – even you think he's a buffoon, and now you're trying to sound like him…"

Mohammad Ali steps up to his daughter and raises his hand. Instinctively she grabs his wrist and pulls it down. Father and daughter, wrist-to-wrist, eye-to-eye…

"Dad, you love this country. And you miss Mum. And you love me. I'll be home soon. We'll know who Arnold's father is in a couple of days. His father will look after him then. And I will come back to my father."

She leans in to kiss him. He starts to pull away, but then his shoulders slump. She kisses his bald forehead. His fingers damp and tight in her own.

"She is sleeping with men in Dubai," he mumbles softly, like a child. "She is having sex with them."

"What? Who? Mum?"

He nods. Awa's twin hands to her mouth, trying to cover her shocked grin. "No, Dad! That's ridiculous. Mum… with other men? She's not. Why do you think that?"

"She is. That's why she doesn't come back. She is sleeping with them and they make her happy."

Awa shakes her head, in disbelief as much as negation, puts her arms out to the small man with the trembling belly. But he ducks past her and hurries away up the stairs.

"Dad!" she shouts after him. "Aba!"

But the door slams. And the house of ghosts is empty once more.

* * *

Julius Miles has held a dozen hands in his life. His mother Wendy, of course, rigid strength – pulling, not coaxing. His father Claudius, softer and more anxious. Granny Miles was a sturdy handholder, grasping young Julius as if he were a small balloon and she a post, embedded far into the earth.

Uncle Gus held his nephew's hand even when Julius went to university and beyond. A lazy promiscuity running through hand-shakes, hugs and shoulder squeezes – nothing sexual, just a Mediterranean comfort in the grasp, hand on body.

Holding Gwendolyn's hand in the early months of their relationship was electricity for Julius. Her slender fingers, like bone china, in his sweaty mitt. He clasped them even deep in his sleep. And in his nightmares they shattered one by one as he gripped them.

And now he holds Arnold's hand. Thrilled and terrified by the small, hot wriggle in his palm.

They reach the school, fifteen minutes before any parents or carers will be there with their charges, toast still being gnashed, hair scraped, teeth foamed, screeches and screams over shoes, packed lunches, book bags, coats. Arnold slows, glancing through the wire gate to the toys discarded after the previous day's games on the playground concrete. Sighs quietly to himself.

"It's early, Arnold. And I've something to show you. Come on, let's walk round the block."

* * *

I follow at my usual distance. The second shadow of Julius Miles, his benevolent haunting. Arnold steps by the large man's side happily enough, but does not look up at him, even though Julius peeks down intermittently, viewing the top of the boy's head and the swirl of dark hair that coils down to his ears. He suspects that the lad needs a haircut, but wonders whether such ragged length could be the style these days – such things having been a mystery to Julius since birth.

We walk past the front entrance to the school opposite the park, down the Victorian terraced street, crossing Old Ford Road by the former gun factory and through the park's east gates. Mothers pushing buggies glance up at Julius and most of them smile at the man and the boy walking to school through a municipal green space in central London, clearly father and son. A reassuring sight.

The sun is hot at 8.30 a.m. Sudden worry on Julius's face. "Did your mother put suncream on you on sunny days, Arnold?"

Arnold shrugs as if he's not going to commit to answering such a difficult question. "Because you know, the incidence of melanoma has doubled in the UK in the last ten years."

Arnold kicks a stick, which snaps in two with a satisfying crack. "What's Melon Moma?"

"Skin cancer. Each year approximately 3,400 British men are diagnosed with malignant melanomas. In 2004 one thousand three hundred and twenty-two men died of skin cancer, one thousand and two of them from malignant melanoma."

Arnold yawns. They walk on, side by side, the boy taking two steps to the man's one. Small clack of tiny Clarks on tarmac. Louder smack of the size-thirteen Timberland Power Loungers. Clack, clack, smack. Clack, clack, smack...

"Mummy died." The boy stops suddenly. Looks up at Julius. "She wasn't a Melon Moma, but she died. Like Grandpa."

"Yes. She did. But like I said at the crematorium, statistically..."

"She sings to me."

"Did she? I'm sure she was a very good mummy..."

"She sings to me from dead land. Every night when I go to sleep." Julius looks down, concerned, but Arnold isn't seeing him, gazing upwards to somewhere past Julius's nose. "Dead land is quiet, she says, so she needs to sing. She knows I like her singing."

Julius nods, unsure whether to engage with the boy's delusions or to follow his instinct to gently but firmly reiterate to Arnold that his mother is no longer able to sing to him at bedtime because she's been incinerated at 450 degrees Celsius.

"Say hello to her, Julius."

Julius smiles, shakes his head. "Arnold, the truth is..."

"Say hello to Mummy."

"I can't, Arnold…"

"Yes you can. She's here, she's right next to you."

Julius feels a familiar sadness well up inside him. Reaches out to pat the boy's head. Arnold doesn't flinch or pull away, the big fingers on his hot hair. "She's not here, Arnold. I'm sorry. She's gone. But she still loves you…"

"No. She's here. I can see her. She's laughing at you."

Julius shivers suddenly. Turns. And looks down. On the tarmac path beside him is a feather, grey and sleek. He peers at it with suspicion. I duck behind one of the large plane trees.

"Mummy says I have to be good when I'm with you," Arnold says. "She says you'll look after me."

Julius smiles wanly. Unable or unwilling to understand that what Arnold is saying is true. His mother *is* standing next to Julius. I see her, not the features or even a shape, this isn't Hollywood, folks, but her presence. Like a haze on a hot afternoon, or steam off ice. The boy is still young enough to connect to such energy, but most of you lose it after the age of four, when memories begin to coalesce and firm, clay setting. Only a rare few – myself, some of the better mediums and psychics, blind girls and Downs-syndrome adults – retain the ability. Perhaps we are the incomplete ones, the ones who do not develop. But I choose to believe that it's the rest of you who have regressed from our more natural state of grace.

The man and boy turn back towards Woodstock Road, another school day beckoning. When they near the South Gate, Julius stops on the grass. "This is what I had to show you, Arnold." Extracts a spoon and six hard-boiled eggs from his backpack. Holds out the spoon that glints in the morning sunshine. Arnold blinks, takes the piece of cutlery with curiosity.

"It's all in your forearm. I've studied it on the internet. The ideal angle is ninety degrees. Lock the muscle at the elbow, but keep your shoulder loose, like this. Don't run, but walk quickly with large steps, see…"

Julius places the egg on his spoon, locks his forearm, keeps his shoulders loose, starts to walk. Giant on the moon. Carrying boiled protein.

I shuffle backwards as Julius advances. He reaches the foliage that conceals me, then turns, striding back towards Arnold. Eyes always focused on the mottled beige egg on the spoon.

Arnold watches him. Smiles. "Can I do it? I want to do it!"

"Absolutely. That's what we're here for. It's your turn." Julius presents another boiled egg. Arnold stares at it, entranced, his spoon hanging limp in his left hand.

"Hold up your spoon! Forearm at ninety degrees! Ninety degrees! Loose shoulder, large steps." The boy does not budge. "Go on! You have to move if you're going to win the race!"

But Arnold is frozen, staring in wonderment at the egg on the spoon in front of him as if waiting for it to hatch. Julius hurries to him, but the moment the big man puts a hand on the boy's shoulder, Arnold takes off, large gangly steps a vague counterfeit of Julius's long strides.

"Wait, Arnold!"

The small boy is striding out of the gate, heading towards the road in front of the school, the spoon held firmly out in front of him, a wand. Beyond, cars are pulling up by the school's main entrance, parents arriving with their children.

Julius drops the rest of the boiled eggs, which bounce and crack open on the concrete path. Dark shell, pale flesh. Hurries, terrified, after the boy. "Arnold! Wait!"

Arnold is moving fast, along the pavement, towards the pedestrian crossing, the egg barely moving in the metal dip, skinny little legs gliding across concrete flagstones. "See!" he declares. "See!"

"Stop, Arnold! The road!"

As Arnold starts across the pedestrian crossing, Julius's shout booms out over even the acceleration of the planes taking off from City Airport, and Arnold hears him, half-turning in alarm, stumbling. The egg falls off the spoon. The boy takes several steps more before he realizes that his spoon is empty. Whips round, seeing the broken egg behind him. Drops the spoon, which clatters to the ground.

A car screeches to a stop at the crossing. Faces turn, mothers gasp.

For a moment Arnold's face is taut, impervious, a wan stone. Then the stone dissolves in a small earthquake.

He crumples to a sobbing heap in the midst of the Zebra crossing. Julius gets to him, unable to quell rising anger. "Don't give up now! It's just your first go! Come on! Try another egg!"

But Arnold continues to wail while London commuters glare, horns honk, parents gaze in disapproval from the main school gate and Julius blushes. They are a scene now, he and the boy, something Julius hates to be.

"Get up!" Julius hisses. "Try another egg!" Brandishes the spoon under Arnold's nose. "Come on. You were doing well! Try another one." Presents the egg, as if it were a votive offering. "Please." But Arnold buries his head deeper in his hands, two words squeezing out through tightly clasped fingers: "Go away!"

From across the road, it seems to me that the boy's reaction is not sincere. I detect a degree of artifice in his posture in the middle of the pedestrian crossing. He's making a point. His mother is dead and his egg is broken and the world needs to know how unhappy these things make him.

"Arnold," sings a man beyond Julius. Julius turns to see Larry Silk approaching. The crisp grey suit kneels, placing a hand on Arnold's shoulders.

"He's fine," Julius hastens to say. Silk nods up at Julius, dismissing him in one slight gesture, reaching in a pocket, extracting a small plastic robot figurine. Larry moves the robot's arms up and down, and the robot starts to chatter. "Intergalactic Superstars activated!" croaks a mechanical voice from inside the toy. Arnold's eyes flicker between his fingers, arms lowering.

"Come on, Captain. Let's get you off this strange planet, away from the aliens and into the mother ship," Larry Silk helps Arnold to his feet, handing the plastic robot to the boy.

"Intergalactic Superstars activated!"

Larry Silk hoists Arnold onto his shoulders, turns and strides up to the school gates, the parents looking on with barely concealed admiration and relief as the warrior and the prince walk away from the stumbling giant into the blinding light of the morning sun.

10

Heavy East London summer rain, tight fists pelt battered streets, shapes under umbrellas dashing through sputtering puddles, cars scything leaden pools of dirty water, crunch of spray. Low dark sky, all the latent anger of tower blocks and bedsits and rusted cars and garbage and broken dreams boiling upwards from the hot concrete. It's thirty-two degrees Celsius and police helicopters churn the skies.

The number 8 bus is a fog of sodden faces, grinding and screeching with every traffic light and metal lake it ploughs through. Don't get me wrong, I like my buses, these lumbering red behemoths, out of time and place however much they update them with CCTV cams and green engines and scented upholstery the colour of ripe aubergines.

Some nights I pop a mazzy and ride the length of the route and back again, top deck, front row. My paradise run, neon and forgiveness, it's cheaper than heroin, and you get to see through first-floor windows, where everything worth knowing happens. Baby suckles breast. Old man sucks oxygen from a tank. Young woman sips whiskey from the bottle. Couple playing darts in 1930s suit and frock, hair parted, hair curled. Priest unties dog collar. Man kisses priest. Old girl in wheelchair pours the tea whilst watching wide-eyed as the bus passes like a chariot in front of her to freedom.

Today I'm up on top, second row back, waiting for my front seat to come free. My old man always grumbled, never wanted the first row. "Most dangerous of all, Kev, all that glass'll crash right through you. And if someone's looking for a slice of trouble, they head for the top of the stairs, plenty of space and an audience, and guess who's first in line?" But he always relented, sat right up next to me, always the aisle seat, one eye down the stairs, one eye on the dullards ranked behind us on the top deck.

I watch the trees whip and tremble in the storm, watch an umbrella snap inside out, exposing sharp entrails to the sky. Nearing Bethnal Green Underground Station the number 8 surges through a deep puddle, and I hear the hiss of water on hot drive shaft and a communal shriek from the bottom deck as water sloshes in across the floor through the back doors. Then laughter.

The bus slows. I find myself staring down the gun-metal cobbles of an old Victorian alley just past the railway bridge, and I see someone I recognize. White Adidas tracksuit, slouched shoulders. Check my journal, his name written in a column next to: *Associates to the murder.* The youth called Trevor Nugent. He's leaning into the window of a car, chatting it looks like, not buying nor dealing. He's not covert, glances aimlessly up at the noise of a plane overhead. Relaxed and smiling. I wonder for a moment if Trevor has a girlfriend or boyfriend, but this sedan doesn't belong to someone who'd sleep with a council-estate donkey like Nugent. It's a black BMW, 760i. A car I know, a car I've seen before. Then it comes back to me: the BMW belongs to Larry Silk.

As the bus jolts forward once more, heading towards Tesco's, the Impressionist painting of white tracksuit, lanky youth and gleaming rain-streaked car is gone.

* * *

I found my bag. On the bus I remembered, remembered that I don't take my bag on the bus, just a plastic wallet, back pocket or coat pocket; keep it lean, don't risk the biscuit, my old man used to say. The bag was under my bed.

Why is my mind the foam on a wave? It feels medical, not psychological. A virus or a curse. So I make an appointment at the surgery in Stepney Green. Dr Fitzgerald listens to my symptoms with raised eyebrows.

"Jesus, Felicity, what have I told you, stop with the fuckin' benzos!" He swears a lot, Dr Fitzgerald, because he's from Cork in Ireland, where he says cursing is taught at school. That's primary school. "Where the hell're you getting them?"

"I'm in pain. So I take painkillers."

"You're addicted."

I shrug. "You smoke."

"Tobacco doesn't cause anterograde amnesia. What are you swallowing, girl, jellies?"

"What's anterograde amnesia?"

"It's when you can't remember recent events. Older stuff, the past, is still clear enough, but you forget what you had for breakfast."

"Shreddies." Dr Fitzgerald's eyes crinkle at the edges. "I had Shreddies for breakfast."

"Is it Temazepam you're taking?"

"I'm fine, Lionel. Really. I'll cut back. Shift down a gear. It's getting easier, the pain's not so bad now."

"Sweet Mary, Felicity, what's the truth? Pain or no pain? You're over eight months post-op, it should be calm and sweet songs by now. Maybe I should refer you back to Dr Pillai?"

"Who's he?" Then I burst out laughing. "Don't worry. I'll see you, Doctor Happy. Call you when the fog clears."

* * *

It's clear that Julius Miles has never bunked off work before. He's not very good at it. Rather than skipping carefree through the large piles of hot summer sunshine, he is trudging morosely through the shadows of the Hernshall Estate towards the park.

His contract with the Hospital Trust is clear. "Unauthorized, non-sickness related absence is cause for termination." Julius has gambled, as we all do, on statistics. His boss, Richard Lovall, has never once contacted Julius during mid-quarter analysis, coinciding as it does with his own mid-term accounting period. On an afternoon as hot as this, Julius has calculated that his boss will remain in air-conditioned isolation with Mrs Aqbal, the pencil-browed financial controller. Julius has bet the farm on neither Mrs Aqbal nor Richard Lovall wanting to work up a sweat trudging down the corridor to Room 717B. He's rerouted his office number to his mobile, in case either of them decide to call him about something.

Victoria Park is my favourite park in the world. Green swathes of swaying grass, two hundred and thirty-two trees, many of them giant plane trees casting their crowns of leaves high above the drunks and the joggers and the mums and the babies who process along its paths and promenades. It's the sort of urban pastoral paradise where you will find love. Or get stabbed. Or both.

Julius heads into the upper park, stopping beneath the shade of one of the plane trees, where he applies factor-fifty suncream to his arms, neck, face and hands. Smiles as he remembers Gus, fifty-something back then in the early 1980s, slapping baby oil onto naked flesh as he stripped down to his Y-fronts on one of the park benches. "Tanned fat's better than pallid fat, *n'est-ce pas*, Julius, *mon brave*? A truth for all nations, no less…"

Two large police horses are exercising on the grass, trotting and galloping, short policemen in short sleeves and riding hats rising and falling in the saddles like puppets. Some tourist is taking pictures, recording this joyfully anachronistic sight.

Julius finds police officers reassuring. Not because they protect us from wrongdoers and ruffians, but because they know their statistics. Like members of the medical profession, the police are faced daily with the patterns and repetitions of human nature. They plot likelihoods and probabilities in their heads based on vast personal banks of prior data before deciding how to act. It might not make them the most innovative of thinkers. But it does make them averagely fair-minded. Or so Julius believes.

The fact that Julius likes policemen makes me like Julius even more. He does not bow to populist chatter. I'm impressed that unlike most people his opinions are not borrowed from newspapers or magazines or television talk shows. I like that he spouts ideas that are firmly his, even when those ideas are inane or belligerent, which is most of the time.

Beyond the police horses, Julius spots the orange cones, sunshades, baseball caps, a gaggle of red balloons tied to the backs of white plastic chairs. A sea of tiny figures dressed in similar white T-shirts, adults buzzing around them, squeezing and spraying suncream onto flailing limbs like farmers marking livestock.

When I get to the tall plane trees bordering the stretch of grass that today plays host to the Woodstock Road Primary School Sports Day, Julius is standing awkwardly close to, but noticeably apart from, the main group of parents. He seeks out Arnold through sweat-beaded eyes. The numerous children are excited, running this way and that, cartwheeling, tumbling onto the grass with happy abandon. So many different skin colours, ethnicities and sizes: all seem wired to the hilt.

I spy Arnold just as Julius does. The boy is standing under a small tree sucking on something, staring out at the other children as if analysing them for some small project of his own. He seems so focused on his own thoughts, so separate from the crowd, that for a moment I think that maybe there could be a chance he is Julius's son.

Julius approaches, affecting nonchalance. "Hello, Arnold."

The boy looks up. "Hello."

"Ready for the big race?" Arnold nods, the popsicle he's suck-ing in a cardboard tube dripping onto the front of his small white T-shirt. Julius looks concerned. "Should you really be having an ice lolly now? Why don't I buy you one after the race?" Reaches out for the tube.

"No. It's mine! Don't touch me!" Arnold ducks under his arm and runs away.

"Excuse me, sir... Can I help you?" A large woman strides to-wards Julius wearing a purple skirt and large red T-shirt that reads "Woodstock Road Primary".

"Er... I'm here to see Arnold... Arnold Perkins..."

The woman stops. The flesh on her vast arms jiggles menacingly as she crosses them across a gigantic bosom. "And you are?"

Julius looks beyond to see Arnold run up to Awa Yasin, who is wearing a long black dress and pink-and-black headscarf. She kneels down, takes the orange popsicle from the boy, gently scold-ing as she rubs at the front of his white T-shirt with a tissue. A man walks up to her wearing jeans, green T-shirt and all-white trainers. It's Larry Silk.

"Excuse me, but I'm Mrs Chambers, the head of Early Years, and I'm afraid I don't recognize you as one of Arnold's caregivers. Could you please tell me your relation to the boy?"

Julius looks back to the large woman. Eyes narrowed. "Professor Michael Adams, Arnold's paediatric psychiatrist. From the Royal London Hospital. His aunt mentioned he was competing today, and I wanted to come and give him my support. After all that has happened."

"Oh. I see. Quite. Well... sorry. You can't be too careful these days." Despite her words, the large woman does not sound apologetic.

"No. You can't." Julius walks quickly away from her, keeping to the fringes of the other parents, who are chatting together in small hearty groups, dads brandishing cameras and video cams, mothers armed to the teeth with high-energy, low-sugar, low-carb sports drinks and spare UV-resistant baseball caps.

Julius looks at them and feels inadequate. Senses that he should have been more worried about Arnold not wearing a hat in this heat. He watches as the boy finishes the popsicle, lifting the end of the cardboard above his nose, pouring melted ice directly down the tube onto his face and chest until he is drenched in sticky orange.

Awa Yasin admonishes Arnold once more, scrubbing again at his T-shirt as the boy stands motionless, taking the vigorous female assault without rancour or frustration. Julius watches as Larry Silk puts a hand on Awa's shoulder and she stops rubbing. Silk pulls something from his bag, taking off the stained T-shirt and slipping a fresh one over Arnold's head.

I see Julius wince, and I too notice the black swoop and the logo on the small, white T-shirt that reads "Nike, Just Do It".

"Ladies and Gentlemen. Next up, Nursery One and Two, egg-and-spoon race. Contestants to the starting line, please!" Gargantuan Mrs Chambers is now armed with a small megaphone that she brandishes like the purser on the Titanic. Her announcement begins a new level of bustle amongst the parents as children are grabbed and slathered once more in factor two hundred, baseball caps tightened, and fathers film themselves giving last-minute instructions in hushed coaching tones.

As Larry Silk kneels by Arnold's side, Julius shuffles towards them.

"…Just go out and enjoy yourself, it's only a bit of fun…" Larry Silk sings in a cheerful tone.

"There's another way of looking at it, Arnold," interjects Julius, bluntly. "You could try and win!"

The small boy looks up. Larry Silk whirls around. "What are you doing here? Awa said you weren't coming…"

Julius ignores the white-haired accountant, continues to address Arnold directly; "Remember what I taught you. Lock the muscle at the elbow, ninety degrees, but keep your shoulder loose, no running, just quick large steps. Breathe regularly, fill the diaphragm – in, out, in, out…"

"Julius, you came!" Awa approaches, clutching her phone, set to video mode, just like a real parent. "I thought you weren't interested…"

Julius kneels by Arnold's side, reaching into his pocket. "Take this…" Thrusts something quickly into Arnold's small palm. The boy looks at it, a small ornate silver spoon, his finger rubbing the bowl. "Is it gold?"

"No, silly. It's silver. It belonged to my uncle. I think it'll work well."

"He can't use that!" Larry Silk is distressed. "It's against the rules! They provide them with spoons! That would be cheating!" He reaches down to take the spoon, but Arnold holds it close to his small chest.

"It's all right Larry," says Awa. "I think he can use his own spoon. It's not exactly the Olympics…"

"Come on, everyone, to the starting line please, we don't want to get behind, we're on a tight schedule!" Mrs Chambers urges.

"But Awa, it says in the programme that the school will be providing spoons; I don't want Arnie getting disqualified just cos Mr Miles wants to offload some family heirloom or other…"

"He's four. I'm sure it's okay. I'll ask Mrs Chambers if he can use it – come on, Arnold, we don't want to miss your race…"

Awa takes Arnold's hand and leads him towards the starting line – a piece of rope held by two young play assistants in matching Woodstock Road Primary School T-shirts. Larry Silk glares at Julius. "He doesn't need to win, he doesn't need that kind of pressure after all he's been through."

Julius nods back at him. "He doesn't need to lose, either."

Arnold lines up behind the rope with two dozen other children – he's one of the smallest in the field – most of the girls are taller and bigger than him, whilst two of the boys look old enough to be at university.

Mrs Chambers waddles along the line handing out spoons and hard-boiled eggs. When she gets to Arnold, he holds up the antique silver spoon. "Can I use this one please?" Mrs Chambers hesitates, the regulation spoon in her hand. Julius watches, eyes narrow, as Awa Yasin steps alongside Arnold for a moment. "His uncle gave it to him, they're very close," she whispers. Mrs Chambers thinks for a moment, nods and moves on to the next child.

Julius tries not to glance towards Larry Silk, but he cannot help himself. The accountant doesn't look up, studiously checking his iPhone.

"Ready everyone? Eggs on spoons."

In the midst of the nervous excitement of children and parents, Arnold remains still. Eyes fixed on the blue sky kissing white clouds. Behind my tree, I sense a sudden breeze. Hold up my fingers, spreading them wide. There are things you know and things you don't. The gust passing my hand is warm, a breath. I've felt it before, many times.

I look back at Arnold and I want to go to him and hug him and tell him: your mummy's here, she's come to you, the air by your ears is her fingers in your hair, the sunshine on your back her cheek against your shoulder blades, the sound in your ears her whisper of love for you.

But I cannot. Because I'm no bridge. No stepping stone. Just a simple connector, A to B, flex into socket. I cannot, must not, be what I am not.

"Come on, Arnold, put the egg on the spoon, put the egg on the spoon!" Larry Silk intones, tearing himself away from his phone. "Don't worry how you do, don't worry about winning, just put the egg on the spoon and enjoy the experience!"

"It's not an experience," Julius counters. "It's a race!"

Larry Silk ignores him. "Come on, son!" he shouts.

Mrs Chambers puts the pink plastic whistle to her mouth and blows. The subsequent noise is deafening. The sound of shrieking, screaming fathers and mothers hurts Julius's ears. He wonders if this is what parents do with children. Fill their offspring with their own hopes and fears, landfills for all the non-biodegradable waste in their own pasts. His own father wanted him to be a history professor. His mother, a surgeon. And both expected grandchildren from their only son, sturdy babies who would rekindle the rosiness of their own flushed breeding years.

I watch Larry Silk, his eyes electric as he bellows encouragement at Arnold, wondering what hole the child fills in him. The small boy is second last, arm held at ninety degrees, delicate brow furrowed in concentration as he takes exaggerated big steps, carefully, one after the other like some underage pantomime villain.

I see several parents notice Arnold and start to laugh, nudging their neighbours and urging them to look. One father swivels round to focus his video camera on him. Julius sees it too and searches out Awa Yasin, who meets his gaze – and there is anger in her eyes, or perhaps just sadness. She starts cheering Arnold more loudly. The small boy is now making some progress with his strange elongated strides, passing three of the fatter girls to join the main pack.

It's at this moment that the race gets interesting. The two gangly boys in the lead are so focused on the eggs in front of them that they fail to see they're both veering off course as if sucked along two lines doomed to meet in a cataclysmic spearhead. Sure enough, despite the shouts and howls from jumping parents and teachers, they collide, knee knocking knee.

A moment of surprise, eyes still boring into the eggs on the spoons held out from their chests, then gravity ensues. And the tall boys tumble, together, heavily onto the grass.

The children who follow behind are unable to stop. They plough into the sprawled boys, tripping and sliding and tumbling, a sudden bouillabaisse of wheeling children. Other contestants manage to pull up short, their eggs flying off into the crashed kids, where they become mashed in a tangle of jerking limbs, pale shell and yellow crumbling yolks.

Mrs Chambers blows her pink whistle until her eyes pop. Several parents run onto the course emitting breathless wails as they seek out their dears.

And then this tiny god appears. Blazing a divine path through the ragged detritus of pitiful humankind. A dark-haired miracle brandishing Uncle Gus's antique spoon before him like a silver sword. Arnold weaves through the staggering children and red-faced parents, reaching the head of the pack. The finishing line within sight. Julius's breath catches in his chest.

"Come on, Arnold, that's it!"

Then one of the tall boys tries to stand, eyes fixed once more on the prize. His spindly legs tremble like those of a newborn deer, his arms outstretch stiffly as if in some low-budget horror film. "Watch out, Arnold!" roars Julius. Audible gasps from the parents as the tall boy loses balance once more and lurches forward, arms windmilling towards the much smaller racer.

But Arnold shifts one way, then the other, arm still held rigidly out in front of him. The outstretched tentacles thrash towards him, but he ducks beneath them without breaking stride. And as the tall boy crashes to the ground a second time, Arnold is free of the pile-up, the grass clear to the finishing line.

He reaches the rope, the two play assistants drop the line, and Arnold crosses it. Parents cheer. Mrs Chambers stops blowing her whistle. Awa Yasin skips across the grass. Larry Silk is red with shouting. Julius continues jumping up and down. But Arnold keeps going. And going.

Adult eyes watch as the boy continues, seeing nothing but the egg on the spoon before him, past the chestnut tree, past the rubbish bin and beyond, towards the ornamental lake. If anything, he is speeding up.

I watch as Awa Yasin dashes after him, skirt and headscarf billowing. She runs well, I think, a natural athlete. Following her, jogging with short skinny strides, is Larry Silk. They reach the small boy, and as Awa touches his shoulder, Arnold stops. The egg tumbles off the spoon. He leans down and picks it up, placing it back in its rightful position.

Still holding the spoon out in front of him, he walks back towards the crowd, flanked by the woman and the man. People start to applaud. Larry Silk grins; Awa smiles. In contrast, Arnold's face betrays no joy, no emotion. He looks ahead – a star athlete for whom this was just another race.

Julius stands alone, watching the boy. Awa gestures towards him. "The magic spoon!" she shouts, reaching down to take Uncle Gus's heirloom from her charge. Immediately, Arnold tucks it behind his back.

"It's mine. I won. You can't have it. Mine."

"Arnold," Awa Yasin begins to admonish him.

"It's mine!"

"It's okay," Julius calls out, approaching, whispering quietly to the Somali woman. "He's had a lot taken from him recently, don't you think?"

Awa watches Julius as he kneels down until his face is level with the boy's. For the first time I notice the bags under Arnold's eyes. Staring up at the bags under Julius's eyes.

"You can keep the spoon, Arnold. Okay?"

"Okay."

Julius reaches out and pats Arnold's head. "Well done."

Arnold smiles. Julius smiles. Hopeless Egg-Walker Becomes Hard-Boiled Superstar Thanks to Big Coach.

"Ladies and Gentlemen! Ladies and Gentlemen!" A whine of feedback, then Mrs Chambers booms out once more. "And now to the most hotly contested prize of the afternoon, always an annual treat, the one you've all been waiting for… the Woodstock Road Primary School Fathers' and Male Carers' Race! Will all fathers and male carers please make their way to the start line now…"

Larry Silk looks at Julius. Julius looks at Larry Silk. They both look at Arnold. I smile. Sometimes I miss the blind idiotic competitiveness of men.

* * *

Two dozen men at the starting line. Some in their twenties. Most are thirty-something. Larry Silk a few decades older than any of them. Julius the tallest in the line-up.

The men who know one another stand in small groups joking, laughing, concealing nervousness and fear of losing behind buffoonery and aping.

Mrs Chambers bustles, lingering with the better-looking fathers, flustered flirtatiousness. "Right, men, enough talking the talk, time to walk the walk, please take your marks…" Her laughter girlish, high-pitched. I feel sorry for her, this highly intelligent woman whose habit is to play dumb and infantile around guys. Maybe it works. Maybe it's where yours truly is going wrong.

Julius and Larry Silk stand side by side, Ogre and Puck. Julius gazes down the one hundred metres of grass. He calculates that his fastest ever time walking the 2.1 miles to work is 26 minutes, a mile every 12 minutes 22 seconds, one kilometre in 7 minutes 42 seconds, one hundred metres in 46.24 seconds. He knows he can run faster than that, but how much faster? Double the speed would put him at 23.12 seconds for the hundred. Which seems fast to Julius, but somewhere in the arrogance that is the male brain, he believes he can do even better than that.

The mighty bosom of Mrs Chambers enters the men's eyeline, the megaphone whines and she shouts: "Daddies, male carers, on your marks, get set…" And the pink whistle blows.

The International Association of Athletic Federations stipulates that any start by an athlete in a race within 0.1 seconds of the start gun is a false start, since this is the time it takes for the sound waves from the gun to travel through the air to the ear, and for the brain to process this information.

It takes Julius a full two seconds to realize the race is under way.

Despite his hesitation, he's not last off the blocks. He propels himself forward like an elephant, lumbering rather than running. His feet pound the grass, arms piston the air, head tossing like a lead weight on broad stiff shoulders. My ancient ponderous beast.

As Julius runs, an article from *The Journal of Modern Statistics* by Dutch maths professor John Einmahl charges through his head. In his paper, Einmahl predicted the maximum fastest times possible for different track-and-field events, given current time records and the limitations of the human body. Dr Einmahl calculated that the best possible time for the hundred-metre is 9.29 seconds.

At this moment, Julius believes he might be getting close to this speed. His lungs are raw. Sweat pours down his pupils. He blinks furiously, but there's no time to wipe, his fists must pump him faster, faster, faster. He looks up. To his surprise, he is last. Barely halfway down the course.

Two runners ahead is Larry Silk, eyes fixed on the finishing line. And beyond him Julius can see the line of open-mouthed, red-faced onlookers at the end of the painted track. And amongst them, the small dark shape of Awa Yasin.

It's her voice he hears above the bellowing crowd and the ringing in his ears. "Come on, Larry!" she shouts. "Come on!"

Julius is surprised to feel shooting jealousy. He pushes harder for the finishing line, and then almost immediately he hears the small Somali woman shout again. "Come on, Julius! Push it! You can do it, Julius!" In front of her, enveloped in her skirts, is Arnold Perkins, turned away from the race, smiling at a dog.

Legs searing, lungs exploding, Julius wants nothing more than to fall down, turn to the sky and gasp air in lungfuls every second of every day for the rest of his life...

"Run, Julius! Run, you big bugger!"

And now I realize this bellow is my own. The cry of a lover or a mother. I shriek again, releasing something. "Go, Julius! Go! Run like the wind!" Heart hammering with excitement. "Run! Run, I said, run!"

He cannot hear me in the din. The crowd erupts as a twenty-something wins the race. Larry Silk comes in sixth out of twenty-four. Julius collapses like a beached whale – not last, but three from it.

Behind the tree I dab the pink handkerchief to my brow, breathless. I know I shouldn't, but I need something to calm me down, and they're burning a hole in my pocket. Just one little pick-me-up. For the road. For the celebration. For the joy of knowing Julius Miles.

* * *

Julius waits until the last evening plane has circled and disappeared west towards Heathrow. It's 8.45 p.m. and he can hold off no longer. He walks next door, rings the bell, and Awa Yasin answers. "It's late, Julius."

"Is it? I suppose it is."

"What do you want?"

Julius stands on the doorstep, hulking, heavy. Thinks he should go. But stays. For once says what's in his heart. "I think I need a beer."

Follows her downstairs. Awa opens the fridge, hands him a can of lager. "He went to sleep wearing his winner's rosette," she says, smiling.

Julius doesn't respond. Takes a large gulp of beer, which goes up his nose and he starts to cough, ale dripping from both nostrils. "God, sorry," he splutters, "sorry…"

Falls into silence, dabbing the beer on his chin with the back of his hand. Awa hands him a paper napkin.

"You know what, Julius?"

Julius looks up. "What?"

"Don't take this personally, but I think I need to point this out to you. Now rather than later." Julius nods, lost as to what's going to come next.

"You appear to the world like a big awkward geek. An introvert. Even a bit of a sociopath."

"I have friends."

"You're hard to talk to. You're intimidating; it's not just your size, it's the feeling people get that you don't understand them."

"I don't."

"Exactly. You might not know this, Julius, but you come across as someone who doesn't care. Who's arrogant and aloof and judgemental. But I had this feeling the first time I met you, and every time I've talked to you since then I haven't lost it. I think inside that big bulk you're different. You do care. You care a lot about people. You care about Arnold."

Julius peers at her. She takes a sip of beer as if it might be holy. "I think maybe you do want to be Arnold's father."

Julius snorts. "No, I don't. And I'm not, I'm not his father."

"You see, to my mind that's looking at it all wrong. It doesn't matter, the fact of whether you are or you're not. I think it just matters that you want to be."

"But I don't want to be." Julius takes his glass from the table and sits down on the sofa.

"Five days and we'll know."

"Five days?"

"That's what the woman on the phone said. Five working days."

Now Awa sits down cross-legged on the rug. Looks up at the big man with tired eyes. "I'm not his mother, Julius. But one of you two monkeys is his father."

Julius nods, drinks beer. Awa Yasin plays with the hem of her headscarf. A bee stuck in the kitchen pats angrily at the window glass. The sun slips finally from the top of the trees, leaving the back gardens in the shadow of dusk.

"I think you'd make a good mother," Julius remarks, quietly.

Awa looks up at him. Brown eyes blinking. "I know you maybe meant it like one, but somehow that doesn't sound like a compliment."

"Oh no. It is. My mother was a good mother. Still is, I suppose. It's rare."

Awa considers this for a moment. "Okay then. I'll take it as such. Thanks."

"You're welcome."

Beyond her silhouette, Julius sees the lights in the tower blocks flickering on between the trees, the final breath of the day leaving the sky.

"My mother's in Dubai. Been there five years. I don't think she's coming back." She doesn't wait for sympathy, continues brightly. "Ever been there? To Dubai?"

"Lord no. Sounds like a hellhole!" says Julius, then realizes. "Sorry, I didn't think, your mother's there."

"And my sister. She lives there."

"Really? Well then, double sorry. I'm sure it's a fascinating place to live. World's tallest building, skiing in the desert, that sort of thing…"

"It's a desert of the heart and soul. My sister loves it. There are tons of Somalis there, all sorts of businesses, airlines, shipping companies, restaurants, it's kind of Mogadishu transplanted."

"Makes sense, I suppose. A business-friendly haven in that part of the world."

Awa shrugs. "Yeah."

"What do you think of it? Do you like Dubai?"

"I've never been. But Mum's found me a husband there." Awa laughs, derisively, walks into the kitchen. "A guy who works at the restaurant my sister and her husband own, they're making him manager when they open the second branch next year…"

Julius nods, tipping his glass to drink, but to his surprise it's empty. Awa takes another can from the fridge, hands it to him. "Daisy's last Grolsch. Enjoy."

Julius holds the cold can. "Would you like some?"

She shakes her head. "Mubarak. That's his name, my husband-to-be."

"Means blessed, or fortunate, doesn't it? I know a couple of Mubaraks who work at the hospital."

She nods. "He's on crutches. Permanently. Had polio when he was a kid. So not entirely blessed. That's why Mum suggested he gets me, you see. Damaged goods. Both of us. Two 'almosts'. We should be very happy together."

"Have you met this blessed Mubarak?"

"No. Just saw his picture."

"Do you like his picture?"

"He's not ugly. And he's smiling, which I think says he's not trying to impress. But he looks... I dunno. Needy?"

"And you're not, are you. It strikes me that you're pretty self-sufficient."

She looks at him, shrugs again, small shoulders. "My dad wants me to fly out there and meet him."

"Are you going to?"

"I don't know. I know I should say no, screw it, I'm little Western Awa from East London. But..."

"But what?"

"Maybe there's something comfortable in doing what's expected of you. In connecting up the dots. Sometimes you don't want to fight, to struggle, you know?" Her voice as tired as her eyes now. "And, probably, most of all, I'm afraid. I've got this thing, this illness..."

"Condition. Officially epilepsy is classified as a condition. What are you afraid of?"

"I don't know. That maybe my parents are right, that I'm not as strong as I think I am. Maybe Mubarak's for me. A new life in Dubai. I'm not scared of things, normally. I'll be fine..."

She tails off. Julius waits. But she does not continue.

"Well..." he says with a cough, "sounds like you've made up your mind. Good luck with it." The clock ticks, Julius counts thirty seconds, but still she does not say anything. So he places the unopened can of beer carefully on the table, heads up the stairs. In the hallway he pauses for a moment, listening for something. But there is only silence.

11

Boys like half-angels in bright white kurtas and taqiyah skull caps hurry giggling through the shopfront door from the hot evening sun. A handwritten sign on cardboard is tacked to the shuttered window: *Jamim Alal Mosque, Tajweed classes 6.45 p.m.–10.45 p.m.*

I watch the last two Bangladeshi boys disappear into the cool shadows, Urdu bickering swallowed by the makeshift mosque, a crumbling shop on the Roman Road that used to be an oil-and-paint seller in the 1920s, then a barber's shop, Carrington's bakers, a video- then DVD-rental place, Songla Bangla Fish Emporium & Cash 'N' Carry. And now a house of God.

The door to the mosque remains ajar an inch; I can see the boys sitting cross-legged on rattan matting, gazing at their instructor as they murmur the verses of the Koran, soft strange words in the cool shadows of the hottest day of the year.

A patter of bare footsteps, a small brown face peers at me, flicker-smiles, and the boy closes the door. I feel warm, inside and out. A sense of sanctity dwelling inside the ramshackle converted shop. The Unseen and the Unknown being worshipped by cheerful children dressed in perfect white.

As far as I can tell, Awa Yasin does not attend any mosque. I am not saying that she's a non-believer, she seems to have a faith in a God of sorts. But rather hers appears to me simply a faith like most faiths in this drifting island – unhitched, listless and grey, assailed on all sides by technology, greed and its roaring nexus – reality TV in which the ugly and the profane are raised up on high and exalted.

It pains me. To feel the lack of God on my streets. Not just because I am one of God's number, His Company if you will, but rather because I think that it reduces us all. In an age in which every human complexity is mapped and delineated and calculated and worshipped, our souls are being ignored, by us and those around us. We are shrinking, until I fear we will become nothing more than commodities ourselves.

I stroll from the shopfront-mosque, trying to remain positive. Awa Yasin's Muslim religion will not, in my professional opinion, be an impediment to a relationship with Julius Miles. Indeed, her spiritual ways, however unaffiliated and unfocused, could fill some of the pores in my big mathematician's heart.

Four doors east of the mosque is the Bow branch of Coral bookmaker's. A boot, heel or hammer has attempted to smash the safety glass in the bottom of the window, a pretty lacework of shatter like a spider's web. The odds for football, racing, Formula One and a couple of popular TV talent competitions shout brazenly from behind the glass, numbers designed to change your life emblazoned a foot high.

More magic. Different spells. I enter and survey the runners and riders for the next race, the 18.50 at Kempton Park. Place £5 on Happy Day at 15/1.

A man glances at me as we watch the race, no one cheering, no excitement in this drab unhappy shop. A bald man, thin moustache, Somali features. I feel I know him, must have encountered him at one time or another on this job, on these streets, because he eyes me more than once. I fear for a moment he could be a fellow love-binder, looks like he could have form, with his shiny egghead and yellowing tobacco-chewing teeth.

But I cannot remember. These gaps in my recollection worry me less now that I have Dr Fitzpatrick's diagnosis. Anterograde amnesia caused by excessive use of benzodiazepines. From what

I've read, when I come off the jells, my memory loss will lessen, my recollections will harden, and I'll return quickly to full cognitive recall after merely a month or two.

Maybe it was the mazzy, but I dreamt of Jay Munnelly last night. We were on a cruise ship, somewhere hot, palm trees in every port, sangria in the morning, you know the style. A thousand passengers or more, most fat and ill-kempt, which is why he stood out, striding down the crimson carpet that descended the double atrium staircase like a hero from Greek myth, if Odysseus wore a white Lacoste tank top and cream Prada shorts.

Imagine my flurry each mealtime through endless wardrobes of dresses, every colour, every cut, every frill and neckline and belt, changing in and out of my beautiful clothes quicker than a Saturday Night drag queen at Madame Jojo's.

Meal after meal I tried to find the courage to speak to him, until the final day of the cruise, somewhere around Grand Cayman, when I approached his table wearing an off-the-shoulder floor-length ball gown, just like the one Halle Berry sported at last year's Oscars.

Jay Munnelly looked up as I handed him his Ray-Ban Aviators.

"I believe these are yours; I think you left them by the First-Class wave pool."

He looked up at me, chuckling. "Thanks, Kev, you always watch out for me, don't you?" His wink and my stomach is Niagara Falls as I lean down to kiss his parted lips... and the cruise liner lurches suddenly, klaxons blaring, passengers screaming, waiters dashing this way and that in a volley of trays and cocktail glasses. Then a thundering wave of seawater crashes through the aft windows and sweeps Jay Munnelly away.

As I drown, surrounded by hundreds of lifeless corpses suspended like pale dead insects in an endless jar of Mediterranean blue-green, I glimpse Munnelly far below me, his hand reaching from the darkness of the sea trench, but I cannot swim to him however hard I struggle. And as the hand slips away into nothingness, I wake, screaming.

And now I am six doors on from Coral's in the Bishmala Internet Café next to an overweight Asian man surfing for nude pictures of Kate and Will and a balding Bulgarian guy on a passionate video conference call with his sullen girlfriend in Sofia.

Who is Jay Munnelly, and why is he taking cruises in my subconscious?

A Google search comes up with little. A reference to a conviction for disarray in a Dagenham nightclub in 2005, six-month suspended sentence. A fuzzy photograph from a mid-Essex newspaper three years ago and the headline: *New Boss of Munnelly Drug Ring?* References to a libel case brought against the same mid-Essex newspaper by the QC Roger Fairbright, one of the best and most expensive lawyers in the country. And notice of the same newspaper's bankruptcy two years later.

Otherwise, nothing. Just other Jay Munnellys at various American high schools and a Jayson Munnelly who runs a print-cartridge refill business in Saskatchewan.

I try a different tack, Google instead the words "Munnelly Family", "Drugs", "Essex" and words rain down from cyberspace. Pages of newspaper articles, many from the national press, fan websites, semi-erudite biographies by former police officers of the main faces of the Munnelly gang.

Here's what I learn: Jay Munnelly has four brothers, twelve male cousins, six uncles. All descendants of Declan Munnelly Senior, emigrated from Mayo in 1913. All appear to have entered various courtrooms in the past ten years, some convicted on long sentences for drug possession with intent to distribute, firearms offences, aggravated assault and, in the case of Damian and Donnie Munnelly, the torture and murder of two "drug dealers" in Hornchurch, Essex, in 2009.

The victims were bound to kitchen chairs and systematically burned with a steam iron... The murders were said to be linked to a police-surveillance operation in Hornchurch in 2007, during

*which the convicted men believed their victims had given infor-
mation to the police...*

You can tell the Munnellys are related. Strong noses, square jaws,
thick foreheads. But none has the beauty of young Jay. Lips always
considering a smile. Grey-green eyes narrowed in thought. Close-
cropped black hair, sheered flint. A body ripped by bar curls and
stomach crunches, as if preparing every day for prison.

I cut and paste text and images into an email to myself. Type
an initial family tree, lines between Munnellys stating familial
links, ages, convictions and reputations. It's second nature to me,
this is what I do in my work – the connections between those I'm
interested in, strengths and weaknesses, their desires and shames.

Jay Munnelly, thirty-seven years old. An impresario in his own
mind, probably watches *Entourage* and imagines himself in Los
Angeles. Strolls, not swaggers. Supremely confident, so shuns the
limelight. Dangerous. Smart. Infective.

I'm about to click off, my hour close to an end, when I come across
an article from the Chelmsford Gazette, May 2010. *Former Essex
police chief employed by PR firm working with Bardots Nightclub.
Drug gang's ties to Essex and Metropolitan Police?* The article
seems light on fact and heavy on supposition. A retired police chief
inspector, Charles Riordan, now works for a Colchester-based PR
firm that helped rebrand a notorious nightclub in Romford that
was closed after a teenager died having popped ecstasy in one of
the bathrooms. The same chief inspector also worked at the time
of his retirement on a special Drugs Action advisory board to
London's Metropolitan Police Serious Crime Directorate.

A few more clicks and I see exactly what I'm fearing. A name on
the same Drugs Action advisory board list: DCI Eddie Knowles.

* * *

Larry Silk lives behind gates, tall black gates topped with gold spear nibs. Behind them is a red-brick housing development on the fringes of Epping Forest. Silk's is one of the "elegant coach houses with terraces overlooking the pristine greens of the North Chingford private-members golf course". The house doesn't have a number, but only a name: *The Fairway*.

I sit in my rental car on the other side of the road. It's 6.30 a.m., but I have a feeling Silk isn't a slumberer. Already six cars have exited the gated "community": four Mercedes, a yellow Porsche Boxster and a white Range Rover with black tinted windows.

I sip my triple-shot macchiato, slowly. Just enough caffeine to sharpen my eyesight, but not enough to give me the jitters like last time. I am, if truth be known, a very nervous driver. And it's my first time behind the wheel since the operation. I am now a "lady driver", my new driving licence firmly in my purse. Now that I'm a she, it remains to be seen whether I can still do a three-point turn.

Larry Silk's black BMW slides through the gates at precisely 7.35 a.m. My palm damp with perspiration, I slip the Vauxhall Corsa into gear and gingerly pull away after him. Let's see if his way is fair.

The roads of London's eastern suburbs are clogged with traffic already. We move slowly west; I'm relieved to see Larry isn't impatient, no rat runs for him racing down narrow side streets, careering through far-flung industrial estates. He keeps to the main roads, always a few miles under the speed limit.

I maintain at least two cars' distance between us, sometimes three, but never four. My digital voice recorder on the passenger seat next to me.

"Most likely heading to the office at Canary Wharf, we're going south-west, probably onto the North Circular for a straight run into the Docklands..."

"He's taking Woodford New Road, so not the North Circular, looks like we're keeping on towards Leyton..."

"Okay, he's stopping, Rahman Newsagents and Convenience Store, number 202, he's stopping, pull in Felicity, come on..."

The BMW parks outside a newsagent's on Grove Green Road. I watch in my rear-view mirror, pulled up outside the squat bulk of St Eleftherios Greek Church. Silk takes his time. Five minutes or so later he exits the shop, a newspaper in hand. From the typeface it looks to me like the *Daily Telegraph*.

"Continuing south, Olympic park on our left, is he going back onto the A12 towards Canary Wharf? No. We're heading off towards Hackney, that's strange…"

Crawling along Homerton Road, pavements on either side swarmed with kids in blue uniforms bustling to the Catholic school, most of them Afro-Caribbean, girls linked arm-in-arm, boys strutting, jabbering, play-fighting, the end of term, beginning of the summer holidays sizzling just over the hill.

"He's stopping again. A.B. Yates & Sons Garage."

A bus honks as I pull in abruptly onto an alleyway with a view of the small garage workshop entrance, a side-street business, nothing fancy, probably a two- or three-man operation. Two cars already up on the hydraulics, boiler-suited youths gazing intently up into their innards. Larry Silk has parked on the street away from the garage, saunters in, fists in pocket. I see him nod at someone in the shadows and disappear.

"Puzzled. Low rent-car repairs, MOTs, bodywork, he's not bringing the BMW here, so what's the story?"

Ten minutes later Larry re-emerges, nothing in hand.

"And we're off again. Continuing into central Hackney – lock your doors, girlfriend…"

Don't get me wrong. I love Hackney, and Hackney loves me. Spent many a crazy night in the shebeens and Rasta dens of Lower and Upper Clapton in my time. Kevin had a soft heart, but a hard desire for garage music and muscles, and Hackney in the early years of the new millennium had plenty of both and more. Still does, for all I know.

Silk's BMW stops five more times. Another convenience store (he exits without a bag). A laundrette. An African tailoring shop,

Beautiful Days, florid robes and dresses and hats in the windows and a poster for Victory Night at the Evangelical Church of the New Light high up on the door glass. A letting agents in Bethnal Green. A nail salon in Dalston, Fine Time Nails, populated by Vietnamese women of a certain age and Eastern European nannies from Stoke Newington.

The BMW pulls into its parking spot at First Financial Services at 11.05 a.m. I've rented the Corsa for the day, so I idle in the parking lot of the Chinese food importers and wait. Silk does not leave his office until 5.45 p.m. He does not stop on the way home. The black gates close on him at 6.52 p.m.

I head home at midnight without seeing him again.

* * *

Julius Miles lies in the bathtub, feet resting up on the nickel-plated taps, toes like washed-up sea creatures gasping on a silver shore. Sudden memory of his father singing to him in the tub while scrubbing his toes with a sponge, a Beatles song, 'Octopus's Garden', the only pop song he recalls his father ever knowing. Wonders now why that one? Ringo Starr's modest contribution to the Fab Four's opus. The odd song out. Odd man out, Julius thinks, hearing his father's singing, even more atonal than Ringo's original.

The recollection sinks Julius deeper into despondency. He should text his parents, at least see how the Southern Hemisphere is treating them, given that they're away for another six weeks. And if the boy by some cavorting miracle turns out to be his? Will he tell his folks? An email?

Hi Mum and Dad, just a bit of news, turns out I'm a father. Of a four-year-old boy. Your grandson's name is Arnold. His mother just died, but it's okay, all's fine. How's Australia, Dad enjoying the wine? See any roos yet? Send me and your new grandson a postcard. Love, J.

170

The bathwater still and cold. Julius sunken, unable to rouse himself. Trying not to listen to noises from next door, taps running, footsteps running, and the mechanical voice, over and over: "Intergalactic Superstars activated!"

He sinks down beneath the cold water once more, staring up through the viscous veil to the dull white ceiling, imagining the sky soaring above into infinity. A whale alone in the depths. Uncomfortably alone.

* * *

Julius walks to work in twenty-five minutes flat. A record. Wonders if he's getting fitter. Fears that the stress of impending paternity/non-paternity is feeding a nervous energy. Breakdown imminent.

Myriad emails bursting through his inbox, one standing out from the usual. Sender: *freakyjon*. Subject: *Are u up for it?* Fearing a virus, Julius does not click it open. Carries on his work, final data on performance versus indicators for the Hyper-Acute Stroke Services trial run by Dr Viktor Naurburger. Then remembers, *freakyjon* is a name he's read before, a name he knows, a name born in the heady crazy days of first-term university life.

John Dunkerman, aka "freakyjon", who became Jon two days into Fresher's week at Gonville & Caius College, Cambridge. The same Jon Dunkerman who came second to Julius in the college trials for the university Chess Cup, then graciously bought the victor a beer to congratulate him, whilst failing to reveal that he'd added two double vodkas to the pint. An omission that led to Julius becoming rapidly intoxicated, falling heavily down their narrow East Wing staircase and dislocating his shoulder – which Julius blames to this day on his first-round Chess Cup exit to a Lithuanian graduate student from St Catharine's College.

The same Jon Dunkerman, who when Julius did his Certificate of Advanced Study in Mathematics, but lost out on a lecturing post to a woman from Calcutta whose father had come second in the

Fields Medal contest of 1976, sent Julius a sixteen-course Indian gourmet takeaway in commiseration.

Julius clicks on the *freakyjon* email. Grimaces.

Dear Julia, How's the heady world of hospital statistics? Short and sweet is I've heard the Call of the Wild once more. This year's BMS is on a nostalgia kick, last day of the symposium there's an I.M.O. for all former Olympians, but first you gotta get through the regionals. I'm there, 23rd July, Old Applied Maths building on Mill Lane, 2 p.m. R u mathman enough? Be there or be a four-sided polygon. Luv – The Freak!

Julius and Jon went to Bulgaria in the summer before their final year at Cambridge, representing the university in the International Mathematics Olympiad. Their team of six came fourth after the Americans, Chinese and the Romanians. Julius got sunburn and Jon managed to sleep with a French mathematician called Sandrine Dellacourt, a young woman so ugly she was beautiful, at least according to Jon.

Julius reads the email one more time, clicks on the British Mathematical Symposium website. At the bottom of the welcome page, after the list of keynote speakers from around the world, and how to get to Warwick University by various forms of transportation, is the flashing icon. "Relive the glory. One day only. International Mathematics Olympiad, all former Olympians welcome!"

As he tries to contain a rising excitement, Julius wonders what Jon is up to these days. The last he heard of Dunkerman a couple of years back was that he was living in Kent and working for some City bank developing algorithms for financial-trading software. Julius wonders whether Jon still thinks of Sandrine. Could it be that the ugliest woman in French history will also be attending the Olympiad? Perhaps Dunkerman's need for his old sidekick JM is more about rekindled dreams of Parisian lingerie than mathematical greatness?

Julius spends the rest of the day with equations and theories spinning through his head like autumn leaves. Imagines winning the trophy. Pictures Arnold Perkins sitting in an orange plastic chair, wide-eyed and applauding, as Julius receives his medal.

The phone rings, interrupting his happy visions. He knows the extension number showing on the little screen. Begum, Rukshana. Hand hovers over the receiver. It could be work-related, he tells himself. Be professional. He clicks on the speakerphone. "Hi, Julius. Know you're on your way out, it being 5.27 p.m. and all. Just a quickie."

"Hm-mm."

"I was... well... What about dinner Friday? Just dinner. Get to know each other. Well, wasn't going to say that, sounds bland, not that it can't be bland... There's a new Sushi place by Aldgate tube. My treat."

Julius is silent. Listens to his own silence, wishing he could prod himself with a sharp stick, wishing he was someone else – his Uncle Gus. Knows he doesn't want to make the small Bangladeshi woman sad or hurt or angry. Definitely not angry.

"Julius, you still there?"

"Er... yup."

"I'm not saying I fancy you, so relax. Just that I want to try a new restaurant and I like talking with you and maybe you haven't got plans Friday, and we could eat and talk, that's what people do from time to time, isn't it? Eat, talk, grow. Look what you've done, I sound like Julia Roberts in some crap movie."

"No you don't."

"Thanks."

"I'm busy Friday. Sorry."

"Oh."

"Sorry." Julius puts down the phone. Cleans the receiver with anti-bacterial wipes. Cleans his keyboards and screens. Puts the wipes in the biohazard bin. Turns off the lights. Double-locks the doors. Gets a bus home rather than walking, feeling suddenly and overwhelmingly exhausted.

* * *

There is an equation that one of my kind came up with once, which some still employ in their early years of mate-matching, just as a guideline until they get their scoring boots on. I'm not sure whether Julius would consider it mathematically sound, but it goes something like this.

Reaction of Person A to a family crisis minus Reaction of Person B to the same crisis, plus a perfect Sunday for Person A minus a perfect Sunday for Person B, plus how Person A would spend a gift of five hundred pounds minus how Person B would spend the same money, plus Person A's reaction to being stuck in a Friday-night traffic jam minus Person B's reaction to the same enforced entrapment in a gridlock situation.

Each element is rated 0 through 5. Therefore if the couple share the same reaction to a family crisis, these two numbers cancel each other out and you mark it as a zero. A small but comfortable difference you mark anywhere between 1 and 3. Total difference is a 5. And so on. The ideal final addition of the four components is 4, just one number's difference between the two parties for each scenario. Such is the gradation of compatibility. A mark of 20 is not good news for two people's future together.

As I watch Rukshana Begum negotiate her way through the crowds at Whitechapel Underground Station, sidestepping, back-stepping, alert and distant to all around her, I wonder whether, despite her dreams to be a writer, she is too much like Julius Miles. Begum would react to a family crisis with a clear-cut plan, and fuss around its edges just like Julius does. Rukshana's perfect Sunday would involve fulfilling a series of small but pleasurable tasks, just like Julius with his *Observer* crossword and cutlery polishing. Rukshana would spend three hundred pounds of the five hundred, save a hundred in tax-free bonds and give a hundred to charity, probably something to do with impoverished children or cripples. And she would fume at being stuck in Friday traffic, but would convince herself that she wasn't showing it. Just like Julius.

If I have a worry it's that Rukshana and Julius would cancel each other out, the statistician and the accountant. Life would be easy for them as a couple, but their hearts would not beat fast.

The sum of Awa Yasin and Julius Miles might end up being a 3.5. I don't think it would be a perfect four, and it could be a 3 or a 2.5. Awa would help Julius polish spoons, then stick one on her nose and tell him a bad joke like: "Two TV aerials meet on a roof, fall in love and get married, the ceremony was crap but the reception was brilliant".

I think she's more like me.

* * *

The door to Domus Decorus is held open by an aquamarine children's stool with pink and yellow flowers painted on the seat. Early morning sun hot on the Roman Road, broken glass, melted chewing gum and gelatinous fried-chicken bones the treasures discarded on the baking pavement by the previous night.

I peer into the shop, seeking out the big shadow of Julius Miles lurking among the furniture and hanging knick-knacks. Surprised that I am able to see the far wall for the first time. Areas of concrete floor free of clutter. And stacked neatly towards the back of the shop, piles of cardboard boxes clearly liberated from some mini-mart or other – Andalusian orange boxes, Pakistani mango boxes, Turkish olive boxes, different logos, different alphabets, global cardboard, one rainforest tree on top of another.

"Hello?" I call, falteringly. "Hello?"

A head appears from between the spider plants now arranged in an exotic tangle on the desk. "Sorry, love. Shop's closed." Trevor Nugent blinks in the helices of dust that dip and soar in the sunlight

175

between us. His white tracksuit piped in green today. Bracelet clink-ing against a faux-Ming vase in his left hand.

"Closed? Didn't say so on the door."

Trevor looks surprised. "Thought I turned the sign." Glances past me, shakes his head. "My mistake. Sorry."

"The place closing down?"

Trevor nods. "Lady that run it died. Tragic. Slipped, hit her head on her own hallway."

"God. That's awful. She was young…"

"Thirty-two. Has a four-year-old kid."

"Shit."

"That's the word for it. Life's a toilet sometimes."

"I met her once, you know, came in for some pottery clogs, Dutch windmills on them."

"Really? Just found some little clogs like that, they're in one of these boxes…"

"She seemed… friendly."

"Daisy? Yeah. Lovely lady. Couldn't do enough for you."

"You miss her."

Trevor peers at me; I've moved carefully into full sunlight, so I'm just a silhouette to him. "Fancy the clogs, love?"

Before I can answer, Trevor starts to rummage in one of the boxes, extracts the porcelain clogs, unwraps them from the crum-pled newspaper. Holds them up for a moment, scrutinizing the tiny painted windmills and the birds flying above. "Nice," he says, emphatically. Glances at the price tag still stuck to the clog bottom.

"How much?" I ask, showing little interest.

Trevor looks at me. "Couple of quid?"

"So cheap?"

Trevor thinks for a moment. "Well, I wouldn't pay more than that for 'em myself." I hand him the pound coins, take the clogs as he continues: "Anyway, everything in the shop's going to a guy in Bexleyheath, house-clearance fella, something like that. Don't think Mr Miles is getting more than five hundred for the lot."

"Five hundred for everything in the shop?"

"That's right."

I sit down in the last remaining armchair.

"I'm really sorry," Trevor said, "but I've gotta finish all this and…"

My hand up, silencing him. Think it through, Felicity, think it through. Jay Munnelly, Larry Silk, Daisy Perkins. Jay Munnelly, Larry Silk, Daisy Perkins. Names, faces, the weak and the strong, the needy and the needed. A dance, round and round.

And then I'm sure. I've figured it. The real reason darling Daisy priced everything in her shop so high. She wasn't looking to sell anything. She didn't need to sell anything. She just needed to pretend she was selling it, all her prohibitively expensive junk, the sales recorded in her neat little account ledgers. Account ledgers signed off for her by Larry Silk of First Financial Services.

Why didn't I see it before? Larry Silk was helping Daisy Perkins launder hundreds of thousands of pounds of drugs money from the Munnelly family through Domus Decorus.

I saw Larry stop at ten small businesses, and that was just one morning of the week. Let's assume he's fabricating for each a turnover similar to Domus Decorus, two to three hundred grand a year, that's up to three million pounds a year in laundered cash. How many more shops does silky Silk visit in the week? How many more single-owner establishments have the Munnellys intimidated to enable Jay's narcotics fortune to leave no trace?

"I'm sorry." Trevor is annoyed with me now. "I'm supposed to bubble-wrap that chair…"

Suddenly I'm afraid. Does Trevor Nugent know about the money-laundering? What is he stewing with silver-haired Larry Silk? Is Julius Miles going to get hurt? Am I going to get hurt?

Without a word I toss the pottery clogs onto the concrete, where they smash in a satisfying crack. I blindside Trevor Nugent's shocked gaze, stride out of the shop and away down the hot street, ignoring the shouts of the outraged teenager, which are quickly swallowed up by the roar of the planes and the buses and the delivery vans and all the expensive cars that sing out the everyday rage that is the sound of London making money.

12

"Eddie, this is Kevin... I mean, Felicity... Charlie's son... daughter... Look, just call me back, I've something for you, something big..."

Five messages left for DCI Knowles. Still no response. His silence as loud as a confession.

I'm not scared any more. At least not for myself – even when they punched and kicked and spat at school it was not fear I felt deep in my core, but sorrow. Forgive them, Lord, for they know not what they do. Long ago learnt to detach body from soul, mind from the mayhem being inflicted upon the flesh. Flesh heals. Spit wipes off, remember that.

The only fear I have is that this detachment I find I'm capable of these days has hardened. That even with my new body I cannot or will not feel, even if someone dares to reach out and touch me. I'm afraid I've become stone like Daisy, dead on the floor.

* * *

Julius goes to Cambridge. I scan the other passengers entering the train carriage with him for signs of Munnelly snouts, but there are no men with shaven skulls, wide brows and long coats in the summer heat. I sit at the end of the adjoining car; Julius is easy enough to watch, his large head high above the seat back, bowed over his mathematical textbook, flicking through everything he once knew in preparation for the competition this afternoon.

Cambridge station is a sweaty chaos of tourists and summer-school students, thousands of bicycles of all sizes and colours crammed in terrifying piles against fences, lamp-posts, walls and cycle racks. I walk hurriedly away from the station clock, caught out by Julius's unanticipated desire to head into the city centre on foot rather than by taxi or bus.

This is not London, especially not the East End of London. There are pretty little shops and no dog shit, and although the faces are from nearly every ethnicity on the planet, most of them wear glasses and carry satchels no doubt brimming with iPads and Ancient Greek dictionaries.

Julius walks slower here. Shoulders slumped, not in defeat but relaxation I think. As if he's come home to a tribe. People like him are everywhere. Men who buy the same shoes year after year, from catalogues.

I follow Julius through some college or other, a place of honey-stone walls, shaded cloisters, immaculate green lawns clearly hand-snipped by highly intelligent dwarves, a fountain bubbling gently to itself surrounded by a riot of pink and white roses. Even the bees seem clever here, buzzing perfect geometric patterns in the lazy lunchtime air.

We end up at the river, a pub spilling across the road onto a bridge across a low weir and grassy riverbanks thronged with people drinking and laughing and playing badminton, a sport people do not play in London, at least not in public.

Julius spies Jon Dunkerman sitting on the bridge wall. Dunkerman is small, slight and bald at thirty-eight, remnants of hair shaved close to his head by the ears. He wears long khaki shorts, short-sleeved patterned shirt, shiny polished hiking boots and small rectangular glasses with sunglasses clipped onto them.

"The man-mountain!" Dunkerman's hug appears genuine, straining up to reach Julius's neck. Julius smiles. The two old friends hug for a moment, perspiration and aftershave.

"How are you, Big J?" Dunkerman beams when he finally lets go, feet relaxing back to earth from tiptoes.

Julius shrugs. "Fine."

"Good summer?"

"Okay, you know. You?"

The smaller man attempts a smile in return. Then sits down abruptly, turns away. Lets out a sigh. Julius's hand goes to his chin, his mouth, as Jon starts to cry.

Julius sits down next to his friend, cheeks flushing red as he imagines everyone on the grassy banks turning to gawp at them. Reaches out a large uncertain hand, then places it on Dunkerman's shoulder.

"What's up, Jon?" Julius asks quietly. "What's happened?"

The smaller man wipes his eyes, takes out a blue checked handkerchief, blows noisily. "My dad died. Two weeks ago."

Julius blinks. He has never heard Jon talk about his father other than to disparage the man's dress sense and knowledge of wine.

"I'm sorry, Jon. Really sorry..."

"Being back here..."

"He went to Corpus Christi, didn't he?"

"About the only thing I ever did right in his eyes was getting into Cambridge..."

Dunkerman tries to smile, to rein in the sobs, but he is forced to turn away once more, fists against blinking eyes in a bid to stem the flow. Julius stares at his hand on the crying man's shoulder, unsure if the weight of it is reassuring or oppressive to his friend.

Finally Jon lets out a long breath, gathering himself. He turns to Julius and his smile is stronger now. "Sorry, Big J. It's just... I never thought I'd miss the bastard this much."

* * *

The contest to select a South-East team for the Olympiad at the British Mathematical Symposium takes place in an airless, whitewashed room in a brick building overlooking a car park just up Mill Lane from the river.

Forty or more people in their thirties stand awkwardly by desks, most of them men, a handful of women, some clutching water bottles, others pencil cases, colourful plastic rulers. One or two brandish mascots, small cuddly toys or plastic Star Wars figurines. Julius side-eyes his fellow contestants, faces who seem to recognize him, so he nods back at them, trying not to think what they see when they look at him, because looking at them makes him sad. Dunkerman seems to read his mind.

"How sick are we?" he whispers loudly. "Almost forty and skittish as freshers. Remember Bruce's song 'Glory Days'?"

Julius doesn't, but he does recall Dunkerman's passion for Bruce Springsteen and his songs of blue-collar America, a place far removed from Dunkerman's own North London Jewish private-school upbringing.

"Basically the song is about this guy who keeps bumping into all these people from his school days – the cute girl, the baseball star – all these guys whose lives peaked at high school. And with all of them he discovers that everything after they left high school was just one big disappointment – the prom queen is divorced with two kids, the baseball star's an alcoholic, that sort of thing…"

"And we're like that? Thanks, Jon. Makes me feel much better…"

Julius sits down at the desk he's been eyeing since entering the room, one back from the front, right-hand side away from the windows overlooking the car park and the chattering tourists ebbing and flowing to the river along the lane beyond. Dunkerman grabs the chair at the desk behind Julius as a man of Chinese origin with a ponytail goes for the same place, the two men locked for a moment like gunslingers before Ponytail exhales fiercely, turns with a swish of mane and relocates to a desk on the far side of the room.

The contest lasts three and a half hours. Four questions are set. Julius stares at the single white sheet of paper, the text and the numbers, and feels the gentle, ever so familiar buzz, the pure simple joy of being in a mathematics exam. The breathless beginning when he stares at the numbers and symbols and nothing makes sense. Followed by the slow, delightful unravelling, as intimate electric connections are made, a holy and thrilling stripping-away, until the naked essence of the problem is laid bare and the solution begins to emerge as if from somewhere beyond his own cerebral cortex.

Each problem, each equation, its own small but fierce love affair. Sex with numbers.

1. *Prove that the set of integers of the form $2^k - 3 (k = 2, 3...)$ contains an infinite subset in which every two members are relatively prime.*

2. (a) *Find all positive integers n for which $2^n - 1$ is divisible by 7.*
   (b) *Prove that there is no positive integer n for which $2^n + 1$ is divisible by 7.*

3. *Prove that for every natural number m, there exists a finite set S of points in a plane with the following property: for every point A in S, there are exactly m points in S which are at unit distance from A.*

4. *Determine all pairs (x, y) of integers such that:*
   $1 + 2^x + 2^{2x+1} = y^2$.

Julius sucks his pencil. Kneads his cheeks. Never looks up, not once. Dunkerman eyes the massive back of his friend in front of him, each time he glances at Julius the sweat patch between the giant's shoulder blades has grown, as if his brain power is seeping out into the very fibres of his shirt.

An hour left and Julius is onto the last question. The words and numbers like a delicious smell, behind them he knows there lies a thrilling taste and, like the explorer he is, he will find it – he will cut through, go beyond, risk it all.

Unlike others, Julius does not scribble on his page. Editing takes place in his head. Pen poised but not descending until the way is clear. As he writes his explanation of the answer with great precision, he senses as if for the first time a presence behind him. Julius turns, squints back. A loud scrape of chair and Jon Dunkerman shifts, head return-jerking to his own sheet of paper, pen scribbling furiously as if he's been writing all this time.

Julius remains half-turned for a moment. Has Dunkerman been cheating? Copying Julius's answer?

The adjudicator bangs down his gavel, 5.30 p.m., contest over. Julius returns to his sheet of paper. Checks his name at the top. Stands and hands it to the academic at the front. Senses Dunkerman approaching behind him, but doesn't stop. Walks out of the room into the bright sunlight and waits for his friend in the car park next to the cycle racks.

* * *

At dinner in the pizza restaurant in which they used to celebrate college-chess victories, Julius and Jon share a Quattro Stagioni in silence. Dunkerman finishes his glass of wine, pours himself another.

"Wasn't so bad, huh?" he offers finally. Julius shrugs, but says nothing. "Felt like the old days. Did you hear the über-geek next to me, Captain Nerd-Ass, talking to himself? Felt like punching his ear!"

Julius sips wine. Chews pizza crust.

"What's got into you, Julius? All whacked-out, mental cogs seized up?"

"Just tired. Work's been hectic."

"Don't know how you do it. Public sector. You're so... powerless."

"I like the hospital. They leave me alone. How's things in the heady world of quantitative trading?"

"Dandy. Didn't you know? Us Quants are the new masters of the universe. I'm writing algos that deal billions of dollars a week."

"Is that good?"

"For me it is. For the market, who knows. Couple of months ago the Dow tanked 700 points in ten minutes, because a bunch of HFT and Quant programs decided to chase each other down the hill, ended up in a self-reinforcing feedback loop. Lucky someone noticed and the major houses overrode the computers, or it'd have been the biggest one-day loss in market history."

"Wow. Scary. What's a self-reinforcing feedback loop?"

Dunkerman smiles. "Hey, remember the first time we ate here?" Julius shakes his head, sincerely. "The first time you saw Gwen, that table over there, with her poetry bitches?"

Julius stares blankly over at a table near the window, where a man tries to persuade two young children to eat salad. Had not remembered anything about back then. Least of all Gwendolyn.

"You saw her and you wanted her, and I found out she was part of the Ballooning Society…" Dunkerman sniggers happily, and Julius wants to stop him, doesn't want to go backwards, but he hasn't the strength and his friend continues, at pace: "So there we are, back row of the BS slideshow, Tuesday evening Lent Term, she's three rows in front, doesn't even watch the bloody slides, remember, some trip the Peterhouse boys made in a Cameron Voyager III in Morocco…"

Julius nods, even though all he is seeing is Gwendolyn Lank, the imperceptible incline of pencil-thin eyebrows, equally slender deepening of the small cleft in her chin. Her hands, like orchids.

"Then the slide got stuck, remember, and I told you – I can still hear my exact words – 'Statistically,' I said, 'statistically, Julius Miles, this configuration of circumstances – your dream girl's presence at a balloon-society slide show, your state of cheap-plonk intoxication that's left you with just the right amount of testosterone in your bloodstream, the slide stuck and Sebastian Mont-something-or-other fiddling with the projector – this will never happen again. You have to act!' That's what I told you. 'Now! Statistically speaking, this is a once in-a-lifetime opportunity!'"

Dunkerman's face, shiny and bright under the low-slung lights. He takes another gulp of wine. "And you did it. Went for it guns blazing. Asked her what she was knitting, and she said leg-warmers for low-income babies in the former Soviet Republics – and you complimented her on her vintage tweed suit, and she told you it was inspired by a photo of Germaine Dulac from 1919... She's getting married, you know."

"Yeah. I heard."

"Some tit at Oxford. Welsh. Won some national Taff singing competition when he was a boy."

"How do you know?" Julius asks, curious. Then realizes. "You Googled him?"

Dunkerman shrugs, grin still fixed to his face. Downs his glass, fills it once more. "He's a prick."

"Because he's marrying Gwen?" Jon doesn't answer. Julius looks at his friend, notices for the first time a clenched fist on the table. "Jon..."

Dunkerman looks up, sharply. "What?"

"Nothing."

"What?"

"Nothing. What about dessert..."

"No. Don't go there, Big J. I don't fancy her. Never did. Too bony – bet she doesn't even get periods, can't even get pregnant."

Julius puts down his fork. Removes hand from chin.

"Jon, are you okay?"

"Piss off, Julius."

"No. Really. You seem... I dunno..."

"I seem what? What do I seem, Julius?"

Julius shrugs. "Dunno... Unhappy?"

"Unhappy? Who's happy? Any of this lot, Saturday night in a poxy, crappy pizza place in podunk Cambridge? No one's happy, Julius. It's just a word."

Julius thinks about stretching out his hand towards his friend's wrist, to stop Jon pouring himself another glass of wine, but Dunkerman carries on drinking and talking…

"Remember Mungle, Julius? Fat sweaty Malcolm?"

Julius nods, sadly, feeling the slide backwards into the distant past as if towards a deep cold chasm. Malcolm Mungle was an American lecturer who used to insist on his students feeling "the emotional quotient to mathematics". Dunkerman loathed Mungle, thought his classes were inane, and frequently told him so (Mungle would grin through white Connecticut teeth and tell Jon that he felt his pain). Julius sympathized with his friend, he too disdained any emotional connotations to numbers, considering them a refuge from the confusing, tumultuous, usually hurtful world of human interaction. Julius had no desire to feel anything for numbers, he loved them precisely because they could be clear and absolute, hard and resilient. Numbers didn't let you down. Not that they gave up their secrets straight away: they challenged you to understand them, but if you put in the effort and were intelligent enough to consider all options, they revealed themselves clearly, and wholly. And once they were revealed, they did not change or backtrack. Unlike people. Unlike feelings.

"The emotional possibilities of the numerical world! Hah! Pile of steaming crap!" Dunkerman sits back in his chair, swilling his wineglass like a retired admiral. "Happy Numbers! Remember that? Happy bloody numbers?!"

Julius nods. Malcolm Mungle was obsessed with so-called "happy numbers", constantly seeking connections between them and the events in both his personal life and the life of the wider planet.

"What was it again?" mutters Dunkerman, "all positive numbers are either happy or unhappy?"

Julius nods, reciting: "A 'happy number' is when – if you square its digits and add them together, and then take the result of that addition and square *its* digits and add them together, and keep doing the same thing over and over again – you end up at the number one, a totality from which you can go no further."

Dunkerman peers at Julius. "Wow. How do you remember that shit?"

"Dunno. Sticks in some part of my brain, I suppose. I don't remember people and what they say, like you do..."

"So how does it work again? To end up at one?"

"Okay, let's take a number – say... Thirty-two..."

"Three squared plus two squared is nine plus four which is thirteen..."

"One squared plus three squared, one plus nine is ten..."

"One squared plus zero squared is one plus zero which is one."

"Thirty-two is a happy number because the sequence ends. It ends at one."

"*Closure...*" sneers Dunkerman, in a poor imitation of Malcolm Mungle's East Coast American accent.

"In contrast, twenty-five is an unhappy number," continues Julius, "it doesn't end up at one but four, before the cycle begins again in an endless loop..."

Julius takes a small gulp of wine. Then realizes Dunkerman is staring at him, a frown carved deep into his shining forehead.

"Are you an unhappy number, Julius?"

"Sorry?"

"Do you feel like you always end up in the same place, your own number four, before looping off again in the same cycle, the same pattern, returning once more, looping off again, never stopping, never happy?..."

Julius stares at Jon Dunkerman. "No," he says bluntly. "Maybe you're talking about yourself, Jon."

The smaller man laughs sarcastically but says nothing, gulping down his wine.

A short while later Dunkerman excuses himself to go to the toilet. Fifteen minutes later, he has not reappeared. Julius goes looking for him and finds the toilet empty.

Julius walks back to the table and realizes Dunkerman's backpack is gone. He sits alone for another three quarters of an hour, but Jon doesn't return. Julius pays the bill on his card.

"How was your meal, sir?" asks the waiter, without much enthusiasm.

"Great," replies Julius, loudly. "Thank you."

* * *

It's late, so the trains are running only every half an hour. Midway along the London-bound platform is Julius Miles. In the pools of light and shadow surrounded by the shabby brick of the train station he looks like a character from a painting in which the meagre splash of neon only serves to accentuate the frightening edges of the darkness beyond his shape.

I stand at the other end of the platform. I doubt Julius finds me menacing, even though we are the only two people waiting for the 22.10 service to London Liverpool Street.

I watch him from a distance, big head bowed in the pool of platform light, face creasing and uncreasing, eyebrows rising, falling, tongue dabbing his upper lip. He looks stressed, talking to himself; he must be worrying about his drunk friend who has vanished into the chattering Cambridge night.

As he begins to rock gently on his heels, I look up; a train is approaching at speed. It's not Julius's train, its coming fast, an intercity service, the Tannoy cackles, preparing to command us to stand back, but instead Julius takes a step forward. And I start to run.

"Wait!" I cry, knowing that this moment has come sooner than I would have liked. "Wait!"

Julius looks up, the train hurricanes past, almost blowing me down. I stagger, stumbling at the big man's feet, but he pretends not to notice me, gazing beyond at the rapidly shrinking tail lights of the disappearing express. Now I'm this far in, of course I have no option but to carry on regardless...

"Sorry... I thought... I thought... you hadn't heard the announcement, you were a bit close to the edge..."

"I heard it. Thank you..." Julius steps away from me, walking farther up the platform. I try to imagine what he's thinking, that I'm homeless, wanting money or mad.

This is rare. Usually my mark is never aware of my influence over their situation. A couple gets together, sleeps together, sometimes marries and procreates without ever knowing that their union was finessed by a minor god.

Once or twice, however, I'm obliged to step into the light. It doesn't scare me. I know what I'm doing. They will never know the real truth.

Julius has returned to muttering gently to himself as he paces up and down a few feet from me.

This close up I notice a grace to his movements that I had not credited Julius with before. He moves with a strange daintiness, large hands painting small watercolours by his side as he unravels some equation in his head.

I approach him once more, speaking brightly. "Do you believe in tarot cards, by any chance?" I barely miss a beat. "The Fool, the Magician, the Hermit, Death and all that?"

"I'm sorry, what?"

"Tarot."

He stares down at me, but I carry on at speed, careful not to sound needy. "The thing is, I'm developing a new act, I'm a performer in this troupe in London, it's not a circus, there are no animals, just twelve of us human beings, performers all, we each have different talents and we're putting together a new show to tour the Far East in the autumn – and well, I was wondering if you would let me practise, just really quickly, on you?"

Julius's wariness billows across his wide face. He glances up at the ticking clock and the countdown to the next train, the seconds clicking past like numbers in one of his sums. I need to close the deal swiftly. "You shuffle the cards, I choose three and I tell you what they mean. It'll take just two minutes tops, you won't miss your train, I promise."

Still hesitates, then nods once and it sends a weird thrill up and down my gut, and for a moment I am a giddy little girl. Hurriedly I reach into my coat pocket and take out a pack of large tarot cards. "We'll just do a simple three-card spread. If you could shuffle the cards..."

Julius takes the cards from me. Shuffles clumsily. Far beyond, from the deepest core of night, a pinpoint of light appears, a magical star in the broad darkness, the train on its way. I take the cards back from Julius and pick out three, face down. I point to the backs of each of the three cards in turn. "This one represents your past. This, your present. And this one your future. Which would you like to see first?"

Julius shrugs, noticing the approaching train, probably willing it to speed up and save him from this madwoman. I answer for him. "Let's go with the present. Less to fear." I ease the middle card from my fingers and turn it over. A man holding a sword and a pair of scales. "Justice," I say. "It represents your conscience. There's something you know you should be doing but you're not doing it. Fate is in play, and the wheels are turning whether you want them to or not."

He nods, looking beyond, watching the light grow stronger, the first soft rattles of wheels on tracks reaching our ears. I pull out the card on the left. "Let's do your past now." I turn over the card. "Ah. The Magician."

The Tannoy scratches out a bored cough, then announces the arriving train.

I hold up the card, the Magician with his long white beard. "You see the Magician has the sword, the staff, the Holy Communion cup and the star, all tools to help him attain wisdom, but they are separate from him, as you can see, therefore he doesn't know how to use them yet." I throw a stern look at Julius. "This means your past is full of untapped potential. You have always had wisdom, but have never known quite how to employ it to its most devastating effect."

The train is almost upon us. Rattling on, I flip over the last card, holding it up so that the brightest of the bright station lights gleams across its plasticized surface, making it shine like treasure.

"Ah-ha ha!" I exclaim, perhaps a little too dramatically. Still Julius is only half-glancing at the card, and this is the one I want him to see most of all. "The Empress!"

A rush of wind and din of metal, and the train pulls into the station.

"The Empress is the Creator. The Giver of Good Things. She is your future. This lovely lady is out there, perhaps you know her already, perhaps you two are still to meet, but the Empress represents love, sex, fertility, happiness, everything. She is good news, young man! The best!"

Only now does Julius focus fully on the card as the train crunches to a stop three feet away from where we are standing. Doors open, passengers get off the train

"Look at her, Julius. At the Empress. She is your future."

I shift the card into Julius's fingers, letting go.

"You go on," I say as amicably as I can. "I'm waiting for the next train; this one doesn't stop at Tottenham Hale. But it's been a pleasure, sir. Thank you for your time."

Julius holds the card limply between his thumb and forefinger, eyes lingering on the Empress. Then he looks up at me. "How do you know my name?"

The breath stops in me. We look at one another for a moment, and I fear that the whole platform can hear the pounding of my heart. Then I turn and stride fast away down the platform towards the safe black night.

"Hey!" Julius shouts after me, but the doors are beeping now and he is forced to turn and dart onto the train. As the carriages pull away, I turn to see him by the doors, looking down at the card in his hand, at the Empress, painted and printed by my friend Lutfur Abbas of BanglaBright Graphic Design in Stepney Green. It doesn't surprise me that Julius is drawn to the image Luftur has crafted, because this Empress is a rare beauty, with dark locks and a heaving bosom. Any man would give her a second glance, even a balding thirty-nine-year-old statistician with seemingly low sex drive.

Yet Julius Miles has more reasons than most other thirty-nine-year-old statisticians to stare at her, since this Empress looks just like a young lady he knows well. A young lady by the name of Awa Yasin.

I walk away from the platform, jauntily down the steps that smell slightly of piss and half-trodden Big Macs, heading to the station café, where I will purchase a bottle of mineral water and pop a mazzy for the 22.21 train back into London. I can still see Julius, his flat yet handsome face staring at the card in his hand – and as the train turns the bend I swear he looks up and gazes back straight into my eyes.

Then the train is gone. But Julius's face remains in front of me like the imprint of sun glare on my retina, staring back at me. Suddenly something strange, searing, flashes through me, and I am forced to clutch my stomach. I breathe in great gulps of air, trying to understand why I feel so sick.

And then I realize, horrified. This is not allowed. This is wrong. Sweat on my hands, and I want to vomit. Oh God. This will not do. This will not do at all.

13

"Hi, Rukshana, this is Julius. I just wanted to… er… what did I want to say? I guess I wanted to say sorry, for the other day, you know, on the phone. I was stressed – possibly – you know, mid-term reporting and all… Anyway, yes… just wanted to say I'm not a huge fan of sushi, but I would be up for eating with you, so don't know if you'd consider coming east and we could go somewhere round here?"

* * *

Julius unlocks the door to Domus Decorus. Surprised that the key turns smoothly in the lock. Steps carefully into an empty room that echoes to his shoes.

Cleared of clutter, the shop feels cold and naked. Ancient rippled floor swept clean. Julius looking down at the faded brick, the dents and rivulets in the ochre a natural history of shuffling feet and fallen objects across a hundred and fifty years. Raises his head, puzzled, to the wooden beam that traverses the ceiling. Never even knew it was there, beneath the unruly plants and grumpy Toby mugs.

Even the desk is gone, the one sacred remnant from Gus's era. Julius had been conflicted about letting it go with the rest of the stuff, but Trevor was adamant: "Drawer's gonna keep falling out, Mr Miles, leg's rickety as hell. If that thing were a dog, you'd put it out of its misery."

Julius traverses the room, one wall to the other. Back again. At the rear of the shop, the shelves are empty and dusted, the cramped toilet scrubbed and scented with some artificial-smelling toilet cleanser.

He opens the back door to the small concrete courtyard. Not even Gus's tattered deckchair remains propped against the fence post. Three brick walls, weeds poking hopefully through the cracks in the concrete level. The premises returned to some kind of natural state. Before all these lives messed it up.

Julius stands in the middle of the small yard. Reaches out his arms like a child playing airplanes, fingertips straining until they touch the warm London brick of both walls. Feels like an interloper, stumbled across the remains of some far-gone civilization that he does not understand. The deserted yard, the shop so full of absence. Daisy's lascivious chuckle. His uncle's giggle. Faced with the bare Victorian brick, it seems to Julius that he cannot even summon up his uncle's voice any more, let alone his face.

As he walks back through the vacuum of limp shadows, he thinks that in this moment he has understood something about Daisy Perkins and her mania for amassing flotsam. He believes now that the jumble of objects that so infuriated and offended him, to the point that he fantasized about firebombing his own property, served a deeper purpose. That somehow all the junk contained a link back to Gus, the objects cheaper and tackier facsimiles of the more beautiful and well-crafted possessions his uncle Augustus Miles had collected over the years.

Was each item in some way a tribute or memento, in Daisy's mind at least, to Gus? Was her inability to stop buying rubbish in fact a highly dysfunctional, but wholly emotional response to her own grief?

At this moment Julius wishes he'd never agreed to Trevor's suggestion to empty out the shop. Gus's nephew lowers his head, and the tears well in his lids.

"Nice and spacious, eh? Came out a treat…"

Julius turns his head away from the voice, rubbing at his eyes with the bent face of each wrist. If Trevor Nugent notices the big man's tears, his tone does not betray it. "Always thought the place was a bit small, you know, compared to other shops round here. But it's got space, it's roomy..."

Julius thanks Trevor for his hard work cleaning out the shop. Hands him his fee in an envelope. Trevor counts the twenty-pound notes with practised dab, forefinger to thumb, forefinger to thumb.

"Mind me asking what your plan is for the place? Sell it, or..."

"I'm not sure, Trevor..."

"Not a great time to offload commercial property, is it? Way things are shaping. But rents are still holding steady in these parts, or so the Bangla boys say, and they should know, right? I mean they've got the whole bloody place sewn up..."

"I don't know what I'm going to do with the shop yet."

Trevor nods. Scratches thigh, hush of fingernail on viscose. "Look, Mr Miles... if you do, you know, if you are looking for another fella to rent the space..." – his voice higher, nervous, maybe – "I'd be interested. You know. In taking it on..."

"You?"

The young man nods.

"The rent's not cheap, Trevor..."

"Grand a month. I know. Wouldn't be a problem for me..."

"Really? What sort of business are you thinking of getting into? If you don't mind me asking?"

Trevor stops scratching his leg. Smooths down his shaven head. Adjusts the bracelet around his slender wrist.

"Gold."

"Gold?"

"Yeah, you know, cash for gold, granny's charm bracelet, grandpa's service watch, that sort of thing. Everyone's selling, everyone's buying these days."

Julius nods, Trevor continues, a speech he's practised. "Uncertain times, safe-haven assets. It's cast-iron. Been saving up, Dad's got some cash, I got good contacts, brother-in-law owns a hock shop in Bermondsey…"

"Who'll keep the books? Read through the contracts?"

Trevor twists on one foot. "I know people, don't worry yourself, Mr Miles," he states quietly. "It'll be kosher, you can get your lip to take a look at the business plan if you like…"

"Lip?"

"Lawyer, solicitor, whatever you call it. You'll think about it, Mr Miles? Will you?"

Julius looks at the thin young man in the white tracksuit. Daisy's sickly cherub. And nods, without much conviction.

From the safety of the phone box outside Coral bookmakers, I watch the two men exit the shop. Trevor looking back once as the big man bends to lock the door.

I think that Julius Miles is unlikely to rent the shop to Trevor Nugent, but I cannot sit back and take the chance. Maybe I should send him an email, anonymously of course, outlining what I've discovered about Jay Munnelly and Larry Silk – how Silk is lining up the gangly infantile Trevor Nugent to take on the lease of Domus Decorus in order to set up another cash business to filter the drugs' cash through. You've got to hand it to Larry, gold is perfect, soaring prices mean the "business" could wash half a million a year without a tax man so much as blinking.

I've been thorough. It's all written down. Every fact I've uncovered, every deduction I've made. Careful notes inscribed on three different black pads. I have a system now, so that I can remember it all: Post-It notes on doors, mirrors, cupboards, a flow chart of my life leading me each time back to the truth. The truth about Daisy Perkins, about Larry Silk, about Jay Munnelly. And about which cupboard the Sweet 'N' Low sachets are in for my morning tea. My daily pattern. My structure. My map of myself.

Then again, telling Julius could be the worst idea. I know him, he'd go straight to the police and show them the email. Not suspecting for an instant that anyone in the Met might be dancing both sides of the line. He's a big clunking innocent, my mark. I cannot drag Julius into this. My job with him is clearly defined. And almost over.

I wait in the fug of the phone box until a minute or so after Julius has slouched away around the corner onto Woodstock Road. Push out onto the simmering street, keep to the shadows cast by the shopfronts. In the window of Coral's I spy the bald Somali man – pencil moustache, worried face staring at a betting slip. Then he looks up, right at me.

For a moment I think he's an Eye, a seer, a human who can sense when those with immortal tendencies pass by. I'm about to turn on my thick wedge heels when a synapse flashes, something double-clicks in my head.

The nose, the chin, the cheeks. The equation the father laid out, that found its solution in the daughter, the Empress of Bow, Awa Yasin.

In my line of work, you think on your feet. I enter the bookies, sit next to Mohammad Ali Yasin, appear confused, and ask him for a tip for the 15.45 at Sandown. He blinks, massive white eyes open and shut, he swallows his reply – he's not much of a gambler, he popped in on the way back from the library, it's just a hunch, but personally he would go for High & Mighty. I ask him if he wouldn't mind placing my bet alongside his; he blushes as he takes my fiver. I stare at his back as he stands at the counter, long enough for him to feel it.

We watch the race together. I feign excitement, my hand flicks across his for a brief moment. He flinches, but does not retract. High & Mighty comes in fourth, but I kiss his cheek anyway, give him a hot whisper.

"You're quiet, Mo, but you're strong. I'll be honest, I love your back, your shoulders, the tendons in your beautiful hands like something carved long ago. If I wasn't married and in love with my husband, I'd take you to a Holiday Inn bedroom in a heartbeat…"

His eyes are still blinking, thin brown owl, as the number 8 bus whisks me out of his dreams and on towards Bethnal Green Underground Station and the future of Julius Miles...

* * *

Julius puts on his uncle's Yves Saint Laurent suit, even though the trouser legs barely cover his shins and he has to pull his shirt cuffs out from the jacket arms and he cannot button either jacket or waist, resorting instead to a large safety pin hidden inside the trouser lining.

Julius loved his uncle Gus in the YSL suit, dapper as any French film star, suntan and chuckle. In front of the mirror he knots Gus's peach-flower Armani tie. Takes it off again. Telling himself he is going to dine with Rukshana Begum because he will find out from the woman in charge of personnel procurement, through guile and charm, whether his job is safe for the following year. Something he has been worrying about increasingly since being told he might be the father of the small boy who lives next door.

He splashes out on a taxi the two miles from Woodstock Road to the fading baroque façade of Il Gerbino, the Italian restaurant off Commercial Road that was favoured by the Krays in the Sixties and was Uncle Gus's second home for much of his life.

I watch him from the second floor of a crumbling multi-storey car park opposite the restaurant. Pigeons squeaking in the concrete rafters. Adjust my binoculars as he pushes through Gerbino's large brass doors.

Julius walks into the small dining room with the high-vaulted ceiling as if walking into a photo album from his childhood. The table by the side-street window where his uncle fed him breadsticks if he clapped his hands like a seal. The bar of dusty bottles – green, brown and orange jewels in the fluorescent spotlights, where he'd watch the ageing bartender mix a Bora Bora under Gus's strict instructions.

Young Julius sipping his "cocktail" every time Gus took a gulp of Martini. Listening to his uncle's tales of the South Seas, convinced that every one was true.

The two black-suited waiters look up as Julius enters, but show no sign of recognition. Why should they, thinks Julius, it's been seven years since he last visited Gerbino's, with his father and mother for a morose and intermittently tearful dinner when they met up after Gus's funeral. He glances at his watch – twelve minutes past, he thought he was being fashionably, daringly late, but the small Bangladeshi woman is nowhere to be seen, even though he's sure he said they should meet at seven. In fact the restaurant is empty except for an old couple sitting in silence over espresso cups in the shadows near the small stage used on Sunday afternoons for jazz and jokes from the age of cigarettes and pinstripe ties.

The maître d' makes a show of looking up Julius's reservation, even though Julius can see on the page that there are only three bookings for this slow Friday in late July, the weekend school holidays begin. With the ambling grace of a man who has spent a lifetime weaving between restaurant furniture, the maître d' shows him to the table by the side-street window.

Julius sits down, flicks through the menu, relieved to see that most of the dishes are familiar, allowing him to recommend to Miss Begum the *strozzapreti al ragù di manzo con piselli* or the *pancia di maiale al forno con purea di mele*. For Gus's delights are now Julius's, as perhaps his uncle intended.

He does not see me enter, the maître d' whisking me quickly to the table at the back hidden behind the end of the pewter counter, tucking the ten-pound note into his breast pocket as he returns to his haunt by the doors. I adjust my seat so that I can see the back of Julius's head in the mottled mirror above the rack of wine bottles that runs the length of the bar.

Julius plays with his napkin, running his finger along the thick metal of the knife and fork. And I imagine Arnold Perkins sitting opposite him, the boy's characteristic frown as he peruses the oversized menu, Julius smiling, offering gently:

"Try the *strozzapreti*, Arnold, it's homemade, and it comes with a beef sauce and the freshest of peas..."

Sudden click-clack of four-inch heels. Julius looks up to see Rukshana Begum in dark-green, knee-length dress pattering towards him. The two waiters turn as one to view her backside all the way to the table as they continue to polish wineglasses by the service hatch.

Rukshana Begum smiles businesslike as she hesitates, then pulls the chair out for herself and sits down. Julius glances at her make-up, finding it overdone but he seems to like her dress: it's simple, understated, classy. Gus would have approved.

"Thanks for coming out east," Julius begins. "It's one of my favourite places, my uncle used to bring me as a boy... It's still a bit undiscovered, you know, a bit of a local secret..."

"*Vogue* featured it two years ago, Julius – it was on Masterchef last season, I think it's Jay Rayner's favourite Italian in London."

"Hmmm. So not so secret?"

She dabs the corner of her mouth with the napkin, shakes her head. "I came to a Glaxo dinner here last Christmas. Had the calves' liver, was a little disappointed to be honest."

His brow wrinkles, wondering why she's being aggressive. But if it's supposed to inflame him, she's come to the wrong bonfire.

"Oh. That's a shame. Why didn't you say so when I suggested it?"

"It was one dish. And you seemed so excited to invite me here..."

Julius cannot help blushing. Looks back at the menu. A waiter trudges over. Rukshana orders a Campari-and-soda, Julius asks for a bottle of still water.

"Dry night? Not drinking?" she teases, with clear disapproval.

"Wine, with the main course."

Rukshana nods, then asks him, matter-of-fact, if Richard Lovall is going away on holiday in August. Julius says he doesn't know. She asks him if he is going away in August, and Julius replies that he is not. After a silence, Rukshana says, "I'm going to New York, do some shopping, see some shows, you know?"

"Isn't that hot? Must be very sticky this time of year."

"Maybe. I think there's a lot of air conditioning."

"Probably. So you've not been to New York before?"

"Only in the winter. Christmas shopping, couple of times. You?"

Julius shakes his head. "It always seems too hectic on the television, a little desperate, if you ask me. My uncle loved it though. 'Gotta take a bite of the Big Apple,' he always said. But so far, I haven't."

The drinks arrive, they toast, Rukshana takes out her glasses and peruses the menu, and Julius suggests the *strozzapreti* and the *pancia di maiale* as a main course. Rukshana fixes him with a wry smile and orders *ravioli al taleggio*. Julius orders *strozzapreti*, feeling deeply slighted. Rukshana ignores his glum eyes.

"So this uncle of yours, was he a maths bod too?"

"How do you know he's a 'was'?"

"Your tone when you mentioned him. It was… wistful…"

Julius sips his water. Shakes his head. "Gus wasn't mathematical, in fact he was hopeless with anything scientific. He was… artistic. You know, one of those people who loved music, art, theatre. He had… taste. I suppose that was the thing that defined him."

"*Gusto*… Isn't that what they call it in Italian?"

"Maybe. Anyway, Gus could see something, hear something and know immediately that it was special. Sometimes you wouldn't see it yourself at first, in fact to begin with it would seem incredibly ugly, or crass, or just not very good, but then, gradually it would grow on you. You know, a painting, a piece of furniture, even a piece of music…"

"What would he have thought of me?" Rukshana Begum peers at Julius over the rim of her cocktail glass. "Would he have thought I was special?"

Julius hand goes to his mouth. "I don't know."

She frowns. "So no, then."

"I said, I don't know."

"So, what, this guy was such a big influence on you growing up? Fantastic Uncle Gus, the Big G, your Uncle Svengali?"

"I loved him. Very much."

"Why?"

"Sorry?"

"Why did you love him very much? I mean I have lots of uncles, too many uncles, uncles I've not even met yet. I don't really love any of them very much."

Julius stares at her, feeling a rising sense of despair that he's let a relative stranger into a precious place in his world, only for her to mock and despoil it.

"What did Gus make you feel?"

"Feel?" Julius purses his lips at the word.

She nods. "Come on, first words that come into your head, what did fabulous Uncle Gus make you feel?"

"Small."

Her look of surprise. "You felt belittled by him?"

"No. I mean… I didn't feel big. I was big, even as a child. Too big. The chairs in class, the desks, the coat hooks, the painting aprons… nothing fitted me. They laughed at me, called me Sasquatch, Yeti, that sort of thing. But when I was with Gus I didn't think about my body. Ideas were everything with him."

"But you said he wasn't mathematical."

"He wasn't. He was hopeless at adding up. I had to do his accounts for him."

"So these ideas had nothing to do with maths and statistics?"

"No. He thought about everything else."

Rukshana nods. Finishes her glass. The waiter appears, serves their main courses. They eat in silence. The pasta with beef ragout sticking in Julius throat. He coughs.

"Well, it is *strozzapreti*…" chuckles Rukshana.

"Sorry?"

"*Strozzapreti*. It means 'priest-choker'… supposedly greedy priests loved this pasta so much, they choked guzzling it down."

"I knew that. Gus told me."

"Sorry. Just making conversation."

They finish their food. Rukshana orders a large glass of Bardolino. Julius asks for a small glass of Chianti Classico. Beyond the window, he watches a young couple walk hand in hand along the quiet street, the girl cooling her laughing boyfriend with a white Chinese fan. Behind the bar I watch him in the mirror, nursing my fizzy water.

"Gus, what was that short for?" asks Rukshana gently.

"Augustus. If it's okay, I don't want to talk about him any more."

"You invited me here – it was his favourite restaurant, you're wearing his suit…"

Julius blushes again. "How did you…"

"Yves Saint Laurent, circa 1987? I don't know much, but I know fashion."

"Congratulations."

"He was Augustus. And you're Julius. What, your family got a thing for the Romans?"

"No. Well, a little bit. My grandfather studied classics at Oxford before he became a doctor. Named his three sons Augustus, Tiberius and Claudius. Claudius is my dad."

"So what'll your son be? Nero? Caligula?" Rukshana Begum giggles.

"I have a son," Julius says, coldly. "His name's Arnold. He's four next week."

Rukshana stops giggling. Tilts her head, lip jutting. "You have a son?"

"Yes. Arnold."

"You said that."

"He looks like me."

"Wow. Julius Miles. Dark horse. Dark stallion, I should say." Rukshana takes a large gulp of wine, something changed in her eyes now.

"You don't believe me," Julius says, "but it's true…"

"I do believe you. Like your uncle I have a talent. I know when people are lying. Jesus, I hadn't thought of it – are you married?"

"No. Of course not. The boy's mother's dead. She died seven weeks ago."

Rukshana looks at Julius. The waiter collects their plates. She nods at her glass for a refill. He shuffles away, knees creaking.

"Hang on. Seven weeks ago? Your girlfriend died seven weeks ago?"

"She wasn't my girlfriend."

"What was she then?"

"My neighbour."

"I've got a neighbour, but I don't have children with him."

"It was a mistake."

"Right. Lucky Arnold, the great mistake…"

"He doesn't know I'm his father."

"Your son doesn't know you're his father? And he lives next door? You haven't told him? His mother never told him?"

Julius nods, sadly. Rukshana laughs, a high-pitched snort. "Sorry, Julius, but… I don't get it. Is this why you invited me? To tell me about your son? A confession of sorts to the nutty nun from the ninth floor?"

"Good lord, no. I…" Julius stammers, feeling sick. "To be honest, I don't know why I told you. I don't know why I'm talking to you…"

"Yes you do. At some level you wanted to talk about this son of yours, and I'm flattered that you chose me…" she looks at him sincerely. "I mean that."

Julius wants to leave, his stomach a raging torrent. Then he barks: "I didn't choose you! I only wanted to talk to you because I want to know if I'm going to have a job next year! That's why I invited you. You must know! You're in those meetings! Is my job safe? That's why I agreed to go out with you, because you know things that I don't!"

Rukshana does not respond at first. Then she puts down her wineglass, dabs her lips with the napkin and says, deliberately:

"Sure. I have been in meetings where cutbacks to personnel have been discussed. And if you want the brutal truth, here it is. I don't know if your position is going to continue beyond Christmas. But

I would say it's unlikely. I'd say even highly unlikely. If you want me to put a figure on it, and I'm sure you do, I'd say there is only a thirty per cent chance you'll be working at the hospital this time next year. There you go. Is that all you wanted to hear?"

Rukshana sips again from her glass.

"Why did you come to dinner with me?" asks Julius. "It wasn't just to chat. Was it to tell me I'm going to be fired? Did Lovall put you up to this?"

Rukshana doesn't answer for a long time. Then she says: "I'm thirty-five years old, Julius. Thirty-six in September. No woman in my family has ever been this old without children. In fact not one of them got to thirty without giving birth. They're all convinced I'm barren."

"Are you?"

"Good old Julius. Never shy except when he wants to be. No, I'm not. I want to have a child. Children. And I suppose I asked you to dinner because deep inside I thought maybe, just maybe, we'd get along, go on a real date, start going out, fall in love. I even thought maybe you might end up being the father of my children."

Julius looks at her. Opens his mouth, but no words come out. She waits, but still he does not speak. "So eloquent, Julius. What would your fabulous uncle have to say about you now, mouth open like some great big guppy fish?"

"You're lonely?" Julius says, closing his mouth.

Rukshana laughs derisively. "Oh Julius…" She pushes back her heavy chair, stands. Hand hard against the table edge. "Stop wearing your uncle's suit. Stop trying to live his life. You're not him. You never will be. And maybe that's okay. Maybe it's not such a bad thing being you."

She picks up her purse and walks out of the restaurant, the two waiters and the maître d' still watching her even as she heads away down the road towards the traffic lights and Shoreditch High Street Overground Station.

14

September 11th 2001. Watched the towers burn and fall. All those Eames, Jacobsens, Saarinens melting into pulp. Picassos, Rothkos, even Impressionist nudes incinerated. Carpets from Egypt, like some of the hijackers. Scrolls from Mecca, like their Prophet. All gone.

Watched people become falling objects. Devoid of anything other than their mass and acceleration. Pure force. That is the brutality of these fascists, to make us like stone. That is the brutality of their hatred.

I want to take my chairs and say to the Bangladeshi boys who glare at me. Sit in my bergère and you will feel your God.

September 13th 2001. Opened DD because I didn't want to. Been wallowing in TV news for 48 hours, night and day. Out into sunlight blinking like a depressed mole. Only one customer all day, a girl named Daisy, and she was straight from Gatsby. *So callous a beauty. A woman buildings tumble for. Said she wanted to buy something beautiful to stop her feeling sad. Sold her a Franco Albini table lamp for £100. Because I want to sleep with her. God told me to.*

Julius flicks back and forth through the first volume of Gus's diary as if pretending Fate is turning the pages, nothing to do with him.

Slowly, as he relaxes deeper into one of his uncle's two antique French armchairs, he relents. Scrutinizes each entry. Swigging from a glass of hot milk.

December 18th, 2001. Daisy visited again today. Taught her about Eero and his buildings. St Louis Arch, Dulles Airport, JFK's TWA terminal, confessed to kissing the big Finn, Chumley's, '58. Never known such a Daisy, she listens like a priest, spits questions like a torturer. Says she's looking for work. Think I have to give it to her. Even the air dances when she walks.

December 25th, 2001. Depressed as a torn balloon, very Eeyore. Watched the Queen's Speech, and she seemed old. First time Liz looks like she's going to die. I'm next. Lunch of foie gras, oysters from Sheekeys, Bollinger '83. Julius the only one to call this year. Precious, troubled boy. Seems lost now the teaching thing has fizzled. Think he should backpack for a year, Gulliver's travels. Come back a scientist. Lovely to hear his voice, such uncertainty, such confidence. Must make sure the will is certified...

Julius remembers that Christmas, that call. His uncle sounded happy, carefree. "Vietnam, Julius dear boy, baguettes, Buddhism and *bahn bao*. Tell that brother of mine to spot you the air fare!"

Julius never went to Vietnam. He's sure there was a reason. But sitting in the dead man's chair, staring out at the rain streaming down the windows, he cannot remember what it was.

* * *

I wake. Glance at my watch. 2.17 a.m. Try to decipher what has jolted me from my White Ace slumber in the doorway of the "For Sale" house opposite number 42 Woodstock Road. It's a braying I can hear, then a high-pitched wail, then intermittent small gasps. The noise stops, starts again. It's coming from the house next door to Julius Miles, streaking out of the open front-bedroom window. Then I realize it is Arnold Perkins, crying.

The crying does not stop, in fact the boy now seems helpless, howls intensifying, louder and more frantic.

I shuffle hurriedly into the shadows cast by the trees and the cars beyond the orange street lamps. Someone is ringing the bell at Julius's door. Awa Yasin in a raincoat and no shoes. She rings again. Julius's front door opens, the chain barring the outside world. Awa's voice cracks: "He's been screaming for an hour. I don't know why. I can't get him to stop."

Julius takes off the chain, opens fully the door. He's wearing Uncle Gus's favourite grey pyjamas, which made Gus look like royalty, but leave Julius looking like a grumpy, sleepy janitor from a '40s black-and-white film.

"I don't know anything about children, Awa."

"Me neither. I just need someone there right now, I'm afraid I might lose it."

"Lose what?"

"Lose it! God, Julius, it's just what people say!" And she's gone, hurrying back next door.

I watch as Julius hesitates, scratching his heavy head on this soporific night. Then, dutifully, he walks down his steps and up the steps to number 40, where the door is wide open, funnelling Arnold's piercing cries into the street. The big man pauses for a brief moment on the doormat, then ventures inside, closing the door quietly behind him.

I listen to his footsteps on the stairs, step closer to the house. The crying is very loud now. No discernible words, but the sobs rise and fall in tone, some wretched, some quite controlled, then long wails that seem to pump all the oxygen from the boy's small lungs, necessitating a desperate intake of breath once more.

I hear Julius knock on Arnold's bedroom door. "Come in, come in!" barks Awa Yasin. I picture Arnold's room, the large photograph of Daisy Perkins by the bed, Arnold's childish scribbling around her head, various coloured crayons creating a ragged halo – the unquestioning worship of a child for a parent, a boy for his mum.

Screaming from the bedroom. "Come on, please, Arnold!" Awa cries. I hear banging, perhaps the boy struggling as he shrieks.

"Arnold, it's me, Julius, from next door…" Julius states with all the enthusiasm of a man delivering a quarterly data report. The small boy continues to cry as if Julius does not exist.

"God, what's got into him?" Awa exhales, "Is he okay? Should I take him to A&E? No, that's silly, isn't it, he's just a toddler having a tantrum…"

"Take a break," Julius declares, firmly this time. "I'll see what I can do."

"But…"

"Go!" shouts Julius, and I hear Awa Yasin's lighter step in the hallway, then descending the top stairs, then the second flight of stairs to the lower ground floor. The television clicks on, the volume turned up loud, to drown out the boy's wailing.

Arnold is screaming even louder now, maybe Julius is trying to hold him in his arms, the boy's breath rate doubling as he strains against the big man's embrace with all his small furious might. A small thud that could be the boy falling off the bed onto the carpet. Silence for a moment, and I wonder if this has done the trick, the shock of the fall has snapped Arnold out of whatever crazed despair he was suffering. Until he starts to scream again, more piercing than ever.

Then Julius starts to sing. It takes me a moment to realize this is what he's doing, for it's not the most tuneful singing I've ever heard, but the song is heartfelt and grows in confidence and intensity as he goes on. A few notes more and I recognize it. I cannot help smiling.

Some talk of Alexander and some of Hercules,
Of Hector and Lysander and such great names as these.
But of all the world's brave heroes, there's none that can compare,
With a tow row row, row row row row
For the British Grenadiers…

I listen more closely, ear to the still-warm wood of the front door. Julius is singing the song in an exaggerated Cockney accent, like some regimental Sergeant Major from Mile End...

> Whene'er we are commanded to storm the palisades,
> Our leaders march with fuses and we with hand grenades,
> We throw them from the glacis about the enemy's ears...

Arnold has stopped crying. A small moment of silence, then the sound of a thirty-nine-year-old man hopping from foot to foot as he belts out:

> Sing tow row row, row row row row
> For the British Grenadiers...

A small giggle. Julius repeats it again. "*Sing tow row row, row row row row, for the British Grenadiers!*" and again Arnold laughs, his voice high-pitched, a little hysterical – but the spell is undone. The man and boy continue like this for a while, a line of chorus, the boy's chuckle. Then silence.

I look at my watch. 2.55 a.m. The television still on in the lower-ground-floor living room. I glance through the railings, Awa Yasin is curled on the sofa. She looks to be asleep.

I take out my credit card, slide it gently down the lock. I push the front door silently and step into the house.

I move without a sound, sweep up the stairs like the sorcerer in *Swan Lake*. Not even a squeak.

No light in the first-floor hallway. I slip into the shadows outside Arnold's room and peer through the open bedroom door.

Julius is standing in the middle of the small room looking at Arnold. "Sleepy?" he asks the boy. Arnold yawns. "Come on. Let's get some shut-eye."

Julius reaches down. To my surprise, Arnold does not flinch. Julius puts his hands under the boy's armpits and lifts him up, placing Arnold on the bed, his back to me in the hallway. Arnold plugs his thumb in his mouth and turns to curl up next to the wall, knees into chest. Julius sits down gently beside him on the bed. Still facing the wall, thumb still stuck in his mouth, Arnold reaches back and drapes his hand across Julius's knee. And closes his eyes.

Julius observes the boy's breathing, the fast rise and fall that gradually slows. It takes a few minutes but then, gently, Arnold's thumb slips from his mouth and his hand wavers for a brief moment in mid-air, before descending softly to rest on the bed sheets.

Arnold is asleep. Hand still draped across Julius's knee.

I remain motionless in the shadows, no breath even in my throat. Watching Julius sitting stock still with the boy curled asleep against him. A big rock.

As the seconds slip by, I expect Julius to get up and exit the bedroom. I am ready to sneak into the space between the chest of drawers and the small hall table. But the giant does not move. He keeps gazing at Arnold, the flicker of the boy's eyelids. Arnold coughs once, but merely turns back to the wall, fast asleep.

Delicately, Julius lies down beside him on the bed. So close to the boy's face that he can feel Arnold's breath on his cheek.

I carry on my vigil, guarding the giant in grey pyjamas and the thin boy in Superman pyjamas lying next to each other on the small bed, Julius's calves dangling far off the end. Could they be father and son? Could they share DNA, spliced from ancestors going back through time to the African plains? Will the boy's small button nose somehow elongate over the next ten to fifteen years and protrude into the big man's curved profile?

Now their two chests rise and dip in unison. Julius has fallen asleep next to the boy. I cannot take my eyes off them. I nearly miss the footsteps coming up the stairs behind me.

Awa Yasin approaches the bedroom door. Hand on door frame. Head to one side as she takes in the two sleeping figures side by side on the bed.

Then she turns once more, heading back down the stairs, passing by my hiding place. Crouched awkwardly between the hall dresser and the banister, I glimpse a smile on her face in the moonlight.

I wait for a short while, listening to Julius's breathing, the boy's breathing. Then I start to creep down the stairs once more, but as I near the raised ground floor I hear the front door open from inside and someone exit, pulling the latch with barely a click behind them. I wait a hundred and twenty seconds, then hurry down to the hallway and open the door a crack. See the silhouette of Awa Yasin disappearing around the corner by the school at the end of the street. And she's gone.

Outside, something has shifted. The night no longer crackles. All of London seems to have tumbled into sleep, as if in some fairy tale. I slip out of the house and away into the night, leaving the man and the boy to their calm slumber.

* * *

The tower block is 3 a.m.-quiet except for the dull thump of bass from some stereo on the fourteenth floor. Awa watches the arrow blinking upwards. Ignores the fresh graffiti scratched into the chipboard nailed to each wall of the lift. *E9 killaz.* The postcode wars between gangs from the area across the park (E9) and the E3 gangs in Bow. So childish it maddens her. And terrifies her. Two deaths this year already, both stabbings, one a boy still in school. Sometimes she fears for Arnold's future, an innocent among these lunatics.

18th floor. Flat 37. Unlocks the door. Locks it again on the other side. Hangs her coat, slips off her shoes, glides along the smooth lino. Closes the bathroom door, washing her hands after the lift – once, twice.

Listens to her father's snoring. Turned towards the middle of the double bed, as every night. Facing the space where his wife used to be.

Awa lies down beside him. Mohammad Ali does not stir. Many nights she has lain here, not knowing if she is doing it for him or for herself. Has fallen asleep listening to his tobacco coughs.

But this night she does not sleep. Lies on the bed feeling like she's falling. As if the eighteen ceilings and floors of steadfast concrete have evaporated and she is plummeting, arms by her side, towards the earth.

Then the opposite seems to occur – she is the concrete, an immovable weight, and it is the rest of the city that rushes towards her in a million strobing lights.

She gets up from the bed, goes to the window, opens it. The city quiet and still on this warm, clear night. Swallows the breeze. Staring down at the rows of Victorian houses far below, the pins of light from the lamp-posts.

Watches a drunk man and woman wind their way down one street and up another to their own front door. Kissing hard against the wood as they fall through into the weekend.

Now she looks down to the third road below the tower block and the backs of the houses. Sees number 40 Woodstock Road. No lights on, the garden dark. Smiles once again as she thinks of the man and boy, sleeping deeply next to one another.

Awa closes the window. Sits down at the computer. Finds the email address in her father's shaky handwriting, Post-It note on the side of the monitor. She types slowly.

Dear Mubarak.

My father wanted me to write to you and say hello. So hello. How's the weather in Dubai? It's been hot here, for England. Crazy-hot, the local shops have run out of blow-up paddling pools. Congratulations on your promotion to restaurant manager. I'm just a teaching assistant at the local primary school, but I want to see about going back to college to train to be a real teacher. I like kids. But I have to tell you this now, if I'm going to be fair – I never want children of my own. Never.

Anyway, feel free to write me back. I've no plans to come to Dubai any time soon, but you seem like a nice enough guy from the photo Dad showed me, and I'm always up for gossip about my sister and her husband. Any juicy stuff will be treated in the strictest confidence.

Best wishes,

Awa Yasin.

* * *

Julius Miles wakes with cramps in his left leg and muscle spasms in his back. He blinks, Daisy Perkins staring back at him, a half-smile playing across her face.

He sits up, alarmed. It takes him a few seconds to realize her face is a photograph and not the real thing. Sees that he is in a child's bed, the boy's bedroom. Staggers downstairs to find a note:

Taken Arnold shopping at Westfield Stratford. He's happy this morning. Have a good weekend.

The clock on the wall reads 9.05 a.m., which is two hours later than Julius has woken up every Saturday for the past twenty-five years.

15

Julius reads Gus's diary once more, he cannot stop. For better or for worse. Picks up 2002, skimming until the beginning of April and the death of the Queen Mother.

9th April 2002. Couldn't get out of bed to watch the funeral. Wallowed for most of the day as glum as Liz in her Daimler. Somehow found energy to mix a little sundowner, Gordon's and Dubonnet, in honour of the Departed, here's to you, Buffy Bowes-Lyon. Hope I don't live till 101. But if I do, dear Reader, it was the G-and-Ds wot done it...

10th April 2002. Bloody awful hangover. Thanks, Buffy. Met her just the once, Aspinalls in Mayfair, some charity casino thing. Eyes like diamonds, hard and bright. Mean streak, I guessed, but which of us has angel wings? This afternoon put in an angry bid for a Mappin silver tea set, 1939 stamp. Beauty is as unshake-able as the numbers Nephew worships on Accounts Monday. Feeling pre-War these days. Called Dr Pettigrew, asked for more bedazzlers. Don't think he's going to oblige, which is regrettable. I sense the Bleakness gathering...

11th April 2002. The Bleakness back. Walked by the school because the children's voices sometimes lift me. Little black boy came up to the gate and smiled. Said his name was Anfony.

*I corrected him and told him it was "Anthony", but he shook
his head, spelled it out like it was me who was the six-year-old.
A-N-F-O-N-Y. Said his daddy got it wrong on the form, but
his mummy liked it so it stuck. He likes it too, he said, thinks
it's original. Who am I to argue with someone so pleased to be
different. Happiest smile in the world – made me think I should
procreate, like Mitterrand, Rod Stewart or Pierre Trudeau. Join
the Ancient Paters Club. Maybe Daisy would oblige? No doubt
she's as fertile as a Friesian...*

Julius flicks on, head jumbled like Daisy's shop, crammed with
unease and worry. A new face of his uncle emerging from behind
the immaculate oil painting in his head, the brilliant jester re-
placed by a lonely and depressed old man with sallow eyes and
bitterness in his heart. Julius finds himself looking more and more
for Daisy's name, because in the paragraphs Gus writes about
her his uncle is more like the man Julius remembers. Sparkier.
Funnier. Happier.

Daisy Perkins mentioned more as summer became autumn, Gus
recording in tight narrow script the clothes she wore to work each
day, her perfume, her shoes. Her boyfriends (numerous), female
friends (few). Her pet hates – cricket, guitar bands, fried-chicken
restaurants. A moment when her hand brushed his.

Whilst reading about Gus leaves Julius wracked with sadness,
Daisy is emerging as a more complex and intriguing woman from
the one he disliked and feared. She has the same face and body
(which Gus never shies away from describing), the same hectic
energy, but beneath the bluster Gus depicts a thoughtful mind,
a gentle heart. A woman who speaks fondly of a Sunday School
teacher and the parables he so vividly recounted. A woman who
takes leftover food from sandwich outlets to homeless people. Who
reads to his uncle from *Heat* magazine every day for a week whilst
Gus is in hospital following a knee operation. Who swims naked
in Hampstead ponds on her birthday every year.

217

Julius scratches his chin, sensing both Daisy and his beloved Gus spinning away from him, their equations shifting and dancing as if to mock him. Then comes the page he is staring at now.

November 16th 2002. Had lunch with Nephew, who treated me to Gerbino's, dear boy that he is. Months since my last appearance so Patrizio treated me as the veritable prodigal. Tipsy just from the hugs. Scaloppine al limone a gobsmacking fanfare. Felt light enough to entertain again, recounted a dozen of my best stories to Nephew, who laughed more loudly than ever. On our way back to the ranch stopped for a tea at DD, Daisy holding the fort, but she seemed surprisingly subdued. When Nephew went for a pee, it all spilt out, as things do with Perkins... She likes him, dear Reader! Can you Adam-and-Eve it? Tells me she cannot stop thinking about my Julius. My Julius! Swore me to secrecy. As if I'd tell the poor lad, it'd send him to Spazzville and back if he knew Crazy Daisy was gunning for him.

Julius downs his milk. Reads the last three lines of the entry, over and over.

I won't tell Nephew. Not because I'm concerned about his reaction, but because I don't want him to have Daisy nor Daisy to have him. Because I am a selfish, bitter old man who does not want anyone to have what I do not, especially not the two souls I love most in the world.

The following nine pages are blank. The next entry begins on the tenth day:

November 23rd 2002. Just back from ringside at the Miss World contest at Alexandra Palace. Ticket thanks to Barney Fothergill and his Soho connections. Turkish girl won. She was a delight.

Looks onwards for Daisy's name, thirsting for another mention of her feelings towards him. By 4 a.m. Julius is up to the end of 2004, has found nothing. Puts the journals back in the shoe box, warms another mug of milk and sits down at his computer, going onto the Toys R Us website. Narrows down his search to "Boys Aged 4". Clicks on "Pretend and Play Space Station", made up of eleven different pieces, including a 35-centimetre-tall space station, a space shuttle, a robotic arm, a land-rover vehicle, four "multicultural" astronauts "and more!"

As Julius peers at the enlarged image of the box, he finds it hard to see what the "more!" refers to other than the cardboard and the plastic the toy comes in.

Julius clicks "Buy Now" and goes upstairs to bed. He falls into a fitful sleep plagued with dreams of Daisy and his uncle making love.

* * *

I wait until 10.30 a.m. and break into number 40 Woodstock Road. Pretending to deliver kebab shop leaflets, stuff one through the letterbox, a quick jab of credit card, and I am closing the door behind me without a sound.

It came to me over my morning breakfast. If Augustus Miles had a diary, so must Daisy Perkins. She modelled herself on him: his taste, his ways. If there's a diary, it will tell me who the father is. The mathematician or the money-launderer. Who would you rather call Daddy?

As I head up the stairs, part of me knows this is dangerous, that I'm breaking and entering again, and if anyone returns to the house it could end badly, very badly. But there are two sides to every moment. There's the strong straight line that puts each instant in order, cause leading to effect leading to cause, on and on up our lives until death. If I break in, I will walk up the stairs and discover something, or not. And leave. Or get caught. But the secret is, every second of our lives has another guise. Each tick of the clock is unique, disconnected. There is no knowledge of where it might lead, so it can lead anywhere. This walk up the stairs can be the most dizzying delicious walk ever. In this moment I am more alive than I will ever be. Bright. Immense. Vital. There is no next.

Softly, I walk into Daisy Perkin's bedroom. It's minimalist, with a feminine touch. The bed is mahogany, the colour of Greek skin, sheets beige. Matching dark wardrobes. Dark-wood dressing table. Her brush lying there, blond hairs swirled in a memorial to a head that is no more. Neat rows of make-up. Some jewellery boxes that look like they might have come from Japan, emblazoned with storks and temples.

All untouched. All awaiting her return. It's clear that the nanny Awa Yasin has not been in here, doesn't dare. Discarded clothes still in the clothes basket; Prada sweater, expensive bra, silk nightdress. Perhaps the very clothes Daisy Perkins wore the morning she died.

I open the double wardrobe. It's full of neatly hung designer clothes. Rub my thumb and forefinger up and down the expensive cloth, a shiver of luxury at the back of my neck.

I unbutton my shirt, lay it on the bed. Step out of my jeans. Fumble at my bra strap, drop it onto the jeans. And step out of my knickers.

Stand in front of the full-length mirror. My body so soft in places, so hard in others. A topography of confusion – breasts and labia, but my hips are slender, calf muscles like a milkman. My flesh a twisted land of contrasts, landmarks sliding into one another. I step back, framed perfectly in the glass.

Am I attractive? As a woman? Who would want me?

I open the dressing-table drawer. Jumbled underwear, I caress the material, finding a pair of silk panties.

Wriggle them up my thighs. Locate the matching bra, breathe in, yank shut the clasp. My breasts shooting upwards, a swelling of silicone.

Stand back once more and smile. I look good. Sexy. Don't I?

Forefinger running the length of the dresses, blouses and skirts. To my eye the priciest garment is an aquamarine dress. Slip it off the hanger, jump into it like a four-year-old in a birthday Cinderella frock.

Jerk it up my body, duck into the straps. Smooth the satin down my sides. Twirl, once. Push up and back my hair, I look fabulous. Unrecognizable. A dream girl.

Giddy, too giddy, I steady myself against the door frame, heart racing with joy. A noise from the street, dustbin lid or car door.

I rip off the dress, stuff it in my bag, keep on the underwear, pulling on my old jeans and sweater. Shut the wardrobe door firmly for fear that I will ransack the joint.

There are some boxes on top of the wardrobe. In between are shoved two small orange inflatable children's armbands, the kind used for swimming, still half-inflated.

It strikes me that these orange armbands are most likely inflated by Daisy Perkins herself. In my estimation each contains maybe half a lungful of her breath, trapped in Chinese plastic.

Snap the top off one of the clear plastic stoppers, squeeze it sharply and suck the air from the first armband. Taste of sweet plastic. I want to believe that it will give me her strength, if not Daisy's fabulous body. You never know how the dead can affect you.

But I'm not selfish. I place the other armband back on the shelf, so that Arnold can find it and suck on his mother's elixir. Four puffs to last a lifetime.

As I position the armband carefully where it will be more easily found alongside the boxes, I feel something hard and square shoved tightly at the back of the shelf. I stand up on tiptoes. It's a brown book. Carefully I take down the volume and stare at the cover.

A diary. Noble Macmillan, leather-bound. An inscription inside the front cover. *To Darling Daisy, Think well. Love, your Gus.* I turn the pages and something falls out. White and square. I place it in my palm.

A phone Sim card. Tesco Pay as You Go. I take out my phone, switch my Sim for the Tesco one, hoping it's not locked – and it isn't. On my phone screen appears a single text message:

Can u meet? Usual place and time. Got what u asked for. All of it this time. I want to help. OK?

I click on the sender; there's just a mobile number. I stare at the digits, at the simple black lines and curves. Something tells me I know this number. I know this number. This number.

Fingers damp with nerves, I snap out the Tesco Sim, replace it with my own. Go to "Contacts". Flicking on down a hundred names or more – I hoard people like some amass coins – finally, I find it. The same number in my own address book.

07703 345 077. DCI Eddie Knowles.

I remember when my old man first showed me a Sim card, told me how the cops could trace everything about someone from their Sim. Chuckled as he explained how the police had started to give their snitches a Sim card, to be used only to contact the police handler. The snitch had to text the handler once a day at lunchtime. From the triangulation of the text message my old man knew where all his snitches ate lunch each day. "You dine with your enemies, but you eat lunch with your friends," he told me, grinning. "It's a gold mine."

And this is when I realize: that there's another way of looking at Eddie Knowles's involvement with Daisy Perkins. What if Eddie isn't crooked? What if he was simply doing his job and doing it well? What if he knew Daisy Perkins's name for a reason, and one reason only? What if she was his snitch?

Could Daisy Perkins have been a double agent? Using her shop to launder drugs money for Jay Munnelly, whilst being a cop snitch providing intel to Eddie Knowles? If so, no wonder she is dead.

* * *

Awa finds the diary lying in the middle of the first-floor landing. She assumes Arnold must have found it and discarded it when he saw that all it contained was handwriting. But Arnold shakes his head when she asks her. "Not me."

She finds the page she's looking for. Kneads her left shoulder with her right hand clasped across her neck as she reads:

27th October. I'm pregnant!! I think two exclamation marks are justified. God, shock. I didn't plan this, did I? Jesus! How do I feel? Different, yes. I knew this morning when I woke up something had changed. A shift. Like I was not whole any more, there was something else. Intangible yet so definite. And the excitement crawling under the skin, back to childhood and Christmas Eve. Not knowing, but knowing it was coming.

At the chemist's, trembling like a schoolgirl. The sweet man behind the counter smiled. He knew. He knew. And he considered it only good.

A blue line on the peed-on stick. The thin blue line. The line that has been crossed.

Wish Gus was here to talk to. Oh God. Why do I keep invoking the Lord? Dad would be furious, the old Bible-basher. Wish he was here. Mum too. No one to tell but you, dear diary.

Okay, want to hear the really bizarre thing? I AM SO HAPPY!! Such a surprise to me, this feeling, this newly created DESIRE! I want everything for this child, this human, this new her/ him. I will give her/him everything. It's all possible, all do- able. Isn't it?

Hallelujah! When I die my child will live on, down the ages. I was lost, now found. What a feeling of connection! To the world!

The absurdity of life. A drunken fumble, a split condom, and the world turns on its axis.

Arnold if it's a boy. Old-fashioned, solid. Margot if it's a girl. Sophisticated, historic. In past daydreams I saw girls, but now a little boy to love his mummy would not be so bad.

Shit. Will I tell him? First reaction… don't want to. Keep it safe, secret, bound up inside you. Woman's privilege. I have enough love stored up for the child, as if in deep wells over the years.

But fathers sing too. The male hug. Nothing like it. Have to tell him, Daisy, have to. Share the love, don't lock it up. Don't be like Dad. God.

He will flip out. Will he flip out?

Dear diary, I will inform him of this development in the morning. WATCH THIS SPACE!!

* * *

"She sounds happy, doesn't she? Her words, they're so energetic, so open, so… real. God, it's… lovely."

Julius is silent, thick forefingers rubbing thicker thumbs.

Awa laughs. "She chickened out, didn't she? Didn't tell you. After sounding so emphatic."

"Probably not. She probably told *him*."

"What do you mean? I don't get it."

Julius does not reply immediately. Sounds hollow, carved-out when he speaks.

"When we… you know… I didn't wear a condom. She's talking about Larry Silk."

16

I call Eddie Knowles eight times in four hours. Eight messages on his answering machine and two emails.

Eddie, I've news. Call me.

Eddie, it's Felicity. It's important.

And finally. *Okay. If you want to chat in person, I'll be at the Costa Coffee on Regent Street at 10 a.m. Tuesday.*

I sit at the rear of the large coffee shop, back to the wall. Scour every face with exaggerated defiance. Minutes click by, still Eddie Knowles does not show. I am worried. My instinct now tells me Eddie is a good policeman, that his presence with dodgy copper Charles Riordan on the Serious Crime Directorate's Special Drugs Advisory Panel and his contacts with money-launderer Daisy Perkins are most likely part of a sophisticated sting operation against the Munnelly drugs gang. If I'm right, maybe someone has intercepted my phone messages and mails. Maybe I've put Eddie in danger. I chug another espresso to stop the shakes. The shakes get worse.

At 11 a.m. exactly, I exit Costa. Head to the Savile Row nick and ask to speak with DCI Knowles.

"Sorry, Ma'am, he's on leave until next week. Gone to see his son in Toronto. Wanna leave a message?" The desk clerk is smiling, but behind him two uniformed officers have not taken their eyes off me since I entered the building.

I hurry from the Row, don't relax my fists until I am seven stops along the Central Line eastbound. Heart thump, sweat on palms.

Back at my flat I write six Post-Its and place them on three mirrors, the fridge, the back of the front door and the TV screen.

Must not, cannot forget anything now.

* * *

In his garden, Julius Miles watches a thousand rainbows dance through the spray from a hose in his left hand. A dozen white and yellow roses shudder with joy as the jets strike their stems.

The roses do not need watering; Julius spent a week in early May creating his own in-line drip emitter that snakes between the bush roots releasing a gallon of water every hour, connected to a timer set for 5 a.m. and 9 p.m. daily. He has decided to risk over-watering Gus's prize rose bushes because it allows him to stand in the garden for half an hour every evening in the hope of seeing Arnold playing next door. But the boy has not been in the garden for several weeks, Julius only ever sees a small shape flitting between the kitchen and the television set that seems to be gleaming more and more these days in the shadows of number 40 Woodstock Road.

Julius puts down the hose. No sign of anyone in the house to-night. He rubs his neck, bitten in several places by the mosquitoes that have materialized out of this strange heavy heat that hangs over the East London evening like the universe is pushing down on everyone, and not just for fun.

Julius gazes at the back of the next-door house for several min-utes, but still there is no movement. Hastily, awkwardly, he clambers over the fence, landing in the long brown grass. Approaches the rickety shed, the door half off its hinges, window cracked. Daisy wasn't much for garden maintenance, her backyard much like her life – unkempt and wildly blossom-filled. Julius pulls out the twig that holds the lock closed and finds the mouldy Flymo beneath a potting compost bag.

He cuts the scraggly lawn. Takes his time, creating neat lines in the grass, back and forth, back and forth. Stands at the centre of the lawn, admiring the straight clean strips.

* * *

The DLR train glides above East London like a lazy dragon. Steel shimmer off the river, the Dome snow-white in the sunshine. Construction cranes spike the blue sky, shells of unfinished apartment blocks cramming the western end of Royal Victoria Dock like enormous carcasses.

A judder as the train slows on the approach to West Silvertown station. I turn my face to the hot window and the view down onto the hulking cube of the Tate & Lyle sugar refinery, the giant golden-syrup tin jutting out from the north-east wall. My old man grew up around Silvertown, remembered the sweet stench of sugar filling his lungs on freezing winter evenings.

"Out of the strong came forth sweetness," he'd quote me as I ladled spoonfuls of honey-slick syrup onto my porridge, staring at the image on the green-and-white tin of the dead lion, the swarm of bees buzzing about his head.

A hush of hot air as the doors open onto the platform. I do not get up immediately; I know the driverless train is programmed to wait exactly ninety seconds at each station. Thirty seconds left and now I'm up and out of my seat, gliding through the train exit as the "door closing" beep begins.

Gasp in the heat. They say it'll break the record today, thirty-nine degrees Celsius, above 102 Fahrenheit in old money. The meteorologists are in a tizzy – is it global warming or the age-old cycle of heat and cold, swirling back and forth across the centuries? No one seems to know, but they're all sweating.

The metal balustrade scorches my palm. Even the old Jamaican ladies are perspiring in the platform shade, fanning themselves with well-thumbed copies of *The Sun*.

I'm wearing Daisy's dress, satin as light as dew on my skin, but this is no fashion show, I'm clothed for business, brand-new trainers and a sports bra beneath the willowy chiffon. We're getting to the sharp end.

I have my target in eyeshot. Wait till he jumps the bottom step, ambles off east, keeping to the shade beneath the raised concrete DLR track. I spring down the metal staircase, the air liquid as I move.

I do not know where Trevor Nugent is going, but he's heading somewhere he's nervous about going to. Keeps twisting round like a cork on a string, white tracksuit dazzling in the hot sun, tugging the baseball cap lower and lower until he seems to have no head at all.

I've had harder marks. Trevor keeps to the cooler shade beneath the elevated DLR track, pausing only to wipe his brow with a crisp white handkerchief. I'm a hundred feet behind, but he glances at me only once, a jerk-eye in my direction, but I'm looking at my DLR map, clearly a West Ender lost and vulnerable in the arenaceous industrial sprawl of Silvertown and East Ham.

Dogs bark lazily in the noontime from behind rusted fences giving onto low-slung warehouses and cracked-roofed distribution shacks. Truck engine idling warily in the thick methane air. Men – always men – in shorts and T-shirts loading boxes into white vans. Radios playing, the heavy beat of garage music, and I find myself longing for more melodic tunes, the happy stupidity of summer pop hits. There is an anger to these streets, these old brick printing works and disused pumping stations and the concrete mixers trundling by in clouds of resentful dust.

We pass an elderly Bangladeshi couple, she a heavy pear in orange salwar, he a slender sage in grey slacks and pale-blue shirt, white beard and no moustache, white taqiyah. Yet it is her, the sad old pear, who whispers as I pass...

"*As-Salamu Alaikum...*" Peace be with you. I murmur back: "*Waalaikum as-Salam.*" And on you be peace. As I glance over my shoulder, the sage and the pear are holding hands, gazing up at a plane roaring skywards from City Airport. And I see their lives, joined since the age of twelve, his shy glance, her soaring laugh under the flame trees in Lahore, the Krishnachura blossom as red as their beating hearts.

It takes my breath away sometimes. Those who connect without the help of someone like me. There is nothing more pure. More true.

Trevor has speeded up, long angular legs striding forth under the DLR viaduct, and I hurry to keep pace, still maintaining my distance. The ground seems to shake as another train rumbles by over our heads.

Ahead is the next DLR station, Pontoon Dock, rising silver and white above the road, surrounded by sizzling pale concrete. Trevor pauses, mops his forehead once more, tugs the cap. He watches for an instant the children as they run in and out of the water jets spurting from the small plaza banked on each side by high concrete walls, dozens of brown-skinned gigglers chasing each other through the fountain spears, screeching, sliding and hugging to stay upright in the splashing water.

I eye Trevor from behind one of the slender trees by the road, and for a moment he looks like he might be about to strip off his tracksuit and run through the fountains himself, so eager and childish is his expression. And I feel for him, the tug of compassion for this nineteen-year-old simpleton, caught, perhaps for ever, between the child and the man, still as much a gangling boy as he is an awkward adult.

Then something seems to click in, a jolt of responsibility, and Trevor is off again, skirting the fountains, keeping close to the high wall and on into the hedgerows and flower beds of the sunken garden of Thames Barrier Park.

The air here heavy with scent, the yew of the gently undulating hedges, the thicker cling of lavender and other herbs – thyme, sage, mint, a swirl of fragrances like an incantation to magic...

Two paths lead south along the hedgerows towards the river. I duck down, speeding up to take the parallel track to Trevor, gaining almost level with him as I keep hidden behind the thick maygreen.

At the end of the sunken garden is a gate and a grassy bank leading up to wide blue sky. Trevor bounds up the grass. I wait until he has disappeared over the lip of the incline, then dash up the wheelchair ramp by the wall.

Gasp of warm river stench. I'm now at a wide wooden swathe of sun-baked decking above the Thames shoreline. Ahead is a tall modernist roof on slim stilts, an ark of shade crammed with over-heated mothers and pugnacious offspring sucking on juice boxes.

And beyond, silhouetted against the shimmer off the metallic Thames, leaning against the thin aluminium balustrade between the park and the drop down to the river, is Trevor Nugent. Talking to the accountant Larry Silk.

I walk quickly up to the mothers and their children. Stand by the flanks of baby buggies, protected within this circle of women. I cannot hear what the two men are saying, especially over the yelling of the mums and the squealing of their kids, but I'm not here for exact details. I take out my camera, hold it slyly by my side, hip height, press the button. Keep the video running on Trevor and Larry's conversation – I'll blow it up later, read their lips via the software programme on my laptop that's as tidy as any the secret services have at their disposal. Once again, in this riotous age you can find anything you want, if you know who to pay.

I am convinced I have enough to go above Eddie Knowles with this, if he doesn't reply to my messages. I am certain now that Daisy Perkins was killed and I'm convinced I know why. Daisy was a police informant, feeding intel about Munnelly's money-laundering and probably much else besides. An attractive woman with a good rack has always been an intelligence asset.

I carve a careful arc beyond the two men talking in hushed tones by the river, ending up at the same balustrade two hundred feet away from them along the bank. The metal hot to my fingertips, the fumes off the Thames thick with summer brine, sea and mud. To my left, the row of steel half-domes of the Thames Barrier itself, London's flood protection, an engineering wonder of the world.

I look down at the silt and shingle; the tide is out, the far-gone history of bilious London dark and ruddy below me, the clay like some timeless gore seeping up from an ancient brooding beast. Yet the sun bakes my face, modern clear white light behind my closed eyelids. I feel like a breeze, swaying gently as the river hushes and shovels against the shingle.

"Hey!" A man's voice shouting to someone beyond. "Hey!"

A seagull cries in sorrow, wheeling and swirling in the afternoon sky. I open my eyes lazily, a smile full across my face, experiencing a moment of well-being I have not enjoyed for months, not since long before the operation. I feel, what?... "Whole", I think, is the word. The sum of my parts. A fluttering heart and a certain mind. I have uncovered the truth about Daisy Perkins. And maybe I have found love for Julius Miles.

"Hey, lady!" The man's voice is close. I turn and Larry Silk is marching towards me, shouting, Trevor Nugent scurrying behind him, eyes hidden beneath the bluntly tipped baseball cap. I pivot and walk quickly away from them, my running shoes slapping the wooden boards of the riverside boardwalk.

I am shocked when a hand clasps my shoulder and spins me around.

"Ouch!"

"Who are you?" Larry Silk barks, and his face is tight, a single bead of sweat easing down the middle of his thin forehead. Still gripping my neck.

"Take your hand off me," I say calmly. "Please."

Larry Silk takes his hand off me. Trevor Nugent peers at me suspiciously.

"That's her. Came into the shop. Got all shirty with me..."

I am trying not to shake. In the pit of my stomach the fire is there, the adrenaline, testosterone bubbling up against the hormones I have been injecting into my belly for what seems like half a lifetime. My fingers flex into a fist and back again.

"Who are *you*? Why are you shouting at me?" I continue, without emotion. "This place is full of people, all I have to do is scream…"

"You've been following me," says Larry Silk, quiet, intense. "I'd like to know why."

"Have I? I don't remember ever seeing you before in my life. You seem a little paranoid, sir…"

He cuts across me, hard: "Last week you followed me from the gates of my house to my office. You waited until I drove home, waited outside the entrance to the place where I live. Now you're here. Come on, lady."

"Coincidence is God's way of remaining anonymous," I reply, stepping back from Larry Silk, smoothing down my dress. "Or so Albert Einstein said…"

"She's Feds, Mr Silk, I tell you, she's Feds…"

Larry scowls at Trevor's clumsy mention of his name. I shake my head, eyes burning.

"I'm not a policewoman, if that's what you mean, young man. Although I have friends who are." The threat implicit. The smile more confident.

"So do I, lady," murmurs Larry Silk. "So do I. That plays both sides of the tracks…"

"Really?" I murmur back at him. "How so?"

Larry Silk does not reply. Reaches in his pocket, takes out his iPhone and snaps a photo of me.

"If I see you again, lady, someone will come calling for you. Okay?" His voice a snarl, and I sense that he is playing the hard-man, his tone and hulking stance a counterfeit of thuggery – he's channelling Jay Munnelly or one of his meatheads. And I feel sudden compassion for the thin accountant, the bright little bean alongside this gang of muscle, the cowering boy who was bullied at school and now lives and breathes for the bullies and the riches they ransack from the weak and sullied of my streets.

"Come calling for me? Now that's a threat," I state simply. "A threat I will be emailing to the people I know, including my solicitor." I hold up my own much cheaper phone, finger on the side button, the digital voice recorder icon on the screen, a red oblong blinking "RECORD".

Trevor winces, but Larry Silk does not draw breath. Suddenly, my hand flies up of its own accord and the phone is gone, Larry Silk flinging it hard, low and fast, a glint of metal against the churning stew of the Thames. And it's gone, no sound. Vanished into the water.

"No!" I exclaim. "My HTC!" My hand rising fast, I'm going to slap him, but he grabs my wrist, turning me with some strength and skill, and I spin, dropping my handbag, which spills onto the wooden decking…

"You all right, madam?" a booming male voice, but this time it's behind me, a large man is approaching, and I turn and my face says everything I need it to say. Help me! Thank you!

My rescuer is six foot five, almost as wide. Face black, broad as a van, arms like nuclear missiles, legs thicker than I am wide. Hands by his side, but there's no doubt he can use them. His left ear curled and serrated, the misshape of a man who knows what it is to be hit. Beyond him a tiny white woman is clasping two small toffee-skinned children to her, watching us intently, clearly his partner, my guess being she's the one who prompted man-mountain to intervene. I smile quickly at her. She nods back at me, once, and I am thrilled by this show of sisterhood, thrilled that she sees me as one of her kind.

My rescuer steps up to Larry Silk and Trevor Nugent. "I suggest you two leave. Now, I think. Go on…" Larry Silk nods without a word, kneels down and picks up my bag, placing back the lipstick, eyeliner. Then pauses at the feet of my hero giant.

"Hey! Are you deaf or something? I said get out of here! Around now!" But still Larry kneels, and only now do I see what he's staring at. A bright yellow rectangle in his hand that he's plucked from the wooden decking. A Post-It note that fell from my bag. A Post-It note that reads:

DP WAS A COP SNITCH.

Larry Silk stares up at me. His eyes churning. "DP. Daisy Perkins?"

I try to conceal my horror, but my face has always betrayed me. From my expression, Larry Silk knows the note is true.

"How…" he stammers, mouth gaping, fishlike. "How do you know? How do *you* know?"

I grab my handbag and run, away along the hot decking to the hot concrete and the hot grass, and I do not stop running until I reach the station. A train is coming high above the simmering streets, and I get on without knowing which direction it's going and I end up in the Underground station at Bank, chest heaving, heart splitting.

DP WAS A COP SNITCH.

I sit in the tinny heat of the platform staring at the curved tiles of the wall opposite as trains come and go, thousands of gasping Londoners busying back and forth from the carriages, seven million faces, all the loved and unloved who ignore the hyperventilating transsexual in the damp blue dress who might have just signed the death warrants of a small boy and the man she's trying to bring back to happiness.

DP WAS A COP SNITCH.

A train approaches, charging slower, implacable anger, furious passengers jostling for the best place by the doors, and as the outgoers bash through the clambering ongoers, I see a vision in flashes between the surging bodies.

A man, lying on concrete, legs tucked up to his chest, elbows joined above his face in some symbol of defiance. As he twists and turns I glimpse injuries, and between his jerking forearms I see in his face a disarray of blood and skin and tissue. He howls in agony as another blow comes down, a shadow above him, punching and kicking as the man rolls onto his stomach. And the punching man turns to me, mouth twisted in rage. It's Jay Munnelly. I close my eyes as the crunch of bone and skin echoes through my head.

When I look up, the train is gone, platform empty, the pale tiled wall facing me blankly. A chattering family with multicoloured backpacks take their place behind the yellow line, excitedly scanning the dot-matrix display for signs of the next train to Woolwich Arsenal.

I am breathless, head throbbing. The clarity of sight and sound, the colours, the gasps from the cowering man that sounded like furniture buckling, the grunts from Munnelly as he punched and kicked like an animal killing animal, these things were real, and true. This was no invention or imagining, but something that I have seen. I was there when Jay Munnelly beat a man, maybe to death.

Was I?

* * *

Julius hears them return shortly after 9 p.m. Listens to Awa Yasin exhale heavily as she lumbers a sleeping Arnold up the steps of number 40, and tries not to jangle the keys whilst unlocking the front door.

Hears her footsteps on the staircase, her grunt as she deposits the boy in his bed, the soft click as she closes the door to his bedroom. Then silence. He does not hear Awa walk back down the stairs, nor go into the spare bedroom. He wonders whether she could have fallen asleep right there on the staircase.

He waits and waits, but still hears nothing. He starts to worry, perhaps something has happened to her, has she fallen like Daisy and expired there on the landing? Panic seizes Julius, his palms and back suddenly wet, and he has to stand upright, because he is feeling dizzy.

Then he hears footsteps, padding slowly down the stairs to the bathroom. Steadies himself, heavy with relief. Listens as the shower powers on.

Julius lies down on his bedroom floor and stares at the damp patch on his ceiling. His breathing returns to normal. He closes his eyes.

The doorbell wakes him. He peeks out through the curtains. Now she is standing at the top of his steps, hand outstretched to the bell. Something in her hand. It must be the DNA results, thinks Julius.

Again she rings the doorbell. Julius waits, frozen behind the curtain. The small Somali woman hesitates, then pushes the envelope through the letterbox.

It takes Julius thirty-seven minutes to pluck up the courage to read the note.

No news, I'm afraid. The results didn't arrive. I called them and the lab is chasing it. They say we'll definitely have them tomorrow, Saturday. Ironic, considering it's his birthday.

Anyway, Larry wants to take him to the Science Museum tomorrow for a birthday treat, some Star Trek exhibit. I said only if you could come too. Will you come? Please? I'm next door all evening. Best wishes, Awa.

Julius takes his iPod from his workbag, the headphones from his amplifier, and climbs back up the stairs to his bedroom. He lies down on the bed, listening to Bach's Violin Concerto number 2. But still he cannot sleep.

17

Larry Silk unlocks the door to his office with a scowl at his reflection in the glass. The keys slip from his trembling fingers to the ground – he curses loudly, but even this expletive does not seem to raise his spirits. White hair vanishes for a moment as he bends to pick up the fob. At a glance you wouldn't know he was in his late fifties, so lean and mean appears his frame in the dark jeans and dark suit jacket. Gaunt and rough-faced, he enters the door to First Financial Services. Angry beeps of alarm being deactivated. Stomping up stairs. Then silence.

Only the gentle sizzle of fresh black asphalt in the midday sun. Another heat record will be broken today.

Maybe you think I should not be watching Larry Silk. Maybe you think that instead I should be intensifying my search for someone for Julius, because he'll be useless on his own if it turns out by some small miracle that he is the father of the boy.

But you're wrong. There's nothing more vital than what I'm doing right now, perched on the window sill in my suite on the thirteenth floor of the Britannia International Hotel, high above Marsh Wall, pair of binoculars trained on the windows of First Financial Services a couple of hundred yards away down the road.

And this is why. When Larry Silk saw the Post-It on the ground at Thames Barrier Park, he was shocked. His pupils dilated, his mouth gaped, he started to sweat, and Larry Silk is no sweater.

DP WAS A COP SNITCH. His face said it all – Larry Silk had no idea that Daisy Perkins was informing to the police. Which means he did not kill her.

Finally the vodka kicks in. And the mazzy. No need to tut, Dr Fitzgerald, this is the endgame. Purity will be forged through fire. There is no other way.

I see no movement behind the blinds of Larry Silk's office. I am sure Larry is slumped at his desk, unable to pick up the phone. I think most likely he is feeling like me – he doesn't know exactly who killed Daisy Perkins, but he's pretty sure Jay Munnelly had something to do with it.

Knock back another Stoli, ice-cold. Air conditioning gives me a buzz. Pour another, drink another, close my eyes, feel my heart begin to swell, open my eyes and he's sitting there, in the purple armchair by the TV cabinet.

"Cin cin, Kevin."

"It's Felicity now, Dad, you know that."

Smiles, teasing. "Flippety Felicity. Suits you, doll."

Fingers twitching against the arm of the chair. Smoker's habit. Yellowing fingernails, teeth. I still weaken when an old-school Lambert & Butler addict passes me on the bus, the wet acridity clinging to thick wool that whispers to me of home. He brushes a hand through thinning grey hair, yellow streaks even there.

This is how my father appears to me. In the body and face he possessed six months before the cancer sucked him brittle. Back when he could still laugh without rattling.

"So, Flippety, whatcha got?" When the stomach hurt, he hid it behind bad American accents based on his favourite actors of the 1970s – McQueen, Newman, Hackman.

"Okay, Dad, we've got Larry Silk sitting on dynamite."

"Yup. He's tumbled onto an angry little secret, you're not wrong there, love."

"So what does he do? Tell Jay or not tell Jay?"

"Tough decision."

"Arnold's in danger whichever way we spin it. Either Jay Munnelly didn't know Daisy was a police snitch – in which case it's unlikely he had her killed…"

"But Munnelly won't want the monkeys knowing that he didn't know…" My father nods, the thin folds of skin at his neck expanding and contracting, up and down. "His instinct will be to lash out, put someone's head on a stick. Fatal for him if he doesn't, can't have the pack seeing you as a fairy hand."

"So he kills the boy. But if Jay was the one who had Daisy taken out because someone tipped him that she was working for the police, and now Larry tells Jay he's discovered this too, Jay will think that others also know – no way they wouldn't," I continue, working it through. "And if others know, and know how Daisy was dispatched…"

"They pushed her down, she cracked her nut?" Dad shakes his head. "What sort of cupcake move was that?"

"Jay risks being a laughing stock."

"And I'll tell you this, Felicity. Jay Munnelly does not like being a laughing stock. He'll slash and burn, send out the message: 'I'm not in the game, I am the game!'"

"They'll go after the boy, won't they, Dad? They'll go after Arnold Perkins."

I wait for my father's reply, but the purple chair is empty. Nothing but a ringing in my ears. My power to raise the dead only lasts so long.

Don't worry. I don't need my old man to tell me what I already know. That Jay Munnelly kills kids. It's perfect PR for a man like him, in his business. Murder Arnold Perkins and the fanged bastards who want your crown will think twice about messing with you. It's been done before, don't think it hasn't. Life is cheap when money sings. Don't forget I grew up out here, out east.

Pour more fizz into the vodka, slam it back. But my hand is steady, don't bet against me, there's "functioning" and there's a low-down pro, and you know I'm the woman with the trophies to prove it.

Arnold has one chance. Everything comes down to DNA – 99.5% match of allele number values or above. The pronouncement of the Gods.

If Larry is Arnold's father, the boy could be safe. Silk might be able to call off Munnelly, depending on how much Jay needs him to keep the money-laundering going. My bet is Larry has been very careful not to share the intricacies of his book-rigging scams: I'd be surprised if he's even written any of it down – what he knows keeps him rich and alive, which are both good things to be. If Arnold Perkins turns out to be his son, I think Larry will plead for clemency and get it.

But if Julius is Arnold Perkins's father, the bottom falls out of the bucket. Maybe Larry might stretch himself, beg for the boy's life. But he'll let Julius take a bullet, I'm certain. Because Larry is on the edge of a rough saw, he wants the boy as his own and will not feel charitable if he's denied such a deep-rent desire.

Let's face it, men don't exactly have a good track record when their children are taken from them, when their hearts are beaten into the ground. You don't catch a mother gunning down her own in the arms of a weeping father, then massacring his entire family before turning the shotgun on herself. You don't find a mother gassing herself in the family car with her little ones reading comics in the backseat. Bloody retribution for heartache inflicted is a male preserve. I think Larry Silk might even enjoy it, the smell of the trigger, the silence that follows. After all, he's been around the real hard men for years, feeling their grins, their winks, their playful threats and frequent snarls just to scare the bookkeeper.

DCI Eddie Knowles cannot help us. He's retired, the desk clerk told me, moved to Spain. Feet up by the pool. Maybe Daisy's death was the last straw. So if Julius is the father, it's down to me to protect him. And I'll do whatever it takes.

* * *

The desk fan sends eddying dust songs through the shafts of late evening sun coming from the slats at the front window. Julius Miles sits in a pair of white pants and white vest. Red welts on his back from the heat. Sunburnt cheeks and nose. Big sore pasty of a face, baked by an afternoon's half-slumber in the deckchair. Ham hock shoulders boiled also, smouldered the tips of his ears. He tried cold teabags, even crushed cucumber, but none of his Uncle's old remedies seem to work on him.

The piles of leather-bound journals. He reads on. Through 2004 with a feeling of coolness in his belly that has nothing to do with the fan, as the days, the weeks, the months pass. Getting closer to October 2005, when Augustus Miles wrote his last word before walking across the park to be hit by a bus. What will that word be?

Through late summer and autumn 2004, through Olympic gold medals in Athens, floods in Cornwall, Fathers-for-Justice campaigners dressed as Batman...

Ironic, the choice of costume. As far as I know, Batman doesn't even have gonads, let alone offspring. The caped Eunuch who comes alive at night seems the very antithesis of warm fuzzy fatherhood...

On and on, past British hostages beheaded in Iraq, the opening of the Edinburgh parliament building, the fox-hunting ban and the Tsunami in Thailand... Julius dabs smarting shoulders with a wet cloth. For all his damp bulk, he feels sickeningly light reading his uncle's musings. Gus's snatches of history make Julius queasy, hand at his midriff. His uncle seems to delight in the disconnects, the randomness of everything. Julius feels unhitched from his mooring, the heavy vessel tossed by giant waves.

Yet still he reads on, into 2005. May has just four entries, each complaining about an ailment – nose, hip, earache, varicose vein in the right calf. June almost as sparse, and July boasting just three entries:

Worse and worse. Is the blackest hour before the dawn?
  Rewrote the will. Much clearer now.
  Bought Zispins online. Reaching up out of the hole. Pray they
kick in...

To Julius's surprise, his uncle does not mention London winning the Olympic bid, nor the terrorist attacks of 7th July, one of which took place barely two miles from his house on Hackney Road. He puts down the journal, looks up "Zispin" on his computer. An anti-depression drug. Julius reads a thread from people taking Zispin SolTabs. Scrolls down post after post that describe the calming influence of the drug, how it aids sleep, but also those who claim side effects – "fuzzy", "dopey", "putting on weight", "bouts of extreme anger"...

Tears well in his eyes. He sighs loudly and his voice seems to echo around the room, knocking against his uncle's most treasured objects, the armchairs, the books, the tea-coloured globe made in 1827 by S.S. Edkins of Blackfriars. Julius returns to the journals, finding one last entry in October:

Saturday 15th
Glass of 1984 Pol Roger. Takeaway from Tre-Viet. Egremont
apple. None as delicious as you'd think.
  All in order, as Nephew will discover. Hoping such structures
slice the sorrow, allow Him to focus on things that ease his heart
– his numbers, his charts, his rules.
  No note. Simply these missives.
  This week, I feel. One morning. When the sun shines...

Two days later, the sunny morning of 16th October 2005, Augustus Miles crossed the road in Hackney and was struck by the number 38 Routemaster double-decker bus. He died three hours later in the Royal London Hospital. It was a Monday, statistically the most popular day to commit suicide, according to a report from the Office for National Statistics published two months earlier. The figure that Julius recalls most vividly is that out of the 35,000 suicides recorded, 27,000 were men and only 8,000 women, making men almost three and a half times more likely to kill themselves.

* * *

I wake up on the floor. Half-light from Whitechapel Road dull at the distant window. Look up for the string of the alarm, but it's so high above, can't raise myself that far. Clock reads 3.15 a.m. Jerry will be asleep, won't thank me for buzzing him, can hear his voice now: "I'm a warden, Felicity, not a bloody dream-catcher! Go back to sleep!"

I've had them before, you see, the nightmares. Buzzed Jerry in his flat on the ground floor more than once, but we're supposed to contact him only for real emergencies. "Life-threatening real bloody emergencies!"

But this feels like a life-threatening real bloody emergency, Jerry. I'm shaking, nightgown soaked in sweat, sheets on the floor around me.

I saw Jay Munnelly again in my sleep. He was younger, maybe a decade or more, bright-eyed, shaven head, Ralph Lauren polo, shorts. Standing with an older man, bullet skull, scar joining one side of his chin to the other – a man I recognized from the newspaper reports, his uncle Declan Munnelly. A third man with them, he's so familiar, the dark hair, big hands, sweatshirt top and jeans. My father, Charlie. But it cannot be my father, because he's young, and ten years ago he was dead. My father keeps his head turned from me, but I know that stance, that bow of the legs as his weight shifts from one foot to the other.

Then Declan Munnelly is chasing me with a meat cleaver. I cannot escape. As the blade sweeps down into my skull, I wake.

* * *

Sun bangs the windscreens of the cars grinding into London on this steaming Thursday morning. Already a low haze across the industrial units and apartment blocks bordering the Olympic Park. Shining white tubes of the stadium like scorching DNA against the muddy blue sky.

I step back on the footbridge over the A12 dual carriageway to let an overweight older Caribbean man on a bicycle wind his way towards Victoria Park. He tips his cloth cap to me, sings "New day, new blessing, new hope!" as he passes. "Give yourself to the Lord this morn, pretty lady!"

I watch him go through the barriers at the end of the bridge and on down the street, still singing, still calling out to passers-by. Turn to look down at the grumbling traffic, the August grind for blank-eyed commuters dreaming of beaches and swimming pools in distant lands.

Glance at my watch. He said 10 a.m., but I'm getting there early. Check out the entrances, exits. I've Street-Viewed the surroundings, walked it on my laptop screen, but who knows what's changed since the little Google car swept by in 2007.

An angry siren from somewhere south towards the Blackwall Tunnel. An ambulance, not a "blues and twos", I can tell. Dab my forehead. I'm wearing a simple skirt, black, white T-shirt and light jacket zipped up.

Come down the ramp from the footbridge, heading along Crown Close, past Abrahams building supplies and the old Dudley Stationery building, its dull beige glass daubed with insolent white graffiti. The pointed façade of the former Victorian church, now the New Bethel Revival Ministry International, next door to EU Car Parts, piles of metal automotive entrails eviscerated beneath a grimy red window, darkened interior echoing to some cheerless pop song and the sound of hammer against chrome.

The old brick warehouses next door are now empty shells, windows smashed. Huge shipping containers, dark blue and fading ochre, stand in silent mourning, emblazoned with exotic words in

Dutch, German, Turkish, Arabic. Lorries rumble by full of earth or clay or some godless mineral dug from the bowels of London to welcome thrusting concrete and steel girders. As if the very core of the East End is churning.

The gates are green and rusted as he said they would be. Beyond, large digging equipment or cranes or some such mechanized creatures are wheezing hotly as they chew at piles of rubble and twisted metal.

9.47 a.m. Just another day in the dust bowl of the Fish Island Redevelopment Zone, a blink from the Olympic Stadium. I push on the gates, shoulder lowered. They swing open with a grieving howl.

No one approaches. I wait by the brick building to the left, half-demolished, only the ground floor remaining. One door still extant, one window not smashed. An office of sorts, with a chair standing jauntily in the entrance. Glimmer of a kettle behind the glass. Page-three girl stuck at an angle to the back of the door, legs spread in her bikini bottoms, breasts dangling like hanging fruit.

As my watch beeps ten, a figure appears from the rubble soot beyond, like an angel or devil striding through the mists of time. The man is small, hunched almost, shuffling towards me in a grey boiler suit and hard-hat.

He nods once, walks past me without a word, past the page-three girl and into the darkness. I follow.

Inside the makeshift kitchen, the stench of urine and Cup-a-Soup. Boaz, the only name I have for my contact, whom I found after a long series of text messages from pay-as-you-go mobiles around East London, takes off his hat, scratches his thick hair wildly, spits into the rusted sink. His face is younger than his stance, maybe early twenties. Lips cracked by drug use. It's beginning to dawn on me that he's not going to speak, perhaps for fear of being taped.

I hand him the envelope from the tote bag. He counts the fifty-pound notes and nods. I follow the direction of his head, he seems to be indicating the first of the shipping containers. A quick motion of his hand, miming "look behind it". I nod. Then he's gone.

It's well rehearsed; every single one of his gestures is ambivalent, any defence solicitor worth a punt could give a dozen interpretations to his body language, even if hidden surveillance footage recorded our entire mute exchange.

I wait until Boaz is embraced by the heat and the dust once more, then step up to the container. Touch the peeling roasting metal. It stings like a snake bite.

A narrow gap along the side of the container, waist-high weeds wilting in the shadow. I peek along the line between the rippled container and the old brick wall. Six feet away, among the nettles and buddleia stems is a crumpled plastic bag. I step into the narrow gap, put on my water-resistant gloves and pick it up.

The bag is heavy. Inside, dark smooth metal. I look over my shoulder, up at the wall, but there's no one, no cameras, no glint of telescope or binoculars. I lift the object from the bag, weigh it in my hand. The casing is scratched, the handle chipped a little, but that's to be expected, given it was used until recently by some British soldier in Afghanistan. I pop out the empty clip, clear it, making sure the chamber's empty. Flick the safety forward, pull the slider back, clicking the safety in the second notch, pushing the small raised knob on the right-hand side of the casing, releasing the slide lock. Pull the slide forward, take out the barrel spring. Check the barrel – it's dull, well maintained. I reassemble the gun, place it in the plastic bag, scrunch the bag deep in my tote.

I'll pick up ammunition later. If I'm stopped by the police and they find the gun on me, it won't be loaded. I'll get six years instead of the twelve for carrying a loaded weapon.

I walk away into the haze of car fumes and heat, ready for the end.

18

Happy birthday, Arnold Gerald Shawcross. Four years old. Forty-eight months. One thousand four hundred and sixty days.

How many of them do you remember? Do you remember your mother taking you swimming for the first time in the crisp blue water of London Fields Lido? Do you remember holding her hand on the stuffy airplane to Corsica? Do you remember winning the egg-and-spoon race at the Woodstock Road Primary School sports day? Do you remember seeing your mother dead on the tiled floor? Do you remember the first time you laughed for Julius from next door, and he felt that if he had achieved something great?

I don't trust memories. People recall moments as if recalling facts. To my mind, memories are merely stories we prefer to other stories, stories that we constantly edit and re-edit like obsessive film directors, adjusting and revising the meaning as the years go by until the film bears no resemblance to the narrative we thought we were telling when we started.

Over time we craft our memories into armour, plate by plate, until they form an impenetrable, ever so comfortable coat. Hard as flint, clear as ice, but these recollections are not based on any objective truth.

If pushed, I suppose I could tell you my first memory. Vague shadows and light, brisk movement, a woman whom I choose to believe is my mother standing over me. Soft velvet of her skirt against my cheek.

I was two when she died. Hit by a drunk driver on a pedestrian crossing. A straightforward story, the policemen didn't have to say anything – my father saw their sunken shoulders and knew the words that were stumbling unspoken through their heads. For the rest of his life on dark evenings he winced at the sound of a revved car engine, even as he neared his own death and his hearing faltered.

If I were Julius, I would wrap Arnold's plastic space station in many pieces of brown paper so that he would laugh as he ripped off each layer in a frenzy of anticipation. I'd take photograph after photograph of the boy's smiling face, print them out and place them in picture frames to line every wall of my house.

Each birthday my old man bought me sports equipment. Metal goalposts or a trampoline or swing-ball set, praying I would run around like boys do. And I would smile and hug him so that his eyes would not fall. I tried, kicking the football at him as he stood in goal in Hendon-issue tracksuit, legs askance, arms flapping like a demented crane. "Come on, Kev, crack one in! Give it a good punt!" – and then "Good one, Kev, nice try!" as I booted the ball yet again into the flower beds.

7.15 a.m. Saturday 21st August. Julius sits downstairs in his uncle's antique armchair already dressed in a sports jacket and blue tie. Arnold's wrapped birthday present on his lap. Train ticket to Warwick in his wallet. Directions to the International Mathematics Olympiad printed out from the British Mathematical Society's website. Twice.

He listens to the clock tick effortlessly on the mantel. Julius's vast face as unmoving as a chalk cliff – except for the blinking, which increases as the minutes pass by. Outside, a fog lies heavy and thick on the street. Unseasonable, unexpected. A cold damp day at the end of summer.

Julius stares out at the thick mist, wondering if it has been born from his own swirling mind. At 7.30 a.m. he gets up, goes to the computer, finds a telephone number. Takes his mobile from his coat pocket and dials. He is not surprised to get an answering machine.

He leaves a short and polite message for the organizers. Then calls Jon Dunkerman. After the beep he leaves another message:

"Hello, Jon, it's Julius, sorry to call so early, but I wanted to let you know I've decided to pull out of the Maths Olympiad this afternoon. I know it's short notice, but you're first reserve – they really need you, Jon, to give the team a chance of winning. Hope you can make it up to Warwick in time. Sorry again for calling before eight. Over and out…"

Quickly hauls himself up the stairs, Arnold's gift under one arm. Rings the bell next door, standing wrapped in fog like an ancient prophet. Awa Yasin appears, dressing gown tight about her. Arnold peers around her side, soft pink towelling tickling his nose, more interested in the heavy mist that obscures even the red and blue doors across the street, caressing the roofs of the cars like fingers. Awa glances at Julius's jacket and tie and just about manages to hide a smile.

"Hi."

"Happy birthday, Arnold," Julius declares, thrusting the large gift towards the boy. Who eyes the package warily.

"What is it?"

"Arnold, don't be rude…" begins Awa, tightening the belt of her dressing gown as Julius's eyes inadvertently lower.

"It's a space station," says Julius, mustering enthusiasm. "It's like a space rocket, but people live in it."

"Why do they live in it?" asks Arnold. Before Julius can answer, the boy continues: "Are their mummies dead, so they have to find somewhere to live for themselves?"

Awa's hand darts to the boy's shoulder. Julius kneels down and nods, once. "Some of them have no mummies, so they have to live on the space station. Others choose to live there simply because it's fun. You can decide which people are which. There are five figurines in the box. They come from many different cultures."

Arnold thinks for a moment, then smiles. "It's my birthday breakfast. It's like tea, but it's breakfast. Would you like some cake?"

Julius glances at the Somali woman. Awa shrugs, jerks her thumb towards the stairs. "Come on down. It's Arnold's day…"

* * *

Julius sits opposite Arnold at the table in the kitchen of number 40 Woodstock Road. The boy does not look up, ladling Coco Pops into his mouth with impressive speed if not dexterity. At one point he takes his right index finger and inserts it carefully into the bowl, stirring the chocolate cereal slowly round and round as if conducting an important experiment into wave function. He glances up once to see Julius watching him, but does not stop. Julius wonders if this is a challenge to his authority, a test.

"Arnold, shouldn't you be eating that, not playing with it?"

Awa Yasin passes behind Julius, positioning a large cup of coffee and a slice of chocolate birthday cake in front of him. Speaking to the boy, as if to herself: "It's okay, Arnie. It's your birthday, you can stir them with your toes if you want…" Arnold chuckles to himself, clearly contemplating the idea, then stops stirring the Choco Pops with his finger and devours the rest without delay.

Mohammad Yasin watches Julius and the boy from the armchair by the French doors. Has not touched the coffee his daughter placed on the low table. Julius feels nervous under the older man's oblique gaze. Wonders if Awa's father sleeps here, or whether he dressed in the brown suit and pale shirt and came, like Julius, purely for this little breakfast party.

Behind the older man, the strange summer fog hangs low from the trees, obliterating the tower blocks beyond. A grey hesitation, an exhaled sigh, held in the air for ever. Two men, a woman and a boy, lost in thought and cake.

"Your daughter is amazing," Julius stammers at last, unable to bear the silence. "Keeping everything going after all that's happened…" Mohammad Yasin shrugs. His words sharp stabs. "She works hard. Like her father."

250

Julius sips coffee, bites cake. "So, you're retired, Mr Yasin?" The older man nods, the flat fog light reflected off the dome of his bald head. Julius finds himself nodding in accompaniment. "Do you ever think of going back to Somalia?"

Mohammad Yasin glares narrowly. "I am a British citizen. A pensioner of the state. Why should I go anywhere else?"

The blood surges from Julius's chest to his neck. Ears tinged red. "I'm sorry," he stammers. "Of course I didn't mean…"

A chair scrapes back suddenly, Arnold taking his plate of chocolate cake, walking over to the television and pressing the "On" button. Screen gulps into life, the one true being. Cartoons blare.

Awa puts her hand on Julius's shoulder and he feels the heat of her palm. Wants her fingers to stay there. He glances from Mohammad Yasin to the boy spooning cake into his gaping mouth, eyes fixed on the pink blobs on the television screen. Suddenly Julius has a burning urge to leave.

"He's not mine," he mutters quietly, even in the speaking of it knowing how childish he sounds.

"You don't know that," Awa counters, and her hand is gone. Then, as if regretting the gesture, she adds: "At the very worst, you'll still see him, he'll still be your next-door neighbour…"

But the big awkward man is already moving up the stairs, boards creaking, banister groaning as he lumbers forwards out of the house. Julius pauses for a moment on the front steps, suddenly oppressed by the thick fog ebbing along the street, enveloping everything in its path until nothing is defined, nothing is solid and nothing makes sense.

Julius hears a noise behind him. Awa is there, standing behind him. She looks up at him and, without a word, puts her arms around his chest. His arm jerks upwards towards his chin, but she stands on tiptoes, leaning back her head, and kisses him.

Across the street I turn away. Those are not tears in my eyes.

"Is he your boyfriend?"

Awa whirls round: Arnold is leaning against the banister, his expression neither inquisitive nor accusing. The Somali woman blinks for a moment, startled hazel, then moves past Arnold and away down the stairs.

The man and the boy regard each other for a moment. Then Arnold says, "Thanks for the space station. It's cool."

"So you're going to the Science Museum?" Julius mumbles, heart a tornado racing.

Arnold nods his head, solemnly. "I don't like Star Trek. Do you?"

"Not really. Too many characters, too many planets…"

The small boy smiles. And in that smile, Julius feels compassion and understanding and some strange yearning he does not understand but owns nonetheless. Feels it like an electric shock. He reaches down, takes the pair of small red Wellington boots from the floor, a green coat, picks up Arnold in his arms and carries him quickly from the house, the boy's small bare feet knocking Julius's giant thighs, once, twice, three times, four, as they descend the steps at speed.

* * *

"This is my house," whispers Julius when they reach the living room below street level. "I mean, it was my uncle's, but now it's mine. What do you think?"

Arnold scratches his head. Gazes around the lower ground floor, analysing chair to chair, past the lion's claws carved into the rosewood table to the tall Chinese vases lining the marble fireplace. Peers up at the leather spines of the books on the teak shelves.

"It's dark," he offers hesitantly, clearly not wanting to offend. "Do you have any games?"

Julius does not turn on the light. He does not want anyone to know where they are. There's a knock at his door, short, sharp, Awa's voice calling, edging towards panic. Arnold glances up at

Julius, but the big man continues to rifle through the top of the kitchen cupboard looking for the old box of draughts Gus used to pull down on wet Sundays.

"It's the world's most perfect game, Arnold, do you know they found a board in Ur in Iraq dating from 3000 BC..."

A crash behind him. Julius whirls round. Sees the boy's face as a stricken map of fear and guilt. The tall vase in front of him smashed to pieces on the stone hearth. Julius stares at the broken fragments.

Yet feels no anger. No grief. No disappointment. Only a fierce desire to make the quaking boy feel better.

"It's okay, Arnold. It was an accident. Just a bit of pottery. I'll clean it up later."

Kneels down beside the child, concerned for bare pale feet amidst the shards of Chinese porcelain. "How about we put on your wellies and go somewhere special? A treat? My treat..."

Eyes peek back through thin fingers. Julius smiles. "Shall I carry you again?"

*　*　*

He does not put the boy down until they are three streets into the fog, standing next to a dark VW Golf, new and glistening. Taps and double-clicks on his phone screen, extracts a small card from his pocket, holds it to the windscreen of the car. The doors snap open.

"What's that?" Arnold asks, gesturing at the card.

"My magic key," chuckles Julius, holding open the back passenger door.

"I don't have my car seat."

"Oh." Julius rubs his chin, eyes creased. "It's okay. The special place isn't far. Just across the river."

"The River Thames?"

"Yes, that's right, clever-clogs. The River Thames."

Julius helps Arnold into the adult seat belt, fumbles with the keys in the ignition, shoves the gearstick into first, slams his foot on the accelerator and the car tears off down the street towards the Roman Road.

I watch him go. My fingers clenched.

19

The postman does not recall such a summer's day in his ten years in London, dabbing his forehead to clear tiny water droplets from the thick eyebrows his wife adores. I watch him take out the next bundle of mail, including a brown envelope with the logo I'm looking for. He stops at number 40, slips the letters through the box with a flick of his practised wrist.

I wait until he's completed Woodstock Road's deliveries, whistling happily as he rounds the corner. I clip on my name badge bearing the same logo as the envelope, ring the door to number 40. Wait. Ring again. She appears at last, headscarf bound tightly about her round face. She wears a long white blue-embroidered kameez and tight jeans. No shoes.

"Hello," I say brightly. "I'm from Leeds DNA Testing Labs, we're really sorry about the delay in getting you the results you ordered. As the company's London rep, head office asked me to check that you've definitely received the letter today."

"Oh. Yes, it came in the post just now as a matter of fact." She nods, cheerfully. I don't want her to be the one. Try to quell the anger boiling in my gut.

"That's marvellous, once again we apologize for the delay..."

"It's okay," she smiles, starting to close the door. "All's well that ends well, hey..." I put my hand on the door frame.

"It must have made Mr Silk's day, finding out he's the father..."

She looks at me, frowns. "He's not the father."

I gulp in air. "Julius is the boy's dad?"

Awa Yasin stares at me. "Sorry?"

"Julius Miles is Arnold's father?"

She tries to shut the door, but I tug the handle, ripping it open, sudden panic surging through my exhilaration. "Have you told Larry Silk? Does he know yet?"

"What? Who are you?"

"Tell me! Does he know? Does Larry Silk know?"

I need to scare her. I grip her arm, pulling her to me. She's about to cry for help, so I slam my palm against her mouth – she's a quivering fawn against my body. "Simple question, Awa. Does Larry know?"

The young woman nods, terrified. I release her, she spins away, running down the hallway towards her advancing father. But I am gone, long gone, down the steps, down the street, and on fast, running to my scooter parked just round the corner.

* * *

"Ladies and gentlemen, you're standing at the centre of time and space. This line is zero degrees longitude. It is 'nothing'! Literally nothing! You have come all this way to see 'nothing'!" The assorted tourists from around the world laugh, politely, in the mist. "Longitude is an imaginary line that runs from the North Pole and runs down the earth to the South Pole. There are 360 of these lines that help us calculate exactly where we are upon the earth. Sometimes, I think knowing where you are is more important than knowing where you're going!"

Julius half-listens to the actor in seventeenth-century costume, massaging his shoulder that aches from carrying Arnold up the steep hill in Greenwich Park. Arnold gazes at the large red ball on top of the brick-and-stucco house within the gates of the Royal Observatory. No one gives the boy in Spiderman pyjamas and red Wellington boots a second glance. Everyone is too busy talking excitedly in the unseasonal fog, taking pictures of each other stand-ing on the metal meridian line that bisects the ancient cobblestones.

Arnold tugs Julius's hand. "What's that big red apple?"

"It's not an apple. It's a ball. Every day at one o'clock it drops down. In olden days ships in the docks on the Thames down there used to set their clocks by it before setting off to sea. At least when the fog lifted."

Arnold gazes up again at the red ball, waiting for it to drop even though it is only mid-morning. Julius turns, looking out at the miraculous August fog that has turned London into a dreamscape of low white cloud, punctured in places by magical towers and skyscrapers. He glances at the boy, uncertain for the first time. Has he committed a crime? If Arnold is not his son, is this kidnap?

Arnold tugs his hand again, asks, "Can I have an ice cream?"

"Now? It's so chilly…" But Julius takes the boy's hand, marvelling at the hot small heat in his cold clammy grasp, leads him carefully up the cobbled steps to the car park at the top of the hill and the ice-cream van that waits forlornly, disappearing and reappearing in the fog…

My eyes never leave Julius and the boy. I walk around them, concentric circles, thirty feet, twenty feet, thirty feet, twenty feet, a protective ring that cannot be broken. Scanning every face loom-ing out of the mist for the vengeful glare of Larry Silk. Reassuring myself with the hard weight of the gun in the bag over my shoulder. Loaded, this time.

Circles and lines, circles and lines. That's what we are, isn't it, just circles and lines. I stand either side of the meridian that pierces the hillside. One foot in the west, one in the east. Thinking, this is how I've always been - part of me going one way, part going the other. In a fog of my own self.

Arnold finishes his ice cream. Julius ruffles his hair. They get into the Golf. I walk back to the scooter borrowed from my neighbour, pizza delivery man Santos, put on the open-face helmet. But as I pull out from the car park to follow Julius, a car cuts in front of me. The man at the wheel is shouting into a mobile phone held tight to his right ear. The man is Larry Silk.

* * *

Cars backed up in the fog. Distant sirens – police or ambulance. The approach to the Blackwall Tunnel like a graveyard of steel and puffing exhausts in the mist. Windscreen wipers sweeping moisture from the glass, heaters on in summer. The world upside down.

I weave between the ghostly cars, headlight full, finger on the klaxon. Pass by on Larry Silk's passenger side, glancing across at the man in the driver's seat. Silk is silent now, staring straight ahead, body hunched. He doesn't even twitch as I pull ahead of him, swinging in behind the Golf, left-hand bumper, where Julius cannot see me.

Julius's head is so high it brushes the roof of the car. I cannot see the boy, he's hidden by the seat. But I can make out their voices. The man and the boy are singing together.

The Golf's indicator starts to blink, Julius trying to turn off the gridlocked road. A few cars later a white van lets the Golf slip onto the side road by the industrial plant. I turn off too. Glancing in my mirror, I notice the black BMW do the same.

We follow Julius along the back streets under the A102, and on east still. Finally we arrive at the Woolwich ferry terminal, only to find another fog-bound traffic jam. I sit two cars back from the Golf, Larry Silk two cars back from me. Silk doesn't seem suspicious of the scooter in front of him – plenty of other drivers have tried the same alternative route to get across the Thames on this heavy twisted morning.

And then we are on the crammed ferry crossing the slow brown river, Julius helping Arnold from the back seat of the Golf, lifting him up to look over the side of the boat. Pointing out the steel teeth of the Thames Barrier and the yawning Dome through the billowing whiteness. But my eyes never leave Larry Silk in his BMW. Heart thumping, knees weak, hand on the cold metal in my bag.

The ferry lets out a long mournful horn, slowing into dock at North Woolwich. Julius and Arnold head back into the car, Larry Silk watching them as I watch Larry Silk.

When we drive off the ferry, I pull back to allow Larry Silk to pass me, before slipping in, two vehicles behind. Ahead in the line of cars, Julius hesitates, uncertain in the white-out, west or east? He turns right, but soon seems puzzled, even though he's following the main road – and fifteen minutes later he's heading anti-clockwise on the North Circular, and he knows he's lost and he turns off onto a small side road, business-park offices looming out of the mist like abattoirs.

Three vehicles driving alone on this forgotten road. The Golf, the BMW and the scooter. As Julius slows, nearing the small bridge across Barking Creek, I pull back for fear that one of them will recognize me. Perhaps Larry is also worried he might be spotted, because at this moment I see the BMW accelerate and try to over- take the Golf, just before the bridge.

But the gap is too small. Larry Silk realizes at the last moment, furiously pumps his brakes – once, twice – hands spinning around the driving wheel as he tries to correct, but the nose of the BMW thumps the back bumper of the Golf, knocking it sideways – left, left, left – until Julius's car smashes hard into the low brick wall and railings overlooking the creek, and is enveloped by the arms of the fog.

20

"It's funny. They all want to protect us – don't they, Arnold? But they can't… It's not their fault. It's just the way people are. We're fragile, and it frightens us."

Blood runs from the gash on Julius's temple. He speaks with impressive clarity for a man who's pinned to his seat by an obese white airbag.

"That's why we create management teams, by-laws, planning applications, speed limits, education league tables, carbon footprints, multiple traffic-light food labelling, mid-quarter orthopaedic-surgery analyses… We need order, we need structure, but there isn't any really, is there, Arnold? It's all out of our control."

No reply from the back seat. Julius strains to see the boy, but the driver's mirror is bent at an absurd angle, reflecting the roof of the car. The side mirrors are gone, just twisted fists of wires. Whispers of creek mist curling through the gaping holes of the windows, as if the car is floating high above the world.

"You see, Arnold, it just happened, with your mother," Julius continues, to keep the boy awake, to keep himself warm. "I didn't really know her, but I admired her from afar, though I never told her that. I wish I had known her better, because she was probably a great woman. You know, in the way Alexander was great, or the Barrier Reef, or the Chinese Wall is great. Your mother was a life force, no one could deny that however they felt about her. It seems absurd that she died so easily. That now she's just an empty space."

Silence in the car. Julius tries to quell rising panic. "Arnold, can you hear me? Please say something. Are you hurt?"

Suddenly there's ringing in Julius's vast ears, dull angry bells. He manages to raise his right hand to his left temple, feels something wet. Peers at the dark-red blood between his fingers.

"It doesn't add up, does it? None of it. That's why I like mathematics, Arnold, that's why I need numbers. Numbers are exact. Irrefutable. Safe. They protect me… With numbers you can see the patterns. The connections. Everything makes sense."

Only now does his voice start to crack. "I have always been a disappointment to myself, Arnold. We think we're the sum of our parts, but we're not. We don't add up. Like in mathematics, just because you want the numbers to connect, it doesn't mean they will – not if you've got the equation wrong."

Julius tries to unbuckle his seatbelt, so he can turn to see the boy. But he's stuck, held in place by the large white airbag and a shooting pain in his spine.

"Do you know what a happy number is, Arnold?" he continues, trying to keep calm. "It's a number where the iterated sums of the squares of the digits terminate at one. The sequence stops. The number reaches happiness. I think you're my happy number, Arnold. I've stopped making the same mistakes over and over. I've stopped with you."

Julius listens hard, but there is no sound, no movement from the back seat. He starts to shake, his words short, sharp, teeth chattering: "I think I would liked to have been your dad, Arnold…"

Sudden roar at his right side. Julius swivels, terrified, and a man is there in the fog, opening and closing his mouth, but no sound is coming out. Julius stares at the man for a long moment before he realizes it is Larry Silk.

Silk is pulling at the door, face wracked with exertion and anguish, eyes brimming with tears. Finally, the door swings open, Larry's hands thrust around Julius's lap, long thumb hooking beneath the seat belt, poking the red restraint release, and Julius spindles from the car like rope. He sprawls, arms to the ground, a rush of storm in his ears, suck of volume, and now he can make out Larry Silk shouting:

"Are you okay, Julius? Please say you're okay…"

"I'm okay!" Julius shouts back. Then cries out: "Where's Arnold?"

Larry Silk does not answer, picks up a brick, brings it round into the glass of the back-passenger door window. The window implodes gently, a spray of glass fragments that freeze a brief instant, a thousand jewels in the blank fog, before vanishing inside the car. Larry reaches in, flips up the child lock, jerks open the door.

Arnold looks up at him, terrified. Blood running from his small nose. A red welt bisecting his neck where the seatbelt gripped him for dear life.

Larry Silk plucks the quivering boy from the back seat. "I'm sorry, so sorry – I'm sorry, sorry, sorry…" he murmurs, lifting the boy down, passing him like a wounded animal into the massive cradle of Julius's arms. Arnold curls instinctively into a ball, and Julius holds him tight, kissing the boy's cold head.

"Here," says Larry Silk, offering Julius a handkerchief. "For his nose…"

Julius dabs at Arnold's nose, but the boy twists away, burying his head deeper into the big man's chest. Julius looks up at Larry Silk.

"Thank you," he says. Then a thought creases his forehead. "What are you doing here, Larry?"

21

I peer at the two men and the boy from the bushes thirty feet away by the bridge buttress, my scooter tucked behind a giant willow whose vast tendrils play among the swirling mists down to the dark creek mud.

Exhaling deeply. My prayers have been heard. I still hold some sway.

Closing my eyes in gratitude, I barely hear the car approach. A silver Mercedes S-500. It purrs to a stop less than ten feet from my hiding place. The front doors swish open, two men exit – a small one with rough short hair, wide shoulders and jacket over his T-shirt, and a tall one, white polo shirt, white jeans, white brogues. A slender angel in the shroud of this place.

As Jay Munnelly passes by, I see the Sig Sauer P226 tucked into the back of his trousers. He approaches Julius without a word, punches him hard in the face, drags Arnold Perkins from his grasp.

In my experience, violence is usually fast and unexpected. Men of violence know this, that they have to be faster and more prompt than the rest. Larry Silk barely has time to look up as Julius thuds backwards, hands full of blood.

Jay Munnelly grips the boy to him, turning sharply back towards the Mercedes, practised hand firm over Arnold's mouth. But he needn't bother – Arnold does not struggle. Rather he has gone limp in Jay's arms, arms and legs dangling like a puppet. Yet I know he's still alive, still breathing, because his dark eyes are wide and imploring, looking straight at me. I do not know how he sees me, concealed in the creek mist. I shrink smaller, slipping behind the willow trunk as Jay shoves Arnold in the back seat of the Mercedes, slamming shut the door and locking it.

Smaller Bull stands over Julius. Kicks the prostrated man hard in the ribs, for the sake of it. Julius groans, rolling over to protect himself, but Smaller Bull evidently considers his job done, because he takes a step back and does not kick again.

"Christ, Jay, no…" Larry Silk is stammering. "I didn't mean for you… Christ, Jay, no… Really?"

Jay Munnelly strides back to Larry Silk. "You better go, Larry…" Voice as flat and calm as his face. But Larry Silk does not go, still cowering. Jay barks, loud. "Go! Fuck off, now!"

Smaller Bull crouches by Julius, hand gripping large shoulder to pull him round. Larry goes to drag the enforcer away, trembling as he pleads, "Leave him, Rory, please. He's done nothing…" – but Rory brushes the accountant's hand from his shoulder as if it were a spider. Glances at his boss. Jay Munnelly shakes his head. "He's the father, Larr, that's why you called me, right? This lump screwed the snake, gave her what she wanted, her beautiful boy, right? Now I get what I want…"

"No!" Larry's voice louder, faltering. "You don't understand…"

"Hate snakes, Larry. Can't abide them. You know that, you of all. Cut off their heads, hang 'em up by their tails…"

"I know. I know that. The thing is…" Hands held out like a statue. "I'm your snake."

Jay Munnelly coughs, crooked mouth that could be amused or full of spite. "Say again?"

Larry takes a step forward, Rory moves quickly between them.

"It was me, Jay," says Larry, "I recruited Daisy for the Feds. I convinced her. She didn't want to. I blackmailed her…"

Jay Munnelly straightens, eyes fixed on Larry. "Okay," he says.

Larry continues, desperately: "She did coke, Daisy liked a snort, I took her to Jumpy one time, snapped a pic of her buying the stuff from him. Said I'd hand it over to Knowles, to SCG, the cops, said her boy would be taken into care. The fix was Eddie's idea…"

"Knowles? Eddie Knowles?"

"Yeah. He ran me. Chief snout wrangler."

"Eddie's gone, Larr. Cutting his bunions in Spain."

"I know. He moved me across is all, some CI called Montagu…"

Rory glances from Larry Silk to his boss and back again, eyes on Larry's hands. Somewhere high above, the mist glows bright, and for a moment the August sun burns a hole, as if in a dream. The cowering accountant nods before he speaks next, as if trying to emphasize the truth of what he is about to say.

"There's a king snake, Jay, you know it. There always is. This time it's me. I'm king snake. Three years. He had me, Jay, Knowlesey turned me over like a towel. Had his unit follow me, film the drop-offs, pick-ups, two weeks straight. Then put traced notes through the Hackney soap shop, I had the dust all over my car. CPS were saying twenty-five years minimum. At my age. You know they'd have got it…"

Larry's voice begging now. Jay Munnelly's half-smile remains, but the muscles are working hard to keep it in place. He exhales through his nose, wipes a hand across his stomach.

"Larry…"

"I'm king snake, Jay. I'm king snake." Larry Silk kneels down, crunch into the broken glass, but he seems not to feel anything. "The boy knows nothing. The father knows nothing. Let them go, Jay…" Bows in supplication, priest to his bishop. Suddenly older than his own skin. Jay gazing down at him, fingers closing and opening like jaws. Silk keeps talking, not to survive but as if to hear for himself the story of how he came to be kneeling in the dissipating brume by a forgotten road amidst the industrial estates on the other side of Barking Creek.

"I spoon-fed it all through the girl, through Daisy. Just enough to keep the cops interested, but not enough to really hurt us, hurt you. You have to believe me, Jay, I'd never hurt you. But then she saw more than she should have, read some papers that none should have seen. So I pulled the plug…"

Jay Munnelly laughs, hand to his mouth. "Don't believe you, Larr. Rory, do you believe this widget?" Rory smiles, shakes his head. Believes only his master. The one true Lord.

Larry Silk puts it simply: "I killed her, Jay. I killed Daisy Perkins. Murdered her in cold blood in her own hallway. To save you. To save myself." He is shaking now. "I killed the woman I loved."

Julius watches Larry Silk through swollen eyes, resting on his elbows in the gutter. Feels as if the world is spinning around this very place, he and these strange men the single core of existence in the fog. In the last few minutes he has come to believe that all surrounding this one fixed point is nothing but a great turning, faster and faster, matter being tossed up and beyond into the very furthest reaches of the cosmos.

In desperation Julius tries numbers, back and forth like ticker tape, numbers rushing through his head – what is the equation that has brought him to this point, what are the expressions between the equal sign, what are the unknowns the knowns are seeking to decide?

Thinks fast, thinks back to the night he shuddered against Daisy, her hands pressing his chest, back through college and Gwendolyn and his first kiss and back to the first time his uncle carried him from the car into the house on Woodstock Road, Gus's booming laugh that lifted him to the sky and back. And before even that to the moment of his own conception and his parents' conception in beds of old springs, damp mattresses, and their parents and their parents and their parents… the ripple of chance upon chance, the impossible maths, the never-ending Pi that proves the probability of what? Who? God?

Julius gathers all his might to pull himself up to fight, but slips down. Tries to speak, but his jaw is swollen tight. Locked into his bulk: arms and sinews and fat and bone rusted into lockdown. Only the tears of grief and terror welling in his eyes, rolling like words down his thick grey cheeks. Praying for the first time in his life that there might be a God to plead with, an eye behind the numbers. But hearing only the man's laughter that rolls through the vanishing fog like a drum.

"You killed the snake, Larr? You?"

"I loved her, Jay. Like no other."

"But you thought the boy was yours. You killed the woman you thought had pushed out your boy? Come about, Larr. Come about…"

Silk's head still dipped, small sobs, his voice barely audible beneath his tears: "I've always made wrong choices, Jay. Every choice I ever made was shit…"

"I don't believe you, Larr. You never killed nothing." Jay Munnelly steps up suddenly to the bowed man. "Make me believe you…"

Larry keeps sobbing, then lowers himself at Munnelly's feet, prostrating himself flat on the ground. Jay shakes his head violently: "Nah, clumpet, get up! Get up, you hear me? Silk? Get up!"

"Always wrong, Jay, my choices were always wrong…"

I screw tight my eyes. Hold the willow trunk against the sickness, rub my palms against the dark rough bark, scrape harder and harder so that I don't have to hear the gun being cocked and Larry Silk's whimper as the trigger is pulled and his brains spray onto the old damp bridge over the foggy mud.

Lids tight against the shouting man, against this bloody world of men who fight and curse – who break, not make. Concentrating, desperate to escape, to see the beautiful things in the dancing lights… and I am watching Julius Miles on the upper deck of the number 8 bus, May Day, fat orange sunlight warm across his wide face. His large flat hands laid across his knees that turn inwards as if trying to protect him, his dull eyes scanning first-floor living rooms and bedrooms and offices from the bus deck. I see his lips move as he calculates the probable average population density per square foot of every building along the Bethnal Green Road between the tube station and Weavers Fields.

See him smile at me as I grab the orange pole near his seat to press the red button, just as the bus judders to a stop for a passing cyclist. Remember my sudden complete surge of love for him, coupled with deep cold panic, the horrible dread that paralysed me because I imagined him hearing what I really was, who I was, this thing, this half-thing, this chimera. Or worse, him seeing the scars and the folds and the fat and the skin and trying to hide the repulsion he would feel at the very sight of me, this man-made monster, stammering as he made his excuses and dashed from me into the spring night.

I see my pathetic smile back at him as the bus pulls into the stop, see myself watching him from the bus stop as he gazes forward once more from his seat, counting the rooms and the people and the square footage until the bus is over the hill and no more.

It was that moment, at the bus stop, when I knew we had met for a reason – and that reason wasn't for me to love him, however much I craved it, but to save him from himself.

Sun warm suddenly on my back. Burning through the white veil. The shouting continues beyond my hiding place, men shouting as only men can. But if I do not move, if I do not open my eyes, nothing can happen to me – and I see Daisy Perkins now standing in her hallway, naked and flushed and scared, and I do not know why I am seeing her like this, as beautiful and vulnerable as a child. Then it becomes clear that the voice shouting at her is mine, it's my voice, my voice shouting at her like the men are shouting, and Daisy is trying to cover her naked body with her fluttering hands, and she reaches for a coat to cover herself, but a hand rips it from her, and the hand is my hand.

"He's Julius's son! You know he is, tart, you must know!" And Daisy is trying to shut the door, but my hand grasps the jamb, I'm strong, never been stronger, because despite my breasts and skirt and bra and blouse I was once a man with a man's snarl and grab.

"Why won't you tell him, tart? I knew the minute I saw the boy. *I* knew. Why won't you tell him the boy is his? He needs to know, tart! He needs to know!"

And now someone is writing circles in the air, circles and lines, circles and lines, and I see that it is Daisy Perkins, her long elegant fingers inscribing great wheels against the rays of morning sun as she topples backwards, naked in her long thin hallway, grabbing for the banisters, grabbing for me, grabbing to save her life, but grabbing at nothing. Her naked body a tilting flail of flesh. And then she is gone. Hard, straight down. The simple crack of her skull against the tiles.

She shrinks instantly, young Daisy, all life gone. The air still vibrating from her fall, but her skin is taut, veins grey, no pulse. Just the blood, a life force of its own now, spreading ever wider from beneath her porcelain cheeks. As I stare down at her still, unmoving body, small footsteps pad up the stairs and Arnold Perkins looks across his dead mother up into my disbelieving face.

I step back from the willow tree. Open my eyes. The mist is clearing. A seagull mewls from the creek bed. I open my bag, tossing it upside down. All my life falls out, my pills, hair clips, scarves, sweets, phones, gun. And many pieces of paper, simple sentences written on each. I scrabble in the dirt for them.

Julius likes almonds.
Boy wets his bed, who can blame him.
Find deodorant with less itch.
You killed Daisy.
And another: *You killed Daisy Perkins.*
And another. *You killed Daisy.*

Dr Fitzgerald sits back in his deep chair, tobacco fingertips joined to make a cathedral roof. "Anterograde amnesia may be drug-induced, Felicity. It can follow a traumatic brain injury or an acute event such as concussion, heart attack or an epileptic episode. Less commonly it can also be caused by shock..."

Jay Munnelly drags the prostrate man onto his knees. "Tell me different, tell me it wasn't and couldn't be you…"

Daisy Perkins lies in a pool of blood while her son stares up at me with uncomprehending eyes.

Larry Silk's head bowed, awaiting execution. Julius Miles trying desperately to get to his feet, murmuring, but Rory pushes him back down with his boot.

"Larr, why? Why are you king snake? Why you?"

Men are loyal creatures. They like it simple. Their games are straightforward, with rules and anti-rules, deeds and consequences. Us women play it differently, with abstraction. With us everything is fluid and nothing is the truth until it is, and the truth does not exist beyond what lies in the depth of our hearts.

As the mist seeps back down the banks to the creek from where it came and the sun begins to bake the damp concrete and brick of East London once more, a man approaches the four figures by the crashed car on the bridge. Average build, trousers, sweatshirt, baseball cap, trainers. A confident slouch.

Rory is the first to notice. Shocked, but not presumptuous enough to comment out of turn. Grunts at his master: "Jay…"

Munnelly turns, steps back. "Oh God," he grunts – or perhaps they are not words, but a sound escaping from somewhere dark inside him. Takes another step forward. Body tense, arms crossing his chest in defiance or protection. "No."

"You're going to let him go, Jay boy, you know you are. Cos you know he's lying." The voice is deep, strained, but measured. The man walks up to Jay, stops inches from him. Eyes bright, hands in trouser pockets. "Remember me?"

Jay shifts on his toes. Mouth a horizontal slit, fighting emotion. Muscles primed, a wholly dangerous instant.

But the man's voice continues evenly. "Hear what I'm saying, Jay. It wasn't the accountant. Maybe he wishes it was, who knows, but an accountant never killed anyone with his bare hands. Not anywhere, anytime."

Jay tilts his beautiful head, jaw clenched like a jewel. "Kevin," he says brutally. "Oh Kevin, Kev, Kev, Kev…"

I nod. Hand on the Browning in my pocket. The mist has cleared and now I can see. So much has been forgotten, lost in a whirlpool of hormones, booze, narcotics. The yearning I felt for Jay when I saw him talking with Larry Silk by the llamas, I believed it then to be a new passion, a breathless stab of instant infatuation. But lost in the mazzies and the vodka I was numb to the truth. That I had always loved him. God, how much had I loved him, that boy, that man, Jay Munnelly. Kevin's boyfriend of fifteen years. Jay Munnelly – the words that used to write silver in my morning sky.

We all remember, eventually. My connection to the Munnellys goes way back, into the pit of my old man's disgust. He loathed the Munnelly clan, called them scum, in public, to their faces. Despised the family's influence on his colleagues in the Metropolitan Police. They way they bought off coppers with cash and coercion.

It was Jay Munnelly's father my old man killed. A bullet in the back outside a club in Mile End. Independent Police Complaints Commission took two years to clear DI Charlie Hopkins. By which time he was finished, a cancerous drunk, the sarcoma just a symptom of the despair that had eaten away his very soul.

I see clearly now as I stand before Jay Munnelly. My vision of Jay joking with the man in the tracksuit, no wonder I never saw his face. Because the other man was not my old man, the other man was me. I desired punishment and abuse for what my father had done to his. But instead Jay took me in his arms and loved me.

My male voice gets stronger as I speak, as if a bad habit surging up at time of stress. "It was me, Jay. Kevin killed the snake. Kevin killed Daisy Perkins. He went to grill her, get out of her what she knew, but she was dumb, Jay, she was a loose dumb scud, she was going to blab to them just to hear the sound of her own voice."

I can be something I'm not. Done it for thirty-three years. I can fake anything I want, just see me weep and shudder. "I did it to protect you, Jay. The last thing I ever did for you."

I wait. He scratches the back of his neck. Reaches behind and pulls the Sig from his belt, points it at me. "Where have you been, Kevin? I couldn't find you. Not nowhere. I looked, of course I did. Where were you?"

"I missed you, Jay. Don't think I didn't. Let it be said, I'm full of regrets about it. But I had things I had to do. Didn't want to bring them anywhere near you; you're a man who understands time and place. Right? Am I right?"

Don't wait for a reply, the moment is now. There are many probabilities, but only one possibility. "The cops don't have it, Jay, they don't have what they need to finish you. I spoke to Eddie Knowles, sipped a latte with him at the Savile Row nick. He didn't have enough, said as much, in as many words. He didn't have shit." I point at Larry Silk, who is still on his knees staring up at me blankly. "The accountant's lying. He's no snake. Followed him myself, watched every cash, every carry. The cops weren't on to him. He's just trying to protect the boy. He loves the boy, you see, Jay, even though he's not his kin. He loves the boy. It's a complicated thing, I know, I don't expect you to understand it. But I understand it."

I reach out and tousle Jay Munnelly's hair, like I used to. He does not flinch. "You see, you have to let them go, Jay. I alone understand that. To save your soul. You have to. Save it, Jay."

Rory sniggers. I round on him. "Don't mock, Monaghan. You know what it is to love. You've loved him as long as I have." Rory's snigger catches in his throat. Hand to his ear, tugging. "Jay only works with those who love him. He has to. He has no choice."

I know Julius's eyes are on me. In this moment I feel so slight I think I might be about to float away through the soft rays of emerging sun, the final heat of summer. I realize now I was wrong to think it was love that I felt for Julius Miles. The truth is this. Real love is the one that breaks us. It happens but once in our lives. And my destruction took place long ago.

"Let it go, Jay. It changes. Everything changes, all things, every one of us. Nothing stays the same. That's what most men never get. Nothing stays the same." Jay's eyes boring into me. In the newborn sun the man in white seems as if he might ignite.

"Go back, Jay. Back to the beginning. You know where that is, you know who you are. Let the boy go, open the door and walk through it. I have freed you."

I start to step towards him, but instead feel the sudden hard steel of the Sig Sauer against my temple. Jay's knuckle blanched on the trigger.

I do not close my eyes. If he reaches out and feels my flesh, my breasts bound tight in bandages, he will know I am no longer male and he will shoot me dead. It's a simple sum. He cannot reach out. I cannot die. I am God.

He does not reach out. Does not even breathe. Lowers the gun, walks to the Mercedes, opens the door, lifts out the boy. "Leave the country, don't come back," he growls to Larry Silk. To Julius, nothing. He cannot, will not look at me.

Dutifully, Rory gets into the passenger seat and Jay revs the Mercedes loudly, swings it round in a jerking arc, speeding away into the now shimmering East End day.

I nod at Larry Silk, at Julius. Bend down and kiss Arnold's warm hair, whisper close to his small ear. "You are daddy's one true love. I thought I could find someone for him, but he found you. I have realized that he has never loved and will never love anyone or anything more than you."

Julius is staring up at me, and I smile. "He's yours, Julius Miles. The DNA is yours. You're the daddy now."

He watches me swing my bag of clothes behind me, get back on the scooter and putter away. Another hot August day. You'd never know the fog had even existed.

22

The City of London Cemetery contains more than half a million graves. Occasional tourist buses pull up at the Victorian Gothic entrance, groups of Swedes, Malaysians, South Africans wandering the grass-verged lanes in search of Mary Ann Nichols and Catherine Eddowes, two of Jack the Ripper's victims. Elsewhere, English fathers drag sons to see the grave of Sir Bobby Moore, England's 1966 World Cup winning captain. From time to time dignitaries and uniformed officers file through the section reserved for members of the Metropolitan Police who have fallen in the course of duty, past the flag pole, the roll of honour, the neatly inscribed names.

Apart from the chattering tourists and hushed groups of family members paying their respects and the odd rustle of birds and small animals in the florid undergrowth, the cemetery is suitably sleepy. A restful final resting place.

Even the solid concrete spaces of the Crematorium Memorial Garden feel tranquil, bees buzzing above the wall of small intimate black plaques. Each niche is lockable and contains enough room for at least two standard-sized urns, so that a couple can sit next to each other for ever in the tranquil darkness as they once sat next to each other every night in the BBC-illuminated darkness of their living room.

The ashes of Daisy Perkins sit alone in her niche, the plaque on the front bearing the simple inscription: *Daisy Perkins, much missed mother*. Every Sunday, Julius and Arnold come to the cemetery to place fresh white roses in the holder on the outside of the niche. Murmur a prayer to the dead woman, "We miss you, Mummy, we love you, Mummy." And Julius lifts up the boy so that he can kiss the plaque at the front of the niche. Arnold waving at his mum, eye to eye.

Then the big man carries the small boy on his shoulders towards the bicycle propped by the entrance and I watch Julius buckle the boy into the child seat, ping the bell once to make him laugh, and cycle away. It's the last time I will ever see them. It's been decided. Time to move on.

I wait until they're long gone before reaching up, plucking one of the white roses from the holder.

"Sorry," I declare to Daisy Perkins, and I mean it. "I did it for love."

I turn down a smaller path deeper into the cemetery and the forgotten corners of this two-hundred-acre site, where weeds and wild flowers dance unfettered by gardening shears and lawnmowers. Far beyond the clipped beech and holly hedges, by a low-slung ash tree under siege from long summer grass pitted with molehills and field-mice communes, is an unkempt grave. Dark headstone threatened by moss and snail slime. The inscription is ornate, but the lettering is already crumbling, the granite eroded by London's acid rain.

Sidney "Charlie" Hopkins,
Detective Sergeant, Metropolitan Police,
Born April 4th 1942,
Died April 17th 1989.
Duty and Honour above all.

I toss the white rose into the long grass that carpets the grave. Hands held tight to my simple yellow dress.

"Goodbye, Dad," I whisper. "Rest in peace."

23

The walkway to the plane smells of damp feet and hairspray. Rain hammering the glass, but no one cares, summer shirts and dresses and shorts impatiently waiting to board. He grips his boarding card like part of himself. Stares down at his shoes, shined many times in the hours before the taxi arrived.

Finds his seat easily. Aisle, not window, nearer to the loo. Arranges the magazines and laminated flight safety sheets. Rearranges them. Unbuttons his grey suit jacket. Feels inside his pocket, the slip of paper.

A receipt for winnings. £10,100. Foxy Laddie at 100-1, didn't have a hope, but against all odds won the St Ledger at Doncaster. National headline news.

He tries not to wish he'd bet more than the hundred pounds in twenty-pound notes that appeared in the unmarked envelope on his doormat the morning of the race. Name of the horse scrawled in childish writing. Senses such thoughts are liable to harm whatever magic is at work. Remembers from his dusty childhood that magic is real in the lives of those who choose to believe.

"Ladies and gentlemen, this is your captain, Farooz Abdullah speaking. I'd like to welcome you on board this Emirates flight from London Heathrow to Dubai. We will be travelling at a cruising altitude of 33,000 feet..."

The heavy throb of the engines judders the window as the aircraft taxis down the runway. Mohammad Yasin closes his eyes, seeing his wife on their wedding day, and smiles...

* * *

Trevor Nugent feels the steam on his face, breathes in the earthy scent of the grinds. Peers at the ancient Gaggia that cackles and billows like some primeval living thing, watching the dark slink of coffee fill the small white cup.

The old man takes the cup between thumb and forefinger, raises it quickly to his lips. Swallows. Trevor watching, waiting, brushing the steam away with the side of his palm. Behind him the framed photograph of the Azzopardi family high up on the wood-panelled art-deco walls.

"*Buono*," the old man nods. "Now, do it again."

Trevor sighs, rolls his eyes, returns to the vast red coffee machine. Feels the eyes of the customers watching this master class. Knowing that in an hour's time Julius Miles is coming to taste the espresso and, if he likes what he drinks, a lease will be granted.

Flicks the lever, tamps down the grounds, shunts the brushed aluminium tamper up into the machine basket, turn-locks it into place. Presses the switch.

"Heard back from the Council yet?" the old man asks, returning to the high wooden stool. Trevor shakes his head. "They said by the end of the week."

"But they say it is possible, no?"

"Yeah. They said they'd agree change of use A1 to A3. Just need the paperwork."

"And the big man, *il gigante felice*, he will pay for the fitting-out, for the work?"

Trevor nods. "I've got a name. Wanna hear it?" The old man nods, patiently. "The Woodstock Café."

"It's good, Trevor. *Molto bello*. The name of the road and the description of the business. Could not be better."

Now it's Trevor's turn to nod, neck flushed with nervous expectation. The espresso is done. The old man takes the cup and sips once more, Trevor watching his eyes, knowing that Julius Miles is a pedant and a connoisseur, and that if the coffee is close to perfect he will say yes to opening the café that will finally bring Trevor his fortune in the new East End of post-Olympic London.

Nonno Azzopardi shakes his head. "Not yet. Try again…"

* * *

They kiss once more, his hand idling over her breasts, her belly. She grips his wrist suddenly and he laughs.

"I'm pregnant." A simple monotone, her default when things get emotional. "Five weeks."

Jon Dunkerman fills his eyes with her face. Blinks. "That first night in Warwick, after the Olympiad?"

Sandrine Dellacourt looks back at him, tears welling. Jon shakes his head vigorously, kissing her lashes. "No, no, no. Sandy, no!" Places his hands both sides of her head, pulling her up to his mouth, but he speaks, not kisses.

"I will never ever leave you…"

* * *

Julius Miles sleeps in the spare room, having no courage to empty the wardrobe and drawers in Daisy Perkins's old bedroom. The doorbell rings, and Arnold scampers downstairs to answer it as Julius elongates out of the small double bed, draws back the curtains. Weak sunshine, autumn on the horizon.

Hears her voice, peals of laughter from the boy, as if created long before any of them were born. Smiles to himself. Wonders at the spinning possibilities that led to all this.

Sits at the kitchen table gulping coffee, toast burning. Glances at her as she makes Arnold's packed lunch, waving him away. "I know you can do it, Julius, but I want to."

He snaps photographs as they pull on the white shirt, blue sweatshirt, blue trousers. Arnold beaming with pride – his first school uniform, first day at big school. Awa photographing the two of them, Julius kneeling down by the boy, getting pins and needles, falling theatrically to the floor.

They walk Arnold to the end of the street in silence, sound of chattering children, shouting mothers, fathers, cars pulling up, bicycle bells. A new school year. A new beginning.

Escort him into the schoolroom, Julius marvelling at the smell of plastic anoraks, clay and cleaning fluids that fills his head with flashes of his own primary school, another city, another age.

Awa kisses Arnold, hugs him, wipes her eyes. The boy tugs at his hair, itching to run free. Julius picks him up, tickles under his left arm, sending the boy wriggling. Kisses his forehead. "Enjoy yourself, Arnold. Remember, the first letter of your name is the shape of what?"

"Julius..." Awa thumps him, but Arnold nods seriously. "A triangle," he confirms, turning on his heels and dashing into the class with his friends.

They walk back slowly. At the steps to number 42, Julius stops. "I'm selling Gus's house," he says falteringly. "Buying Daisy's place next door."

"Oh. Wow. That's perfect..."

"Yeah, Mrs Eaves, the owner, was a friend of Gus's. I'm giving her a fair price."

"Well, at least you won't have to pay a removal company. Just carry everything down one lot of steps, up the next."

"I don't know how much I'll move. Think maybe I'll sell a lot of it."

Awa looks at him. "Your uncle's stuff?"

Julius nods. "Yeah. His stuff." Screws up his toes in his shoes, hoping this will make him strong. "I was wondering… while your dad's in Dubai… would you like to stay with us? For Arnold. For the boy…"

Awa looks away, watching the mother hurrying her two late children up the road to the school like a dog chasing rabbits. Julius looks the other way, seeing three birds cut across the blue sky, green flash of wings.

"All right," he hears her voice say. "I'll come and stay with you."

*　*　*

Adem Yilnaz sits at his desk in the new classroom, barely able to breathe. Waits until registration is under way before daring to flick his eyes behind him. Electricity deep in his belly. He cannot believe it, but she's looking back at him. Hand wiping a stray curl from her forehead. She doesn't look away but holds his gaze, flickering smile.

He can still feel the press of her lips against his. A miracle, at the dog end of August, a party his parents dragged him to, Turkish friends of Turkish friends in South Woodford, semi-detached, usual lamb on spit, usual sparking fire pit. She couldn't unscrew the top of an Orangina bottle and by some fluke he succeeded, first time. They talked, and towards the end of the evening as the music got louder and the parents danced and smoked, they found themselves next to each other by the embers, and after they had talked for a long while she leant close and kissed him.

"Adem Yilnaz?"

"Here, Miss Jenkins."

It's going to be a good year, he thinks, maybe the best he's ever had…

*　*　*

First snow. A sense of relief, winter boots plucked from cupboards, down jackets fluffed from vacuum-packed bags, skates lifted from basement hooks, skis waxed. Thoughts of hockey matches, weekends up country.

Larry Silk shivers in his English mac and Chelsea boots. Knows he must get kitted out; a guy at the accounting firm said they'd take him to Holt Renfrew after work, help him find footwear, a good Canadian coat. Slams back his coffee, finishes his doughnut. Watches his breath in the air, mixing with the fat white flakes that are getting thicker by the second, deadening the horizon.

His fine aquiline features achingly beautiful against the vast cold of the immense Canadian sky.

I watch him hurry into the gleaming skyscraper in the Financial District near the lake. Tighten my scarf, pull on my gloves. Don't worry, don't be sad. My numbers are different to yours, never reaching one but continually looping away in an eternal circle. I find happiness elsewhere.

Keep the world turning, Felicity, balance the books. It's what we're here for. To solve the sum of your lives.

It's going to be a long Toronto winter, but I will find Larry Silk love if it's the last thing I do...

Acknowledgements

Thanks to Andrew Dechet for your encouragement and incisiveness that helped me move on when I was flagging. To Anthony Wimbush for your insights and positivity. To Daniel Smith, particularly for all things NHS and statistics. To Martin Billington for backup and inspiration. To Corey Milner, for the magic and the maths. And to Dudi Appleton for all your wisdoms, patience and understanding.

Thanks to my agent Caspian Dennis, for unravelling the knot. To Alex and Elisabetta at Alma Books for your enthusiasm and diligence. And to my parents for not questioning their eldest when he first set out on the journey.